The Ottoman Excursion

TIM PELKEY

The Ottoman Excursion, Published April, 2020

Editorial and proofreading services: Kellyanne Zuzulo, Susan Strecker, Stephanie Peters, Karen Grennan
Interior layout and cover design: Howard Johnson
Photo Credits: Front and back cover images: Ganbat Badamkhand, Ulaanbaatar, Mongolia.

 **SDP Publishing**

Published by SDP Publishing, an imprint of SDP Publishing Solutions, LLC.

ISBN-13 (print): 978-1-7342402-5-2
ISBN-13 (ebook): 978-1-7342402-6-9

Library of Congress Control Number: 2019919106

To Mom and Dad

PROLOGUE

1938
Southeastern Turkey

Colonel Muhammed Tunç strode past the collapsed and burning buildings. His gaze fell on the silhouettes of the dead and dying. Though none wore the drab olive of the republic, his anger mounted with each lifeless body.

In the Great War, the Kurds of this village and many like it had fought under the Ottoman banner. They'd helped push the Russian and Armenian hordes from the banks of the Tigris. Almost a million had given their lives. Even more were left homeless.

Is this their reward?

Tunç stopped at the village mosque. Its walls and roof had collapsed. Its single minaret was burning. Inside were old men, women, and children, their limbs angled grotesquely, their faces frozen in horror.

"'Let not the worldly life deceive you,'" he said, quoting the Quran. "'Allah causes you to live, then causes you to die, then assembles you for the Day of Resurrection.'"

From the ashes of the Ottoman Empire had risen the Turkish Republic. The leader of the republic, Mustafa Kemal Atatürk, forced his fledgling nation on a course of rapid Westernization. A constitution soon replaced the sacred words of the Quran. Islamic schools were outlawed; sharia courts and mullahs were removed from the judicial system; and Caliph Abdülmecid II, their holy leader, was exiled. But Atatürk's most sweeping changes were reserved for the Kurds. Their political parties, language, and schools were banned. Their leaders were executed. Their very existence had become unforgivable.

A gunshot was followed by a victory flare arcing overhead.

Tunç's men appeared on the streets. Laughing, they clapped each other on the back and fired their guns into the air. Another Kurdish rebellion, another cry for freedom had been crushed.

"'Forgive us our sins and remove from us our evil deeds and cause us to die with the righteous,'" Tunç said, again reciting from the holy book.

Mustafa Kemal Atatürk. *Blasphemer. Heretic. Infidel.* The cirrhotic, self-proclaimed 'Father of the Turks' would soon be dead, killed by his own vices. But his followers would live on. And the most loyal of those followers, those who would work most zealously to preserve his ideals, were the most powerful men in Turkey—the Army High Command. It would take a legion of Allah's followers to stop them. It would take time. But it had to be done.

A cry came from the depths of the mosque.

Tunç turned toward the sound and began running. Ignoring his men's objections, he burst through the mosque's crumbling front door.

The sound pulled him down a partially collapsed, smoke-filled hallway to a back room. In the room was a crib. Among the blankets was a shock of black hair.

As Tunç lifted the squirming pile of blankets and put it to his shoulder, the crying stopped.

Part

1

"Nationalism is an infantile disease.
It is the measles of mankind."

— **Albert Einstein, 1921**

1

Present Day
Western Turkey, field hospital

D r. Michael Callahan stared down at the blank post-op note. The strain of the last twenty-four hours returned. The OR had provided temporary sanctuary. Out here, he was helpless.

He slipped off his sweat-soaked cap and ran his hands through his hair. He had to focus. Another case would soon be starting. Grabbing a pen, he began writing.

Rain drummed against the tent's canvas roof. The steady patter was joined by the distant sound of women's voices. The voices became louder. They made their way into his consciousness, their melodic rise and fall melding together into an odd singsong intonation. He'd grown accustomed to the habitual, guttural call to worship, but it was too early for the midday prayer, and the sound was different.

Setting down his pen, he walked to the recovery room. His previous case, a boy, was resting peacefully. The mother sat quietly at the bedside. She smiled at Callahan before tilting her head toward the voices. Following her gaze, Callahan walked to the tent opening and pushed back the flap.

In the rain, an old man sat at the front of a wooden cart pulled by a donkey. The cart was draped by a black tarp. Several veiled women, the source of the cry, filed behind.

With a flick of his reins, the old man brought the donkey to a stop. Slowly, he turned and looked back at the rain-splattered tarp.

His gut wrenching, Callahan pushed past the tent flap and sprinted through the rain, splashing through puddles in the well-worn grass. He stopped at the back of the cart.

Shouts came from adjacent tents. Others poured outside.

Time slowing, his chest pounding, Callahan squinted up into the cloud-filled sky. He felt the rain on his face, wishing it could wash away this moment.

His gaze dropped to the others who now surrounded the cart. He then looked down at the familiar running shoes that jutted from beneath the rain-splattered canvas.

As the women's voices resonated, growing louder, he reached out and pulled back the tarp.

2

Twenty-seven days earlier
Day 1

The Airbus climbed from Istanbul Atatürk Airport. The plane carried members of the World Health Organization's Disaster Relief Team. Two days earlier, an earthquake had struck Turkey's western coastal city of Izmir. From their homelands, the relief team members had flown into Istanbul and caught the early-morning charter flight to Izmir.

Callahan, a surgeon from the University of Michigan, sat between Bryce Jones, a pediatrician from the University of Oxford, and Eric Haas, a surgeon from Pittsburgh's Allegheny General Hospital. The three stared out the window.

"The Golden Gate," Bryce said, pointing from his window seat.

"It doesn't look like a gate," Haas said, leaning across Callahan.

"There once was an open archway through that wall," Bryce said. "A Greek legend said when the Ottomans conquered the city, an angel turned Emperor Constantine into marble and placed him under the wall. When he returns to life, he'll retake the city— his Constantinople. The Ottomans blocked the gate to prevent Constantine's return."

Haas laughed. "Who was she?"

Bryce looked quizzically back.

"That sounds like something you'd learn on a tour," Haas said. "And if you went on a tour, I'm guessing a woman was involved."

11

"I was a history major," Bryce said. "Istanbul is literally the focal point—"

"Believe it or not," a voice said, "people do fill their minds with something other than Ben Roethlisberger's quarterback rating."

The three physicians turned.

Brooke Johnson, the nursing training director at the University of Iowa, stood in the aisle. Over the past few excursions, Brooke and Haas's on-again, off-again relationship had played out like a soap opera. She motioned toward a young woman next to her. "I'd like to introduce Amanda, our top nursing graduate this year. She'll be joining us."

Haas stood from his aisle seat and took Amanda's hand. "I'm Eric." A few inches shorter than the nurses, Haas had brilliant red hair and the muscled physique of a gymnast. "If you're ever in need of surgical advice, I'm always available."

"I'm afraid he is," Brooke said. She pointed. "That's Dr. Jones by the window. There's Dr. Callahan. And—" She paused, looking toward the row behind them, where a young man sat by himself. "We haven't met."

"Scott Adams," the young man said, standing and shaking the nurses' hands.

"You're tall," Brooke said.

"Scott's our new tentmate," Haas said.

While waiting for the charter flight, the team members had selected roommates to share the four-person tents where they'd be staying.

"You're the one from Alabama," Brooke said, "the infectious disease specialist."

"That's correct," Adams said with a Southern drawl. "I'm from Tuscaloosa."

"Tusca-loosa," Brooke said, letting the word roll off her tongue.

Haas patted Adams's shoulder. "Scott's married, with two kids."

Adams pulled a photo from his wallet. "My wife, Lil, along with our girls, Sara Beth and Ann. They're two and four. We have a third on the way."

The nurses cooed in unison.

"Welcome to the team," Brooke said. "We certainly could have used an infectious disease expert on past excursions." Leaning forward, she spoke quietly. "Too many surgeons." After a nod to the others, she led Amanda away.

"You have to love her," Haas said when the nurses were out of earshot. "How many women even know the Steelers quarterback?"

"I take it you didn't visit her," Bryce said. "Like you said you would."

"I thought about it," Haas said. "I even looked into a flight. But—"

"There were no flights between Pittsburgh and Iowa City?" Callahan asked.

"Not direct ones. Also, I would have had to meet her parents."

The others laughed.

"She seems like a nice girl," Adams said. He held up the photo. "If you're worried about commitment, don't be."

"*Two* kids with another on the way?" Haas said. "How old are you anyway?"

"Old enough to meet someone's parents," Bryce said.

Alin Tevfik, a surgeon and the team's leader, rose from his seat in the front of the cabin. He held his arms out wide. "Welcome to Turkey."

The team members applauded.

"More than three decades ago, on our first excursion, our relief team consisted of three physicians and two nurses," Alin said. "It's with great pride I see what we've become. The largest excursion assembled to date, we have forty-three providers. We represent eleven countries: Australia, Brazil, Canada, England, France, Hungary, India, South Africa, Sweden, Turkey, and the United States."

The applause as the members heard the name of their country built to a crescendo that continued long after Alin finished. The roll call of nations celebrated the nationalistic pride of each of the relief workers but also marked their transition to operational members of the World Health Organization.

Alin took it all in. Approaching the eve of his seventh decade, he deserved moments like this. While he could have been enjoying a well-earned, peaceful retirement, he spent his days pandering to pharmaceutical companies for dated medical supplies and bureaucrats for funding.

"I'd like to thank our Turkish colleague, Dr. Safiye Özmen, for working with local officials to select the site of the field hospital," Alin said.

The team members clapped as a woman in the front row briefly stood. Safiye Özmen wore a heavy sweater and glasses with thick frames. Her dark-brown hair was pulled into a bun. Callahan recalled Safiye had been on three or four previous excursions. He'd forgotten she was from Turkey.

"Any advice regarding working in Turkey?" someone asked.

Born and raised in Istanbul, Alin had emigrated to the United States, where he'd spent a long and productive career at the University of Michigan. A year earlier, he'd moved to Manhattan to work full-time for the WHO.

"Safiye and I would recommend avoiding all forms of confrontation," Alin said. "Turks can be very friendly, but relations can quickly swing the other way. Arguments can become heated, even violent. And if you have hopes of converting anyone to Christianity, abandon them now. Foreigners have been arrested for such activities. If you enter a home, take off your shoes. When eating in public, use your right hand, since the left is considered unclean. If you're offered tea, I recommend accepting it or they may take offense."

Safiye turned from her seat. "And I wouldn't drink alcohol in public."

There was laughter as everyone looked toward Haas, who stood and bowed.

"When we arrive, we'll have our work cut out for us," Alin said. "The residential districts have been devastated. Five thousand are reported dead with more injured. Over 400,000 have been left homeless. The city, still suffering from aftershocks, is being evacuated. Most of you know what we're in for. We're going to be busy."

Alin paused. "As many of you know, I'm a US citizen. I view America as my home. But I've always been very proud of where I've come from. Atatürk's reforms, made almost a century ago in the remains of an empire that had a sultan, a caliph, and sharia, were incredible. He built a western-style democracy, reformed the education and judicial systems, and changed the language and alphabet. In a Muslim country, he separated mosque and state and abolished the sultanate and caliphate. He outlawed the harem, veil, and fez, ended polygamy, and gave women their freedom and the right to vote."

The female team members applauded.

"My father worshipped Atatürk," Alin continued. "That's why I'm glad he doesn't have to witness current events. Like many countries, Turkey has moved backward. President Cebici and the members of his Islamist party are dismantling Atatürk's reforms. They've pushed back against secularism and reinstituted mandatory religious education, religious dress codes, and the Ottoman language. Cebici's government has held corrupt elections, used strong-arm tactics to remove dissent, and jailed tens of thousands of political opponents and journalists. They've moved Turkey away from representative government, away from NATO, and away from the European Union."

A grim smile crossed Alin's face. "We've all read the travel brochures. Turkey geographically straddles Europe and Asia. They do so ideologically as well. Pulled by Islamic fundamentalism to the East and modernization and democracy to the West, they're struggling with a synthesis." He paused, nodding. "What my old country does is important. They're more than just a bridge between East and West. They're a microcosm. If they can't arrive at a peaceful solution, the rest of the world may be in trouble."

The Airbus touched down in the town of Sasalı on the broad Aegean peninsula northwest of Izmir. Two buses took the relief team members past Izmir's outskirts.

Rising columns of smoke fed a gray blanket that covered the city. Cars loaded with belongings crept slowly, filling all lanes of the jammed highway. Along the side of the road, pedestrians pulled carts stacked with furniture, clothes, and food.

"It looks like a war zone," Callahan said.

Moving slowly with the traffic, the buses headed east. They eventually passed from the smoke-blanketed city to clear air and a green, mountainous countryside. They stopped at the fringe of a rolling field that was surrounded by wooded hills and covered by scores of conical white tents.

The neat rows of tents reminded Callahan of Civil War photos of Union encampments. But instead of dreary, black-and-white images of muddy fields filled with soldiers, he saw men wearing skullcaps, women wearing bright headscarves, and a field carpeted with emerald-green grass. The still-frame image was thrown into motion by children running among the tents.

The relief team members stepped from the buses, carrying duffel bags and backpacks. Haas held his phone into the air. "No signal." Others also checked their phones with similar results.

Following Safiye, the team members passed in silence through the tents. The tent city inhabitants stared back, disoriented and fatigued, possessing the universal look of those overcome by recent events. Were the newcomers here to help or take something away? Was this real or just a bad dream? Was this the end of something or just the beginning?

The assembly team had arrived the day before. Medical supplies were stacked in an open area on the eastern side of the field. A dozen large tents had been laid out. Two were up.

Hundreds of bedraggled people were lined up at the edge of the site. Some stood with the support of crutches; others wore ill-fitting bandages wrapped around injured heads, arms, or legs.

"We're going to have to jump right into it," Alin called out, stepping onto a crate. "Primary care teams, take care of the wounded with what you can dig out of the supply crates. Specialty teams, let's help the assembly team with the installation. First priority is the triage tent and then the inpatient tents."

Alin scanned the field. "And remember," he said, wiping the sweat from his brow. "One patient at a time."

3

Nineteen months earlier
Grozny, Chechen Republic

Major Vladimir Petrovich sat at the head of a three-truck convoy. He extended a pack of cigarettes toward the driver, Yenkov.

The nineteen-year-old private shook his head. "No, thank you, Major."

Petrovich lit a cigarette and took a deep, relaxing drag. He opened his window and exhaled. Yenkov shivered as cold air rushed in.

"It'll keep you awake," Petrovich said.

"If I don't freeze, Major."

The caravan passed a pier where an elderly man was ice fishing. Petrovich remembered a similar pier on Lake Ladoga where his grandfather had taught him to fish and mesmerized him with tales of how he'd fought the Germans and liberated Leningrad. Petrovich's boyhood had been an idealistic time, not only for him but all of Russia. The country had been at the height of its power. The Cold War had been raging, and foreigners were despised—especially by young boys who devoured the propaganda from Moscow. The world had been black and white.

On the narrow icy road, a black sedan drove past.

"There they go again," Yenkov said, waving a hand in frustration, "breaking protocol."

The Mercedes GT sedan held four nuclear reactor technicians from the United Arab Emirates. Over the past week, Petrovich and his men had ferried the technicians to secret Russian missile silos and supervised their dismantling of aging warheads. The technicians were harvesting plutonium for use in their reactor in Abu Dhabi. It was an easy method of acquiring plutonium for the Emirati and a source of revenue for the ailing Russian military.

Petrovich glared at the Mercedes. *The sons of bitches.* The Soviet Union had lost the Cold War. The economy was in turmoil. And now, like conquerors in a vanquished land, these smug Arabs were plundering Russia of its valuable resources. With the transfer of the plutonium, so went the honor of the old Soviet guard and everything for which his grandfather had fought.

"Try to keep up," Petrovich said.

The old Kazak diesel, stinking of oil and exhaust fumes, shouted its opposition as Yenkov pushed it forward. But despite the diesel's best efforts, it wasn't long before the sedan had disappeared ahead into the glare of the newly fallen snow.

The road led into a valley. As the convoy descended, turning tightly around the bend of a hill, Yenkov jammed on the brakes. The truck came to a stuttering stop.

Petrovich watched in his rearview mirror as the other trucks came to similar sliding halts.

The Mercedes had stopped in front of a landslide. Fallen trees and dirt blocked the icy road where it was cut from the side of the hill. The four technicians emerged from the sedan and began walking back toward the trucks.

Petrovich's gaze, however, wasn't on the technicians. He was scanning the woods.

This wasn't a landslide. There was too little dirt, too many trees. At the base of a fallen tree, he spotted it—a pile of sawdust.

He began rolling down the window. "Get back in the car," he yelled, knowing it was already too late.

A harsh metallic staccato filled the air. Bullets tore through the Arabs, who collapsed. The truck's windshield shattered. Yenkov slumped forward.

Petrovich felt sharp pains in his right shoulder and cheek. Falling against the door, he pulled the handle. The door opened, and he tumbled, slamming hard against the gravel.

His second-in-command, Lieutenant Andrei Popov, led the men from the rear of the second truck. There was another barrage.

Popov and the men fell. Popov managed to climb to his feet. He limped to the side of the road.

An assailant, a camouflaged mountain guerrilla, appeared at the edge of the woods. Several more followed and soon over a dozen stood at the road's edge, watching as Popov struggled through the knee-deep snow.

One of the guerrillas raised a pistol.

"Andrei," Petrovich yelled. "Down!"

His cry was drowned by a high-pitched crack as the guerilla's Luger kicked back. Popov fell face-first beneath the virgin canopy.

The assassin turned. His face wasn't that of a rugged mountain fighter but of a young man, almost a boy. It was the same with the others.

The young men walked toward Petrovich. The assassin crouched. He picked up Petrovich's cigarette and held it to his lips. "Russian," he winced, tossing it aside.

The others laughed.

The assassin's eyes were blue and radiant. They desperately searched Petrovich's face for something: pain, fear, death?

The major glared resolutely back, betraying nothing.

The assassin pursed his lips and blew a column of smoke into Petrovich's face.

Again, the others laughed.

Petrovich's eyes burned. As his blood pumped onto the icy road, he drifted slowly, inevitably, away.

4

"Mankind is a single body and each nation a part of that body. We must never say 'What does it matter to me if some part of the world is ailing?' If there is such an illness, we must concern ourselves with it as though we were having that illness."

—**Mustafa Kemal Atatürk,** founder of the Turkish Republic

Day 2

"We're off to a great start," Alin said, standing at the front of the mess tent.

The day after their arrival, the relief team members were eating lunch—their first official meal.

"Thanks to the assembly team for setting up the kitchen so quickly," Alin said.

"A mixed blessing," Haas mumbled to Callahan, swirling his spoon through a bowl of watery tomato soup.

"Our most critically ill patients have been stabilized," Alin continued. "The installation is going well. The triage tent is up and running. Equipment has been installed in the adult inpatient and pediatric tents. The intensive care and surgery tents are still being worked on." He looked toward Callahan. "Michael, when will the ORs be running?"

"Sometime tonight," Callahan replied.

"Good," Alin said. "Last night, everyone set their tents north of the field hospital. That's where we'll have the Cloister."

The Cloister was where the relief team members would stay. Two years earlier, Haas had coined the term after they'd camped on the grounds of a Bosnian monastery.

"I met with city officials this morning," Alin said. "As tremors continue, so does the evacuation. The officials estimate the tent city's population will more than double over the next few days."

There was a sudden commotion in the back of the tent. Amanda rushed in. "Dr. Jones needs help," the young nurse called out.

Callahan, Haas, and Safiye followed Amanda to the pediatric tent. Brooke was ushering a woman outside. The woman was in hysterics, screaming, "Bebeğim, bebeğim benim."

Amanda led them into an exam room.

A girl lay unconscious on a table. She was wet, her skin blue. Bryce held the girl on her side, suctioning blood from her mouth. "She's not breathing," he said.

The physicians swarmed the table. Safiye grabbed a pair of scissors and cut through the girl's shirt. Callahan inserted an intravenous line. Haas placed EKG pads and hooked up the leads.

"She needs fluid," Bryce said to Amanda. "Get a bag of lactated Ringer's. And crossmatch two units of blood."

Callahan drew out a vial of blood from the line and handed it to Amanda, who rushed from the room.

"Heart rate, 180," Haas said as the EKG monitor came alive.

Safiye held her finger on the girl's carotid artery. "Nothing."

All heads turned toward the EKG, which was still picking up a heart rate of 180.

"She's in PEA," Bryce said.

Pulseless electrical activity occurred when the heart muscle failed to contract despite normal electrical signals from the heart's natural pacemaker.

Safiye began chest compressions. Bryce tilted the girl's head back and intubated her. Callahan hooked the breathing tube to the ventilation machine. Once Amanda returned with a bag of fluid, Haas attached it to the line.

As the fluid poured into the girl's IV, the others watched as Safiye continued chest compressions.

"What happened to her?" Callahan asked.

"Not sure," Bryce said. "She collapsed in the triage tent. They brought her straight here."

The EKG showed a heart rate of ninety-seven.

"Still no pulse," Haas said, holding the girl's wrist.

"Epinephrine," Bryce said to Brooke. "Quarter milligram."

Brooke grabbed a medicine bottle from a cabinet. Drawing a small syringe of fluid from the bottle, she injected it into the line.

Moments later, Safiye stopped the compressions.

Brooke gasped, but Safiye—her hand flat to the girl's sternum—shook her head. "It's beating."

Haas, still holding the girl's wrist, nodded. "I feel it."

Over the next minute, the girl's heart rate and blood pressure normalized. Her color returned.

"I can take it from here," Bryce said. "Thank you, everyone."

"Labs?" Callahan asked.

"Good idea," Bryce said.

Callahan drew off two vials of blood through the IV. Carrying them outside, he stepped across a swath of green grass into the adjacent tent.

Thomas Wilkins stood by himself surrounded by an assortment of equipment and crates of supplies. A full-time WHO employee, the South African was Alin's assistant in Manhattan. During excursions, he served as the team's head laboratory tech and supply chief. His tent performed similar double duty, respectively functioning as medical laboratory and storage depot.

"Michael, what do you need?" Thomas asked, pushing back a row of dreadlocks.

"A metabolic workup, CBC, and cultures: aerobic, anaerobic, mycobacterial, fungal, and viral," Callahan said, handing over the vials.

"Is this from that little girl? Nata?"

Callahan nodded.

"I'll run 'em, stat," Thomas said, stepping to a nearby machine.

Back outside, Callahan found Safiye talking to the girl's parents. Despite the summer heat, Safiye wore a heavy sweater underneath a lab coat.

"Doktor, sağolun. Allah'a şükür, kızımı kurtardınız," the mother said to Callahan. She was thanking him.

Callahan gave an exaggerated, deferential bow in Safiye's direction. "I help—*yardim Doktor Özmen, yardim.*"

This wasn't the first time Callahan had seen a female doctor mistaken for a nurse.

"*Doktor?*" the woman asked Safiye.

Nodding, Safiye glanced up at Callahan above her glasses. "You didn't have to do that."

He smiled. "What happened to their daughter?"

"Before she became sick, she was playing and running—a perfectly healthy eight-year-old."

"Why was she wet?"

Safiye spoke briefly to the parents before turning to Callahan. "She was playing in the river."

That night, Callahan carried a box of equipment into the pediatric tent. Safiye stood at a bedside, scribbling into a chart.

"Some pediatric equipment got mixed in with ours," Callahan said, holding up the box.

"Set it here," Safiye said, pointing to a table. "I hear one of the ORs is running."

"Haas is operating now," Callahan said. He set down the box and looked over the room. "I've never seen this many injured kids before."

"Thirty have been admitted to the ward, but we've already treated and released twice that many."

In the midst of rounds, Bryce was moving from bed to bed, giving orders to two of the nurses while speaking with the kids in Turkish.

"He hasn't stopped since we arrived," Safiye said.

"A full Oxford professor by thirty-three. Over a hundred research publications. Sometimes I think he only sleeps to pacify the rest of us."

Bryce walked toward them. "Come here. I want to show you both something."

They followed him into the intensive care room. The room was quiet with the exception of the steady electronic ping of the heart monitor and wheeze of the ventilator. Nata lay sedated, wrapped in blankets, tubes coming from her mouth, nose, and arms.

"I did a bronch," Bryce said, turning on a monitor.

On the screen, they watched a video of a fiber-optic tube moving down the girl's throat, past the milky white bands of her vocal cords, and into her bronchus. The smooth pink mucosa of the bronchus was interrupted by bright-red ulcers.

"It looks like she aspirated battery acid," Callahan said.

"It's most likely an inhalation injury," Bryce said, nodding. "A bad one."

"Did you do a lavage?" Callahan asked.

"And biopsy. Thomas sent everything off for analysis."

On the screen, the scope moved farther into the girl's airway, which branched into multiple small passages. The ulcerations increased.

"I can't imagine an infection doing this," Safiye said. "Or an autoimmune process or malignancy."

"We'll have to wait and see what the lab results show," Bryce said. "At this point, whatever the etiology, the best thing we can do is support Nata and hope she starts to heal herself."

5

Day 4

allahan sat at the edge of his cot, dressing. Adams had left moments earlier for a run. The tent flap swung open. The morning light followed Bryce inside. He collapsed face-first onto his cot.

"When's the last time you slept?" Callahan asked.

"Yesterday, on an inpatient bed," Bryce said.

"Did you eat?"

"Oatmeal. Must have been left over from last summer."

The tent city's muezzin sounded the call to prayer—a shrill electronic recording.

Haas pulled his pillow over his head. "Do they have to do that every morning?"

"And five times a day," Bryce said.

"We're late," Callahan said to Haas.

The two were scheduled to take over for the night-shift surgeons.

Callahan headed toward the field hospital. As the muezzin continued, he looked down the rows of tents. Muslim faithful were outside their tents on prayer rugs, kneeling and facing Mecca.

In the surgical tent, the night-shift surgeons were in the ORs finishing early-morning cases. With patients pouring unabated into the field hospital, the ORs had been booked to capacity. Callahan spent the next half hour rounding on the post-op patients. Afterward, he walked toward Mrs. Bagley, the chief nurse.

An elderly Englishwoman, Mrs. Bagley stood outside the clinic rooms, writing on her ever-present clipboard. Like Alin and Thomas Wilkins, she was also a year-round WHO employee but was based out of the London office.

"What do you have?" Callahan asked.

"And a good morning—" Mrs. Bagley began before looking up. "My goodness, Dr. Callahan. It looks like you just crawled from bed."

"Not a coincidence," Callahan said, trying to pat his hair down. "I thought the showers would be running by now."

"They are," the elderly nurse said. "Some local men assembled them last night."

Despite an outer shell of a humorless disciplinarian, Mrs. Bagley was a pleasant woman who enjoyed her unofficial role as the team's matriarch.

Haas entered the tent. Freshly showered and shaved, he patted his chest. "Feel like a new man."

"Regrettably, Dr. Callahan is not able to share your sentiments," Mrs. Bagley said.

"You missed rounds," Callahan said.

"Yes, Meredith," Haas said, ignoring Callahan. "I see why."

Haas was the only team member who called Mrs. Bagley by her first name. He pulled a Pittsburgh Pirates baseball cap from a back pocket and set the bright-yellow hat firmly on Callahan's head.

Mrs. Bagley rolled her eyes. "If you two find yourselves so inclined, we're in desperate need of someone to see patients." She looked down at her clipboard. "Dr. Callahan, room C. As for you, Dr. Haas, there's a patient in room A. Let me know if either of you requires an interpreter."

The team members had picked up basic Turkish medical terminology, such as *ağrı* for pain and *ilaç* for medicine, but they still relied heavily on interpreters recruited by Safiye. Fluency in Turkish was difficult without prolonged study. It used the Latin alphabet but was an agglutinating language. Phrases were frequently all one word constructed by stacking different endings on a primary word. Vowel harmony was required in selecting the endings. Sentences also began with the subject followed by the object and then verb.

Callahan and Haas spent the morning between the clinic rooms and ORs. At noon, they sat across from each other, writing post-op orders.

Brooke and Safiye stepped into the tent.

"Anyone for a late lunch?" Brooke asked, casting a hopeful look toward Haas.

As far as Callahan knew, Brooke and Haas hadn't spoken since being on the plane. Brooke was extending an olive branch.

"Some restaurant workers have booths set up on the other side of the tent city," Safiye said. "The food is good."

They all stared toward Haas, who continued writing.

"Go ahead," Callahan said. "I'll cover."

Haas shook his head. "Just ate, thanks. I've got a patient waiting." He stood and walked into a clinic room.

Brooke, her jaw set, marched outside.

"What's up with him?" Safiye asked.

"Playing hard to get, I guess."

"The offer for lunch stands."

Callahan looked in Haas's direction. "I *am* hungry. But I don't want to get into the middle of anything."

Safiye shrugged. "Into the middle of what?"

"Good point."

Callahan walked with the two women from the field hospital.

The population of the tent city had more than tripled since the relief team's arrival. Many of the tent city's inhabitants sat around slow-burning campfires. Children, like schools of fish, ran between the tents.

On the far side of the field, they came to an area swarming with activity. The smell of tobacco mixed with the scents of roasting beef and lamb as large hunks of meat turned on spits over open grills. Boys hawked a myriad of knickknacks, jewelry, and watches. Outdoor furniture, cigarettes, blankets, and clothes were for sale.

"Buyurun. Buyurun," peddlers called out, pointing toward a variety of wares.

A man approached Callahan and thrust a forefinger toward a distant tent, where young women waited with knowing eyes. Callahan waved him off.

The three of them bought shawarma and sat in an open area on the grass. Conversation filled the air around them as men huddled in small groups, drinking tea and smoking cigarettes. Nearby, a group of old men passed around the hose from a hookah.

"That was quite a trip," Callahan said, looking back in the direction of the field hospital.

Safiye nodded. "Men and their *genelevs*."

"Their what?" Brooke asked.

"Genelevs," Safiye said. "Public houses, brothels."

"You make them sound legal," Brooke said.

"They are," Safiye said.

"I'm surprised a Muslim nation would allow it," Callahan said.

"There's no more reconciliation with the Muslim faith than there is with the Christian," Safiye said. "The genelevs exist, well, because they've always existed."

Brooke eyed Callahan's baseball cap. He'd slipped it on during the walk. "The 'Picksburg' Pirates," she said, imitating Haas's accent. Reaching over, she flicked off his hat.

The men around the hookah looked at them. One stood.

Callahan put the cap back on. "It's all right," he said, holding up his hands. "Yatişmak. Yatişmak."

After a few moments, the man sat. He and the others returned to their conversation.

"What was he going to do?" Brooke asked. "*Beat* me?"

"Maybe," Safiye said quietly. "Our little city seems to contain many rural Turks. Some are refugees from Syria and Iraq. Some are Kurds. Many have a less than enlightened attitude regarding women's behavior."

Brooke looked at Callahan's hat. "It figures I'd almost get stoned to death because of *his* hat. Did you know he told Alin he wasn't leaving Pittsburgh during football season, or if the Penguins or Pirates made the playoffs?"

"Eric's a good guy," Callahan said. "He's just—"

"Juvenile, self-centered, obnoxious," Brooke said.

"Depending on the day," Callahan said. "But he can also be a good friend. You know that. Last year, I tore my ACL. When I woke up after the surgery, Eric was at the bedside. He'd found out I was having surgery when someone wished me a fast recovery on Twitter. He'd driven from Pittsburgh and smuggled a six-pack of beer and pizza into post-op."

"Why can't he be like that more often?" Brooke asked. "The good Eric."

"There's a price to being friends with Eric," Callahan said. "But when he decides to be your friend, he's a great one." He paused. "You realize why he didn't come to lunch, don't you?"

"Because he's a jerk."

Callahan shook his head. "I'll deny I ever said this, but when you were flirting with Scott on the plane, Eric was jealous."

"Your *so* tall," Brooke said. "I thought I was being over the top. He didn't realize that?"

"Apparently not," Callahan said.

"If Eric was jealous, why wouldn't he come to lunch with us?" Safiye asked.

"He was scared," Callahan said. "Eric likes to appear as though he's above it all. Being jealous means he's not. Being jealous means—"

"He cares," Brooke said, breaking into a broad grin.

6

Thirteen months earlier
Burdenko Military Hospital, Moscow

Petrovich peered into the blue, radiant eyes. He'd looked into the eyes of grizzled combat veterans, cold-blooded killers, and suicide bombers. He'd seen schizophrenia and fanaticism of all kinds. This, however, was something different, something more—the accumulation of all of them but none of them.

"Vlad? Vlad?"

Ignoring the beckoning voice, he welcomed the frigid touch of the icy road. He let the cold course through him, envelop him.

On that morning in Grozny, the cold had saved him. It had slowed his metabolism and cooled his brain, allowing him to survive despite the blood loss. But while the cold had saved him, it was the lasting image of the young assassin that had given him a reason to live. Revenge made him endure the guilt of living while Yenkov, Popov, and the others under his command had died. Revenge made him endure the countless surgeries and the excruciating pain.

"Can you hear me? *Vlad.*"

The voice returned. Insistent, it pushed aside the assassin's face. It pushed aside the cold, the guilt, and the pain.

He opened his eyes. A blurred figure stood over him. He blinked, his eyes adjusting.

Tatiana.

For the first time since Grozny, something within him began to thaw.

"What are you doing here?" he asked.

The patchwork of skin grafts had left a maze of scars over the right side of his face. It was more than anyone should have to gaze upon—particularly Tatiana.

"I see a few bullets haven't changed you," she said, wiping away tears. She bent down and kissed his forehead.

"You're right. I'm the same. Exactly the same."

Tatiana lingered over him. She took in everything: the scars, the guilt, the shame. She managed a smile.

"Thank you for coming," he said. "When I get out of here, I'll give you a call. We'll do something fun."

Tatiana was shaking her head before he finished. "No, Vlad. That's not how this will work. You're not the same, not even close. But with help, you can be."

He started to object, but she put a finger to his lips. "For the first time in your life, Vladimir Petrovich, you need someone else. You need me."

"In spite of everything, I am certain we are moving toward the light. The strength which animates my faith derives not only from my infinite love for my dear country and people, but from the young people I see, who are moved purely by love of country and of truth in their efforts to find and to spread light amid today's darkness, immorality, and fraud."

—**Mustafa Kemal Atatürk**

Day 5

Callahan walked from the OR. He pulled off his surgical gown and cap. "What's next?" he asked Mrs. Bagley.

"Would you believe nothing?" the English nurse said, looking up from her clipboard.

For the first time since the ORs had started running, the waiting room was empty.

"Really?"

"You're free to go," she said.

Callahan stepped out from the tent. He breathed in the warm summer air. It was Friday night. It was only his fifth day in Izmir but felt like his fiftieth. His time here formed a continuum with previous excursions and identical field hospitals in Eritrea, Bosnia, Nicaragua, Guatemala, and Israel. It was hard to believe he'd first heard about the earthquake only one week ago.

"Fundic, tubal, ovarian," Callahan recited softly beneath his surgical mask as he identified the sutured branches of the elderly woman's left uterine artery.

Earlier in the evening, the woman had come to the emergency room complaining of abdominal pain. An ultrasound detected a large cystic ovarian tumor. Callahan, the night's on-call attending surgeon, had taken her immediately to the OR, where his suspicions were confirmed. The ovarian tumor had ruptured. After siphoning off more than a liter of blood and dissecting the adhesions between the ovary and pelvic fossa, he was able to remove the twenty-five-centimeter tumor, which now sat inauspiciously in a plastic bucket at the foot of the table.

Callahan looked across the patient. The resident, holding the retractors that kept the incision open, stared blankly into the incision, subtly moving his head in rhythm with Green Day's "Basket Case" blaring from a speaker in the corner of the OR.

"It's okay to close," Callahan said. He tore off his gown. "Give me a page if you have any problems."

Unaccustomed to being anything but a bystander during most OR cases, the first-year resident appeared surprised. As if for the first time, he looked into the incision.

"I can stick around," Callahan said.

Pulling himself from his sleep-starved haze, the resident stepped forward. "It's a simple closure." With a firm tone he turned to Cindy, the scrub nurse, and held out his hand. "3-0 Velcro."

Cindy snapped the handle of the preset needle driver firmly into the resident's open palm.

Callahan smiled. There were moments in a resident's training when progress was almost palpable. He held up his cell phone. Cindy nodded. If there was a problem, she'd call.

Before leaving, he walked to the ovarian tumor and

cut into it. As it fell open, he saw a disorganized soup of brain, hair, skin, and teeth. It was a teratoma.

It was almost 3:00 a.m. as Callahan stepped into the surgery suite. He knew he couldn't sleep. He was too wired from the surgery and would be for at least an hour or two. By then, it would be time for morning rounds.

He flopped down on the couch in front of the incessantly running television. On his phone, he scrolled through Facebook and Twitter and then picked up the remote and flipped through several channels. Nothing was on. A few donuts from the previous morning sat in a cardboard box. Warily, he picked one out and walked to a window.

It was Friday night. The campus lights gleamed yellow in the distance. Many of that night's parties would still be going. The undergraduates were celebrating the end of spring term. Some were savoring the last moments before graduate school or work.

He recalled his own college days. Friday nights and weekends had been a time to relax. In medical school, they became a time to study. The comfort he associated with Friday nights and weekends disappeared entirely during his residency as life became a three-day cycle, when he and his colleagues were known as the pre-call, on-call, or post-call resident. The importance of names, days of the week, and even holidays drifted away as vacations and good friends were replaced by conferences and coworkers, and football games and parties were exchanged for mortality conferences, tumor boards, and rounds.

Since finishing his training, he'd climbed the academic ladder. After he was promoted to assistant professor, the next step was an associate professorship. But as the once distant pinnacles of full professorship and tenure approached, they began to look more like plateaus. From those plateaus, the other pinnacles he imagined—friends, family, and a life outside the hospital—seemed out of reach.

Stepping from the window, he threw the stale, half-eaten donut into the garbage. On the television, CNN was preparing to broadcast a special report. Static filled the screen as they cut from the Atlanta newsroom to a satellite feed from Turkey's western coast. A camera was filming a large fire. The camera panned to an English reporter.

"Disaster has struck on this early Saturday morning in western Turkey. A large earthquake has hit the coastal city of Izmir."

There was footage of an airplane swooping low over the fire and dropping chemical foam.

"It's still too early to know the extent of the damage, but thousands are dead with many more injured. Thus far, there's been no official word from Ankara."

Callahan's phone dinged. He walked toward the OR, his thoughts turning to the resident. It wasn't a message from Cindy, however, but a WHO group text message.

Izmir. We're on. Travel info to follow.

He stopped and poured himself a cup of coffee. Returning to the window, he looked over the campus.

The excursions had always been a welcome break. They'd provided a change of scenery, a rejuvenating escape. Right now, however, he didn't need to escape from his life. He needed to invest time into making one.

"Are you okay?"

Callahan remained outside the surgical tent, stretching his hamstrings. He straightened as Safiye walked toward him. "I'm fine," he said.

"What is it?" she asked, seeing his smile.

"Did you ever find yourself in the last place you ever expected to be?"

"More times than I care to think about," she said. "Why? I hope you're not having regrets about being here."

"No, I love the excursions. But I've begun to realize there's a whole lot of stuff, important stuff, I'm missing out on."

A group of boys ran by. One threw a ball to Callahan. He caught it and rolled it back and forth in his palm. "I promised myself I'd spend more time outside the hospital. This is a heck of a way of doing it."

Safiye looked toward the boys. "Your being here makes sense to them. For them, it's the difference between life and death." She nodded toward the ball. "And it looks to me like you're having a good time."

"That's the problem," he said, throwing the ball back. "I am."

They watched the boys.

"How about you?" he asked. "When have you found yourself in the last place you expected to be?"

"Right now. As you saw yesterday at lunch, my country can be repressive for women. One of the reasons I joined the relief team was to get away."

"Then we've both failed."

"If I look back and see this as a failure," Safiye said, "I believe I'll have lived a pretty good life."

Callahan softly elbowed her. "I was kidding."

Safiye smiled. "That's another reason I wanted to get away. There's not much sarcasm around here."

Mrs. Bagley emerged from the surgical tent.

"Is it time?" Safiye asked.

The elderly nurse nodded. Callahan and Safiye followed her to the mess tent.

Alin had called a meeting of the team's administrative council. He'd named Callahan and Safiye as physician representatives to the council, which also included Mrs. Bagley and Thomas.

Alin began the council meeting with an update. As the aftershocks from the earthquake diminished, the mayor had lifted the evacuation order. Residents were returning to the city. Izmir University Hospital, overwhelmed with patients, had requested help.

"I was impressed during my visit to the hospital," Alin said. "It's state of the art. For now, we'll stay in the call rooms, but I hear they might be getting rooms at the Büyük."

"The Büyük?" Safiye said. "That's a five-star hotel."

"We'll see," Alin said. "Either way, we start on Monday. I promised them four physicians and a nurse." He looked toward Callahan and Safiye. "I was hoping you two would take charge of scheduling. I thought we'd permanently loan them Scott Adams and Ramish Mahindra. The hospital is understaffed in their specialities: infectious disease and pulmonology."

Thomas handed out a list. "These are the supplies we have on order. Is there anything else we need?"

Donated supplies were stockpiled at WHO headquarters in Zurich. As they ran low during excursions, supplies were either shipped from Zurich or purchased using discretionary funds.

"Bottled water," Safiye said. "After Nata became ill, we placed quarantine notices by the river, but many are getting their drinking water from it."

"How is she?" Callahan asked.

"Stable but still sedated and requiring the ventilator," Safiye said. "The good news is she doesn't appear to be getting worse."

"See what we can get," Alin said to Thomas, "but supplying the entire tent city with bottled water is beyond our means. I'll bring it up in my next meeting with city officials."

Once the meeting adjourned, Callahan and Safiye stayed to work on the schedule. Afterward, they walked to the supply tent to make copies. As they neared the tent, the smell of tobacco permeated the air. Inside, the tent was hazy with smoke.

Thomas and Haas—cigars clenched between their teeth—were playing poker with Ramish and Brooke. Amanda stood behind Brooke.

"It's mine, all mine," Thomas cackled as he raked in a handful of change.

"We started without you," Haas said to Callahan.

Haas opened the refrigerator and picked out two beers, handing one to Callahan. "I'm buying." He extended the second bottle toward Safiye, who shook her head.

Haas opened the bottle. "Tonight, we're gonna take some rupees from Ramish and—" He turned to Brooke. "What do they barter with in Iowa? Cattle, corn, overalls?"

"Surgeons," Brooke said. "But they're really not worth much."

As everyone laughed, Brooke glanced at Callahan and Safiye and smiled. For better or worse, she and Haas were back together again.

Callahan took a swig of beer. He looked at the bottle's label. "Efes?"

"A Turkish beer," Haas said. "I picked it up in Ottoman Square."

Brooke turned toward Callahan and Safiye. "Ottoman Square is Eric's term for the market on the other side of the tent city."

"When you're there, don't you feel as though you just walked into the middle of the nineteenth century?" Haas asked.

"In many ways," Safiye said.

"Well, it's not Arn City," Haas said, raising his bottle. "But, when in Rome."

"You mean 'Iron' City?" Brooke asked, referring to the Pittsburgh-brewed beer.

"You'll be calling it Arn after you drink one," Haas said.

"Is that an invitation to 'Picksburg'?"

As Brooke's question hung in the air, everyone looked to Haas, who suddenly appeared flustered. He cleared his throat. "Sure," he said. "You're all invited. It'll be like Ottoman Square but better. We'll go to Primanti Brothers. We'll get pierogies."

Brooke's gaze narrowed. Standing, she turned to Callahan. "You can take my spot. Amanda and I are going to Ottoman Square."

"You'd prefer spending your evening with hookah-toking, turban-wearing misogynists?" Haas asked, his cigar clenched between his teeth.

"Beer-drinking, stinky cigar-smoking cretin versus Islamic fundamentalists," Brooke said. She held up her hands, weighing the choices. "Toss up." She looked to Safiye. "Interested?"

Safiye nodded.

"Anyone else?" Brooke asked. "You're all invited."

With no takers, the women left.

Ramish turned to Haas. "You handled that well."

Haas waved a hand. "We're better off without 'em."

The four continued to play poker, finishing off Haas's stash of beer. After the game broke up, they made their way to the Cloister and joined a group around the fire. Brooke, Safiye, and Amanda had returned from Ottoman Square and were there along with several others.

"There you are," Haas said. He flopped onto the grass at Brooke's side and set his head on her thigh.

In imitation, Callahan threw his hands up. "There you are," he said. He set his head on Brooke's other leg.

"My lost boys," Brooke said, patting their heads.

Alin was in the midst of a story. As Alin continued, Callahan stared into the fire, his head buzzing from too much beer.

"We were in Zimbabwe," Alin said. "The country was suffering from a horrid famine. A month before most of the men in the tribe had been killed in a fight with another tribe. There was no one to hunt. We had six team members. In the group was Dr. Henry Mack, a surgeon from Oklahoma. Henry was about six foot five. Henry decided that since he was going to Africa, he was going on safari. I think he'd read a little too much Hemingway. He smuggled a rifle and ammunition through customs. When we arrived at our encampment, the first thing Henry did was take off into the bush. A few hours later, he returned with a gazelle thrown over his shoulder. The villagers grabbed the animal and skinned it. Within ten minutes, it was on a barbecue spit.

"That whole month, Henry never operated once. The people were in more need of food than a surgeon, and Henry happily obliged. He brought back antelope, boar, kudu—anything he thought was 'big game.' The health of the village improved. I have no doubt it had more to do with Henry's hunting than our doctoring."

8

Day 6

allahan and Adams stepped from their tent. It was Saturday morning, a few minutes after dawn. Bryce and Haas stood outside in the dew-covered grass, talking quietly. The four began jogging, moving silently through the rows of tents. They followed Adams, who already had a route. North of the field, they headed east along a wooded trail.

"Do you really believe God wanted Henry VIII to establish a church?" Haas asked Bryce, continuing their conversation.

Bryce was a member of the Church of England. "Every other religion was started by men," he said. "Ours is no different. But you can't focus on the offenses of clergymen. It's the ideals they teach that we should strive for."

"I just can't believe a church was started because a king couldn't get a divorce," Haas said. "The founders of every religion are thought to have been inspired by God, but nobody thinks that about the monarchy—at least, not today."

"Are you suggesting Peter and Paul or Muhammad received more divine inspiration than Henry VIII?" Bryce asked. "Or for that matter, Martin Luther or Joseph Smith?"

"I'm not," Haas said. "But their followers do."

"You realize religious arguments are destined to go in circles," Adams said.

"Let 'em go, Scott," Callahan said. "Trust me. They can go on like this for hours."

Haas laughed. "Don't let Callahan kid you. He enjoys our verbal sparring matches as much as anyone. He pretends to be a spectator, but before you know it, he's rolling around in the muck with both of us."

The tentmates crossed a narrow bridge that passed over a river. Turning north, they ran side-by-side along a gravel road, which paralleled the river.

"For me, the church is a vehicle," Bryce said. "It provides a forum for thinking about important questions. Is there a god? How should I behave?"

The land surrounding the road transitioned from woods to farmland. Callahan looked toward the river—the river Nata had been playing in before she became sick. A constant southerly current kept it clean and free from stagnation. Nothing seemed out of the ordinary.

"Lil and I are bringing our kids up in the church," Adams said. "It has so many good lessons."

"I agree," Haas said. "The problems occur when people take it too seriously, when they use something they read in the Bible or Quran as justification for going on holy wars, stoning someone, genital mutilation, or doing whatever crazy shit enters their minds."

"The Church of England has backed off from a literal interpretation," Bryce said.

"The church has backed off on many things," Haas said. "They've been backpedaling for a few hundred years. And churchgoers have gone along with every step back. At heart, they know the Bible is just a collection of stories. They don't think the pope is infallible or the clergy has divine guidance."

They came to another wooded area. The woods were demarcated by a chain-link fence topped with swirling rows of rusted barbed wire. The river continued beneath the fence, disappearing into the thicket while the gravel road turned to the right.

The physicians continued along the road. After a short distance, they came to an intersection. "This way," Adams said, pointing them left onto a paved road.

The road led them deep into the woods. After a few hundred yards, the fence—which continued along the left side of the road—was interrupted by a gated entrance and a sentinel building.

They ran past the gate. Fifty yards later, they came to a stop.

A fissure crossed the road. Several inches high, its edge was a slope of broken pavement, roots, and mud that had been partially flattened by heavy-machinery tracks.

"Damn," Haas said.

"I thought you'd get a kick out of it," Adams said. "The earthquake's epicenter was downtown, but there must be a branching fault line that extends out here."

The fissure extended into the woods as far as they could see in both directions. Muddy tire tracks led back along the road and turned into the gated entrance.

"You've been quiet through this whole discussion," Adams said to Callahan. "Do you have any thoughts?"

"I think they're going to need to fix their fence," Callahan said, looking to where the fence buckled as the fissure passed beneath it.

"Seriously," Adams said.

"I think you're right," Callahan said. "All conversations about religion are destined to go in circles."

"You must have *some* thoughts," Adams said. "Do you believe in God?"

Callahan smiled.

"Answer him," Haas said. "You're not one of these useless talking heads running for public office."

"I'm an advocate of the Golden Rule," Callahan said. "Almost every situation can be solved if you simply put yourself in the other guy's shoes. But you're right. The church has many good messages. Behaving like Jesus or striving for your personal nirvana are good things."

"Michael thinks we should all be Buddhists," Haas said.

Callahan nodded. "Religion is Bryce's vehicle for meditating and thinking about the world. That's how it should be. Religions fail when they try to govern. They fail when clergymen try to impart knowledge or define the unknown. In that respect, I agree with Eric. The church has thrived on ignorance. They've claimed to know the nature of the universe, how the world was created, and how life started. But they've been repeatedly proven wrong. Not too long ago, they thought the earth was flat, propped up on four pillars, and created in seven days. Even today, religions claim they know what awaits us in the afterlife: a day of judgment, a heaven or hell, a reincarnation. But they don't."

Hans began clapping. "See, I told you. There he goes, diving right into it."

"In my opinion, the church's inability to embrace science has killed their credibility," Callahan said. He shrugged. "But, there's a universal need for religion. People have an inherent need for a higher power to consecrate special events and tell them there's a meaning to life. They want to be part of a community, and they want an afterlife, where their loved ones still exist and where they can live forever. When they pray, they want to believe someone is listening."

Day 8

The penetrating headlights of the late-model bus and the shrill whine of its overworked engine were an unwelcome intrusion upon the tranquil predawn countryside. Izmir had resumed its normal bus schedule, adding three routes a day to the tent city.

Waiting at a makeshift bus stop in the glow of a single bare light bulb were Callahan, Safiye, and the other relief team members scheduled to work at University Hospital: Haas, Brooke, Adams, and Ramish. After the bus came to a halt, they climbed aboard. The bus headed west.

Rays from the rising sun skipped tangentially across the countryside, creating a kaleidoscope of night and day. The team members, content to wrap themselves in what remained of the night, peered silently out the window as the land's ordered segregation into fields of tobacco, cotton, grapes, and figs was unveiled.

The bus made a slow descent from the coastal mountains into a long, sloping valley filled with low-lying, red-roofed buildings. On the distant horizon, the Aegean appeared. Against the sea's azure backdrop, Izmir's skyline, punctuated by high-rise buildings and numerous pointed minarets, came slowly into focus.

The city proper was filled with activity. Bulldozers knocked down compromised structures while pile drivers hammered out new foundations. Trucks carried away detritus while others brought in girders, rebar, and sheets of drywall, granite, and glass. Like all great cities following a disaster, Izmir was undergoing a reptilian transformation, tearing away its weakest parts and replacing them with something stronger.

The bus detoured around work zones, stopping several times in the shop-lined eastern districts before making its way downtown. When the bus stopped in front of a large building with a sterile white façade, Safiye stood. "This is it—University Hospital."

They walked inside. In the house staff office, they were given ID badges, beepers, and a brief orientation before they dispersed to their assigned locations.

At the fifth-floor surgery desk, Callahan and Haas read the names of their contacts from slips of paper to the receptionist. She repeated the names into a phone—her voice booming seconds later over an intercom.

An older man wearing a white coat appeared from a room and walked toward them. He had a full head of unruly graying hair and a bushy mustache.

"Gandalf," Haas mumbled.

"Turkish Einstein," Callahan countered.

The man appeared overworked with dark circles beneath penetrating but warm eyes. He stopped in front of them. "I'm Mavik Kuval, director of Surgery," he said in heavily accented English. He was Callahan's contact.

"Your contact should be here shortly," Kuval said to Haas after introductions. He then motioned for Callahan to follow.

"Alin assured us you're an excellent vascular surgeon," Kuval said. "Our vascular specialist, Bilecik, may he find peace with Allah, was killed in the earthquake."

"I'm sorry to hear that," Callahan said.

"Bilecik had done our vascular cases for the past twenty years," Kuval said.

The Turkish surgeon headed down a stairwell and then pushed through a doorway. He pointed toward a row of sinks next to double doors leading into an OR. "You can scrub here. They should be ready inside. The case is an aortic dissection. If you have questions, ask Kadri—the resident. I'll be in OR nine." Backing away, he gave a brief wave and then disappeared around the corner.

Callahan looked up and down the empty hallway. In Ann Arbor, aortic repairs and other complicated vascular cases were performed by fellowship-trained surgeons. He'd participated in a few emergency repairs during his general surgery residency, but it had been a while.

Tentatively, he donned a surgical mask and cap and scrubbed. He took another look up and down the hallway. Was this really happening? Was he starting a complicated surgery without having seen the patient? Without having reviewed his chart?

He backed through the doors, hands raised.

On a table in the middle of a white-tiled room, an anesthetized patient lay draped for surgery. One of several blue-gowned nurses rushed toward Callahan and handed him a sterile towel. A surgeon, already gowned and gloved, was looking at an X-ray in the view box. He turned. "Dr. Callahan?"

"Kadri?" Callahan said.

"Evet," the resident replied.

A nurse held up a gown, which Callahan slipped into. After tying it, she pointed to a cabinet containing gloves.

"Eights," he said.

The nurse raised a questioning eyebrow.

Callahan walked to the cabinet and pointed toward gloves. "Sekiz."

The nurse pulled the gloves from the cabinet and held each out as Callahan snapped his hands into them. Kadri and the two nurses then moved into a semicircle.

"What do we have?" Callahan asked, looking toward the patient.

Kadri didn't respond.

When Callahan repeated the question, Kadri motioned Callahan toward the view box.

"Ingilizce biliyor musununz?" Callahan asked.

"Hayir," Kadri replied.

Callahan pointed to the nurses.

"Hayir," Kadri repeated.

No one spoke English.

"Ingilizce biliyor musununz?" Callahan repeated.

Kadri shook his head.

Christ. This was too much. He couldn't operate like this.

As Callahan backed toward the doors, Kadri thrust a gloved forefinger toward the X-ray and spoke rapidly in Turkish.

Callahan paused. The X-ray showed fractures of the first and second ribs, a widened mediastinum, and loss of the aorta's normal contour—features consistent with a dissection. He looked toward the surgical table.

The patient's torso was draped in preparation for a left fourth intercostal thoracotomy. The anesthesiologist, peering at Callahan over the patient's head drape, gave a reassuring nod. Kadri walked to the surgical tray and picked up a scalpel, which he extended toward Callahan.

The situation was appalling. But what were the alternatives? An aortic dissection was a medical emergency. And Bilecik, the hospital's only vascular surgeon, was dead.

Callahan walked to the table. He imprinted the radiologic findings on the draped body. Looking toward Kadri, he reached out and took the scalpel.

The surgery began awkwardly. Callahan had to repeatedly walk over and sort through the instruments. But the scrub nurse, Suray, soon picked up on his terminology and began smartly snapping instruments into his hand.

It was also soon clear that Kadri was one of the best residents Callahan had ever worked with. Their hands moved in concert as they made their way through skin, muscle wall, and fascia into the patient's thoracic cavity.

When the anesthesiologist collapsed the left lung, the surgeons clamped the damaged section of aorta above and below the dissection. They replaced the damaged vessel with a Dacron graft. Standing back, they released the clamps.

Callahan held his breath as the graft grew taut with blood. The sutures held. No leaks.

Reversing the order of the surgery, they reinflated the lung and closed the chest wall. As they removed the surgical drapes, the OR doors swung open. Kuval entered.

Callahan tore off his gown and mask, his mind flooding with everything he'd wanted to say. Instead, he held his tongue.

"They're setting up a vascular case in room eight," Kuval said. "Another surgical team is waiting."

"I'd like to continue working with Kadri and Suray," Callahan said.

"I promise the other residents and staff are—"

"If this is going to work," Callahan said, interrupting, "and unless some of your residents speak English, I need to work with the same team."

Kuval looked toward Kadri and Suray, who were busy with the

patient. After a moment, he nodded. "The resident will bring you and Kadri up to date."

"And Suray."

"Yes," Kuval said. "And Suray."

And so it went for the rest of the day. Whenever the three of them were at or near the end of a case, Kuval appeared and directed them to the next room.

Late that night, after what Kuval promised would be their last case, the three of them wheeled the patient from the OR. In the post-op unit, Kadri began a surgical note. Suray checked the patient's vitals. Falling into a bedside chair, Callahan closed his eyes. As he began drifting to sleep, he was jarred awake by a familiar voice.

"There you are."

It was Kuval. "I'm sorry, but there's one more case," he said. "He's a fifty-nine-year-old male with a triple A. He had a bad fall. It's five centimeters and growing." He extended a chart.

A "triple A" was an abdominal aortic aneurysm. At five centimeters and growing, the aneurysm could rupture at any moment.

Callahan turned to Kadri and Suray. "Did either of you have anything else planned for tonight?" When Kuval interpreted, the two laughed.

Callahan reached for the chart. "He's in OR?"

"Five," Kuval said.

"And he's already on the table?"

"Yes," Kuval said. "Thank you."

10

Day 9

Callahan felt a nudge on his shoulder. After a few seconds, another. He opened his eyes.

"Uyan, uyan." Kadri was leaning over him, motioning him toward the door.

Callahan looked around the darkened call room. The other relief team members were still sleeping.

"Acil bir iş çikti," Kadri whispered.

It was 4:06 a.m. Callahan had been sleeping for less than three hours. He slid from his bunk and walked with the resident to the surgical floor.

In an OR, orthopedic surgeons were pinning the femur of a patient with an open fracture. Callahan had been called in to repair the femoral artery, which had been severed by the broken bone.

Two and a half hours later, the artery repaired, Callahan walked from the OR. Seeing no signs of Kadri, who'd left to answer a page, he headed toward the cafeteria. On the way, he spotted Adams, who was walking with a resident.

"Mike, hold on," Adams said, his pager beeping. "I need to tell you something."

Callahan followed Adams into a radiology room. As Adams answered his page on a house phone, the resident extended a hand. "I'm Emir Aksu."

"Mike Callahan," he said, shaking his hand. "You speak English?"

"Yes," Emir said. He slapped a chest X-ray into a view box. The X-ray contained dense infiltrates throughout the lungs.

"Besides rip-roaring pneumonia, what's wrong with him?" Callahan asked.

"He's a thirty-five-year-old male who presented with fever and cervical lymphadenopathy," Emir said. "He was initially placed on broad-spectrum antibiotics, but his lymph nodes kept enlarging. He was then admitted and treated with intravenous antibiotics without relief. When his lymph nodes began ulcerating through his skin, the infectious disease team was called in to consult."

Adams hung up the phone. He pointed at Callahan. "The relief team members are going out for dinner tonight. The plan is to meet Safiye's friends. Whoever's interested should be in the call room at six."

"I'll try to make it, but if I see the sun today, I'll consider myself lucky," Callahan said. "I feel like a cog in an overworked assembly line."

"Same here, but the cases are incredible." Adams turned toward the X-ray. "This guy's the most interesting of all."

"Emir was just telling me," Callahan said. He turned. "I presume his wounds were cultured?"

Emir nodded. "We just came back from the microbiology lab. A technician gave us her preliminary results. The cultures were positive for *Yersinia pestis.*"

Callahan recalled a distant medical school lecture. "The plague?"

"Bingo," Adams said. "Would you like to see him? We were on our way."

Callahan, pushing aside thoughts of food and more sleep, nodded.

The three physicians walked through the hospital to a quarantine room. They slipped on gowns, gloves, and masks before stepping inside.

A nurse sat at the bedside. She was fully gowned and wearing a face mask and gloves. With a scalpel, she scraped away dead tissue on the man's neck. He was sedated and snoring loudly.

The room was under negative pressure. Air was being pumped from the room to prevent the spread of airborne pathogens. Still, the room smelled of decay.

"The bubonic form of the plague affects the lymph nodes,"

Adams said. "The pneumonic form affects the lungs. He's got both."

"How'd he get it?" Callahan asked.

"Fleas are the vector for the bacteria, which are endemic in certain species of rodents and ground squirrels," Adams said. "He must have been bitten. He's a farmer."

"Emir said his lymph nodes kept enlarging even though he was given broad-spectrum antibiotics," Callahan said.

"That's what doesn't make sense," Adams said. "*Yersinia* should respond to most antibiotics, but this strain hasn't. The microbiology tech said it's resistant to everything they've tested it against. That's why she would only give me a preliminary read. She needs to run the results by her supervisor."

That evening, despite a busy afternoon, Callahan finished in time to join the team members for dinner. Adams and Ramish were still working, but Safiye along with Brooke and Haas were in the call room.

They set out on foot from the hospital, heading west.

A salty breeze rolled in from the Aegean, which peeked at them between shoreline buildings. As they stepped out onto the Atatürk Caddesi, a wide four-lane boulevard that ran along the bay, the coast came into view.

"In the summer, pleasure boats dock at the harbor to the north," Safiye said. "Tourists spend the day shopping and eating along the shore."

As the city unearthed itself from the quake, the scene before them looked quite different. No cruise ships were docked in the harbor. No tourists were in sight. Many shops and restaurants were closed. Except for the occasional passing car and rare pedestrian, the seaside street was deserted.

They walked north along the boulevard. Scattered groups of salesmen and maître d's sat lazily in front of their establishments, talking among themselves.

After several blocks, they turned inland. At a row of buildings, they followed Safiye through an unmarked door and down a hallway. They were struck by scents reminiscent of Ottoman Square: olive oil, cardamom, tobacco, and garlic. Hearing the clink of silverware and the buzz of voices, they emerged through an open doorway and found themselves in the midst of a busy upscale restaurant.

"This is it," Safiye said.

Tuxedoed waiters scurried among well-dressed patrons at linen-covered tables.

"I hope they don't have a dress code," Haas mumbled, looking at himself and then the other team members—all adorned in an assortment of surgical scrubs, tennis shoes, T-shirts, and jeans.

The maître d' approached wearing an apron and black bow tie. "Kaç kişi?" After he and Safiye spoke, the maître d' led them to a private room. As the team members sat around an oval table, the maître d' popped the cork on a bottle of wine and filled their wineglasses. "Şerefe," he said, raising his own glass.

"Elinize sağlik," Safiye replied.

Everyone drank.

"What did he say?" Brooke asked after the maître d' left.

"'May there be appetite,'" Safiye said. "And *elinize sağlik* means 'health to your hand'. It's a common courtesy to say to someone who fixes your food."

As waiters brought baskets of pita bread and olives, Brooke turned to Safiye. "Tell us about your friends."

Safiye had largely kept to herself during previous excursions. This trip had been different. Perhaps it was because they were in Turkey and Alin looked to her for leadership. Perhaps she was becoming more comfortable with the group. Either way, everyone welcomed the change.

"Ayla and I grew up together in Izmir," Safiye said, peering at them above her glasses. "We were best friends."

"Didn't you go to school in DC?" Brooke asked.

Safiye nodded. "I went to undergrad at George Washington and finished med school and residency at Georgetown." She smiled. "During the summer, Ayla would visit. Once, we went to a function at the Turkish Embassy. That's where Ayla met Mehmet, who's also from Turkey. He was working at the National Institutes of Health. They fell in love. She stayed into the fall, and they were married."

"How did two girls from Izmir end up attending embassy events in Washington, DC?" Haas asked.

"Eric," Brooke said, slapping his shoulder.

"That's okay," Safiye said. "My father was the Turkish ambassador."

"That's amazing," Brooke said.

Safiye nodded. "Living in Washington was a great experience."

"Your friend's husband must be a top-notch researcher," Callahan said. "The NIH is a high-powered place."

"Mehmet's incredible," Safiye said. "Beyond incredible. He and Ayla returned to Izmir when he had a chance to start his own lab. He was tired of working for someone else."

"Very tired."

Everyone turned toward the voice.

A man stood in the doorway. Gray around the temples, he wore a blue blazer, tan khaki pants, and a white sports shirt. "Safiye, I hope you're not telling all my secrets."

Skipping across the room, Safiye embraced the man. She then turned to the others. "This is Mehmet Koba."

As Mehmet bowed, a balding man with a graying goatee entered the room with a woman wearing a tan head scarf. Mehmet turned toward them. "I'd like to introduce Dr. Yalçin Kaldırım and his wife Berna."

Another woman appeared in the doorway. She and Safiye ran into each other's arms.

"Ayla, look at you," Safiye said. "You look wonderful."

Ayla Koba wore a brown dress with an open back. Breathtaking, she had turquoise eyes, silky dark hair, and unblemished skin. The team members couldn't help but agree. Ayla Koba was beautiful.

After introductions, everyone sat.

"On behalf of my country, I would like to say thank you," Mehmet said. "What you're doing here is incredible. It makes me feel as though I'm not doing enough, and I live here."

"It's a beautiful city," Brooke said.

"I'm impressed by how open everything is," Callahan said. "It's so much more modern-looking than Istanbul."

"That's because of the Great Fire," Ayla said.

"Fire?" Brooke said.

"After World War I, the Greeks were allotted Izmir and Turkey's west coast, but when they marched into central Turkey and crossed the Milne Line, Atatürk and his soldiers drove them back into the Aegean. During the fighting, several fires started. No one knows exactly who was responsible, but Izmir burned to the ground. Afterward, the city was rebuilt along more modern lines."

"Ask Ayla anything about Turkish history," Safiye said. "I've learned more from her than all my teachers combined."

"Will Turkey ever be allowed into the European Union?" Haas asked.

"*History* question," Brooke said.

"That's okay," Ayla said. "It's a great question. When the EU formed, the answer would have been no. Then came the 1999 Helsinki decision allowing Turkey in as a candidate member. A major obstacle to full membership has been our constitution. President Cebici has made changes, but they've been terribly self-serving. Emboldened by populist support, he's broadened his powers, decreasing the influence of parliament and the judiciary. His actions have not endeared Turkey to the EU." Ayla smiled. "But Cebici is getting old. He's said he won't run in the upcoming elections. The wolves are already circling. The country's path, and how strongly we pursue EU membership, will largely be determined by our next president."

All eyes turned to Safiye, who broke into a broad grin. As everyone began to laugh, Safiye wrapped an arm around Ayla. "I told you. She's incredible."

Waiters entered the room and began taking orders. Callahan, sitting next to Mehmet, turned. "How long did you work at the NIH?"

"Ten years," Mehmet replied.

"It's an incredible institution. Was leaving hard?"

"Not too hard. After Ayla and I were married, an opportunity presented itself to come back to Turkey."

"To run your own lab?" Callahan asked.

"As they say, it was an offer I couldn't refuse. But I loved DC. I look back very fondly on my time in the States, for a number of reasons." Mehmet took Ayla's hand and kissed it. The gesture, however, went unnoticed as she and Safiye continued talking.

"I should know better," Mehmet said. "When they're together like this, they're nonstop."

Throughout dinner that night, Callahan's gaze repeatedly wandered toward the two women. Ayla Koba was not only beautiful but also extremely personable. Most interestingly, she drew out similar traits in Safiye. Based on initial impression, the two women could not have appeared more unalike. Safiye wore one of her thick sweaters, and her hair was pulled back into a maintenance-free bun. But as the dinner progressed, Safiye's shy demeanor and even her bookish appearance melted away.

"You're from Ann Arbor?" Mehmet asked Callahan.

"Yes."

"It's a fine institution. I was there once for a conference. What kind of research are you involved in?"

"Cancer research," Callahan said. "Mostly clinical trials using immunotherapy—tumor-directed antibodies."

"What antibodies do you work with?"

"I'm involved in a few clinical trials, for one, antibody to Hu-689."

"From Kinmesta Pharmaceuticals?" Mehmet asked.

"Yes," Callahan said. "You're familiar with it?"

Mehmet nodded. "Hu-689 is overexpressed on the membranes of some adenocarcinomas, but it's also expressed in normal liver tissue."

Callahan stared back in disbelief. A few days before the excursion, he'd received word the first clinical trial using the Kinmesta antibody had been discontinued. Patients with late-stage gastric carcinoma were experiencing liver failure. "How'd you know about the cross reactivity with the liver?"

"In our lab, animal models allow us to test our hypotheses," Mehmet replied.

"You have the antibody?"

"No, it's not commercially available. But we have an accomplished immunologist in our group. A few years ago, he developed something similar to the Kinmesta antibody."

"Have you published?" Callahan asked.

"We haven't." Mehmet gave a doleful smile. "I'm afraid if we reported all of our failures, we wouldn't have time for anything else. In our experience, we've found the early optimism associated with new antibodies is often unfounded."

"Yes," Callahan said. "The antibodies never seem to be as specific as initially hoped."

Mehmet nodded. "So often there's an unforeseen cross-reaction. It's no good to kill the tumor while knocking out the liver, heart, brain, or another vital organ."

Ayla wrapped her arm around her husband. "You men look so serious. Please, no talk about attacking organs or killing tumors. Tonight is a night to relax."

Mehmet laughed. "As usual, you're right." He kissed her cheek.

Across the table, Brooke and Haas were talking to the Kaldırıms.

"Last night, the tremors caused a container of solvent to fall and break," Yalçin was saying. "But otherwise, there were no problems."

"Every patient on our floor hit their call button," Brooke said. "But I can't blame them. It was scary."

"You needn't worry," Yalçin said. "During the earthquake, the hospital went undamaged. Residual tremors shouldn't be a problem."

"You work in the hospital?" Callahan asked.

"Yalçin is the director of the microbiology lab," Mehmet said.

"Microbiology?" Callahan said. "Then you must have seen the *Yersinia* cultures from the patient in quarantine."

Yalçin dabbed a napkin at the corners of his mouth. "Well, yes and no," he said. "The bacterium was misidentified by one of our laboratory technicians. It's not *Yersinia pestis*, but *Pasteurella dagmatis*. The correct report went out this afternoon."

"I was surprised by the bacteria's antibiotic resistance," Callahan said. "Is *Pasteurella* typically resistant to so many antibiotics?"

"If you treat the patient with Zagam, one of the new fluoroquinolones, he should improve," the microbiologist said. "The antibiotic is available in our dispensary."

"I'll tell Adams," Callahan said. "Thanks."

The waiters cleared the plates. Trays of Turkish delight and slices of baklava were brought in. The maître d' poured glasses of port. As he had prior to each new course, he held up a glass in a silent toast. When he drank, the others did likewise.

"He's trying to get us drunk," Brooke said when the maître d' left.

"It's working," Ayla said.

Safiye raised her glass. "This has been a great dinner. To Izmir and friends."

"To Izmir and friends," everyone toasted.

Ayla held her glass up to the light. Swirling the wine, she gave it an appraising look. Safiye did likewise.

"Good legs," Ayla said.

"Very good," Safiye said. "And good color."

Mehmet ran a hand over his face. "Oh no."

Ayla held her glass beneath her nose. "Aromatic."

"A rich, deep bouquet," Safiye said.

They took sips.

"And lively," Safiye said.

"Very," Ayla said. "When it touches your lips, there are hints of peppercorn and vanilla."

"As it moves over your tongue, it transitions to raspberry and coffee," Safiye added. "A good mouthfeel."

Berna Kaldırım leaned toward her husband. "What did she say?"

"I sense hints of South American rain forests, Swiss mountain streams, and Belgium wheat fields," Ayla continued.

"With a harmonizing symphony of redwood, maple, and oak," Safiye said.

"They're drunk," Haas said.

"It only takes about a glass—" Mehmet began before Ayla clamped her hand over his mouth. "That's paired well with cambozola, taleggio, or asiago," she said.

"It recedes," Safiye said, "to a citrusy explosion of tangerine, mandarin, and pomelo. Accented with a sweet aftertaste of forbidden love and summer nights."

"At some point, these two had way too much time on their hands," Haas said.

"Weekends in Georgetown," Mehmet said. "They've been like this ever since we went wine tasting in Virginia. When the steward began describing the wines, they started giggling and couldn't stop. When the wine began bubbling through their noses, we were asked to leave. They've been wine-label connoisseurs ever since."

Safiye and Ayla turned toward each other and raised their glasses.

"It ends in a velvety, lingering crescendo," Safiye said. "That's easily paired with a wide variety of desserts."

"Enjoyed now or cellared for an encore performance," Ayla said.

The two women gave deep contented sighs, their shoulders drooping in mock exhaustion.

After a round of applause, Safiye and Ayla clinked their glasses together. Feeling the effects of the wine, their eyes sparkling, they giggled uncontrollably.

11

Day 10

After the ruthless efficiency of University Hospital, Callahan felt sluggish during his return to the field hospital. By noon, he'd finished only a single case. For lunch, he joined a group heading to Ottoman Square. Spotting Bryce walking by himself, he jogged to his side. "What's up?"

The normally well-groomed Oxford grad, surprisingly unshaven, stared somberly ahead.

"Nothing," Callahan said, filling the silence. "How are you?"

"Did you hear what happened?"

Callahan's stomach sank. "No."

"Nata died."

"I'm sorry to hear that. I'm so sorry. But she was a sick girl. A very sick girl."

"Her pulmonary function went to hell," Bryce said. "I should have seen it coming."

"You did an incredible job with her. Under the circumstances, she received the best of care."

"That's just it. *Under the circumstances.* I should have transferred her to Ramish's care at University Hospital. She would have had access to better facilities."

"The hospital was crazy," Callahan said. "Everyone was overworked. They had supply shortages, tremors. Keeping her here, even in retrospect, was the right decision."

Bryce shook his head. "I forgot rule number one. Know when

you're in over your head. I thought I could take care of her myself. My ego killed her."

Callahan knew there was nothing he could say to make Bryce feel better. Good doctors agonized over their decisions even when the outcome was a success. An unexpected death, particularly a child's, was devastating. Bryce had lost patients before. They all had. Still, Callahan had never seen Bryce like this.

"Did her blood work show anything?" Callahan asked.

"Her cultures never grew anything. We sent one of her blood samples to the reference lab in Paris for analysis but haven't received the results."

"What about an autopsy?"

"Her parents wouldn't consent," Bryce said. He looked up toward a nearby hill. "We buried her this morning."

That night at dinner, Callahan sat with Safiye, Brooke, and Haas in the mess tent. Adams joined the group.

"They let you out?" Haas asked.

"For the moment," Adams replied.

"How's your quarantine patient?" Callahan asked. "The farmer."

"He's improving. He's responding to Zagam."

"Dr. Kaldırım was right then," Callahan said. "It's a *Pasteurella* infection."

Adams shook his head. "I don't think so. The farmer's symptoms—the pneumonia, the buboes—are textbook for *Yersinia*, which would also respond to Zagam."

"Hasn't the plague been wiped out?" Brooke asked.

"Infections still exist, but they're rare," Adams said. "*Yersinia* is no longer a significant pathogen because it responds to most antibiotics. The last epidemic was in Asia in the early nineteen hundreds."

"You said the bug infecting the farmer was resistant to most antibiotics," Callahan said. "Would that be typical for *Yersinia*?"

"No, but it's not typical for *Pasteurella* either," Adams said. He set down his fork. "What really bothers me, however, is how did Kaldırım know the bug was susceptible to Zagam?"

"He must have tested it," Callahan said.

Adams shook his head. "When the lab tech gave us her

preliminary report, she said she hadn't shown the culture plates to her director. She said it was resistant to everything she'd tested it against. But at that point, she hadn't exposed it to Zagam. That's what's strange. It takes at least a day to run susceptibility tests. They couldn't have found the bug susceptible to Zagam by dinner."

"How else would Kaldırım have known then?" Safiye asked.

"Good question," Adams replied.

"I don't see why you're so concerned," Haas said. "The head of the microbiology lab identifies a bug, recommends treatment, and the patient is getting better. Chalk one up for the good guys."

Adams took a bite of food and nodded.

Haas shrugged. "Now that your patient's responding to the antibiotic, the bacteria are no longer recoverable. You'll never know whether or not it's *Yersinia*."

"True," Adams said, a glint in his eyes.

"Then why so happy?" Haas asked.

"Perhaps it would have been a good idea to take another set of cultures before starting the Zagam," Adams said.

"You didn't," Haas said.

Adams smiled. "I did."

"You devious bastard."

"That's why I came back," Adams said. "I just gave the cultures to Thomas. They're on their way to the lab in Paris."

That night, Alin held an administrative council meeting. Afterward, Callahan and Safiye remained in the mess tent to update the schedule. Administrators from University Hospital had requested help in orthopedics. Callahan and Safiye added the team's two orthopedic surgeons to the rotation. They also began assigning team members their allotted one day off per week. Thus far, everyone had been too busy to take it.

"On Saturday, I'm going sailing with Mehmet and Ayla," Safiye said. "Would you like to go?"

"Where?"

"They have a cottage on the coast. North of here."

He began leafing through the schedule. "Saturday?"

"Yes," she said, "If you'd rather not, I'd understand."

He pointed. "It's open."

"Are you sure? You don't have to."

As he considered his reply, Callahan's thoughts traveled back to the Guatemala excursion, four years earlier. He'd become involved with Jenna—an internist from Boston. Toward the end of the excursion when most relationships fizzled, theirs intensified. They spent their free moments in each other's arms, savoring each touch, each smile, each kiss.

Two weeks after the excursion, he called Jenna and told her he was flying to Boston for the weekend.

"To visit *me*?" she asked.

"Of course."

"You—you can't."

"Why not?" he asked.

"I'm seeing someone."

Everyone had a past. He couldn't expect her to discard it—not yet, at least.

"An old boyfriend?" he asked.

"No, someone new—a cardiologist from the hospital."

A wave of nausea swept through him.

Someone new.

At that moment, he realized Jenna did have a past. Him.

Without another word, he ended the call.

For many, the excursions were an altruistic break before marriage, kids, and career took over. The thrill of being in a foreign country combined with the camaraderie built by days and nights of working together fostered fast fraternization that often led to intimacy. From one excursion to the next, however, the relationships didn't last. His experience with Jenna had not been uncommon.

"We can work at the hospital on Friday and have Saturday off," Callahan said, tapping his pencil on the schedule. "It works out perfectly."

"Great," Safiye said.

Callahan looked up toward Safiye. Before last night, the thought of anything romantic between them would have seemed crazy. Now, he wasn't so sure.

A day of sailing sounded like fun. But he wondered if this would be like his relationship with Jenna. Was it something he should end before it ever had a chance to start?

12

One year earlier
Republic of Dagestan, Russia

Petrovich maintained almost perfect plank position: his palms flat to the floor, elbows locked, and back straight. His neck was bent, however, as he looked out the glass door onto the rolling waves of the Caspian.

Tatiana had taken him from Moscow's Burdenko Military Hospital to Makhachkala in the northern Caucasus region. The seaside town was a site where the Russian elite vacationed. But their time here had been anything but a holiday.

"Plank, not upward dog," Tatiana said.

Petrovich straightened his neck.

"Chaturanga," she said.

Petrovich bent his elbows until his face was a few centimeters from the floor. As he held the position, sweat dripped from his nose onto the mat.

"Upward dog," Tatiana said.

They raised their heads and bent their spines back, trying to look skyward.

"Plank," Tatiana said after several moments.

They straightened their backs.

"And chaturanga."

Petrovich collapsed onto the mat. "I can't do it."

"Five more reps and we're done."

"Then what?"

"Weight training."

Petrovich rubbed his shoulder. "This can't be good."

"You need to break up the scar tissue. Range-of-motion exercises are good. Pain is good. So is the weight lifting. You've atrophied."

He flexed his bicep. "You think so?"

"You spent over six months in bed. What did you expect? Come on. Five more reps."

Petrovich pushed into plank position.

"Keep your back straight," she said.

"When are we eating?"

"After weights."

"What are we having?" he asked.

"Burgers and salad."

"*Tofu* burgers?"

"Yes," she said.

"Please, Tatiana. Let me take you out. We need real food."

"You need to cleanse your system. All those painkillers they gave you at Burdenko are terrible. And you were smoking again, weren't you?"

Petrovich began to speak, but she waved a hand. "Don't bother. I know they gave you nicotine patches to wean you off the cigarettes. I also saw what they fed you. I can't believe they expect sick people to get better on fried food and soda. It's no wonder you gained weight."

"You're saying I'm fat *and* weak?"

"And, most unfortunately, lazy."

13

"Everything we see in the world is the creative work of women."

—**Mustafa Kemal Atatürk**

Day 12

"We'll have another case ready shortly," Kuval said to Callahan. "After that, there are only two more patients for you."

Callahan was at University Hospital. After finishing a case, he'd found Kuval scrubbing outside the adjacent OR.

"Take some time off," Kuval said. "Enjoy the city. It's Friday. Students from the music conservatory are putting on free concerts in Konak Square's amphitheater. It's their way of helping the city return to normal." He raised a dripping forefinger as he backed from the sink. "And, if you only go to one restaurant while you're here, I recommend Lysimakhos Lokantası." With a nod, he disappeared into the OR.

Callahan headed toward his next case, believing he'd be working late into the night. As Kuval promised, however, he had only two more cases. That evening, he checked in at the Büyük Hotel. The five-star hotel had reopened and was letting the relief team members stay rent-free. He showered, dressed, and then walked down to the lobby.

The team members had met the last couple of nights in the

lobby before heading out for dinner. Callahan waited until several minutes after six p.m.—the previous meeting time. Not seeing anyone, he bought a newspaper and headed toward the hotel restaurant, resigned to dinner alone.

A woman emerged from a hallway ahead of him and walked toward the restaurant. She wore a black dress with a flared skirt and had a thin waist and lean, athletic legs. She stopped outside the restaurant. Callahan continued past her, trying not to stare.

"*Michael?*"

He was startled to recognize the woman. It was Safiye. Her hair, long and silky and no longer confined to a bun, fell just beyond her shoulders. Her shoulders, except for the thin straps of her dress, were bare.

"Hi." He pointed. "No glasses."

"Contacts."

For the first time, he noticed her eyes were a deep green.

"Are we still on for sailing tomorrow?" he asked.

"Still interested?"

"I am. I even stopped in the hotel's shop and bought a swimsuit."

"I had to make a few unexpected purchases myself," Safiye said, glancing down at her dress. "When I packed, I didn't expect to go sailing or to be frequenting nice restaurants."

"You look great."

"Thank you."

"Where's the crew?" he asked.

"Amanda and Eric headed back to the field hospital. And I know the orthopods have a late OR case."

"I saw Ramish and Scott earlier. They said they were too busy for dinner."

The two smiled at each other.

"I guess you're stuck with me," Callahan said.

"Likewise."

Safiye turned toward the hotel restaurant. "We could eat here."

Callahan flipped the newspaper on a bench. "Follow me. I have a better idea."

Outside, Callahan waved down a taxi. He spoke briefly with the driver before sliding into the back seat next to Safiye.

"What was that about?" she asked.

"You picked the site of the field hospital. The least I can do is pick where we're going for dinner."

"And that is?"

He smiled. "A surprise."

Twenty minutes later, the taxi came to a stop at a restaurant on a large hill in Izmir's eastern district. "Mount Pagus," the driver announced. "Lysimakhos Lokantası."

"Have you been here?" Callahan asked.

"Once," Safiye said. "It's a wonderful restaurant."

They were seated on the second-floor balcony. After giving the waiter their orders, they took in the coastline.

Safiye pointed to the crumbling remains of an ancient stone tower. "The Citadel. The restaurant is named after its builder—Lysimachus, one of Alexander the Great's generals. After Alexander died, Lysimachus named himself king of Lysimachia, a territory centered in Istanbul."

"This was before Constantine named the city Constantinople?"

"The area has *never* suffered from a shortage of narcissists."

Their waiter brought their food. As they ate and continued talking, Callahan noticed Safiye's attention frequently wander across the balcony. After one of her prolonged stares, Callahan followed her gaze to an empty table. "Is everything okay?" he asked.

"Sure. Why?"

"You seem distracted."

Safiye gave a melancholy smile. "I've been debating whether I can get through dinner without mentioning this. I guess I can't."

Callahan raised an eyebrow.

"I owe you a little more history." She took a deep breath and turned. "That table is where my fiancé proposed to me."

"Fiancé?" He glanced around. "Will he be making an appearance?"

Safiye laughed. "The engagement ended a long time ago." She looked toward the table. "I just can't help but keep imagining myself sitting there. I was so different then. I was eighteen. Like most young Turkish girls, I only wanted to marry well. I—" She paused. "I'm sorry. This must be boring."

"Not at all. I take it the engagement was before you went to Washington?"

She nodded. "My father's appointment came at the perfect time. I needed to get away. In the States, everything changed for me." She surveyed the restaurant. "Being here again, I feel as though I've come full circle."

"Is your father still ambassador?"

"He passed away several years ago."

"I'm sorry."

"Don't be," she said. "He lived a very full life."

"And your mother?"

"She died while giving birth to my brother."

Callahan cringed. "I'm making you relive your lowlights."

"It's fine." Safiye summoned a smile. "How about you? Are your parents still living?"

"Retired. They spend their summers at a cottage on Green Bay, their winters in Florida."

"Any siblings?"

"A younger sister, Kate," he said. "And you?"

"Just the younger brother."

They sat quietly for a few moments before Safiye broke into a broad grin. "You know what I'd like to know?"

"What?"

"What happened to you and Jenna."

Callahan groaned. "You've got a good memory."

"It was my first excursion. You two made quite an impression."

Callahan couldn't remember Safiye being in Guatemala, but then he could hardly remember anyone but Jenna being there. "Let's just say things didn't work out," he said.

"They worked out for a while. I thought you two were connected at the hip. Seriously, I thought you'd last."

"Not even for a month after the excursion."

"I'm sorry," she said.

"It's like your engagement. Something that ended a *long* time ago."

They sipped their wines.

"Speaking of relationships," she said. "What you said to Brooke about Eric the other day was nice."

Callahan shrugged. "They would have gotten back together again anyway."

Safiye threw him a quizzical look. "Did you see what happened?"

"No."

"Brooke was so touched by what you'd said about Eric being jealous, she marched into the surgical tent, wrapped her arms around him, and gave him a kiss."

"I missed it," he said, laughing. "Don't quote me on this, but

I'm getting the feeling Eric is starting to think about settling down. He's not exactly a spring chicken anymore."

"He just acts like one."

After dinner, they walked outside to a waiting taxi. As Safiye slipped into the back, Callahan spoke quietly with the driver.

"Another surprise?" Safiye asked once he was seated beside her.

"I have to redeem myself. But if I manage to dredge up more painful memories, promise you'll stop me."

"I made it through dinner sitting two tables away from where I was engaged. I'm sure I'll make it through whatever comes next with flying colors."

The taxi took them back downtown. Passing into the heart of the city, they turned onto a narrow street filled with peddlers.

"This was once called the street of the Mevlevis," Safiye said.

"*Mevlevis?*"

"Sufis—Islamic mystics. You probably know them as 'whirling dervishes.'" She pointed. "Some are performing now."

A dozen men stood in an open area. Wearing white shrouds and large cylindrical hats, they were spinning, arms extended as they looked skyward.

"The ritual brings them closer to truth and perfection," Safiye said. "To achieve them, they have to set aside ego. Their hat represents ego's tombstone. The white robe represents ego's death shroud."

"And they're whirling because?"

"That represents the planets spinning around the sun. Their open hand, facing skyward, represents their openness to God."

They watched out the rear window until the men disappeared from view. Moments later, the driver brought the taxi to a stop at the edge of an area that opened to the bay.

"Konak Square," Safiye said.

Music filled the air as they stepped from the taxi.

"Have you been to the amphitheater?" Callahan asked.

"During field trips when I was a girl. Is that what you were planning?"

"If it's okay?"

"It's more than okay," she said.

Callahan extended his elbow. Safiye wrapped her arm in his.

"You surprise me, Michael Callahan," Safiye said as they walked across the square. "Good food and now good music. I hereby relinquish all future planning to you."

"I can't take credit. They were recommendations from Dr. Kuval—my contact at the hospital."

"Tell him he has excellent taste," Safiye said.

As the sun set over the Aegean, the music from the amphitheater stopped. Silence momentarily hung over the square before a high-pitched muezzin sounded the call to prayer. Dozens of people filed in and around an ornate domed octagonal building. Setting down their rugs, they knelt and began their prayers to Kaaba.

"Do you need to—?" Callahan asked. He couldn't recall seeing Safiye perform the namaz.

"I'm fine," she said. "I was raised as a Muslim, but let's just say I'm not a strict worshipper."She motioned toward the crowd. The majority were ignoring the call to prayer. "Like most."

They sat and watched as the Muslim faithful performed the sunset prayer.

"That's Yalı Mosque," Safiye said, pointing toward the octagonal structure. "It was built in 1750." She nodded toward a stone tower. "And that's the Clock Tower. It was a gift from the German emperor to the sultan. The mosque and the tower were the only buildings that survived the Great Fire. Afterward, the city was built around them."

When the prayer ended, the horizon glowing red, Callahan and Safiye continued to the amphitheater and found seats. The orchestra, which had resumed, was playing Beethoven's "Pastoral."

Safiye closed her eyes and moved her head in rhythm with the music.

"That was beautiful," she said when the piece finished.

They stayed for the remainder of the concert—a Middle Eastern homage to Beethoven. When it was over, they filed with the others from the amphitheater toward a queue of taxis. Neither wanting the night to end, they veered away from the taxis and strolled along a bayside pathway.

The pathway led them to a harbor. At the end of a dock, they sat on a bench overlooking the bay.

The moon hovered over the bay. Waves and a light breeze rocked the boats, causing their lines to clang lazily against the masts.

"That sound reminds me of my childhood," Safiye said. "We used to sail on the Aegean. At the end of the day, we would dock the boat and swim. My father would sit back and watch me and my brother with our friends. It was the only time my father wasn't in motion. But when I think of him, that's the image I recall."

Callahan set his arm around her. She set her head on his shoulder.

A large pleasure boat circling the bay made its way slowly toward them. On deck, dozens danced as a band played.

"Beethoven and now Green Day," Callahan said.

Onstage, a Billy Joe Armstrong look-alike sang.

The boat pulled alongside the dock. "*Altin Yol,*" Callahan said, reading the name on the bow.

"'Golden road,'" she said. "It's named after an ancient road built by the Romans south of Izmir."

A few groups who were congregating on the dock boarded the boat. One of the men remained behind, looking anxiously toward the parking lot. When the ship's horn blew, he ran toward them and held out two tickets, speaking rapidly in Turkish.

"Some of his friends didn't make it," Safiye said. "He says it's a two-hour ride."

"Sounds perfect," Callahan said.

The man handed his tickets to Safiye. Callahan pulled out his wallet to pay, but the man waved him off and ran back to the boat. Callahan and Safiye ran after him, leaping onto the boat as it left the dock.

Safiye took Callahan's hand and pulled him onto the dance floor. After dancing to several songs, they wandered the boat, finding a bench on the empty rear deck.

"In the OR, late at night when I need an adrenaline kick, I listen to Green Day," Callahan said.

"I love them," Safiye said. She'd sung along to all of the songs.

"You don't seem like a punk rocker."

"If Green Day is punk rock, then I guess I am," she said, her chin jutting defiantly.

He smiled. "Okay."

She looked across the water. "I like Green Day because they remind me of Washington. When I first went to the United States, my college roommate and her friends took me to a Green Day concert. It was an incredible time. The people I met that night ended up being my friends for the next four years."

The boat continued its leisurely circuit around the bay. It was a warm summer night, but the wind off the bay was cool. Callahan again wrapped his arm around Safiye. She set her head on his shoulder. As they stared contentedly toward the city lights and their rippling reflections on the water, the tent city was suddenly a thousand miles away.

The boat made several stops but too soon found its way back to their dock. Leaving the boat, they strolled hand-in-hand to Konak Square, where they caught a taxi back to the hotel. They walked through the lobby to a bank of elevators.

"I had a wonderful time tonight," Safiye said.

"I'm sorry about the restaurant. I hope the memories weren't too bad."

"Now I have good ones to replace them with."

Neither moved.

"We should probably call it a night," Safiye said.

"We should."

Safiye looked inquisitively down the hallway. "Did you see the pool?"

Callahan was in the water by the time Safiye appeared in her bathrobe. A couple was in the hot tub. Otherwise, the deck was empty.

Safiye took off her bathrobe. Wearing a one-piece white suit, she walked to the edge of the pool and dove in, splashing Callahan when she surfaced.

Callahan returned the splash. He swam underwater and grabbed her legs. Picking her up, he flipped her into the water. After a few minutes of playful swimming, they came to a stop. Their backs to the pool wall, they looked across the shimmering water.

"Does this seem like an excursion?" Callahan asked.

"At the moment, no."

They looked toward the hot tub. The couple had left.

"We chased them away," Safiye said.

"All part of my plan."

He leaned toward her. They kissed.

"That was nice," she said, their lips almost touching.

They continued kissing. Beneath the waterline, their bodies drifted together.

After several moments, they looked into each other's eyes. They were pressed together, his arms holding her tight, her legs wrapped around him.

"Let's go," Safiye said.

Callahan nodded.

Climbing from the pool, they slipped into their bathrobes. They walked hand-in-hand back into the hotel. Safiye pointed. "My room's just—"

"Safiye."

Turning toward the voice, they reflexively let go of each other's hands.

Brooke was walking from the lobby. "I've been looking all over for you," she said to Safiye. "They told me you left the hospital. I—" She stopped. "You two went swimming? At this hour?"

The field hospital suddenly wasn't so far away.

"Where's everybody else?" Brooke asked.

Safiye shrugged. "We're it."

A grin spread across Brooke's face.

"Where's Eric?" Callahan asked.

"He had a late case at the field hospital," Brooke said. "Since I work at University Hospital tomorrow, I thought I might as well stay here." She looked toward Safiye. "I *was* hoping to room with you, but if you have plans here with tall, dark, and handsome, I understand."

Callahan bowed. "Have a wonderful night, ladies." He hit the button for the elevator.

"Seriously," Brooke said. "I'll get my own room."

Safiye grabbed Brooke's forearm. "Can you wait a second?"

Brooke nodded.

Stepping toward Callahan, Safiye slipped her arms around his neck. "I had a wonderful time tonight—tall, dark, and handsome."

Callahan wrapped his arms around her waist, and they kissed.

14

Day 13

Callahan and Safiye stood in the Büyük's entrance as the Kobas pulled up in a white Land Cruiser. Safiye stepped ahead and waved. Once again, she looked terrific. Her hair was tied back into a short ponytail, and she wore a red-striped nautical shirt and white slacks.

Safiye hugged Mehmet and Ayla, then turned toward Callahan, who was carrying their bags. "You remember Michael."

"Dr. Callahan," Mehmet said, surprised. "Yes, of course, it's good to see you again."

"I *told* you Safiye was bringing someone," Ayla said. She hugged Callahan. "You'll have to forgive my husband—the quintessential absentminded professor."

"At times, I'm one myself," Callahan said.

Mehmet opened the rear hatch of the SUV. He and Callahan slipped the bags into the compartment while Safiye and Ayla sat in the back.

"I'm glad you're here," Mehmet said, winking as he closed the hatch. "With these two, I'll need all the companionship I can get."

They drove north from Izmir and stopped in Bergama for groceries. As they left the city, Ayla pointed toward crumbling buildings. "The remains of the Red Basilica. Saint John refers to it in Revelations as the throne of Satan. It was built in tribute to the Egyptian gods." She pointed toward a bluff. "And there's the acropolis. The ancient city of the kings of Pergamon."

"Ayla should have continued her studies," Mehmet said. "I've never seen someone get so excited about a bunch of holes in the ground."

"It's not the holes," Ayla said. "It's the stories in them. Civilizations, their highs and lows, are there to see." She pointed to a small collection of ruins on an otherwise barren hill. "There's something our doctor friends would be interested in—the Asclepion. It was a site of healing named after Asclepios, the son of Apollo. According to myth, he used the blood from Medusa to bring people back to life. Once he began charging gold for his services, Zeus struck him down."

"So it was okay to bring people back from the dead, just not get rich from it?" Mehmet asked.

"Maybe Zeus was trying to combat rising health-care costs," Callahan said.

"Or he may have been a proponent of socialized medicine," Mehmet added.

"Very funny," Ayla said. "I can see you two are going to make quite a pair. Doctors shouldn't try to play God. I believe that's the message."

They traveled from Bergama to the coast, where they passed along a scenic seaside road. They finally stopped in front of a ranch that overlooked a small bay. A schooner was buoyed offshore.

"It's not grand, but it's ours," Mehmet said.

"It *is* grand," Safiye said. "The cottage, the beach and water—they're all beautiful."

The four of them prepared a cooler of snacks and drinks. Afterward, Mehmet rowed them to the schooner.

Onboard, Callahan and Safiye remained in the cockpit, doing their best to stay out of the way as the Kobas went about a well-rehearsed routine of rigging the boat. Once the sails and lines were secure, Ayla skipped nimbly across the deck and raised the sails, shrugging off Callahan's request to help. Mehmet took the rudder and turned the boat away from the wind. As the sails filled, the schooner cut smoothly through the water.

Ayla sat at Mehmet's side, curling up next to him.

"You two make quite a team," Safiye said.

"We try to get away as often as we can," Ayla said. "When we're on the boat, he's entirely mine. No phone calls, no research."

"There's been too much work," Mehmet said. "It sneaks up on

you and squeezes everything else out. I'm sure our researcher from Ann Arbor knows what I mean."

"It makes you forget there's more to life," Callahan said.

Ayla opened the cooler. She pulled out wine coolers for herself and Safiye and beer for the men. "Here's to not forgetting," she said.

They clinked their bottles together.

Nearing a regatta, they watched as a dozen small sailboats tacked sharply about a mark. Soon, the schooner was in open water, and Callahan and Mehmet were listening as the girls reminisced.

"My family moved to Izmir when I was ten," Ayla said. "I remember how proud my father, a mere high school teacher, was when he learned we lived in the same neighborhood as the great Professor Kizeel Özmen. When he found out the Özmens had a son, he wanted to make introductions. He was heartbroken when he discovered Safiye's brother was only four."

"Instead, her father had to be content with a match with Kizeel Özmen's daughter," Mehmet said.

Ayla reached out and squeezed Safiye's hand. "He didn't have a choice."

Over the next couple hours, the wind carried them across the channel that separated Turkey's western coast and the Greek island of Lesvos. Mehmet tacked along the island's southern coastline until it opened into a wide bay. Hills ringed the bay and a quaint village.

"Kólpos Kallonís," Mehmet announced.

Ayla dropped the sails as Mehmet started an outboard motor and steered toward the harbor.

"What time is it?" Ayla asked.

"Almost noon," Callahan said.

"Perfect," Ayla said. "We have time for a little shopping."

"There's always time for a little shopping," Mehmet grumbled.

"You're welcome to join us," Ayla said to Callahan.

"Oh no," Mehmet said. "We have better things planned for our good man from Ann Arbor."

"Mehmet prefers to go for a drink at Aristotle's while I shop," Ayla said. She turned to Mehmet. "Should we meet you there when we're done?"

Mehmet didn't respond. Instead, he was looking intently toward the harbor, a hand raised to shield his eyes from the sun.

A mix of sleek fiberglass yachts and old wooden fishing boats filled the harbor. Mehmet's gaze was on the largest of the yachts. Two figures stood on the rear deck. One of them, a well-dressed man, was waving.

"Mehmet," Ayla hissed. "Did you know about this?"

"It'll only take a second," Mehmet said under his breath.

When they neared the yacht, Mehmet slowed the motor and returned the man's wave. "Iskender, hello," he called out with an exaggerated smile.

The man named Iskender had black hair that was slicked back. He wore a light-blue blazer with an oversize yacht club insignia on the breast pocket. He stood by a young deckhand.

Mehmet turned off the motor. As the schooner glided alongside the yacht, the deckhand grabbed the approaching bow pulpit and stopped the boat.

Iskender boarded the schooner. "Mehmet, Ayla, it's good to see you." He shook hands with Mehmet and kissed Ayla on the cheek. He then turned toward Safiye, who'd remained sitting. She was looking over the side of the schooner.

"Hello, Safiye," Iskender said, a tentative note in his voice.

Not acknowledging the greeting, a vacant look in her eyes, Safiye stared into the water.

"Iskender," Mehmet said, clearing his throat. "This is Dr. Michael Callahan. He's from the United States. Michael, this is Iskender Tunç."

Tunç turned appraisingly toward Callahan. "The United States. You must be one of the volunteers who's come to the aid of our poor, helpless country?"

"I am," Callahan said. "But your country is far from helpless. It's quickly returning to normal."

A coughing sound came from the yacht.

A blond, unshaven man emerged from below deck, a cigarette pinched between his lips. Stopping halfway up the stairs, he peered through thick glasses at the newcomers before disappearing back down the stairs.

"Your boat is beautiful," Callahan said. He pointed toward the name written on the stern. "*Potansiyel.* What does it mean?"

"'Potential,'" Tunç said. He glanced toward Safiye. "It serves to remind me of what can be. Our world is full of so much potential, wouldn't you agree?"

Callahan nodded as Safiye continued her trancelike stare into the water.

"I hope you can join me for lunch," Tunç said to the Kobas. "My chef has—"

"No, thank you," Safiye said.

Tunç held out his arms. "Mehmet? *Ayla*? The food is ready." He motioned toward his boat. "We could—"

"No," Safiye snapped.

As Safiye's acrid tone washed over the group, Tunç's eyes shifted back and forth, searching for a way out of the situation. Finding none, he shrugged. "Then perhaps another time." To no one in particular, he gave a brief mechanical bow and strode from the schooner. He grabbed the pulpit and shoved the schooner off with one furious heave.

Set adrift, Mehmet pulled the motor's starter rope. The engine didn't catch. After a few more pulls, the engine roared to life. Turning the schooner away from the yacht, Mehmet steered them to the other side of the marina.

Callahan looked back and forth at Mehmet and Ayla. Both avoided his gaze. Meanwhile, Safiye continued staring into the water.

Mehmet directed the schooner into an open slip and cut the motor. Callahan hopped onto the dock and stopped the boat, holding it in place as Ayla fastened the lines.

"We'll see you at Aristotle's," Ayla said after the boat was secured.

Safiye stood. Callahan held her hand as she stepped onto the dock. "You okay?" he asked.

On the verge of tears, Safiye gave a slight nod before she and Ayla walked away.

Mehmet pulled two beers from the cooler and snapped off their caps. He handed a bottle to Callahan. "It's a long story, my friend. It's a story that begins and perhaps ends by saying Iskender and Safiye were engaged."

"Safiye told me she was engaged. She didn't tell me the name of her fiancé, but for some reason the Tunç name seems familiar."

"It's one of the most well known in Turkey," Mehmet said. "Iskender's father, Muhammed, was a Turkish general. After his retirement, he started a textile company, which he ran until his death about a dozen years ago. Under Iskender's guidance, the company has grown into one of Turkey's largest conglomerates. He has his hands in everything now: transportation, electronics, defense, even medical research."

"Is that how you know him?"

Mehmet nodded. "If not for Iskender, there'd be no Koba Laboratories. Tunç Corporation is my one and only benefactor."

"You're not affiliated with the university?"

"We're a private lab. We have no teaching duties. It allows us to concentrate on our research."

"An offer too good to pass up?" Callahan asked.

"It was."

The two sipped their beers.

"Safiye doesn't readily talk about her engagement," Mehmet said. "She must really trust you."

"The topic came up last night when I made the mistake of taking her to the restaurant where he proposed."

"The breakup was very hard on Safiye. She not only had to contend with an angry ex-fiancé but her own father. He felt the broken engagement brought shame on the family. On top of all that, Safiye had to deal with the death of her good friend Rabia." Mehmet paused. "I'm guessing she didn't say anything about her?"

"No."

"Rabia committed suicide the day after Safiye ended the engagement. When Ayla first told me about it, she said the suicide had nothing to do with the broken engagement. When I started asking questions, Ayla became emotional and simply stopped talking. Even then, several years after the suicide, the subject still bothered her. I've learned to not talk about it."

Callahan and Mehmet finished their beers and headed to Aristotle's. Not long after, the women arrived, carrying shopping bags.

"Would you boys be interested in a lunch date?" Ayla asked. She slid into the booth next to Mehmet as Safiye, who appeared in better spirits, sat next to Callahan.

"Two dates in two days," Callahan said. "Sounds great."

Ayla sat forward. "I'd like to hear about the first one."

"It wasn't a real date," Safiye said.

Callahan grabbed his chest. "Dinner, music, dancing, a boat ride. I'm afraid that's the best I can do."

"But it was so impromptu," Safiye said.

"Safiye," Ayla said. "Those are the best kind."

Safiye nodded. "You're right. I had a good time—a great time." She looked apologetically toward Callahan. "I'm sorry. And I'm sorry for—"

Callahan held up his hands. "You don't have to say a thing."

"Thank you." Safiye pulled a T-shirt from one of her bags and handed it to Callahan. "It was the least touristy one they had."

On the back of the shirt was a drawing of Lesvos. "Kólpos Kallonís" was written above it, with a big star on the site of the marina.

"It's great," Callahan said. He leaned toward her and kissed her cheek. "Thank you."

Safiye blushed as Mehmet and Ayla looked on, smiling.

Their waitress approached. Ayla scooped up their menus and handed them to the young girl. "We'll have sardeles pastes and ouzo," she declared. "For all four." She turned to Callahan. "When you come to Lesvos, they're a must."

"*Sardeles pastes?*" he asked.

"Sardines," Safiye said.

"They're the best in the world," Ayla said. "And the ouzo is the best in Greece."

When the waitress brought them their food and drinks, Ayla raised her glass. "Ya mas."

"Ya mas," the others said, clinking their glasses together.

The four enjoyed their lunch.

"I never thought I could make a meal of sardines," Callahan said as they left. "But you were right, Ayla. That was good. Thank you."

"The ouzo helps," Ayla said.

Mehmet held his arms out wide. "Ouzo *always* helps," he said, his voice booming.

Back at the schooner, they untied the lines and pushed the boat from the slip. Motoring through the harbor, they looked in the direction of the *Potansiyel*'s empty rear deck.

"I wish we could stay longer," Ayla said, filling the silence. "Lesvos is the birthplace of Aristotle and Aesop. It was once inhabited by the greatest Greek philosophers and writers— Theophanes, Pittacus, Sappho, and Arion."

When Mehmet rolled his eyes, Ayla jabbed his shoulder.

After they were out of the harbor, Mehmet turned into the wind and cut the motor. Callahan motioned for Ayla to remain seated and raised the sails.

The brisk northwesterly wind carried them quickly back across the channel. When they neared the coast, however, the wind died and the sails went slack. But no one noticed. Safiye and Ayla had resumed their reminiscing.

"The embassy events were boring," Safiye said, recalling the night when Mehmet and Ayla met. "Their pageantry was interesting for a while, but they were so formal. That's why I was surprised when Ayla was so giddy when she came home that night." She looked toward Mehmet. "What did you do to her?"

Mehmet shrugged. "We barely spoke. We danced for a few songs and then went our separate ways."

Safiye turned to Callahan. "When Ayla came back, she told me she'd just met her husband."

"She should have told me," Mehmet said. "It would have made my life a lot easier."

"But not *nearly* as interesting," Ayla said.

Mehmet looked up at the sagging telltail. "Shall we motor the rest of the way?"

"Wait," Ayla said. She ran to the bow and pulled off her shirt and shorts. Underneath, she wore a black bikini. She paused briefly to model it. "Do you like it?"

"It looks wonderful," Mehmet replied. "But I thought you already had a black one."

"I do, but it was getting worn," Ayla said before diving into the water.

Safiye walked to the bow and also slipped from her clothes, revealing a red bikini. Ayla whistled from the water.

Imitating Ayla, Safiye turned to the men and put a hand on her hip. "Do you like it?"

"I thought you already had a red one," Callahan called out.

"I do, but it was *so* worn," Safiye said. With a flip of her hair, she dove in.

After the girls' swim, Ayla dropped the sails as Mehmet started the motor. Fifteen minutes later, they were on the beach, carrying their supplies into the cottage.

"We know you have to work tomorrow, but we were hoping you could stay the night," Ayla said. "We could grill some steaks from the freezer and drive you back early in the morning."

"Staying sounds great," Safiye said looking expectantly toward Callahan, who nodded. "It does," he said.

"Perfect," Ayla said.

They ate dinner on the deck. Mehmet opened a bottle of wine. They toasted Sappho, Lesvos, and sardeles pastes. "To the most beautiful bikinis I've ever seen," Mehmet said after opening a second bottle.

"I thought alcohol was taboo in a Muslim nation," Callahan said. "But it doesn't seem to be a problem here, even in public."

"It's a Muslim tenet most Turks overlook," Mehmet said. "My father was devout, but he had a shot of raki every night with dinner."

"Alcohol consumption has always been a part of Turkish culture," Ayla said. "The Ottoman sultans drank. Atatürk drank."

"The other night at dinner, I noticed the Kaldırıms didn't touch their wine," Safiye said.

Mehmet and Ayla looked at each other and smiled.

"They're *very* devout," Ayla said.

"Don't take this wrong," Safiye said. "But they're not exactly a couple I imagined you two socializing with."

Mehmet cleared his throat. "The Kaldırıms are a couple whom I ask Ayla to endure every few months or so. The unfortunate part about running your own lab is that sometimes you're forced to play politics. Yalçin was a close adviser to Iskender's father. He's not as close to Iskender, but he still advises him on medical topics."

"When you're as good as you are, you shouldn't have to worry about funding," Safiye said. "If Tunç Corporation doesn't fund you, somebody else will."

"That's nice of you to say, but in today's economic climate, it's an option I'd prefer not exploring," Mehmet said. "What's the saying? 'Keep your friends close and your enemies closer'? Yalçin and I aren't enemies, but I guess I'd like to keep it that way." He looked toward Ayla. "And with respect to Tunç Corporation, I think my wife will agree, they've been very generous."

"I can't complain," Ayla said. She gave a coy smile. "But I still might, every now and then."

Safiye waved a hand. "When it comes to Iskender Tunç, feel free."

The two women clinked their glasses together.

Following dinner, the four of them played cards on the patio table. Afterward, they turned their chairs and looked out over the bay.

It was dark. The stars were bright. They talked, the sounds of the water lapping onto the shore as a backdrop.

"There's Asclepios," Ayla said, pointing skyward. "He's saving Orion by stepping on Scorpio, the red star. There's his head and foot." She traced her finger across the sky. "He's holding the serpent that gave him the elixir of life—the elixir from Medusa's blood."

"Wasn't Hippocrates a descendent of Asclepios?" Safiye asked.

"Yes," Ayla said. "The original Hippocratic oath began with an appeal to the Greek divinities: 'I swear by Apollo, the physician, and by Asclepios.' The symbol of modern medicine, the staff with the snake twisted around it, was a symbol of Asclepios's followers."

"If anyone finds this elixir, let me know," Mehmet said. "We could use it at the lab."

It was well after midnight when they stepped into the cottage. Ayla brought Callahan and Safiye to the guest bedroom. Twin beds were separated by a night table.

"I can sleep on the couch," Callahan said, looking back toward the main room.

"Your chivalry is duly noted, Dr. Callahan," Ayla said. "But I've seen your doctor's call rooms. If we drove you back tonight, you'd sleep in the same room anyway." She winked at Safiye. "If there's a problem, just yell."

"I'd prefer if there was no yelling," Mehmet said, leaning over Ayla.

"Shush," Ayla said, pushing him back into the hallway.

Ayla turned toward Safiye. The women hugged.

"Thank you for a wonderful day," Safiye said.

"It's nice to share this with you," Ayla said. "I hope you can visit more often." She looked toward Callahan. "Both of you."

Ayla disappeared with Mehmet into the adjacent bedroom. Callahan and Safiye took turns changing in the bathroom. When Callahan climbed into the bed by the window, Safiye was already under her covers with the lights off.

The moon's reflection, coming through the window, partially lit the room. Safiye was turned toward him, her eyes open. "Goodnight," she whispered.

"Goodnight."

He looked across the divide separating them, trying to figure out a way across it. It was then he heard Mehmet and Ayla talking. The walls were paper thin.

Callahan summoned his fortitude and rolled over. It had been a perfect day. The Kobas were the perfect couple. Intelligent and interesting, they maintained a playful, confrontational banter that was akin to two puppies wrestling.

Callahan felt a hand on his shoulder.

"I just wanted to say I'm sorry about Kólpos Kallonís," Safiye whispered after sliding beneath his covers.

"Don't worry about it."

"Mehmet told you about Iskender?"

He nodded.

"Seeing him brought back so many emotions. I'm sorry for acting odd."

"There's no need to apologize."

Safiye nodded. She propped up her chin on her palm and stared out the window, her eyes flickering in the moonlight.

"I like your friends," he said.

"They like you too."

He reached out and ran his forefinger along her cheek. Her skin was smooth and warm. He smiled. "Last night, we gave Brooke quite the shock."

"We did."

They kissed.

Safiye lay back. He moved over her and they continued kissing. As they became more heated, their bodies grinding together, a loud snapping noise came from the bed.

"What was that?" Safiye asked.

"I think it was a spring."

Through the wall, they heard muffled laughter. The sound was agonizingly close.

They looked into each other's eyes.

"Thank you for spending the day with me," Safiye said.

"Thank you for inviting me."

They held each other tight.

"You'd better get back," he said. "Otherwise, I hate to think what we might do to this bed."

After a long kiss and a final hug, Safiye slipped from the bed.

15

Day 14

With no scheduled surgeries at University Hospital on Sunday, Callahan spent the day on call. While not in surgery or rounding on in-patients, he caught up on his journal reading in the cafeteria, where he kept an eye on the door, hoping Safiye might join him. She never did.

In the afternoon, Callahan stopped by the pediatric clinic, but Safiye had already left. After his shift ended, he and Adams took the late bus back to the tent city.

It was dark as they exited the bus and walked to the field hospital. While Adams stopped at the supply tent to talk to Thomas, Callahan continued to his tent and unpacked. He then joined Brooke, Haas, and several others around the Cloister's fire pit.

"This is nice," Callahan said, falling into a flimsy patio chair.

"Eric bought them in Ottoman Square," Brooke said.

"Ten bucks for the lot plus quarter a beer," Haas said. He reached into a foam cooler and pulled out a beer, tossing it to Callahan. "Including the cooler."

"Eric has become *quite* the negotiator," Brooke said.

Haas winked. "If you need something, talk to me."

Brooke sat forward. "So, where's Safiye?"

Callahan looked toward Haas. He and the others stared into the fire, doing poor jobs of holding back grins. Courtesy of Brooke, word of his romance with Safiye had spread.

Callahan turned toward Safiye's tent, pretending he hadn't already noticed it was dark. "She's not here?"

"Maybe she's doing something with Ayla," Brooke said.

Adams appeared from the darkness, clutching a fistful of paperwork. "*Yersinia*," he said. "The culture results came back from Paris. The bug was resistant to everything except Zagam."

"At least Kaldırım got that right," Callahan said.

"Could the hospital have confused the two organisms?" Haas asked.

"They're too distinct," Adams said. "From a diagnostic standpoint, there's no way that should happen."

"Why would Dr. Kaldırım falsely report the bug as *Pasteurella*?" Brooke asked. "What would he gain?"

"Maybe he figures he's doing the city a favor," Haas said. "One disaster is enough for the month. Earthquake, plague . . . what's next? Locusts?" He handed a beer to Adams.

Callahan set his bottle with the other empties. "Take my chair," he said to Adams. "I need to stretch my legs." He flipped a quarter to Haas.

"First one's on me," Haas said. "I'll take this as down payment on a second."

Callahan walked to the field hospital. In the surgical tent, Alin was on his phone. He'd been gone the last few days on a whirlwind fund-raising tour, traveling to London and Paris. Fund-raising was a necessary function of the director. Unfortunately, there was no better time for it than the middle of a catastrophe.

Alin wore scrubs and running shoes, his feet up on a desk. Callahan smiled to himself. The image reminded him of their first meeting. It had been during the final year of his residency. He'd been near the end of his rotation through the gynecologic service. Alin, his attending, asked to meet him in his office.

Callahan arrived first. As he waited in the doorway, his attention was drawn to photographs of Alin with his family, other faculty members, and past residents, but many were also with important dignitaries: two US secretaries of state, Al Gore, and even Britain's former prime minister, David Cameron.

In one photograph, Alin was receiving a medal. Below it, the medal hung in a glass case with an engraving:

WORLD HEALTH ORGANIZATION
LIFETIME EXCELLENCE AWARD

"My wall of vanity caught your eye."

Stepping to Callahan's side, still wearing his scrubs, Alin proudly pointed at one of the photos. "My son and daughter. He's a banker and she's a lawyer. I'm afraid the apples have fallen far from the tree."

"They may have landed in a better place."

Alin laughed. "That's possible, Dr. Callahan," he said, motioning him toward a chair. "That's very possible."

Callahan liked Alin. Everyone did. He was a soft-spoken, fatherly type who took a strong interest in teaching. Since he put in the extra effort, his residents did likewise, their performance always peaking under his tutelage.

"First of all, I'd like to commend you on your performance, not only during this rotation, but throughout your entire residency," Alin said, after sitting behind his desk and putting his feet up. "You prepare well for cases. The attendings and residents trust and respect you. And so do your patients. In my mind, no greater compliments can be paid to a surgeon."

Callahan nodded. "Thank you."

"We can go over your evaluation later, but I called you here for another reason. Every few years, the members of the surgery department offer an instructor position to an outstanding fifth-year resident. This year, we've decided to offer that position to you."

Callahan was planning a career in academics. He'd thought it would require additional training beyond his residency—a fellowship. The instructor position, however, would function as a fellowship while getting his foot in the door within a highly respected department.

"I—I'm honored," he stammered.

"The position can be a stepping stone to great things," Alin said. "You'll eventually be able to pick your area of interest. You . . ."

As Alin expounded on the virtues of the department, the implications of the offer washed over Callahan. In one stroke, his future had fallen into place. "I accept," he blurted.

Alin laughed. "I haven't finished my song and dance."

"You don't have to, Dr. Tevfik. I'm familiar with the department's reputation."

"Okay, but take some time to think about it. You have a few months before you have to officially reply to the offer."

"I don't need time. This is what I want to do. I know it."

"Are you sure?"

"Yes," he replied.

Alin stood and extended his hand. "Then let me be the first to welcome you to the department, Michael. Congratulations." They shook hands. "And please, call me Alin. We're colleagues now."

When their conversation concluded and Callahan walked from the office, he stopped by the glass case. "Do you mind if I ask what this is for?"

"Almost thirty years ago, I became involved with the World Health Organization's disaster relief team," Alin said, walking around his desk. "Once a year, we travel across the globe when disaster strikes. Would you be interested?"

Callahan scanned the photos on the wall. "Yes. But I'm not sure how the publish-or-perish mentality of academia would mesh with volunteer work."

"It's meshed well for me. I love working here, but it can be a bit of an ivory tower. Sometimes I need something different. Working for the WHO has been an extraordinary life opportunity. It's a highly skilled team that's placed in difficult situations. It's provided me with the chance to contribute on a global scale." Alin paused. "I'll tell you what: Consider yourself officially invited. If you decide not to go, that's fine. This is a standing offer distinct from the instructor position."

A month later, as Callahan returned his signed contract to the department chairman, he passed Alin's office and peeked inside.

Alin looked up from his desk. "Michael, to what do I owe the pleasure?"

"I was just returning my contract. I wanted to say thank you."

"You're welcome. But thank me in ten years. I hope we're a match."

"I think so," he said. "Thanks again. By the way, when are we leaving?"

"Leaving?"

Callahan pointed toward the glass case. "The next excursion. You did say it was a standing offer."

"I did. But I also said the offer to work at the university is distinct. You shouldn't feel compelled."

"I'm not. How about this? Let's see how the first one goes."

The first excursion went well, as did the next four. The excursions were hard work, but Alin had been right. They were extraordinary.

"I take it they put up a cell tower," Callahan said when Alin ended his call.

Alin nodded. "This morning."

"How's New York?"

"Life is different. I take the subway to work and Uber everywhere else. But after so many years of the same routine, it's good to be doing something different. When you get to be an old-timer, you should think about doing something like this." He dropped his feet from the desk. "Tell me. How's the department? Your research?"

"We have a great crop of new residents," Callahan said. "They're working out well. With respect to my research, it's good but hectic. The chairman has hinted at a promotion to associate professor, but I'm not holding my breath."

"Just keep working," Alin said. "Looking back, I'm not sure how I did it all: clinical work, research, teaching, volunteer work. It's all a blur. But when you're young, you have the energy."

They sat quietly, lost in their thoughts until Alin's phone rang.

"I'd better take this," he said, checking the caller ID. As Alin stood, Callahan waved him back down. "I was just passing by."

"Thanks, Michael. We'll talk later."

Outside, Callahan took a step toward the Cloister but stopped. Feeling restless, he turned and walked into the tent city. He wandered aimlessly between the rows of tents. At the edge of the tent city, he came to a stop. He looked up into the night sky.

Just keep working.

Was Alin right? Was more work the answer? Would he find answers in his teaching? His research? Here?

He scanned the stars, his gaze settling on Asclepios. His head swimming, he could taste cabernet and hear Mehmet and Ayla laughing. In the same stream of consciousness, he could smell Safiye's perfume and feel her lips on his.

He'd spent the previous two nights with Safiye, drinking wine and staring at the stars. She'd let her hair down, literally and figuratively. He liked what he'd seen. Despite all his trepidations, he'd entered the roller-coaster ride of another excursion relationship.

There was the crackle of tires on gravel. A black limousine appeared. Glistening, it moved slowly along the road, the purr of its engine barely audible. It stopped beneath the bus stop's bare light bulb. From its shadows, a man exited. He turned and extended his hand.

A woman stepped from the car. Her face appeared in the light.

It was Safiye.

Safiye wore her black dress. She embraced the man. They held each other for what seemed an eternity before she finally walked away, disappearing into the night.

The man climbed back into the vehicle and shut the door. The limousine pulled away.

Hidden in the darkness, Callahan stood motionless, staring at the vacant bus stop. Before the man had slid back into the limousine, the light bulb had briefly illuminated his face.

The man in the limousine was Iskender Tunç.

Part

2

"Growth for the sake of growth is the ideology of the cancer cell."

— Edward Abbey

16

Koba Laboratories
Izmir, Turkey

An international group of eight scientists sat around a conference table. Dr. Tanik Goya, the most senior of the researchers and Mehmet's longtime friend and colleague, began the Monday morning meeting with his article review.

Over the last few years, Tanik's updates had grown progressively shorter. This was not because he'd become delinquent in his duties. Tanik was extremely thorough. His updates had grown shorter because the current literature was becoming more and more irrelevant. That morning, as the Ph.D.s sipped their coffee and listened to Tanik, they were confident they'd left conventional research far behind.

"Silverstein ends his editorial by hypothesizing the key to understanding malignancy is not to merely catalogue the myriad of genetic defects found in different cancer cells but to better understand the mechanisms controlling cell behavior," Tanik said, concluding.

Everyone turned toward Mehmet. He was incredulous. "Silverstein has shown the ability to be flexible, to change his viewpoint." The others broke into laughter.

From the lab's inception, the scientists' tireless pursuit of the holy grail of medical research—a cure for cancer—had been fueled by contempt for conventional research. For Mehmet, this disdain was embodied in one person, Dr. Saul Silverstein, the director of

99

the lab where he and Tanik had worked during their tenure at the NIH and the author of that morning's article.

"Are you saying cancer *isn't* a result of genetic mutations?" The question came from the summer intern, Farrat Badem, who also sat at the table.

"Silverstein, like most cancer researchers, is a proponent of the genetic theory of malignancy," Mehmet explained. "He believes cancer is derived from an accumulation of mutations. As more data has been gathered, however, it's become clear many of these same mutations can also be found in normal cells. If these mutations can be found in normal cells, clearly something else is involved in determining malignant behavior.

"An opposing hypothesis on the origin of cancer is the epigenetic theory. It proposes cell behavior is a result of the complexity of interactions between the cell and its environment. The theory is best summarized by a quote." Mehmet pointed to a plaque above the chalkboard.

A lifetime study of the internal combustion engine would not help anyone to understand our traffic problems. A traffic jam is due to a failure of the normal relationship between driven cars and their environment and can occur whether they themselves are running normally or not.

Sir David Smithers, 1962

"There's data to support Smithers's viewpoint," Mehmet said. "When cancer cells from mouse germ-cell tumors are introduced into mouse embryos, the cancer cells form normal tissues. In humans with germ-cell tumors treated with chemotherapy, the cancer cells transform into normal tissues. Most researchers consider these events as nothing more than a curiosity. But it's in these phenomena we believe the essence of cancer is apparent. In both examples, despite whatever genetic defects exist, the malignant cells become normal. Malignant cells *are not* inherently malignant. The process resulting in the formation of a malignant cell can be reversed."

As Farrat stared back, slack-jawed, Mehmet turned toward the others. "Let's start with the team updates. Frank, go ahead."

Frank Loy, a former researcher from the University of Alberta, slid forward in his seat. "As you recall, we've identified thirty different types of DNA selectin within cell nuclei." He looked around the table. "But, we've found the important one. In malignant cells, only one form of selectin is activated—selectin C-22."

"What do you mean by *activated*?" Tanik asked.

"In our cancer cell line, when we broke down the tumor cells, only selectin C-22 was bound to the DNA," Loy said. "All other forms of selectin were unbound or dormant, inactive and free floating in the nuclear matrix."

"Is selectin C-22 ever activated in normal tissues?" Tanik asked.

"Yes," Loy said. "In embryonic cells."

All eyes again turned to Mehmet Koba. Loy had told him of the discovery, but it was the first time the others had heard. Despite Mehmet's attempt to prevent it, a smile slowly burned its way across his face. He didn't say anything. He didn't have to.

When Mehmet founded the lab, he made several hypotheses that laid the foundation for their research. The idea that cancer cells were normal cells that had simply regressed to an earlier stage was one of them.

"What do embryonic cells have to do with cancer?" Farrat asked. "Cancer occurs in older people."

"Think of the earliest cell—the fertilized egg," Mehmet said. "As it starts to divide and forms a cluster of cells—the blastocyst— its only function is to survive. Similar to cancer cells, the cells of the blastocyst do this by multiplying rapidly and invading the surrounding tissues in search of nutrients. Different from cancer cells, however, something in the blastocyst's environment triggers its cells to stop growing, stop invading, and proceed to the next step. In other words—to mature. The identical multipotent cells of the blastocyst shift their behavior, transforming into the billions of specialized cells working in concert to form a living organism. If there's a miracle to life, then this coordinated, beautifully orchestrated shift in cell behavior is it."

Mehmet paused. "Think of it this way. Cancer cells are like a computer that's had a catastrophic error and fallen back into a default setting. The default setting is an embryonic survival mode that runs only its most basic program, telling the cell to divide, conquer, and metastasize. If a cancer cell can be rebooted and kicked out of this survival mode, it might behave normally." He pointed up at the quote on the wall. "If the cell can run a different program and mature in the right direction, Smithers's traffic jam can be undone. Cancer can be cured."

After lunch, Mehmet stood in front of two empty chalkboards in his office. With no scheduled meetings, his Monday afternoons were a time of pure, unadulterated thought. Allowing his mind to roam free, he picked up a piece of chalk and began writing.

His telephone rang. His secretary was supposed to hold all calls. "I know it's Monday afternoon, but it's Iskender Tunç," she said when he answered the phone. "He's on line one."

Things had not gone well in Kólpos Kallonís. Mehmet had been expecting the call. He hit the button for line one. "Iskender, how are—"

"Who is Tanik Goya?" Tunç asked.

"My associate lab director."

"Do you need him?"

"He's an integral part of the lab," Mehmet said.

"Farrat claims he's making him wash dishes."

"Instruments. He's washing instruments. It's part of his orientation. We've all had to do it."

Tunç had insisted Farrat be allowed to work at the lab during his summer break. Farrat was the lab's first and only intern.

"Farrat doesn't need to wash dishes," Tunç said.

"We're gradually immersing him in the lab's operations. By the end of the summer, he'll be amplifying DNA."

"I want him involved in cutting-edge research. You *are* involved in cutting-edge research, aren't you?"

Before Mehmet could respond, the line went dead.

Mehmet took a calming breath. Still holding the phone, he hit the button for Tanik's extension.

"First, let me say I agree with you," he said when Tanik picked up.

"This is about that little shit, isn't it?"

"Can you make sure he gets involved in something."

"Doing what?" Tanik asked. "He can't do anything. He's a sophomore undergrad. Yet, he walks around here like he owns the place."

"Let him do some old experiments that worked. Just let him think he's contributing."

There was a moment of silence before Tanik sighed. "I'll find something."

"Thanks. To be honest, I feel sorry for him."

"What happened to him anyway?" Tanik asked. "The technicians are afraid of him."

Farrat's forehead and chin were covered with numerous deep-pitted scars.

"I'm not sure," Mehmet said. "But just grin and bear it. When his summer break is over, everything will return to normal."

"Is that a promise?"

"It is."

Mehmet set down the phone and returned to his chalkboard. Once again, he cleared his thoughts. As he began writing, his office door swung open. Farrat entered. The intern walked across the room and sat in a chair by Mehmet's desk.

The secretary stuck her head in the doorway. "Sorry," she mouthed.

"I had a few questions about this morning," Farrat said, opening his notebook.

"Come on in," Mehmet said. "Have a seat."

Farrat looked up, not registering the sarcasm.

Mehmet could see why the others were afraid of him. Farrat's scars and empty stare were unsettling.

Mehmet forced a smile. Deciding to take his own advice, he walked to his desk. "Now, what were your questions?"

It was an hour before Farrat left.

Mehmet locked the door behind him. Anyone else who came through his door this afternoon would have to knock it down. He unplugged his phone and without further interruption, spent the rest of the afternoon and early evening writing down his ideas, losing himself in what he loved to do. He filled both chalkboards, outlining a series of experiments that would lead to a fuller understanding of selectin C-22.

When he arrived home that night, he felt higher than his research had ever taken him. Ayla always said he glowed on Mondays, typically insisting they make a night of it. But it was too late for the dinner reservation she'd made—something that had become all too common in the last few years.

Standing at the kitchen window, eating the kebap Ayla had left for him, Mehmet watched as she worked in the garden under the backyard light. Ayla was the only thing he loved more than his work, but the work had always come first. She, ironically, was the one who'd made his work in Izmir possible. During his rough times at the NIH, she'd given him the confidence to stand up to Silverstein and explore his own ideas.

Ayla turned and waved. After seven years of marriage, her smile still cut through him.

He cracked open the window and held up his plate of food. "Thanks."

"You're welcome. Another late night?"

It was more statement than question, but he nodded. "Did you have a good time this weekend?"

"I did," she said. "Safiye and Michael make a nice couple."

"They do."

Ayla looked at her garden. "Let me finish here, then I'll be in."

As Mehmet watched Ayla work, he couldn't suppress the feeling he'd let her down. He'd promised her they'd soon get started on the family he knew she so desperately wanted. But "soon" had become a point in time permanently fixed in the future. They were on the verge of something big at the lab. He'd be working more than ever. His promise of a family would have to remain on hold.

17

Nine months earlier
Republic of Dagestan, Russia

P etrovich and Tatiana jogged along the beach. "Makhachkala," Petrovich said. "How did a city get a name like that?"

"It was once named Petrovsk after Peter the Great," Tatiana said. "When the Romanov monarchy collapsed, it was renamed after a revolutionary."

"Petrovsk ... It has a nice ring to it."

Shaking her head, Tatiana picked up her pace.

Petrovich maintained his position at her side. "They didn't shoot me in the leg," he said.

She surged ahead. By the time he caught up with her, they still had a kilometer of beach left.

"I'll race you back to the condo," he said. "If I win, you have to let me take you out for dinner."

"And if I win?"

"I won't complain for two weeks."

Tatiana considered this for a moment before breaking into a sprint.

After several strides, Petrovich was next to her. They remained side-by-side, arms and legs churning. As the stairs leading to the condo approached, he accelerated ahead. Taking the stairs three at a time, he ran into the condo and collapsed on a chair.

Thirty seconds later, Tatiana strode into the room, her mouth pressed into a tight line.

Petrovich smiled, knowing she hated to lose. To his surprise, she walked straight toward him and sat on his lap, straddling him. She tried to kiss him, but he turned away.

"What is it?" she asked.

When he didn't respond, she grabbed his chin and turned his head toward her. "You don't get it, do you?" she said. "I still love you, Vlad. A few bullets couldn't change that."

He looked away.

Tatiana placed her hand gently on the right side of his face. She ran her fingertips over the maze of scars. "Is it these?" she asked. "These are nothing. Skin sewn together. I don't see them, only you."

She kissed his cheek and ran a hand over his shorts, pressing her palm against him. "I see this isn't a problem. But it never was."

She slipped out of her clothes. Moving back over him, she pulled down his shorts and guided him into her.

In the four months since he'd left Burdenko, hardly an hour had gone by when he didn't imagine being with Tatiana, doing this. He wanted to stop her, to look away, but couldn't.

"Please, Tatiana. You don't have to do this."

She rocked against him, her lips parted. "But, we are."

The frustration of the past nine months built within him. Grabbing her by the hips, he began thrusting into her. Tatiana met his force with her own, moaning with pleasure. They were soon climaxing together.

Not yet satiated, he stood from the chair and lifted her. Stepping out of his boxers and shorts, he set her on the exercise mat and entered her.

Tatiana raised her hands above her and pushed against the mat, bucking her hips against him. This time, after his second orgasm, he collapsed onto his elbows over her.

Tatiana reached up and wiped the sweat from his brow. She kissed his cheek, his chin, and then his lips. She glanced down as he remained within her, her legs still wrapped tightly around him. "Maybe I should take advantage of that," she said, a playful look in her eyes.

"Is this what I've been training for?"

"No, Major. Think of it as reward for good behavior."

She turned her hips and rolled him onto his back. Placing his hands on her breasts, she began grinding against him. She threw her head back and groaned, her orgasm working its way through her.

Reinvigorated, he began moving with her. They moved in rhythm, their bodies writhing, driving each other to frenzy.

When the last traces of pleasure had left them, they came to a stop, exhausted. With a whimper, Tatiana fell to the mat.

Petrovich looked up at the ceiling. As he caught his breath, his chest heaving, he realized something was different.

A crushing weight was gone. He felt no more guilt, no more fear, and no more pain. The visions that had tormented him since that icy cold morning in Grozny were pushed aside, not forgotten but no longer incapacitating.

Tears filled his eyes. His hands, his arms, and then his entire body began to shake. He covered his face and sobbed.

Tatiana wrapped her arms around him and held him.

18

"*My people are going to learn the principles of democracy, the dictates of truth and the teachings of science. Superstition must go.*"

—**Mustafa Kemal Atatürk**

Mehmet sat behind his office desk. Dr. Niles Vandegut and his team sat on chairs throughout the room. Vandegut, a Swedish immunologist, had worked at Stockholm's respected Karolinska Institutet before joining Koba Laboratories. It was Vandegut and his team who'd developed the antibody to Hu-689 and discovered its cross-reactivity with the liver.

"How's the viral model coming?" Mehmet asked.

Despite the promise of immunotherapy, Mehmet didn't believe it would provide a universal cure. Cancer was too diverse. Too many different antibodies would have to be raised against an infinite number of tumor types. Mehmet believed, however, Vandegut's knowledge of cell membrane dynamics could still prove useful. He'd encouraged Vandegut to start experimenting with gene therapy—using viruses as a vector for introducing therapeutic DNA into cancer cells.

"The viral model is complete," Vandegut said. "The parvovirus we selected has successfully installed DNA into several different tissue cultures."

"Why did you choose parvovirus?" Mehmet asked.

"It's harmless," Vandegut said. "In children, it causes slapped cheek syndrome—a rash involving the face. It itches for a few days before the virus is cleared. By adulthood, everyone has been exposed to the virus and acquired an immunity."

"You don't think a high-dose infection will be a problem?" Mehmet asked.

"Not in immunocompetent adults."

"Then you're happy with the gene-therapy model?"

Vandegut nodded. "It's ready. Now it's just a matter of determining which DNA sequence to infect with." He smiled. "We have the gun. We need the bullet."

"A minor detail," Mehmet said.

When the meeting concluded, Mehmet stood in his doorway, saying his goodbyes. His arms raised, he tapped a plaque above the door. The plaque had been a fixture in his office since he'd returned to Izmir.

> *"The key to treating cancer is to redirect the cancer cell,*
> *not destroy it."*
> Morticai Valance

While at the NIH, Mehmet had come across the quote in an old medical journal. Intrigued, he began working his way back through Valance's articles. In the 1990s, Morticai Valance had single-handedly revived the epigenetic theory of cancer. Valance's inspired stream of articles came to an end, however, after several condemning editorials. The most damning of which had been written by Saul Silverstein—Mehmet's boss at the NIH. Silverstein's editorial had put the epigenetic theory and Morticai Valance to rest, relegating them to nothing more than historical footnotes in the rapidly changing world of molecular biology.

Mehmet, however, was captivated by epigeneticism. During the day, he went through the motions in Silverstein's lab. But at night and on weekends, his imagination went wild. He expanded on Valance's ideas, envisioning a whole new set of experiments. When he brought his plans to Silverstein, the lab director said he thought the experiments wouldn't pan out. Silverstein was interested in guaranteed results. Results led to publications, and publications led to funding. Silverstein didn't want to do anything that might compromise funding.

After Mehmet's attempts to redirect Silverstein's lab failed, he decided to offer his services to Valance.

Following a pleasant drive from Washington, DC, through the rolling Virginia countryside, Mehmet walked across the grounds of the University of Northern Virginia, thrilled at the prospect of meeting the world's most published epigeneticist.

As he stepped into Valance's lab, it was motionless. It smelled of mildew. Rusting equipment was strewn across tabletops. Dirty, encrusted beakers sat in sinks under a film of scum.

In the back of the lab, a man sat at a table surrounded by stacks of books and journals. As Mehmet walked up, he could see the man was playing poker on his computer. His graying red hair was pulled into a ponytail. A box of powdered mini-donuts sat on the table next to him.

Mehmet looked toward the nameplate outside the adjacent office.

MORTICAI VALANCE, PHD

"Excuse me," Mehmet said. "I have an appointment with Dr. Valance."

Most research assistants caught playing computer games at least tried to hide it. This guy didn't seem to care. He continued playing the game. Finally, the word BUST flashed across the screen.

"Dammit," the man said, waving a hand in frustration. He turned. "You must be Mehmet Koba. I'm Morticai."

"Dr. Valance?"

"In the flesh," the man said. He stood and looked at his open palms, sprinkled with powdered sugar. He wiped them on the lapels of his lab coat and then extended his hand.

Valance wore a white lab coat over a Hawaiian shirt. His beard was unkempt.

After they shook hands, Valance lifted several dusty, yellowing journals from a nearby chair and tossed them on the floor. He fell back into his chair and motioned for

Mehmet to sit. "My secretary said you're from Saul's lab. How's that old dog these days?"

"You *know* Dr. Silverstein?"

"Sure do. Went to school together at Stanford. After that, we both ended up at the NIH. I worked there for a few years before deciding I'd rather be a big fish in a small pond." Valance spread his arms out wide. "Welcome to my puddle."

Mehmet looked down at the chair. A single journal remained. He picked it up. The journal was two decades old. He dropped it onto the pile with the others and sat.

"What does ol' Saul have you working on these days?" Valance asked.

Mehmet told Valance about the latest gene defect they'd discovered in lung cancer cells. Expecting a vindictive response on the futility of such endeavors, he was surprised when Valance just shook his head and smiled. "Saul's really done well for himself."

Mehmet hadn't come here to discuss Silverstein. He explained to Valance he'd read his papers on epigeneticism. The papers had sparked an idea for a series of experiments. He wondered if Valance might be in need of a collaborator.

"You must be into ancient history," Valance said. "I haven't published anything in over ten years. Look around: this isn't exactly a hotbed of activity."

Mehmet's gaze wandered over the lab, unable to hide his disappointment.

"I've got tenure," Valance said. "And until something better comes along, I'm ridin' this gig out." He shrugged. "I'm sorry, but epigeneticism is dead."

Valance grabbed the box of donuts and extended it toward Mehmet. When Mehmet shook his head, Valance picked out a donut and plunked it into his mouth. He then turned back to the computer and hit a button on the keyboard, refreshing the screen. As the card game reappeared, Valance began tapping the keys.

Mehmet watched, his anger building. "Dead? *Why?*"

Valance turned. "Think about it," he said, his eyes coming alive. "We live in a fast-food society. We want everything quick and easy." His gaze narrowed. "Do you know who's responsible for handing out grant money?"

"The government."

"Right. And who runs the government?"

"Politicians."

"That's right," Valance said. "They're either dangerous or stupid. Most are both. Meanwhile, we, the scientists, have to beg, grovel, and kiss their fucked-over asses for money."

Valance sat back in his chair. "When you're a hotshot young researcher, you want the golden prize. Get a lab, get big money to support you, publish, and *boom*—you're famous. The pot of gold is waiting." He traced his hand along an imagined rainbow. "The molecular geneticists have capitalized on the fast-food mentality. Everyone would like to think the cause of cancer is a simple genetic defect. Figure out what it is, fix it, and then *boom*—no more cancer. We're almost there, they say. Just a little bit more time and a little bit more *money*," he said, rubbing his thumb and forefinger together. He eyed Mehmet. "What if the public were told that even if we did miraculously figure out a cure for every known form of cancer—knew every possible mutation and how to fix it—new cancers would still pop up?"

"They'd be disappointed."

"They would be," Valance said. "Fighting cancer is like signing up to be Sisyphus. No matter how far you push that rock up the hill, at the end of the day, it's coming back down. Cancer will never be eradicated. No matter what therapies you come up with, the cells will find a whole new way to flip out. It's Darwinian theory applied to malignancy. The cells will adapt."

Mehmet watched as Vandegut and his team disappeared down the hallway. Returning to his desk, he looked up at the plaque above the doorway.

The cells will adapt.

He agreed with Valance. Cancer would always exist. The cells would find new ways to become malignant. But Valance had ignored the practical side of things. Many cancers were treatable. Advances were being made, but current therapies were aimed at killing the tumor cells. Mehmet believed a universal cure would only come by employing the epigeneticist's creed that cancer cells were good cells behaving badly. They had to work with the cancer cells, not against them.

"Iskender Tunç, line one," his secretary said, her voice sounding from his desk intercom.

Mehmet picked up the phone. "Iskender, hello."

"Could you come over? I'm in the administration building at Turkish Sky," Tunç said. His voice sounded strange. It took a moment for Mehmet to realize why. It was a question, not a command.

Vandegut and his team had been the first of Mehmet's morning meetings. His remaining meetings would have to be postponed.

"Yes, Iskender. I'll be right there."

It was raining as Mehmet drove his SUV on a one-lane road into a wooded thicket. The clouds and trees worked in concert to block the sunlight. Turning on his headlights, he drove slowly, braking frequently while traversing the innumerable roots pushing through the crumbling pavement. As he emerged into a clearing, the looming buildings of Turkish Sky Manufacturing came into view.

After all these years, Mehmet was still overwhelmed by the sheer size of the facility. Its dilapidated state and catacomb-like stillness only magnified his discomfort.

Following World War II, Turkish Sky had been conceived as a vital component of the country's national defense. The first fighter jet to roll from its bays, the THK-1, was state-of-the-art. In the midst of the escalating Cold War, however, Turkey found itself an ally of the United States, which was all too eager to stock the country with missile bases and jets. Demand for the THK-1 diminished, and the jet was soon obsolete. Over the next half century, Turkish Sky struggled to find its niche, having little success building transport aircraft and even less when it turned to commercial jets. The company went bankrupt in 2001. Several years later, the facility was purchased by Tunç Corporation. In the time since, not a single airplane had rolled from Turkish Sky's bays. The acquisition had been recorded, thus far, as one of Iskender Tunç's few failures.

Mehmet pulled into the parking lot outside the three-story brick administration building. The lot, like the service road leading into the facility, was in disrepair, its pavement cracked.

Parking near Tunç's limousine, the only other vehicle in the lot, he ran through the rain, slipping inside the building past two large wooden doors, one of which had been cracked open.

Dull gray shafts of light seeping in through windows above the doors were the only source of illumination in the high-ceilinged entrance hall. As Mehmet's eyes adjusted to the darkness, he saw Tunç's bodyguard and driver standing against the opposite wall. Above and behind them, a faded mural of Atatürk with a Turkish flag waving in the background consumed the wall. Much of the mural had peeled away, but Atatürk's penetrating eyes remained. So too did his quote.

The future is in the skies.

Mehmet shook off the rain and walked from the entrance and down a dingy, dust-filled hallway. He passed several empty offices and stopped at the end of the corridor. Knocking quietly at a closed door, he opened it and stepped into a well-lit room.

On the far side of the room, Iskender Tunç stood in partial profile. He stared out the window at the river as it was pelted by rain. Wearing a blue pinstripe suit, his oiled hair combed perfectly back, he was well tanned after the weekend on the boat.

Mehmet had met Tunç here a few years earlier. He looked toward the glowing wall sconces, desktop lamp, and chandelier— surprised the room had electricity. Along with the new lights, the office had since been paneled and carpeted.

Another new addition hung on the wall—an oil painting of Alexander the Great. The Macedonian leader sat high on his horse in the midst of battle. Alexander looked down on his men fighting and dying beneath him. The image reminded Mehmet of Tunç, not because the two men were heirs to power at a young age or for similarities in leadership skills, charisma, or ambition, or for any other reason Tunç wished to impart. It was the indifferent, above-the-fray portrayal of Alexander that reminded him of Tunç.

Mehmet scanned the room, wondering why Tunç had bothered with the upgrades. The office still had the same feel of abandonment that pervaded the rest of the facility. Linen sheets covered the tables and chairs. Dirt had accumulated in the room's corners and crevices.

Mehmet cleared his throat.

Turning, Tunç made a seamless return to the room. Without a word, he walked purposefully across the room and out the door, waving for Mehmet to follow. In the hallway, they took the stairs to the third floor, which was similar to the first: dirty, empty, and dark.

Tunç strode to the end of the corridor and opened a door. Like Tunç's office two floors below, the room was well lit. But instead of a mahogany desk and the other fine appointments of Tunç's office, there was a bed. A man lay in the bed. Hooked to an IV, he clutched a bedsheet to his chest.

An elderly man sat at the bedside, squinting through bifocals as he wrote in what appeared to be a medical chart. A second man, who appeared to be in his midtwenties, sat at the end of the bed, reading a book.

"This is Enver and Beyir," Tunç said, motioning respectively toward the two men.

The elderly man didn't look up but continued writing. The young man nodded, his eyes calm and observing.

Tunç walked to the bedside. He bent down and spoke softly. "Savon, this is Dr. Koba."

The man, thin and jaundiced, raised a bony hand. Mehmet took it.

"May Allah guide you," Savon said. He squeezed Mehmet's hand with surprising strength and pulled him closer, his eyes bulging as he strained to sit up. Beyond Savon's yellow sclera, his irises were a penetrating blue.

"That's okay," Beyir said. The young man was suddenly at the bedside, supporting Savon. "Relax," he said, his voice soothing. "Let go."

Mehmet looked back and forth between the two men. They could be the same age. Beyir, however, was the picture of health. He was tall and sinewy, his arms rippling with muscle.

Beyir carefully lowered Savon back to the bed and then returned to his chair.

Tunç motioned Mehmet from the room. They stepped into an empty office across the hallway. Tunç continued to the far side of the room and looked outside through a dirty window. "His doctors say he has pancreatic cancer. They predict he'll die soon—*very* soon." He turned. "He's like family to me. I want you to cure him."

"Shouldn't he be in a hospital?"

"Nobody must know he exists," Tunç said, shaking his head. "He doesn't exist."

"Has he seen an oncologist?"

"Enver is a doctor. He'll answer all your questions." Tunç held out his arms. "Now, Mehmet. Can you do me this favor? Can you cure him?"

"I can't go back to the lab and just grab something off the shelf."

"But you'll try? You'll try to find something? If you do, I would consider the money I've invested in you—the money I'll *continue* to invest—as worth it."

The request was absurd. Advanced pancreatic cancer was a death sentence. The facts, however, were insignificant. To say it was impossible would be considered mutiny. There was only one answer—the same he'd always given.

"Yes, Iskender. I'll try."

"Good," Tunç said. "Wait here. I'll get Enver."

Moments later, the elderly man passed through the doorway. In eerie imitation of Tunç, he walked to the far side of the room and looked out the window. His hair was thick and white. Like Tunç's, it was well oiled and combed back. Removing his wire-rimmed bifocals, he began cleaning them with a handkerchief.

"Two weeks ago, Savon was seen for progressive abdominal pain," the man said. "An ultrasound detected gallstones. His gallbladder was removed. Intraoperatively, irregularities of the pancreas and liver were biopsied. The tissue diagnoses returned as pancreatic adenocarcinoma with liver metastases." He slipped his glasses back on and turned. "At this point, Iskender came to see me. I'm Enver Pasha, a doctor and longtime friend of the Tunç family."

"Are you an oncologist?"

"No, but I'm familiar with the options. Savon is inoperable. Chemotherapy and radiotherapy may extend his life for a few months, but they won't cure him."

"I don't have an answer," Mehmet said. "You must realize that."

Enver nodded. "Yes, but you're closer than you think. Current medicine provides no acceptable options, which is exactly why you're here. You're a cancer research scientist. *You* are Savon's only hope."

19

Day 18

ollowing a late dinner in the mess tent, Callahan walked toward the Cloister. It was Thursday. After watching Tunç's limousine disappear into the darkness on Sunday night, he'd avoided Safiye. Monday at breakfast, he watched from across the mess tent as she ate, laughing and talking as if nothing had happened. Tuesday and Wednesday, he'd avoided the mess tent altogether, eating in Ottoman Square. Earlier today at lunch, their eyes met briefly, but he could only look away, the image of her and Tunç's late-night embrace still etched in his thoughts.

Bryce stepped from the pediatric tent. He extended a paper. "Thomas just brought me the final lab results for Nata's blood work."

The paper contained chromatography data. Somebody had circled the peak of a spike on a graph and written: Trichothecene region, 140 µg/ml.

"What are trichothecenes?" Callahan asked.

"I was hoping you might know."

Callahan shrugged. He handed the paper back and continued walking.

"How are *things*?" Bryce asked, jogging to his side.

Callahan had confided the weekend's events to Bryce.

"I still can't help but wonder why," he said. "In Kólpos Kallonís, Safiye couldn't even stand to look at Tunç and then—" He shook his head. "The whole sailing trip was a charade, and I was some kind of prop to make Tunç jealous."

"I think you're missing something."

"I would have been missing something if I didn't just happen to walk by the bus stop on Sunday night."

"I know Safiye," Bryce said. "She's the best. That's the beauty of the excursions. The work, the living conditions, the stress—they push you. Fairly soon, you see what people are like. I can't believe Safiye would use you."

"You always look for the best in people."

"You know, my friend, it sounds to me as if she may simply have decided to give this Tunç fellow a second chance. You may have found yourself a little competition."

"Then I forfeit," Callahan said. "In three weeks, we'll all be back home."

They entered their tent. Adams and Haas were inside. Adams was pacing while Haas lay on his cot, his hands behind his head. "He's a son of a bitch," Adams said. "I don't trust him."

Haas raised his arms. "A plague is upon us."

"I thought your farmer was better," Callahan said.

"He is," Adams said. "But yesterday, he came back with his wife and daughter. They had the same symptoms: lymphadenopathy, fever, chills."

"Did you culture them?" Callahan asked.

"Yes," Adams said. "And started them on Zagam."

"Let me guess," Callahan said. "Kaldırım reported the cultures as *Pasteurella*."

"That's right." Adams pulled two vials of blood from his breast pocket. "I took additional cultures from the mother and daughter. I'll have Thomas send them to Paris."

"And when the results come back as *Yersinia*, what will you do then?" Bryce asked.

"That's what I was just asking," Haas said, "The moment we leave Izmir, your complaint will be shit-canned. You can file a report with the WHO, but we know from past experience the last thing they want to do is ruffle feathers."

Adams looked down at the vials. "I don't know what I'll do. But I'll be damned if I do nothing."

20

It was early Friday morning as Mehmet drove along Turkish Sky's rut-filled access road, headed toward his last and least anticipated meeting of the week. Emerging into the clearing, he turned away from the administration building and crossed a bridge over the river. He stopped at a gated fence that cordoned off Turkish Sky's three hangars and typed a code onto a keypad.

The gate slid open. He drove past the first two hangars and turned into the third hangar through an open door, parking next to Tunç's limousine. Behind him, the door began to close. Exiting the vehicle, he began the long walk to the far side of the hangar.

The once-refined synchrony of the hangar's assembly lines had long ago given way to the chaos before him. Portions of a fuselage, a few engines, a wing, and innumerable other rusting airplane parts were strewn about in suspended states of disassembly. Desks were blanketed with yellowing blueprints. Patches of mud, washed in by the recent flood, covered the once-immaculate floor.

A casual observer would say the three hangars were identical. All three mammoth rusting shells stood as monuments to a bygone era. All three smelled of an odd combination of grease, a reminder of a productive past, and mildew from the mold now sprouting from the mud-covered floor. All three were similarly inundated with once-valuable machines and parts that time and the elements had turned to junk. But there was a difference.

In the first two hangars, the vaulted, rusting sheet-metal roof was visible from the shop floor. In the third hangar, the roof was blocked from view by a black-painted ceiling.

Mehmet walked to the far corner of the hangar and climbed

a ladder. The ladder, crudely cut from a supporting beam, led him through a small opening in the ceiling. He stepped from the ladder and walked across a dimly lit room to a door. When the door's lock buzzed, he opened it.

In the next room, a guard sat behind a desk surrounded by video monitors. Mehmet continued past the guard into a room lined by lockers. From a locker, he removed a hooded bodysuit and mask. After putting them on, he stepped into a tiled shower stall. Ultraviolet bulbs lining the stall lit up. He rotated with arms extended as a mist hissed from several ports. Once the hissing ended and the mist dissipated, he opened a door.

A vast room filled with low-hanging fluorescent lights ran the remaining length of the hangar. The fact the room existed was sickening. The fact it existed because of him was even more appalling. His shame gave way to anger, anger at Tunç, but mostly himself and his own naïveté. His mind had taken him so far. At his most critical juncture, however, it failed him.

Five years earlier, Tunç invited him to lunch. While they ate in Tunç's downtown office, Tunç inquired about the lab's progress.

Mehmet painted an honest picture of a hardworking group of researchers.

"Is there anything the lab needs?" Tunç asked.

Mehmet had chosen not to tell Tunç their progress was slower than envisioned. The lab was floundering. The benchwork had become all-consuming. More technicians were needed for the more mundane work to free up the PhDs to interpret data and set up the next round of experiments. But he didn't want to burden Tunç with this information—not yet, at least.

"Could you use more equipment or more space?" Tunç asked.

"Neither. Things are going well."

"How about more technicians? More PhDs?"

As Tunç pressed, Mehmet couldn't help but wonder if extra funding was simply his for the asking. "We're fine . . . but, a few more technicians would help."

"They're yours," Tunç snapped. "And PhDs?"

"Well, with a few more, the lab could make giant leaps forward."

Tunç smiled. As if for the first time, he gave Mehmet an appraising look. He stood and began pacing. "The Tunç Corporation is the third-largest company in Turkey. We're the country's largest private contributor to medical research. What's good for the Tunç Corporation is good for Turkey, right?"

Mehmet nodded.

"Despite this, there are operations the public cannot know about," Tunç said. "I think you're capable of taking the next step in our organization. Before you do, however, I must ask for your utmost discretion."

"You know you have it."

"Recent events have exposed certain *inadequacies* in our operations. If you accept my proposal, I can double current funding to Koba Laboratories. You can have your technicians, a few more PhDs, and then some."

Mehmet set down his fork, wondering if he'd regret his next question. "What operations?"

Mehmet walked down the central aisle of the sprawling attic room. To his right were rows of stainless steel cabinets. Through their glass doors, he saw culture plates containing *Bacillus anthracis*, copper-colored colonies of *Yersinia pestis*, and chocolate agar plates coated with *Francisella tularensis*—the deadly agent of tularemia. Incubating in similar cabinets to his left were toxin-producing varieties of *Staphylococcus aureus* and a miscellany of virulent bacteria, including *Vibrio cholerae*, *Salmonella*, and *Shigella*.

The next and largest section of the room contained a sea of broad, waist-high tables. The thousands of petri dishes spread over the tables contained bacteria incubating in growth media infused with the latest antibiotics. The bacteria, already resistant to most antibiotics, were being exposed to new drugs until a resistant strain emerged. If cultured long enough and often enough, a resistant strain would develop. One always did. The strain would then be grown and a subculture exposed to the next new antibiotic. By simple repetition of these procedures—a perverse adaptation of survival of the fittest, an unnatural form of selection—they'd created legions of super-bacteria that could turn the simplest infection into deadly, antibiotic-resistant disease.

The last third of the room was devoted to viruses. African

Rift Valley fever, smallpox, and Ebola viruses, along with orthomyxo, influenza, picorna, corona, and pox viruses incubated in temperature-controlled cabinets. By altering viral nucleotides, he'd been able to incorporate various traits into their genomes: increased reproductivity, vaccine resistance, and improved virulence.

Mehmet continued down the central aisle, his thoughts returning to his lunchtime meeting with Tunç.

"We essentially act as a clearinghouse for rare micro-organisms," Tunç said. "By providing the organisms to select groups, we promote Turkey's interests."

"Rare microorganisms? What types?"

Tunç gave a dismissive wave. "Bacteria, viruses, natural substances."

"How are they used?"

"That's not our business," Tunç said, an edge to his voice. "But if these groups didn't get them from us, they'd find them elsewhere: the Balkans, Russia, Iran."

"Are they used as weapons?"

"They function strategically. They work by inflicting fear." Tunç paused, looking warily at Mehmet. "Before I go any further, I need to know if you're with us."

"I am. But I'd like to know more. Is this a government operation?"

Tunç proceeded to wrap the star and crescent of Turkey's flag around his microbial clearinghouse. Its affiliation with Turkish Sky, once a symbol of the country's military strength, only supported his illusion of patriotism.

"Throughout history, these organisms have been a standard part of the armamentarium of many countries," Tunç said. "In the Middle Ages, plague victims were routinely catapulted over city walls to spread disease. The United States gave handkerchiefs and blankets from smallpox wards to Native Americans. Many countries in the Middle East have had productive biowarfare facilities at some point in their histories. As we saw recently in Syria, many still do. These activities can be unpleasant, but they're necessary."

"What would be my role?"

"We need you to oversee the facility. We have technicians who would do most of the work, but we need someone at the PhD level to direct them."

Tunç walked to the window and looked outside. "In the twelfth century, Frederick Barbarossa, the emperor of the Holy Roman Empire, used the bodies of dead soldiers to contaminate drinking wells during the Battle of Tortona. Barbarossa did what was necessary to win. We have a responsibility to do the same. We can no longer be bystanders and look to NATO for protection. We must be prepared to stand by ourselves. I like to think of our operations as our own Little Tortona." Turning, he held out his arms. "Now, my friend, are you with us?"

Mehmet had no reason not to trust Tunç. The *Gazete İstanbul* had recently referred to him as the "Prince of Turkish industry." The son of one of Turkey's greatest generals, the Izmir businessman had given him the chance to run his own lab and was paying him an exorbitant amount to do so. He now offered to double funding.

"Yes, Iskender. Of course."

Mehmet opened a door in the back of the attic room. He stepped into a windowless room. It had an exposed plywood floor and was lit by a bare light bulb hanging through a hole in a drywall ceiling. In the middle of the room, two card tables sat side by side.

Tunç and one of his bodyguards, along with the three technicians, sat in folding chairs around the tables. They also wore bodysuits, their hoods pulled back. To Mehmet's surprise, Yalçin Kaldırım had joined them.

Tunç's comments five years earlier about the inadequacies of his Little Tortona had been a direct reference to Yalçin, the facility's director at the time. A year before Mehmet took over as director, the lab's entire population of exotic and deadly bacteria had been lost after a common bacterial strain contaminated the growth media. Years of painstaking work were eliminated. This and a few previous events had called into question Yalçin's fitness to head the facility. But the final blow to his directorship came when Farrat Badem, Koba Laboratories' current summer intern and the son of Little Tortona's head technician Hacek Badem, developed skin lesions. Farrat's mother took him to University Hospital, where the lesions were cultured. With Yalçin's blessing, his own microbiology lab had reported the cultures as a "smallpox-like virus."

Smallpox had existed in only a few research laboratories following its worldwide eradication from humans in 1979. After they'd acquired the virus through the black market, Hacek unwittingly contaminated himself with the virus and brought it home. Hacek informed Yalçin the patient in the hospital with the smallpox-like virus was Farrat. Within the hour, Yalçin had revised the lab's interpretation to a "flu-like virus".

Mehmet closed the door behind him. He pulled back his hood and sat next to Hacek. The head technician and his son had survived their smallpox infections. Like Farrat, however, Hacek's forehead, cheeks, and neck were pitted with smallpox's numerous telltale scars. The scars had served as a never-ending reminder of Yalçin Kaldırım's incompetence.

"Before we start," Tunç said, "Yalçin asked to attend today's meeting. He has something he'd like to update us on."

"Last week, a culture at the university grew *Yersinia*," Yalçin began. "One of my technicians gave a preliminary report of *Yersinia pestis*. When I discovered it, I changed the interpretation to *Pasteurella dagmatis*, a similar gram-negative rod." He paused, wanting everyone to know he'd learned from the smallpox incident. "However, because of the unavoidable difference between the preliminary and final reports, the American doctor caring for the patient sent another sample to a lab in Paris for clarification. The Paris lab reported the sample as being positive for *Yersinia*."

Mehmet recalled the dinner conversation with Safiye and her colleagues. At the time, he'd taken Yalçin at his word—that the patient in quarantine was infected by *Pasteurella*.

"This could just be a sporadic infection," one of the technicians said. "They do occur."

"It was one of our strains," Yalçin said. "It was resistant to everything we tested it against."

"How is the patient?" Hacek asked.

"I recommended treatment with Zagam. He's doing well."

"A single inconsequential *Yersinia* infection shouldn't raise much suspicion," a technician said.

"That's true," Yalçin said. He cleared his throat. "Unfortunately, the farmer's daughter and wife were admitted this week with similar symptoms."

Hacek groaned. "This farmer," he said, rubbing his temples. "Do you know his name?"

Yalçin slid the patient's hospital data across the table. Hacek picked it up. "His last name is Tatvan." He turned to his fellow technicians. "Sound familiar? Neighbors? Friends? *Family*?"

The technicians shook their heads.

"Where does he live?" Mehmet asked.

"873 Belekara Pasa, Ulücuk," Hacek said. He looked up. "That's just downstream."

Throughout Little Tortona's existence, its wastes had been sealed in metal barrels and buried in a field on the grounds of Turkish Sky. The recent earthquake and the resulting rift through the river had caused a flood that unearthed many of the barrels.

"Even with the flood, I don't understand how this could have happened," Mehmet said. "Everything we dump is irradiated. Even if some of our wastes leaked into the river and made it downstream, our bacteria shouldn't be able to infect anyone."

When he'd become director, Mehmet established procedures to ensure contaminants wouldn't enter, exit, or spread throughout the laboratory. Bodysuits and air filters became standard issue and special washing procedures mandatory. Prior to being placed in metal drums, all wastes were now irradiated, preventing the discarded organisms from being able to reproduce and become infectious.

Hacek turned toward Yalçin. "You said the *Yersinia* was resistant to everything you tested it against?"

"In our initial panel. We then tested it against a broader panel of antibiotics and found it susceptible to Zagam."

"But you recommended Zagam before you knew it was susceptible? *Why*?"

"Since Zagam is a new antibiotic, I knew the bacteria hadn't been exposed to it," Yalçin said. "It would still be susceptible."

"Our *Yersinia* strains have been exposed to it," Hacek said. "We developed a resistant strain last year."

Yalçin didn't respond, sweat beading on his forehead.

"If it's one of our strains," a technician said, "it would have to be over—"

"Five years old," Hacek said. "Before a Zagam-resistant strain was developed . . . and before we started irradiating our wastes."

There was a moment of silence as all eyes turned toward Yalçin.

"Tell me more about this curious American doctor," Tunç's bodyguard said. "The one sending specimens to Paris."

Following the meeting, Mehmet drove from the third hangar. He passed through the gate and over the bridge. Instead of following Tunç's limousine and Yalçin's sedan back along the access road, he turned toward the administration building.

Inside the building, he found Savon sleeping in the third-floor room. Enver Pasha stood at the bedside with another elderly man, who wrote something in Savon's chart and then left.

"The oncologist?" Mehmet asked.

Enver nodded.

"I still think this is for the best," Mehmet said. "There's nothing we can do."

During their first meeting across the hall, Mehmet had convinced the old doctor a miracle cure was too much to expect. Enver had then persuaded Tunç, who'd turned Savon's care over to the oncologist.

A nurse entered the room. Preparing to place an IV, she pushed back the left sleeve of Savon's gown, exposing a tan patch over his lateral bicep. As she began to peel off the patch, Savon jolted awake. He pushed her away.

"It's fine," Enver said. "Leave it."

The nurse smoothed the patch into place. Finding a vein, she placed the line and hooked it to a bag of yellow fluid hanging from a bedside pole. She opened the valve and then left.

The two men watched as a third course of chemotherapy dripped into Savon's veins.

"After six years of research, the fact you have nothing to offer is unfortunate," Enver said. "Iskender's venture into medical research has been a failure. I'm afraid the direction of his philanthropic efforts will have to change."

21

Day 20

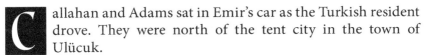 allahan and Adams sat in Emir's car as the Turkish resident drove. They were north of the tent city in the town of Ulücuk.

"Here," Adams said, pointing. "873 Belekara Pasa" was handwritten on the side of a mailbox.

Emir turned onto a dirt driveway. The drive, flanked by fields lined by orderly rows of crops, led to a modest farmhouse and barn.

Adams's former patient, his neck wrapped in bandages, emerged from the barn. After the farmer's illness, his work clothes were now two sizes too big, but his grip was firm as he shook hands with the doctors. He handed a bag to Adams and bowed. "Sağ olun."

Adams pulled a tomato from the bag. "Sağ olun," he said, returning the farmer's bow.

Emir spoke in Turkish and explained to the farmer that his wife and daughter were doing well. They would have to stay in the hospital, however, until they'd finished their antibiotics and were beyond the stage of contagion.

The farmer was ecstatic to hear the news. Waving the physicians forward, he gave them a tour of his fields, proudly pointing out his various crops. As they walked, Adams intermittently stopped and collected ground samples.

By the time they circled back to the barn, the farmer was breathing hard. He leaned against a rusted barrel and caught his breath.

Callahan noticed an insignia on the barrel. Most of the

barrel's paint had chipped off, but the image of an airplane with a flag waving in the background was discernible. The image seemed familiar. "What's that?" he asked, pointing.

"Türk Gök Fabrikası," Emir said after speaking with the farmer. "It's the symbol for Turkish Sky Manufacturing, a local company that's upstream from here. The barrel washed up in one of his irrigation channels after the earthquake. He would have brought it back, but the company has gone out of business."

Callahan looked to the river. On the other side of it was a road. It was the road Adams had taken them on during their run.

"Look familiar?" Callahan asked, motioning toward the barrel when Adams returned from collecting his samples.

"Near the rift," Adams said, nodding. "It's the symbol on the sign by the sentinel building."

Callahan turned to Emir. "Turkish Sky didn't appear to be out of business."

Emir spoke with the farmer. "It closed about fifteen years ago," he said afterward. "Several years ago, it was purchased by Tunç Corporation."

"Tunç Corporation?" Callahan said. "As in Iskender Tunç?"

Emir nodded. "When the plant closed, many in the area lost their jobs. After it was purchased, everyone hoped they'd start rehiring. They never did."

22

Six months earlier
Republic of Dagestan, Russia

Petrovich watched as Tatiana slept, her breathing regular and deep. After an abrupt inhalation, she opened her eyes.

"Good morning," he said.

Tatiana blinked away the sleep. Even now, as she woke, she was beautiful.

"Do we have anything to do today?"

She gave a carefree shake of her head. "Nothing, nothing at all."

"Then we can spend the entire day in bed?"

"We can."

He reached out and ran a finger along her cheek. As he leaned in to kiss her, Tatiana's cell phone rang.

Neither moved. After several rings, her reply sounded.

"*I'm not available. At the beep, please leave your name and number.*"

"Tatiana," a male voice said. "Are you there?"

Petrovich flopped onto his back.

She pushed up onto an elbow and looked expectantly toward him as the voice continued.

"Tatiana? Tatiana Andropovna?"

After a few moments, Petrovich gave a reluctant nod. As she took the call, he recalled the first time he'd heard that name.

Tatiana Andropovna.

Petrovich, a sergeant in the Russian army, stood at attention outside the Smolny along Nevsky Prospekt. It was roll call during the first day of officer training. He and the other seasoned military men were already in formation when the captain called her name. She was the first of the intellectuals to be summoned—one of the newly commissioned officers from the university.

When the captain repeated her name, Tatiana warily walked from where she stood with the others and joined the line. For the benefit of her colleagues, she snapped her heels together and mockingly puffed out her chest.

The captain looked her up and down, his gaze settling on her blouse and its plunging neckline. He began yelling, telling her she was a disgrace to the Kremlin and the memories of Alexander Suvorov and Georgy Zhukov, the great Russian generals. He ordered her to stand at attention, straighten her uniform, and button her shirt.

Tatiana stared ahead, the captain's spittle drying on her face. With steady hands, she buttoned her shirt. "You forgot Kutuzov."

"What?"

"General Mikhail Illarionovich Kutuzov," she said. "He defeated Napoleon."

"I know what he did," the captain screamed. "*Silence!*"

As the captain called the remaining intellectuals, they joined Tatiana in line and followed her example, snapping to an overly eager attention. After roll call, the captain put the entire group through a twenty-five-kilometer run.

For the next twelve weeks, the captain extracted his revenge. But while the other intellectuals washed out, Tatiana couldn't be broken.

Basic officer training was followed by six months of advanced training. He and Tatiana excelled and were among the few selected for two years of training with the Glavnoye Razvedyvatel'noye Upravleniye (GRU), the country's military intelligence directorate.

Until then, the disparity between their backgrounds had kept them apart. But with Tatiana's unexpected mastery of the physical aspects of training and his equally unexpected grasp of its finer academic points, a mutual respect formed. They soon transitioned from colleagues, to friends, and then lovers. For those two years, their days belonged to the GRU, but their nights belonged to each other.

After concluding their training, Tatiana joined the Sluzhba Vneshney Razvedki (SVR), the foreign intelligence service and the former KGB's first directorate. He returned to the army. They took the separation in stride, naively believing their best years were ahead of them.

Over the next dozen years, their careers and other lovers kept them apart. They occasionally rekindled their romance during weekends in Saint Petersburg or Moscow but afterward always went their separate ways.

Tatiana set down her phone, breaking Petrovich's reverie.

"Yasenevo?" he asked.

She nodded.

They were calling Tatiana back to work. SVR headquarters was located in Moscow's Yasenevo district.

Petrovich moved back against the headboard. Taking a deep breath, he gave a tentative but accepting nod.

"Is that it?" she asked, her eyes accusing. "'Thank you, Tatiana. The last seven months have been great. I'll see you again in a year or two.'"

"No," he said. "It's not like that."

"It's *exactly* like that," Tatiana said. She held out her arms. "Is there something wrong with me?"

"No, Tatiana. You're perfect. More than perfect. But your career. You need to get back."

"I'm thirty-eight years old. Do you think I give a damn about my career? Did it ever occur to you I might want to have children someday, that I might want to get married?"

He looked down.

"A few months ago, I said I loved you. I've said it at least five times since, and you haven't said one word in return. I've never asked for a commitment, Vlad. But tell me, do you love me?"

Once again, he was silent.

"*Do you?*"

He shook his head.

"I want to hear you say it."

He looked her in the eye. "I don't love you."

She flew across the bed in a rage. He covered his head as she pounded him with her fists. "You love me," she screamed. "You love me."

When she stopped, out of breath, he lowered his hands. Given an opening, she slapped him hard across the face. She raised her hand to strike him again.

He stared back, hands still lowered, blood trickling from a scar on his cheek.

She collapsed onto the bed and began crying, burying her face in the sheets.

His heart ached. He wanted to hold her, to offer her some sympathy, but knew he couldn't.

When she finally looked up, eyes red, she shook her head. "You love me. You can't tell me you don't."

"Yes, Tatiana. I love you. But before I can think of a future, before I can think of anything else, there's something I need to do." He held out his arms. "I need to find who did this to me."

"Your assassin is a ghost." She reached out and wiped the blood from his cheek. "Popov, Yenkov, the others, they're dead. Let them go."

"I can't."

"This assassin, these guerillas, they were only soldiers, like you. They were doing someone else's bidding. They stole *plutonium*. They have access to a nuclear program. They have money and backing. You're in over your head."

"I have to try," he said. "I have to. Afterward, I'll come back to you. We'll get married. We'll have children."

She shook her head. "You won't come back, not from this." She reached out and gently brushed a strand of his hair back. "If we go our separate ways, it's over. If you do survive, if you do come back, I won't be waiting."

23

"*Science is the most reliable guide for civilization, for life, for success in the world. Searching a guide other than science is meaning carelessness, ignorance, and heresy.*"

—**Mustafa Kemal Atatürk**

Day 22

"I thought you had today off," Haas said to Bryce.

Callahan along with Haas, Bryce, and Adams were taking the Monday morning bus into Izmir.

"I do," Bryce said. "I wanted to see if I could find more information on trichothecenes at the hospital."

"Trico-*what*?" Haas asked.

"Trichothecenes," Bryce said. "So far, I've learned it's a toxin produced by *Fusarium*."

Adams looked up from a journal. "*Fusarium*? Here?"

Nodding, Bryce turned to Callahan and Haas to explain. "The fungus is typically only found in jungle climates."

"Weren't Nata's cultures negative?" Callahan asked.

"Yes," Bryce said. "But while she was in the river, she may have been exposed to the toxin but not the fungus."

"Exposed to the toxin . . . but not the fungus," Haas repeated. "Is that possible?"

They all looked toward Adams, who shrugged. "Chromatography tests are extremely sensitive. It could be detecting only trace amounts of toxin."

"Nata's blood level was 140 micrograms per milliliter," Bryce said. "That's very high."

"Maybe the farmers use it as a pesticide," Callahan said.

"That's why I wanted to learn more," Bryce said. "Thus far, the only information I can find on trichothecenes is its use for biowarfare purposes."

"Biowarfare?" Haas said. "We're not exactly in the middle of a war."

"But we *are* in the Middle East."

"Where would it be coming from?" Adams asked.

"We already concluded Nata likely aspirated something in the river," Bryce said. "And we are near a large military complex from which rusting barrels were floating downstream just a few weeks ago."

"An *inactive* complex," Haas said.

"Turkish Sky could have produced mycotoxins in the past," Bryce said.

"Okay," Haas said, nodding. "Let's say you're right. Let's say they manufactured this toxin. What are you going to do about it? It's like our good Dr. Adams's attempts to do something about Kaldırım. We're powerless."

"I'm required to write a postmortem report for the WHO," Bryce said. "I can send a copy to the city of Izmir. In the report, I can postulate the elevated trichothecene level, as Michael suggests, is the result of a pesticide."

"Which would raise the question of where it's coming from," Callahan said. "Which would lead to some sort of an investigation."

"Your postmortem report will just be distributed a little more widely than usual," Adams said.

The four physicians exchanged glances, nodding.

As the others continued talking, Callahan's attention drifted.

A ray of light from the rising sun danced its way over the heads of the passengers to the front, where it settled on the back of Safiye's neck. It'd been just over a week since his vision of Safiye had come crashing down. He didn't want to admit it, but seeing her with Tunç had hurt.

"Let's say they *were* producing bioweapons at Turkish Sky,"

Adams said. "That could explain the illnesses of the farmer and his family. Our antibiotic-resistant *Yersenia* might be manufactured."

"Maybe," Haas said. "But you'll need more evidence before you convince anyone of that."

"We should contact the Paris lab and ask them to test the samples you took for trichothecenes," Bryce said to Adams. "The irrigation ditches were fed by the river. If it's in the river, it should also be in your samples."

"Is this seat taken?"

Callahan's gaze had strayed out the window. He turned toward the voice.

Safiye stood in the aisle. Without waiting for a response, she sat next to him. "When are we going to update the schedule?"

"I presumed after the next administrative council meeting."

"The council met last night," she said. "I came looking for you. Where were you?"

"I went for a walk."

"To where?"

"Ottoman Square."

"Are you mad at me?" she asked.

"What makes you think that?"

"We haven't talked in over a week," she said, her voice low. "You've been avoiding me. After the weekend, well, I thought we had something."

So had he.

"I'm not mad," he said.

"In that case, I'm meeting Mehmet and Ayla for dinner Wednesday night. You can join us."

"Are you serious?"

"See, that's what I mean," she said. "What's changed? If you have cold feet about a relationship, that's fine. If you're worried about the end of the excursion, that's fine too. But I can't just act as if nothing has happened between us."

Callahan's tentmates, sitting in the two rows in front of them, had stopped talking. They looked stiffly ahead, pretending not to listen.

"Are you sure you wouldn't rather invite Iskender Tunç?" he asked.

"Iskender? You know how I feel about him."

"I thought I did. Until I saw you—together."

Safiye's face went pale. "When?"

"When he dropped you off at the bus stop. In the limousine. You were wearing your new dress."

"Is that what this is about?"

"It appeared very intimate—nothing impromptu about it."

"It was *not* a date," Safiye said, speaking quietly. "It was anything but. I was saying goodbye to him—forever. After we drove back from the cottage, Ayla dropped Mehmet off at his lab and then returned to the hospital. She told me Iskender had been putting pressure on Mehmet to arrange a meeting between us. Kólpos Kallonís was a setup. That's why she told me to bring someone. She knows I hate Iskender. The best way of fending him off was to tell him I had a boyfriend."

Callahan tried to clear his thoughts. In his mind, his relationship with Safiye was over.

"After Ayla left the hospital, I called Iskender," Safiye said. "We met for dinner. I told him I'm not the girl he knew. I told him my life is my work, that there isn't room for anything or anyone else. What you saw that night, our embrace, was our final goodbye."

24

Mehmet stood in front of his office chalkboard, his mind racing. It was Monday afternoon. At the morning meeting, Frank Loy reported he and his group had found the site where selectin C-22, the type of selectin activated in malignant cells, bound to the DNA. The Canadian researcher had even given selectin C-22 a name, Primidin, reflecting Mehmet's hypothesis that cancer cells were recapitulating the behavior of "primitive" cells.

Loy had concluded his update by telling them the next step was to characterize the cascade of events following Primidin's activation. What Mehmet remembered, however, wasn't so much Loy's update, but the statement Tanik made afterward.

"Now that we know the binding site, we're one step closer."

One step closer to what?

Finding Primidin was important. But even after further characterizing it, there'd be much more to understand. There always would be.

Mehmet's thoughts turned to Savon. As he reflected on the dying young man, he was forced to step from the mind-set of a research scientist and think as an oncologist.

He raised a piece of chalk and scratched an X over the line connecting Primidin to its binding site on a helical strand of DNA. If Primidin's activation was the initial step in the malignant transformation, they didn't need to characterize the cascade of events following activation. What happened afterward didn't matter. If they could simply block Primidin from binding to the DNA, the malignant transformation could be stopped.

Tanik had been right. They were one step closer to under-standing cancer. But the cure was no longer hidden in some unimagined, distant revelation. It was right in front of them.

At University Hospital, Callahan, Safiye, Adams, and Haas ate lunch in the cafeteria. Emir and a group of residents sat at the adjacent table.

"I talked with Kaldırım again about the Paris lab results," Adams said. "He still says they're wrong." Imitating Kaldırım, he continued with a Turkish accent. "Diagnostic microbiology is a tricky business. Many traps can lead to an incorrect typing. The Paris lab fell into one. It—"

Adams stopped when Safiye elbowed him. The residents, who'd been talking among themselves, had grown silent.

"You realize a Southern guy trying to do a Turkish accent sounds terrible," Haas said.

"And inappropriate," Safiye quietly added.

"I'm sorry, but this guy is hiding something," Adams said. "He could make a preacher cuss."

"There's the Tuscaloosan," Haas said. "The madder he becomes the more it comes out."

"What is Dr. Kaldırım hiding?" a resident asked.

"Nothing, Öktem," Adams replied.

"No, I want to know," the resident said. "Why would Dr. Kaldırım be hiding something?"

When Adams didn't reply, the resident stood. "Everything I've heard about Americans is true. You sit in front of us and insult one of our most senior professors. You act before considering the effects."

"You're right," Adams said. "I was out of line. I'm sorry."

"You're callous," the resident continued. "You ruin lives and then go back home and pretend it didn't happen, thinking you did us some type of great service. Well, no thank you." He walked away.

By now, the whole cafeteria was watching.

"I'm sorry," Adams said, standing. "Öktem. *Öktem.*"

Pushing through the cafeteria doors, the resident disappeared from view.

Mehmet remained in front of his board, tracing lines over the X between Primidin and the helical strand of DNA, trying to figure out a way to prevent the two molecules from meeting. In the quiet of the office, the solution hit him.

Vandegut.

Mehmet walked to the Swedish researcher's office. Finding Vandegut at his desk, Mehmet closed the door. He sat and began talking.

Nature, through viruses, had developed a perfect system for introducing foreign DNA into cells. With Vandegut's virus-driven gene-therapy model, they could use their virus to insert a strand of DNA containing the Primidin binding sequence into tumor cell nuclei. Their DNA would then bind to the Primidin, preventing it from binding to the native DNA and initiating the malignant cascade. The Primidin would be rendered useless.

"If the Primidin is already bound to the native DNA in tumor cell nuclei, why would it bind to our DNA?" Vandegut asked.

"Once the tumor cells start dividing, the Primidin will have to release the native DNA," Mehmet said. "If there's enough of our manufactured DNA in the cell, it will bind to the unbound Primidin. It will also bind to the Primidin in the sister cell after the division."

"Which would stop the tumor from growing," Vandegut said.

"And if it's not growing," Mehmet said, "it's dying."

"We should test this in one of our mouse tumor models."

Here was the tricky part. If this was going to work, Vandegut had to know the truth, or at least something close to it.

"What if I told you we had a patient?"

"Patient?" Vandegut said. "*Human?*"

"A brother of a friend was recently diagnosed with metastatic pancreatic adenocarcinoma. He's received chemotherapy and radiotherapy without response. When his doctors sent him home to die, my friend asked if we had any experimental drugs that might help."

"Did you tell him that even if we had something to offer, it would be unethical *and* illegal to use it on his brother?"

"I told him we had nothing to offer," Mehmet said. "Which, at the time, was true."

Vandegut and Tanik were the most vocal of the researchers. Tanik would have reservations but would eventually come aboard. Vandegut's reaction, however, was more unpredictable.

"Experimenting on humans," Vandegut said. "We'd be risking everything. The lab could lose its accreditation."

"If we did this, I would make sure my friend and his brother understood that whatever we tried would be experimental. If it doesn't work, there'd be no finger-pointing."

"Have you said anything to the others?"

"You're the first," Mehmet said.

The Swedish researcher slipped off his glasses and pinched the bridge of his nose. "If we did this, we would have to coat the parvovirus with an antibody. We don't have to infect all the patient's cells—just the cancer cells."

Mehmet stifled a smile. Vandegut was in.

"Do you have an antibody in mind?" Mehmet asked.

"CA19-12," Vandegut said.

"How specific is it?"

"Besides binding to pancreatic carcinoma cells, it also binds to cells in normal salivary gland, gallbladder, and pancreas, but it'll miss everything else."

25

Three months earlier
Sakarya, a Turkish province near Istanbul

P etrovich stood on the top floor of an eight-story office complex. Wearing a suit and tie, he looked outside through the structure's plexiglass façade. On the street below, he saw the top of an older-model silver BMW.

"How are you?" he asked, holding his phone to his ear.

"Fine," Tatiana replied from the BMW. "But hurry up. I feel naked sitting out here."

"If there's something that would make me hurry up, that's it."

Tatiana's ultimatum in Dagestan had taken him by surprise. Unable to bear the thought of losing her, he'd gone with her to Yasenevo. They'd persuaded the SVR hierarchy they could find the 300 kilograms of stolen weapons-grade plutonium. They were given one year to do so.

"Did I ever tell you how much I hate fieldwork?" Tatiana said.

"Most intelligence types do. You have to be patient. We're almost through the list."

On that winter morning in Grozny, in addition to the glare of the sun on the newly fallen snow, Petrovich recalled the glint of new guns. The assassin and the young members of his supposedly ragtag group of guerrillas had been carrying expensive Walther MPL-2 semiautomatics.

Petrovich and Tatiana had traveled to Hamburg to visit the manufacturer of the guns. After a few well-placed bribes, they obtained a list of shipments. They'd since systematically tracked down the shipments throughout Eastern Europe and the Near East. Often, they only had to drive into a parking lot or walk into a reception area to see guards carrying the guns. Other purchases took more effort. When they came upon a shipment of two dozen guns to a private security agency in the Turkish province of Sakarya, they found the agency—an offshoot of a local law firm— no longer existed. It never had.

Posing as an entrepreneur interested in forming his own security agency, Petrovich had called the law firm looking for legal advice. After setting up a meeting with one of the firm's lawyers, he now bided his time in their posh waiting room, several minutes before the appointment.

"We've been doing this for *three* months," Tatiana said.

"Let's just finish with the list."

She didn't respond.

"I love you," he said.

"You don't have to tell me that every day."

"I'm making up for the times I didn't."

"How about this," she said. "I'll tell you I love you when you come down here."

"Are you still naked?"

"Ugh," Tatiana said, ending the call.

Smiling to himself, Petrovich slipped his phone into a pocket. He walked to the inner wall of the waiting room.

The plexiglass wall overlooked a column of escalators rising through the center of a busy atrium. The atrium was ringed by a multitude of professional offices. Well-dressed men and women made their way up and down the escalators, filing in and out of the offices.

Petrovich watched a group of young men step onto the escalator to the top floor. Wearing suits, they talked and laughed, playfully jostling each other. They looked more like students on a field trip than businessmen. When the young man at the front of the group turned and looked up toward the law firm, Petrovich almost fell to his knees.

His memories of Grozny always ended with that face . . . and those eyes—staring down at him, waiting for him to die. As the blue-eyed assassin had led the band of irregulars in Grozny, he also led this group. The others sought his eyes and gauged his reaction to whatever it was they were saying. When he laughed, so did the others.

The young men stepped from the escalator onto the eighth floor and headed toward the law firm.

Petrovich turned away. In the reflection of a framed print, he watched the men enter the firm. His thoughts turned to the handgun in his armpit holster. His instincts were to pull the gun and start shooting. Instead, he stood frozen, his adrenaline pumping as the men walked past the receptionist and down a hallway, disappearing into conference room B.

He walked to the reception desk, his legs weak. "My meeting with Mr. Miculka," he said in English. "Is it in room B?"

A cold drop of sweat rolled down his forehead.

"Are you okay?" the receptionist asked.

He pulled a handkerchief from his pocket and wiped his face. "I'm fine."

"Help yourself to a beverage," the receptionist said, pointing toward a utility refrigerator.

Petrovich glanced down the hall. He saw two men talking. One of the men was Emil Miculka, the lawyer he was scheduled to meet. The men broke from their conversation. While the other man stepped into room B, Miculka headed toward him.

"The appointment?" Petrovich said. "Was it in room B?"

The receptionist refreshed her computer screen and tapped at her keyboard.

Impatient, Petrovich leaned over the desk. On the receptionist's screen was an appointment calendar.

12:50 p.m.
1:00 p.m.   B: Rulon/EMİN A.Ş.
1:10 p.m.   C: Miculka/

In room B, a lawyer named Rulon was meeting with members of the EMİN Corporation.

"Your meeting is in room C," the receptionist said. "It's not scheduled to start for another ten minutes. But if you'd like, I—"

Petrovich walked away.

"Here's Mr. Miculka now," the receptionist said.

Petrovich pushed through the firm's glass entrance.

"Sir," the receptionist called out. "*Sir.*"

As the door closed behind him, the receptionist's voice fading, Petrovich stepped onto the escalator.

26

"In human life, you will find players of religion until the knowledge and proficiency in religion will be cleansed from all superstitions, and will be purified and perfected by the enlightenment of real science."

—**Mustafa Kemal Atatürk**

Mehmet sat in a chair in the third-floor room of Turkish Sky's administration building. Savon writhed under sweat-soaked linens, his eyes sunken and lips blistered. It was Wednesday. In the five days since Mehmet's last visit to the room, Savon's hair had thinned, and a shade of gray had washed over his jaundiced skin.

Is it even reasonable to hope?

On Monday, he and Vandegut had talked with Tanik and Loy, who'd also bought in. To minimize the chance anyone outside the lab would learn they were treating a patient, the four of them had decided not to tell the other PhDs or their teams what they were doing. But Vandegut's team members had developed the virus-driven gene-therapy model. If the lab was going to produce the quantities of medicine required within the necessary time frame, his team had to be involved.

The four PhDs and Vandegut's team had since worked day and night to produce the first gene therapy dose, which now sat in Mehmet's lap. Within the bag of fluid were a billion parvoviruses—

each containing multiple copies of the Primidin DNA binding sequence and each coated with CA19-12 antibody.

A nurse entered the room. She pulled down the shoulder of Savon's gown and injected the contents of a syringe into a port. She then left.

Mehmet noticed Savon's shoulder was still exposed. Setting the bag of viral solution aside, he walked around the bed.

The patch previously covering Savon's arm lay on the bedsheet. On his shoulder was a tattoo: a simple drawing of a hawk in flight.

Mehmet dropped the patch into the garbage. He picked up another patch from the bedside table. Removing the adhesive backing, he pressed the patch gently over the tattoo, doing his best not to wake Savon.

"What are you doing?"

Mehmet turned. The oncologist walked toward him, scowling beneath thick, bushy eyebrows.

"His patch," Mehmet said. "It fell off."

The oncologist looked suspiciously at the patch and then up at Mehmet. Unfurling a stethoscope from his coat pocket, he began examining Savon.

Mehmet returned to his chair.

A minute later, Tunç and Enver arrived. Mehmet walked with them and the oncologist to Tunç's first-floor office. Tunç took his place behind his desk while the others sat in opposing chairs.

"We hear you've been busy," Tunç said.

Mehmet walked them through the last two days at Koba Laboratories. When he concluded, he placed the dose of viral solution in the middle of the desk.

For a few moments, they stared at the bag of rust-colored fluid.

"Aras," Enver said. "What do you think?"

The oncologist shrugged. "I'm a simple physician. I'm familiar with the everyday practice of medicine, but not this—not gene therapy."

"Please," Enver said. "Does it *sound* feasible?"

Aras reluctantly looked at his notes. After a moment, he spoke. "His GI tract has been compromised by the chemotherapy. Will this therapy further attack the gut?"

"The CA19-12 antibody coating the virus will direct it toward the tumor, allowing a more targeted effect than chemotherapy," Mehmet replied. "It will miss the GI tract. The virus *will* bind to his salivary glands, gallbladder, and pancreas, but these will only result in mild infections. The parvovirus we're using is innocuous."

"How do you know all the tumor cells will be reached?" Aras asked.

"The initial dose won't infect all the tumor cells. As in any infection, however, the virus will replicate and infect surrounding cells. With this replicative effect and enough infusions, we hope all the cancer cells will be reached. We're not sure how many doses it will take."

"If normal cells are infected by the virus, what will blocking Primidin do to them?"

"Primidin is normally only activated in embryos. It's dormant at all other times. Blocking Primidin in normal cells should have no effect."

"If this works and the cancer cells are destroyed too rapidly, the release of their contents into the bloodstream may be lethal," Aras said. "Savon could die of a simple potassium overload."

Mehmet smiled. The oncologist was asking all the right questions. "That's an advantage of this type of therapy. It won't kill the cancer cells but change them."

"Into what?"

"Normal cells."

"Which ones?" Aras asked.

"That's the big question. Blocking Primidin in cancer cells will force another selectin to be activated. We don't know which one. We hope the cells will become normal. We hope they recognize where they are and blend in with the cells around them. But we don't know what will happen. We have to believe, however, the cell's new path of differentiation will be better than the one it was on."

Aras looked at his notes. He grumbled as he flipped the paper over and back.

"My old friend," Enver said to Aras, "Savon will continue to need the care of a good oncologist. The question is: Do you think the gene therapy will work?"

"Miracle cures come and go," Aras said. "This one has its strong points. But due to its experimental nature, I would have to say no."

They all turned toward Mehmet. He wanted to convey to the three men the logic behind the therapy. At the same time, however, he knew there was nothing to be gained by raising their expectations too high. Before proceeding, they had to buy into the risks and accept the continued likelihood that Savon would die.

"Most supposed miracle cures never make it out of the laboratory," Mehmet said. "Most that make it into clinical testing, don't work either." He looked toward the bag of viral solution. "By using this on Savon, we'll be taking a medication straight from the research bench to the bedside without testing. Optimal dosage, rate of administration, duration—none have been optimized. Unforeseen side effects will occur."

"In other words, Savon will be your guinea pig," Aras said.

"He will be."

Enver turned to Aras. "With the current treatment, how long do you think Savon has?"

"If he survives the chemotherapy, he could live for a few months. Maybe more."

"Then, the best case scenario is several months?"

The oncologist looked down and nodded.

Enver stood. Reaching out, he pushed the bag of viral solution toward Aras.

Two hours later, Mehmet stood at the bedside in the third floor room, watching as the last drop of viral solution entered Savon's IV port. The young man slept peacefully, his vitals stable.

A wave of nostalgia swept through Mehmet as he realized the work culminating in this moment. Morticai Valance had led him to this point. Although the epigeneticist would no longer recognize his remote speculations within the viral solution, Mehmet knew they were at its essence. The Primidin-based gene therapy was *their* work.

He walked from the room. Enver stood in the hallway, waiting. "I must commend you," the old doctor said. "Your ideas are brilliant. But I should apologize. We're pushing you much faster than we had a right to expect."

"And further. Perhaps I should be thanking you."

Enver smiled. "Maybe you were closer than you thought."

"We were." Mehmet raised an eyebrow. "How'd you know of our work?"

"Over the years, the Tunç family has come to me for advice on a variety of medical topics. When Iskender was looking to start a world-class research facility, he gave me the responsibility of finding someone to direct the lab. I made inquiries with the heads of the world's major research institutions. Your name filtered to the top."

"How? I was unknown."

"Dr. Silverstein knew you."

"*Saul* Silverstein?" Mehmet said.

"Yes."

"Saul Silverstein recommended *me*?"

"No one spoke more highly of a protégé than Silverstein of you," Enver said. "Why? How'd you think you got the job?"

"I presumed because I was originally from Izmir. Or because Iskender knew Ayla."

"My search was unbiased by such factors. When I concluded it, I brought a list of five candidates to Iskender. He asked only one question: 'Who's the best?'" The old doctor smiled. "By the way, most of the others on the list are now working for you."

Mehmet fell back against the wall, his head reeling. During his last days at the NIH, he and his old boss had fought like dogs. When Mehmet left, Silverstein had mocked him.

Your ideas won't amount to much. When you finish chasing your unicorns, you and Tanik can always return to the NIH.

Saul Silverstein was confrontational. Those under his charge either rose to his challenges, setting out to prove him wrong, or were crushed. Either way, Silverstein always left a lasting impression. The full extent of that impression was only now apparent.

Mehmet's mission since leaving the NIH had been to prove Silverstein wrong. He'd done so, but it was Silverstein who'd provided the opportunity.

Day 24

Callahan and Safiye stood outside the hospital entrance, waiting for the Kobas. After talking on Monday, they were friendly again, but their romance hadn't rekindled. As fast as the chasm between them had closed, the approaching end of the excursion pulled them apart.

When the Kobas turned into the parking lot, Safiye and Ayla took their positions in the back of the Land Cruiser. Callahan sat in the front with Mehmet.

"How's the world of research?" Callahan asked Mehmet.

"Busy, my friend."

"Too busy," Ayla said. "He's spent the last two nights at work. Or so he tells me. I'm starting to hope it's another woman. At least then I could compete."

Everyone laughed. At dinner that night, however, neither Mehmet nor Ayla appeared interested in their usual banter. Safiye and Ayla talked while Mehmet struggled to keep his eyes open.

When there was a break in the conversation, Callahan looked to Mehmet and Ayla. "Have either of you heard of Turkish Sky?"

"The airplane manufacturer?" Ayla said. "Yes, why?"

"The other day, we passed it while jogging north of the tent city," Callahan said.

"Didn't Iskender buy them?" Ayla asked Mehmet.

Mehmet cleared his throat. "I believe so," he said. "But I think they've gone out of business."

"It appears they're back in business," Callahan said. "There were heavy machinery tire tracks at the entrance along with guards."

"Iskender is probably using the facility for something," Ayla said.

"Speaking of Iskender," Mehmet said, a pained look on his face. "I should apologize to both of you. Kólpos Kallonís was an uncomfortable situation—for all of us."

"I'm the one who should apologize," Safiye said. "He was *my* fiancé. I don't blame you a bit. Your work shouldn't be compromised for something so trivial."

"There are many things more important than my work," Mehmet said. "Your friendship is one of them."

"Thank you," Safiye said. "I just hope Iskender realizes we're over. I hope he leaves you alone."

Ayla raised her wineglass. "To Iskender leaving everyone alone." They clinked glasses and drank.

The restaurant was a block inland from the bay. After dinner, the couples strolled to the harbor. The Kobas walked to the end of a dock, arm-in-arm, and looked out over the moonlit bay. Callahan and Safiye trailed behind. They sat at the same bench where they'd sat after strolling from the concert.

It was another star-filled night. The sound of music drifted from the conservatory, blending with the clang of lines against the masts. The spirit of their night together was as tangible as the bench. Callahan could almost feel Safiye's head on his shoulder, her hair against his cheek. "I wonder where the *Altin Yol* is tonight," he said.

As his words dissipated into silence, a cool wind blew in from the bay.

"Are you cold?" he asked, turning toward her.

Instead of looking up at him, her eyes expectant, she stared flatly ahead. "I'm fine," she replied.

He followed her gaze, suppressing the impulse to wrap his arm around her. With each passing moment, the spirit of their previous night together drifted further away.

Mehmet and Ayla stood at the end of the dock, whispering to each other as they looked over the water. Meanwhile, Callahan and Safiye sat in silence.

When Mehmet and Ayla headed back down the dock, Safiye followed.

Callahan stood and took one last look over the bay.

The *Altin Yol,* as well as their former romance, was nowhere in sight.

Mehmet drove them back to the tent city. At the bus stop, the four of them climbed from the Land Cruiser.

"Michael, my friend," Mehmet said. "It was good seeing you again."

"It's been a pleasure," Callahan said as they shook hands.

Mehmet and Safiye hugged. Callahan and Ayla turned toward each other and also embraced. "Don't give up on her," Ayla whispered.

Callahan nodded.

The Kobas then climbed into their SUV and drove away.

Callahan and Safiye walked back toward the field hospital.

"Thanks for inviting me," Callahan said.

"You're welcome."

They walked in silence. When they neared the field hospital, Callahan stopped. "Now it's my turn to ask. Are you mad at me?"

"I don't appreciate you interrogating my friends."

"It wasn't an interrogation."

"How do you think they'll feel when they learn the truth about why you were asking about Turkish Sky?" she asked.

"What do you mean?"

"Öktem and a group of Turkish residents registered an official complaint at the hospital about Scott Adams. If there's another incident, our invitation to work in the hospital will be rescinded. This could be a huge embarrassment for the WHO. It could turn into an international incident."

"What happened with Öktem was unfortunate," Callahan said. "But you can't expect Bryce and Scott to stop caring about their patients. The plan is to simply inform the authorities about the illnesses. No one is pointing a finger."

"It doesn't matter. Your allegations of bioengineering are out there. They're spreading." She paused. "Does this have anything to do with Iskender?"

"*Iskender?*"

"You didn't talk to me for a week because you thought I was back with him," she said. "Now, you explain these illnesses by connecting them to one of his companies?"

"Are you serious? I admit the whole thing with Tunç bothered me, but I'm over it. I'm over—"

The harsh look in Safiye's eyes softened. "Me," she said, finishing his sentence.

As Safiye continued walking, Callahan jogged in front of her. "That's not what I meant."

When he blocked her path, she looked defiantly up at him, her eyes brimming with tears.

Callahan went to hug her, but Safiye extended her arm, planting her palm firmly in the middle of his chest. "In a couple of weeks, you'll be back in Ann Arbor. I'll be in Istanbul." She summoned a half-smile. "At least you and Jenna were returning to the same time zone. That relationship had a chance."

Lowering her arm, she walked past him.

This time he watched, letting her go.

28

Mehmet drove along Turkish Sky's rut-filled road. After dinner with Michael and Safiye the night before, he'd dropped off Ayla at home and returned to the lab. He and the others had then worked through the night to create a second dose of viral suspension, which now sat on the seat next to him.

The Land Rover emerged into the clearing. For the first time Mehmet could remember, he was happy to be here. He looked forward to seeing how Savon was doing.

He parked outside the administration building. After gulping down his coffee, he lifted the second dose from the seat and entered the building.

As he ascended the stairs, the stench of feces hit him. On the third floor, a harried nurse walked past him, carrying a bundle of soiled sheets.

In the room, Savon lay under a thin blanket, shivering, his cheeks bright red. The tall, sinewy young man who Mehmet had met during his first visit to the room was at the bedside, grasping Savon's hand. "Don't let it win," the young man was saying. "You can beat this."

Mehmet stood at the end of the bed, watching the two young men. As he did, he realized his mistake.

Vandegut had selected parvovirus to serve as the infectious agent because of its innocuous nature. Once the virus entered the bloodstream, the patient's immune system would attack it. As in any normal low-grade infection, the inflammatory response would eliminate the virus. By the time the virus was eliminated, however, it would have implanted the Primidin-blocking sequence into the cancer cells.

But that was in a normal person. Savon had been given the viral suspension after his seventh day of chemotherapy. His immune system had been wiped out. The normally docile parvovirus would replicate with little, if any, immune response. What should have been a harmless low-grade infection was now consuming him.

The oncologist entered the room. Mehmet met the elderly physician's gaze. "His immune system, it—it—"

"—was compromised," Aras said, finishing the sentence. "Savon has symptoms of a florid parvovirus infection."

The nurse entered with a cart loaded with ice. She dumped it into a tub partially filled with water.

Aras pulled back Savon's blanket.

Savon, wearing only a pair of boxers, was little more than yellowing skin draped over bones. Bright-blue sutures traveled across his abdomen, closing his surgical wound. The rash from his parvovirus infection extended from his cheeks and down his neck and chest.

"Beyir, let's lift him," Aras said.

The young man easily lifted Savon by himself, cradling him to his chest.

Beneath the left arm of Beyir's shirtsleeve, Mehmet glimpsed the lower half of a tattoo. It was the same as Savon's—a simple drawing of a hawk in flight.

Beyir set Savon into the bath. When the young man stood, his black T-shirt slid back into place, covering the tattoo.

Mehmet retreated to a chair. He watched as Savon's care was thrown back into the world of conventional medicine.

The oncologist was fortunately adept at his trade. By the time Mehmet left the administration building late that morning, Savon's temperature had started to drop.

Back in his office at Koba Laboratories, Mehmet sat in quiet fatigue.

When you finish chasing your unicorns, you and Tanik can always return to the NIH.

Had Silverstein been right? Had his research culminated in Silverstein's predicted dead end?

Tanik stepped through the doorway, proudly holding up the third dose of viral suspension. His smile disappeared when he spotted the second dose sitting in the middle of Mehmet's desk. "What happened?"

Mehmet ran a hand over his face. "Round the others up. They should hear this too."

Mehmet walked to the conference room table and sat. Vandegut and his team, along with Tanik and Loy, soon sat around the table, looking expectantly toward him.

"In just three days, you've taken a concept and made it reality," Mehmet said. "You've brought us from the bench to the bedside, producing three doses of the gene therapy: three billion copies of the Primidin-blocking sequence, three billion parvoviruses, and tens of billions of copies of the CA19-12 antibody. You've met our challenge. However . . . I've failed you. I forgot to account for the fact our patient was immunosuppressed. The virus, unchecked by an immune response, has spread."

He'd been too focused on the gene therapy. The therapy would alter the tumor cells. He didn't realize it would also kill the patient.

"If my friend's brother is to survive, he must clear the virus," Mehmet said. He shrugged. "I'm sorry, but it's over. Everyone can go home."

As Mehmet walked from the room, Vandegut, Tanik, and Loy followed him into his office. "You should have seen him," Mehmet said, falling into his chair. "The virus was consuming him."

"He has stage 4 pancreatic cancer," Loy said. "Did you really think he had a chance?"

"I have to admit, part of me did," Mehmet said.

"We all wanted it to work," Tanik said. "I feel terrible it didn't. But we're not surprised."

"Under these circumstances, in this patient, there's no way it would have worked," Vandegut said. He pointed toward the two bags of viral suspension on the desk. "But these are incredible. Your idea to block Primidin is brilliant."

"Mehmet," Tanik said. "Ever since you started scribbling in your notebooks at the NIH, this is the quantum leap you've been searching for. This patient may die, but this isn't the end of something. It's only the beginning."

29

Day 25

T he relief team members met in the mess tent. Alin had called an after-dinner meeting. Callahan, sitting with Adams, Haas, and Brooke, looked toward Safiye, who sat in the front row.

Safiye's lab coat, stuffed with medical paraphernalia and handbooks, was a thing of the past. Callahan realized the coat along with her thick sweaters had been a coat of armor. But they'd not only shielded her from the outside world, they'd created an inner sanctum—a place into which she could retreat. It was a place she appeared to no longer need.

"Are you going to talk to her or just keep staring?" Haas asked.

Callahan shrugged. "There's nothing to say."

"I respect Michael and Safiye for backing off," Brooke said. "They're probably doing the most prudent thing."

"When I die, I don't want people saying I was prudent," Haas said.

"I do have to commend Michael for one thing," Brooke said. "Without those terrible sweaters, with the contacts and with her hair down, she's stunning."

"I had nothing to do with any of that," Callahan said.

"Oh," Brooke said. "I think you did."

Safiye was talking with a rotund gentleman. His shiny pate was covered by a thin comb-over, and he had a pencil-thin mustache.

"Who is that guy?" Adams asked.

"Alin mentioned someone from city hall would be here," Callahan said.

Bryce entered the tent. He dropped into a seat in front of them. "The results from Nata's specimens came back from the Paris lab," he said. "Nothing! Not a trace of trichothecenes."

"What about the water and ground samples from the farm?" Adams asked.

"Negative for trichothecenes and *Yersinia*," Bryce said.

"All of them?" Adams asked.

"Yes," Bryce said. "With respect to Nata, all we're left with is a single elevated trichothecene level."

"Remember," Haas said. "You still have the culture results for the farmer and his family. The goal of a report is to induce an investigation. Enough data exists on the farmer and his family to do that."

Bryce shook his head. "The culture results from the farmer's wife and daughter also came back."

"As what?" Adams asked.

"*Pasteurella*."

"Bullshit," Adams said. "If the farmer had a *Yersinia* infection, so did the wife and daughter. They had the exact same symptoms."

The room had grown quiet.

Alin stood from the front row. He shot a darting glance at Bryce and Adams before forcing a smile. "Welcome to day twenty-five." He scanned the room. "To those scheduled to fly home in the next few days, I commend you on a job well done. Thank you for your hard work. To the others, keep up the hard work. Don't forget those remaining in the tent city. They're the homeless and unemployed, the old and sick. We must do what we can for them. Before proceeding with our agenda items, I'd like to introduce our guest. Mr. Ançak Barhal is a city councilman in charge of land appropriations. He was instrumental in securing the site of the field hospital and making our work here possible. Mr. Barhal."

With the use of a cane, the man next to Safiye stood to a polite round of applause.

"On behalf of the city of Izmir, I would like to thank you," he said. "Your work has helped restore our city's most precious commodity—the health of our people."

Everyone clapped.

The councilman summarized Izmir's recent reparations. As he did so, he repeatedly raised a handkerchief to his brow, dabbing at sweat running down his face. He concluded by again thanking them for their contributions and asking if he could do anything to help during the remainder of their stay.

Bryce stood. "Are you aware of health problems affecting those living in this area?"

Haas buried his face in his hands and groaned.

"I am not," the councilman said.

"Recently, a previously healthy little girl suffered massive pulmonary hemorrhage and died after she swam in the river," Bryce said. "The incident raises concerns about toxins in the river."

"I'm sorry to hear this," Barhal said. "If you could provide me with the information you have, I can pass it on to our health department."

"There's an industrial facility upstream from here," Bryce said. "Turkish Sky Manufacturing."

"That facility hasn't been in operation for almost two decades," the councilman said.

"Yes, but barrels have recently—"

"Excuse me," Alin said, standing. He directed an apologetic look toward the official. "Mr. Barhal, our team will continue to do our best to care for the residents of Izmir. While doing so, we will bring any appropriate concerns to your attention."

The councilman nodded.

"On behalf of our team," Alin said. "I'd like to thank you for coming here tonight. We're honored to be a guest in your country and happy to help Izmir in the face of this crisis."

The councilman turned toward the group and gave a humble bow.

Safiye escorted the slow-moving city official from the tent. When they were gone, Alin turned to Bryce. "I know you're distraught over Nata's death. We all are. But for the first time ever, the relief team is on the verge of being asked to *leave* our host country. Our existence, all the good we do, depends on maintaining positive relations with our host countries. If we're perceived as having any other intention than to help, we've failed."

"How is hiding the fact a little girl may have been poisoned in anyone's best interests?" Bryce asked.

"And the fact an entire family contracted antibiotic-resistant plague?" Adams added.

"They're not," Alin said. "But neither is making unfounded accusations. Submit your report. If the allegations are legitimate, they'll be pursued through the proper channels. To make such allegations, however, one should be in possession of irrefutable proof. And correct me if I'm wrong, but from what we all over-heard a few minutes ago, that's not the case."

30

The aroma of steak and eggs mixed with the fragrance of lilacs from the garden as Mehmet and Ayla enjoyed a relaxed Friday morning breakfast on their back porch.

"This is incredible," Mehmet said. "Thank you." The steak and eggs had become a habit of his while he was in the United States. Ayla fixed them for him at least once a week.

Ayla nodded, turning her attention to her conventional Turkish breakfast of warm bread and cheese, a boiled egg, and a fresh tomato from the garden.

Mehmet watched her eat, realizing how lucky he was. Ayla could have been whatever she wanted in life. She still could. Intelligence and an unswerving will were more than enough to push her through the glass ceilings of Turkish society. Like her father, she'd always wanted to teach at one of the great universities. Instead, she'd met and fallen in love with him. Graduate school, only months away, and dreams of teaching were put aside.

He found a pen and paper in a nearby drawer. Back at the table, he scribbled a picture of a hawk in flight and slid it toward Ayla. "What would you say if you saw this as a tattoo on a young man's arm?"

She looked at the drawing for a few moments. "It reminds me of the Ottoman insignias. They often used animals to designate their units or battalions."

"It's a military symbol?"

"Perhaps," Ayla said. "I don't recall that specific marking, but it's similar to the tattoos the Janissaries wore."

"The Ottoman soldiers?"

"*Slave* soldiers," Ayla corrected.

"That's right. They were kidnapped, weren't they?"

Ayla smiled.

"You know history's not my strength," Mehmet said. "Can you tell me more?"

Ayla sat forward, curling her hands around her coffee. "In Ottoman times, conquering armies took young boys from Christian families in the Balkans. The boys were put through a rigorous training program. They became excellent soldiers and faithful Muslims. After their training, they would not only fight Christians, but even former friends and family."

"Complete brainwashing."

"Total. At the time, to be a *kul*, or slave, was a source of pride. They weren't slaves as we would define them today. They were paid a salary and were upwardly mobile. They became so well respected that Muslim families began sending their own sons for enlistment along with bribes for acceptance. They effectively became a class of nobles who were powerful enough to dictate Ottoman policy and engineer palace coups when the sultan's actions opposed their own. When they were finally overthrown by Sultan Mahmud II, it was described as the sultan's coup against the Janissaries."

Mehmet pointed at the drawing. "What would you say if a coworker had one of these?"

"An Ottoman tattoo, with all its Islamic connotations, could easily be interpreted as a display of worship. Is he making a religious statement?"

"I'm not sure."

"In the not too distant past, government officials lost their jobs for such displays of worship," Ayla said. "But I would say it's no big deal with an Islamic party in power."

Mehmet nodded thoughtfully. Standing, he began picking up dishes.

"I was wondering how long your break would last," Ayla said.

"I have a meeting I scheduled weeks ago. I need to go." He set the dishes in the sink and walked behind her, wrapping his arms around her. "I'll be back this afternoon."

"Do you want to go to the cottage this weekend?"

"To be honest, after this week, I'd like nothing more than to stay at home, relax, read, and talk to you."

She nodded. "You've had a hard week."

He kissed her on the cheek. "You're the best."

Thirty minutes after his breakfast with Ayla, Mehmet walked through the attic of Turkish Sky's third hangar.

In the back of the attic room, he looked at several harmless-appearing newts, *Taricha granulosa*, in a terrarium. As he thought of their deadly neurotoxin, he recalled the moment the realities of Little Tortona had been thrust upon him.

After Mehmet had served for a year as director of Little Tortona, his redesign of the attic room had been built, his decontamination procedures implemented, and the previously lost antibiotic-resistant microorganisms replaced. He couldn't help but feel a perverse sense of pride. Organisms that were once the scourge of civilization were under his control. He was producing them and their toxins in massive quantities. And his work at the biowarfare facility, as Tunç had continued to reassure him, was for the good of the country.

It was a Monday night. As usual, Ayla had planned a night on the town. After returning home and changing from his work clothes, he passed the television.

On the screen was the image of a bus and the words "Live—Downtown Tel Aviv." Police officers wearing gas masks carried draped bodies past quarantine ropes. The camera turned to a BBC reporter.

"An hour ago, an explosion brought this bus and its passengers to their final stop," the reporter said. "By the time police arrived, good Samaritans were removing bodies from the smoke-filled bus. Several volunteers complained of numbness. When a volunteer collapsed and began convulsing, the area was evacuated. Police believe a neurotoxin-containing bomb was responsible. A Palestinian militant group has claimed credit for the bombing." A photograph appeared on the screen. "The group known as Fatih is headed by this man, Hamid Sumay."

Mehmet froze.

"Sumay is happy with our product."

Tunç had spoken those words to his bodyguard

before Little Tortona's previous Friday morning meeting. When Mehmet had overheard him, he'd presumed it was small talk regarding one of Tunç's legitimate ventures.

"The attack occurred during peak afternoon traffic," the reporter said. "Twenty-nine are dead."

A Palestinian militant group . . . twenty-nine are dead.

Mehmet had thought his work at Little Tortona was for the good of the country. As he watched bodies being carried from the bus, he realized that wasn't the case.

The following morning, he walked into Tunç's office and handed him his resignation letter from Turkish Sky. Tunç went on a cursing rampage, telling him he could never resign from Turkish Sky, that the fate of not only Koba Laboratories, but his and Ayla's lives depended on his work at Turkish Sky. "This is bigger than you," Tunç had said. "It's bigger than Tunç Corporation. Little Tortona is just the beginning."

He'd glared back. "The beginning of what?"

"Do you know Shirō Ishii?"

Mehmet didn't respond.

"He was a Japanese physician commissioned to build his country's bioweapons program during World War II," Tunç said. "Under Shirō Ishii's guidance, Japan's biowarfare program employed more than 3,000 staff. It included *eighteen* facilities." He paused. "If our country is to once again become a force, like Emperor Barbarossa, like Ishii, we must take advantage of the tools that Allah places among us."

In the four years since his unsuccessful attempt at resigning from Turkish Sky, Mehmet had searched for a way out of his obscene pact with Tunç. But there was no way out—at least none that didn't risk his and Ayla's lives.

He opened the door in the back of the attic room and stepped inside. Tunç and his bodyguard sat around the card tables with the three technicians. Yalçin had once told him the technicians had simply appeared one day. Though weak on general scientific knowledge, they had an intense work ethic. Their willingness to accept additional responsibility had allowed Mehmet to hand over many of the lab's duties—something he'd been eager to do.

The technicians began the meeting with their updates. Hacek went first. "In an attempt to produce a more concentrated cyanide, we've been working on a hybrid of the bamboo plant."

"Cyanide isn't already potent enough?" Tunç's bodyguard asked.

"Yes, but an oral route has always been used," Hacek replied. "With a more toxic form, a transepidermal route can be employed."

The choice of words made it seem more akin to a surgical procedure than the act of killing.

"The puncturing device, a small dart, is coated with the concentrated cyanide," Hacek said. "Once in the skin, the toxin gets into the bloodstream. We estimate incapacitation in minutes."

"Why would cyanide be used instead of ricin or some other poison?" Tunç asked.

"Ricin blocks protein synthesis," Hacek said. "It takes days before it has an effect. Cyanide acts immediately by blocking cellular respiration. The respiratory drive will be paralyzed, and death by suffocation will occur soon thereafter. It mimics a heart attack."

Beyond Hamid Sumay's bombing of the Tel Aviv bus, Mehmet didn't know of any other deployment of the lab's bioproducts. He had little idea to whom they were sold. For his own sanity, he preferred not to.

The door opened. Yalçin stepped inside. He sat and pulled back his hood.

"Now that we're all here," Tunç said, "I want to bring you up to date on the events we discussed last week. The situation with the foreign doctors is under control. Our operations will not be compromised. We've seen to it the specimens sent to the Paris lab were returned as negative and that all further tests will be negative."

"How?" Yalçin asked.

Tunç scowled. Mehmet wondered if that was the true reason Yalçin had been replaced as director. Yalçin didn't understand protocol. When Tunç said something, and so definitively, it wasn't open to question.

"EMİN," Hacek said, answering the question.

When Mehmet had taken control of the third hangar, funding for Koba Laboratories doubled, as Tunç had promised. The extra money didn't come from Tunç Corporation, however, but one of its subsidiaries—the EMİN Corporation, a nationwide courier service.

Hacek turned toward Mehmet to explain. "The samples the foreign doctors are submitting to the Paris lab pass through their courier in Ulücuk."

Mehmet couldn't help but appreciate the irony. In Turkish, the word *EMİN* meant secure.

"The doctors are left with only the single positive *Yersinia* culture and the trace trichothecene level," Hacek said. "Combine that with a multitude of negative and conflicting results, and what they're left with is a confusing mess."

After the meeting, Mehmet drove to the administration building. As he stepped onto the third floor, his nose again burned but this time from the smell of bleach.

The room was oddly still. Savon lay peacefully, his eyes half open, the fingers of his jaundiced hands entwined over clean linens. On his cheeks, there was only a hint of his previous rash. Mehmet read the writing on the medicine hanging from an IV pole: ".01percent morphine."

Savon extended his hand. This time, as Mehmet took it, the young man's grip was almost nonexistent. "Doctor," Savon said, his voice barely a whisper.

"How are you?" Mehmet asked.

"Good."

"I'm sorry my medicine didn't work."

Savon gave an indifferent shrug. His morphine was well titrated.

Mehmet looked toward Savon's left shoulder. "I saw your tattoo. It's nice."

Savon nodded.

"Beyir has the same one," Mehmet said. "I've seen it before. It's a symbol of the great Janissaries."

Savon's right hand moved across his body, coming to rest over the tattoo. "I only regret I won't be alive to see it." His eyes filled with tears.

"See what?" Mehmet asked.

The young man raised his head. He strained to sit up before collapsing on the pillow, his jaundiced blue eyes directed skyward.

"See *what?*"

A noise behind Mehmet snapped his head around. It was Enver. He stood at the end of the bed.

"I was apologizing," Mehmet whispered, walking to the old doctor's side.

Enver nodded, accepting the explanation.

The two men looked down at Savon, who was already breathing deeply, his eyes closed.

"He's in multiorgan failure," Enver said. He motioned toward the bag of morphine. "We're making his last hours as painless as possible."

After leaving Turkish Sky, Mehmet drove straight to the university library. He sat at a row of computer terminals and typed "Janissary" into the search engine. He hit Return.

A list of articles and books scrolled down the screen. After collecting a few of each, he found a desk and began reading.

Formed under Sultan Murad I in 1362, the Janissaries were just as Ayla described. Every five years, the sultan's men searched the vanquished Balkan territories and selected the most intelligent, handsome, and athletic of the Christians' sons as *devshirme*, or draftees. One boy was taken from every forty families, brought to Istanbul as one of the sultan's slaves, and taught to say the *shahada*: "God is but one, and Muhammad is his Prophet."

Once initiated in the true faith, the boy was sent to live with a Muslim family for five years. Afterward, he attended the *acemioğlan*, or freshman schools, to receive a basic education and military training. Those who excelled were selected for the highest honor—to be educated in the Enderun Mektebi, an elite palace school.

At the Enderun, students were placed under the tutelage of the chief eunuch—the *kapı ağasi*. Along with continued military training, they learned at least three languages and were schooled in the sciences, mathematics, geography, history, and law. They were taught to be frugal, diligent, and clean. An importance was placed on good manners, self-control, honesty, and loyalty.

After their training, the young men became members of the Janissary corps—Europe's first standing infantry. The Janissaries were the first to make widespread use of hand grenades, cannons, and guns. They were the first to use alternating lines of volleying fire and the first to have specialists: explosives experts, sharpshooters, and engineers.

The Janissaries were instrumental in the Ottoman conquests

of Constantinople in 1453, the Egyptian Mamluks in 1517, Vienna in 1529, and Buda and Pest in 1541. With their victories came increasing influence. In 1556, they assumed the rights to marry, become tradesmen, and own land. In 1568, they began letting their sons into the corps—bypassing the rigorous selection process and the harsh training of the *acemioğlan*.

As the Janissaries' lifestyle improved, their effectiveness declined. In 1622, when the Turks lost a battle against Polish forces, Sultan Osman II blamed the Janissaries for the defeat. When Osman II attempted to disband them, the Janissaries imprisoned and killed the sultan. In 1807, Sultan Selim III attempted to modernize the Turkish army. Rather than accepting a diminished role, the Janissaries killed the sultan.

In 1826, in what became known as the Auspicious Incident, Sultan Mahmud II announced plans to replace the Janissaries with a European-style army. Determined not to repeat his predecessors' mistakes, the sultan set a trap for the Janissaries. After the announcement, when the Janissaries predictably marched on the palace, they were ambushed by Mahmud's European mercenaries and defeated.

Mehmet leafed through the magazines and books, unable to find mention of a modern-day corps. The Auspicious Incident appeared to mark their end.

In one book, he came across a table with a variety of Ottoman-era symbols. They were the unit insignias Ayla had described. The table contained rudimentary drawings of weapons and animals. As he turned to the final page, his pulse quickened.

A full-page illustration contained an exact replica of the young men's tattoo—the image of a hawk in flight. Underneath it was a caption.

İç oğlanar, insignia of the Sultan's elite.

31

Day 26

As a teen, Bryce Hamilton Jones III was diagnosed with obsessive-compulsive disorder. The diagnosis came after his mother found him repeatedly washing his hands even though the skin on his palms had already been rubbed raw. Treated with behavioral modification, he'd been fine since. But certain compulsions remained. He had a tendency toward excessive cleanliness. And he could never rid himself of the sensation that those close to him were in need of protection. These compulsions had not been debilitating. In fact, during the care of his patients, they were often an attribute. Today, however, hadn't been one of those days.

He'd floundered through the day, performing his tasks out of habit while his mind obsessed about Nata. He'd failed her. And he still didn't know why she died. When would the next Nata be carried to the pediatric tent, her airway ulcerated and bleeding, unable to breathe? When would the next little girl or boy who needed his protection die?

It was late at night as Bryce lay on his cot, listening to the relaxed breathing of his tentmates. Once he was sure they were sleeping, he slipped from his cot. Dressed in a long-sleeve black shirt, a pair of black sweatpants, and his running shoes, he grabbed his backpack, stepped outside, and began walking through the tent city.

The night was pleasant. The sky, lit by a full moon, was clear. Occasional groups sat quietly talking around small fires, but most were inside their tents.

He entered the woods along the well-worn trail and followed it to the river. After crossing the bridge, he broke into a jog and headed north on the Belekara Pasa.

To make such allegations . . . one should be in possession of irrefutable proof. And correct me if I'm wrong, but from what we all overheard a few minutes ago, that's not the case.

The sting of Alin's rebuke had not worn off. But Alin had been right. The links between the illness of the farmer and his family to a bioengineering plot were weak. The links between Nata and foul play were even more tenuous. They needed proof. For too long, they'd danced around the real issue.

His feet landed unsteadily in the darkness. He turned his ankle several times over unseen potholes or rocks. Without serious injury, however, he made his way to the fence at Turkish Sky's southern border. Following the road to the right, he continued to the intersection, where he stopped to catch his breath. Turkish Sky's entrance, lit by two lampposts, was visible in the distance.

He walked into the woods and followed a semicircular path opposite the entrance. His feet crunched over the bed of dried leaves. He slowed, trying to be as quiet as possible, but couldn't avoid the noise. When he was directly across from the sentinel building, its door swung open.

He crouched as two guards emerged from the building and walked in his direction, rifles slung over their shoulders. They stopped beneath a lamppost and lit cigarettes.

Bryce remained motionless. After the guards finished their cigarettes and returned to the building, he continued his path through the woods. He passed over the fissure, which the rains had reduced to little more than a bump, and emerged from the woods near Turkish Sky's northeast corner. He ran across the road and followed the fence along the northern border of the facility to the river.

He removed his clothes except his boxers. Pulling a garbage bag from the backpack, he put his clothes into the bag and sealed it with a twist tie. He returned the bag to the backpack and slipped the backpack over his shoulders. He then stepped into the river.

The cool water sent a jolt through his sweating skin. When the water was chest high, he relaxed and began floating, letting the current carry him. It carried him under the fence into a heavily wooded area.

The trees blocked the light from the moon and stars. For the next few minutes, enveloped by darkness, his only sensation was the pull of the river.

A light appeared, its candescence multiplied by its reflections on the water. As he came closer, he saw the light emanated from a three-story, redbrick building.

He floated steadily past the building, scanning its oily black windows. There were no signs of life. On the opposing bank, he made out three large buildings, their silhouettes highlighted against the star-filled sky. He traveled under a bridge and was soon back in the thicket. Climbing up the bank, he walked back to the edge of the woods and looked out onto the clearing. He shivered as a light breeze passed over his wet skin.

From the woods to his right, a narrow road emerged. On the road, the muddy residue of heavy-machinery tire tracks was visible.

He stepped from the woods and followed the tracks over the bridge, where they veered into the grass, leaving deep furrowing ruts. He walked along the ruts.

The night's quiet was disrupted by the gentle chirp of cicadas. Because of the recent rains, the air was humid, the grass cool and moist against his feet.

At a line of trees marking the western border of the clearing, the ruts headed north. He followed them, passing the three large buildings.

At the northern border of the clearing, he came to a field. From beyond the nearby woods, he heard the gentle flow of water. He'd almost circled back to the river.

He pulled a penlight from the backpack and turned it on, directing it over the ground. The tracks led into a muddy field, where they disappeared in a whirling maze of ruts.

Stepping into the field, his bare feet sank just beyond his ankles in the mud. He was no longer overwhelmed by his childhood compulsion toward cleanliness, but he still shuddered as the mud squeezed up between his toes.

In the middle of the field, he removed a plastic bag containing three sterile cups from the backpack. Holding the penlight between his pursed lips, he unscrewed the lid on a cup and broke its seal. He bent down and filled the cup with mud and water.

He took several steps through the field. Opening a second cup, he scooped up more mud.

His penlight reflected off a metallic object. He tried to pick it up, but the object was fixed to the ground. As he began smearing away the surrounding mud, the object took shape. It was the edge of a barrel.

Straightening, he directed the beam of light over the muddy field. Numerous small metallic reflections winked back at him. The field was filled with partially unearthed barrels.

He walked to the next barrel and stuck the third cup through a rusted-out hole. His hand sank into a jellylike substance. Removing the cup, now filled with brown mucoid material, he screwed on the lid and set it into the plastic bag. He shook the mucoid material from his hand, making a note to start a course of Zagam when he returned to the field hospital.

With the three cups full, he returned the plastic bag to the backpack. He slipped on the backpack and looked in the direction of the river. He would return to the river, where he'd let the current carry him back through the clearing and eventually to the southern border of the facility.

A light suddenly appeared. He flicked off the penlight and knelt. Someone was in the grassy field, walking toward him. The figure held a flashlight. The light swept across the ground, its beam settling on him.

"Dur," the figure shouted.

Bryce ran toward the river. Moving slowly through the mud, he took solace in the fact the figure remained stationary at the edge of the muddy field, content to simply follow him with the flashlight.

As he neared the woods, finding traction on solid ground, a blinding light filled his vision.

"Teslim olmak," a voice barked.

Coming to a stop, Bryce raised his hands.

32

Day 27

A nurse handed Callahan a chart. "Michael, there's a boy in room two. Be prepared."

Callahan scanned the triage note before stepping into the room. A squirming six-year-old boy sat on his mother's lap.

"Merhaba. Neyiniz var?" Callahan asked.

The mother pointed. On the right side of her son's neck, a tennis ball-size lesion protruded from the angle of his jaw.

Callahan reached out to examine the lesion, but the boy slapped his hand. The mother scolded her son.

Callahan set his stethoscope on the boy's foot. The boy watched, amused, as Callahan moved the stethoscope to his knee and then elbow. When Callahan set the stethoscope near his neck, the boy lunged out.

Callahan leaped back, dodging the child's foot as it swung toward him. Standing safely out of reach, Callahan smiled. The boy returned the smile. From appearances, albeit distant, it appeared the boy had a branchial cleft cyst. It was a benign lesion but fairly large.

"Kusura bakmayin," Callahan said to the mother before walking from the room and outside. In the pediatric tent, he found Brooke at the on-duty desk. "Can I steal one of your pediatricians?" he asked.

Before Brooke could respond, Safiye stepped from a clinic room.

"Can I get a consult?" Callahan asked. "It'll take just a second."

Safiye looked toward Brooke. "Do I have a second?"

Brooke held up a forefinger. "One. Several patients are waiting."

In the surgical tent, Callahan introduced Safiye to the mother and son. Safiye removed a sucker from one of her coat pockets. Unwrapping it, she held it out. The boy grabbed it and began sucking vigorously. As he did, Safiye palpated the neck mass. After several seconds, she stepped back.

The mother and Callahan began laughing.

"What?" Safiye asked.

Callahan shook his head. "Nothing." He waved her from the room.

"What do you think?" he asked when they were in the hall.

"It looks like a branchial cleft cyst. It's a big one. You could drain it, but it'll probably recur."

"So you'd take him to the OR?"

"For one that big, yes."

"Thanks." He pointed toward her pocket. "You wouldn't happen to have extra?"

She removed several suckers and slipped them into the breast pocket of his scrubs.

"I'm sorry," he said. "You were right. The other night, I should have been upfront with Mehmet and Ayla."

"You should have," Safiye said, arranging the suckers in his pocket. "It was dishonest."

"And deceitful," he added, a smile creeping across his face.

Safiye took a deep breath, resting her open palm over his pocket. "You were just doing what you thought was right."

"Thanks," he said. "And thanks for the consult."

Safiye looked up, their eyes meeting briefly. "I've got a lot of patients. I'd better go." She began walking away but stopped and turned. "Have you seen Bryce?"

"No."

"We scheduled him to work here today, didn't we?"

"Yes," he said. "But he might have gone to the hospital."

"We paged him there. He hasn't replied. We also called his cell, but he didn't answer."

"If he shows up, I'll send him your way," Callahan said.

When Callahan woke that morning, the fact that Bryce was gone wasn't unusual. What was unusual was that his sleeping bag wasn't neatly rolled up.

Callahan stepped outside with Safiye. As she returned to the pediatric tent, he walked to the Cloister. Inside their tent, Bryce's sleeping bag was still in disarray.

Callahan reached beneath Bryce's cot and picked up his folded white coat. Bryce's WHO identification badge was fastened to the lapel. The relief team members were supposed to carry the badge at all times.

As he pulled Bryce's wallet from a coat pocket, there was a beep. He reached into another pocket and removed Bryce's phone—the source of the noise. Several messages were waiting.

Callahan set the cell phone, wallet, and coat on the cot. He and Bryce had talked about visiting the volcanic tuff pyramids in central Cappadocia or the scenic Bay of Ölüdeniz. Given recent events, however, if Bryce thought he had the day off, he most likely would have visited the university library to do more research on Nata. But wherever Bryce went and whatever he did, he would have taken some combination of the items that now lay before him.

"Councilman Barhal said authorities don't initiate a search until someone's been missing for twenty-four hours," Alin said after ending a phone call.

After Callahan raised an alarm that Bryce was missing, he and Alin had organized the relief team members into search groups. The groups had already left for the tent city, Ulücuk, and Izmir.

With a grim nod, Callahan turned toward the mess tent's opening.

"Where are you going?" Alin asked.

Callahan held up a stack of missing persons flyers that Thomas had printed. "To distribute these," he said. He stepped outside.

The air was thick as the day's heat and humidity still hung heavily in the air. He began jogging. Once the field hospital was no longer in view, he flipped the flyers into a garbage can and picked up his speed, his thoughts fixed on Thursday night's meeting.

Recently, a previously healthy little girl suffered massive pulmonary hemorrhage and died after she swam in the river. The incident raises concerns about toxins in the river.

At the northern edge of the tent city, he headed into the woods, where he passed over the river. He turned onto the Belekara Pasa and ran past the farmer's field. When he reached the fence at

Turkish Sky's southern border, he followed the road to the right.
At the intersection, he turned left.

To make such allegations . . . one should be in possession of irrefutable proof. And correct me if I'm wrong . . .

Sprinting now, his lungs and legs screaming for oxygen, he
heard a rumbling sound. The sound grew louder. Realizing its
source, he jumped into the grass.

A car skidded to a stop next to him.

"A little late for a jog," Adams said, leaning from the open
passenger window of Emir's car. The resident was driving. Haas
sat in the back.

Callahan bent over and gasped for air.

"What were you going to do, Rambo?" Haas asked through
his open window. "Take them yourself? Come on. Get in."

Callahan slid into the back. Emir drove to the entrance.

A guard wearing camo fatigues walked from the sentinel
building. He had a rifle over his shoulder. The butt of a pistol
protruded from his waist holster.

"Looks like he's ready for World War III," Haas said.

Emir rolled down his window and handed a flyer to the guard.
After a short conversation, the guard shook his head.

"He's been on duty since six this morning," Emir said. "He
hasn't seen anyone fitting Bryce's description. The night guards
also didn't report anything unusual."

Emir took the flyer. He wrote down a number and handed it
back to the guard, who returned to the building.

"He'll leave the flyer inside," Emir said. "If anyone has
information, they'll call me."

33

Two months earlier
Istanbul, Turkey

Tatiana sat in a darkened room in front of a computer. It was 3 a.m. She clicked on an icon: "Find Wi-Fi."

A list with six local networks appeared. She'd already hacked into the first four. Highlighting the fifth, she hit Return.

The "Enter password" prompt appeared. She clicked on another icon, activating an encryption program. Sitting back, she waited as the program began testing billions of passwords.

"Tatiana?" came Vlad's voice in her headphones.

"Yes," she said into a microphone.

"I'm putting the last bug in."

The EMİN Corporation was a nationwide delivery service headquartered in the Levent—the business district on Istanbul's European side. Tatiana and Vlad had moved into an apartment across the street from EMİN's main offices. Vlad was now tapping their office phones.

Tatiana looked toward the row of speakers next to the computer. "Got it," she said as a reception meter jumped. "Go ahead, say something into the phone." She slipped off the right ear of her headphone.

"I'm on my way back," Vlad said, his voice sounding from the speaker.

As Tatiana adjusted the volume on the speaker, one of the other reception meters jumped. A male voice sounded from the speaker.

"Vlad, someone's there." She reached toward the window and cracked open the blind. "Someone just picked up a line."

Across the street, EMİN's offices were located on the top floor of a seven-story building. An office light was on.

"The west corner office," she said.

"What are they saying?"

Tatiana turned up the volume and listened as two men spoke in Turkish. Tatiana was fluent in the language.

"Kabul, it's me."

"Beyir?" a sleepy voice said. "What time is it?"

"It's late. Who was the last to leave the office yesterday?"

"One of the secretaries," Kabul said. "Why?"

"I just walked in," the man named Beyir said. "The security system was off."

"What are you doing there?"

"I'm picking up some of Savon's personals. I'm taking him to Izmir."

There was a moment of silence.

"When do you think you'll be back?" Kabul asked.

"I'm not sure," Beyir replied.

"This is terrible. Of all the people to get cancer."

"I know. He's the last one you'd expect."

"Keep me up to date," Kabul said. "Good luck."

"Thanks."

Tatiana heard an electronic click, the call ending. The light in the corner office went off.

"The conversation is over," she said. "When he leaves, he'll turn on the security system."

There was no reply.

"Get out of there," she said. "You can't be in there when he turns it on. You'll be trapped. Vlad? *Vlad*?"

Hearing a noise behind her, she spun.

A shadowed figure stood in the doorway.

"Don't do that," she said.

"Sorry," Vlad said, stepping into the light. He walked to her side and motioned toward the computer. "Have you found it?"

Tatiana turned toward the screen.

The encryption program had stopped. A prompt had appeared.

```
Password found. Do you want to log on? Yes/No
```

Highlighting Yes, she hit Return.

Moments later, the Wi-Fi network's home page appeared.

EMİN Corporation
A faster way of doing business

"We're in."

34

"Where there is no freedom, there is death and destruction."

—**Mustafa Kemal Atatürk**

"It's probably a good thing we didn't go to the cottage this weekend," Ayla said. She stood at the kitchen sink looking outside as it rained.

Mehmet sat at the kitchen table. He set down the Sunday morning paper. "I agree." His gaze wasn't directed outside to the rain pooling on the deck but across the table to Bryce Jones's image on the missing persons flyer.

The previous evening, he and Ayla had helped Safiye and her colleagues distribute the flyers throughout downtown Izmir. Mehmet learned a young girl—a patient of Bryce's—had died of pulmonary failure after swimming in the river. A blood test had shown an elevated trichothecene level.

Tunç had said his workers had cleaned up the mess caused by the flood at Turkish Sky. But if antibiotic-resistant *Yersinia* and fungal toxins had leaked into the river, what else had escaped? Thousands lived in the tent city. How many more would get sick? How many more would die?

The house phone rang.

Ayla quickly dried her hands and answered the call. Safiye was supposed to call with any word on Bryce. She extended the phone, a disappointed look on her face. "It's for you."

185

"Dr. Koba, this is an old friend," said a familiar voice. It was Enver Pasha. "I apologize for bothering you at home. I called to tell you of an expected passing."

Savon was dead.

"I'm sorry to hear that," Mehmet said.

"I also called to tell you our mutual friend doesn't hold you responsible."

That news would have been cause for celebration just a few days ago. But now, as Mehmet looked toward the missing persons flyer, he wasn't sure how he felt.

"I'm glad we finally had the chance to meet," Enver said. "I hope our paths cross again under more favorable—"

"I understand you had some excitement yesterday," Mehmet interrupted.

"Excitement?"

"At the facility."

If Bryce had gone to Turkish Sky and something had happened, Enver would know about it.

The old doctor's voice took an icy tone. "You shouldn't concern yourself with these matters."

The line went dead.

The boy with the branchial cleft cyst was the first of Callahan's Sunday cases. Anesthetized, he'd been prepped for surgery. His neck lesion was now a sterile, iodine-stained mound that protruded through an opening in the blue surgical drape.

Callahan turned to Mrs. Bagley, the scrub nurse, and held out his hand. She snapped a scalpel into it. "Do you know when this is supposed to end?" he asked, nodding skyward as rain pounded the tent's canvas roof.

"Not until tomorrow," she said.

Callahan started the surgery with a transverse incision through the iodine-tinged skin. As blood pooled, he cauterized vessels and extended the incision, making his way through skin and fascia. After exposing the lesion, he began the slow task of shelling it out. With the tip of his scalpel, he cut through the wispy, weblike adhesions between the outer wall of the cyst and the surrounding soft tissues. It was imperative he not rupture the cyst and spill its contents into the boy's neck. Even though the cells lining the cyst were benign and didn't have the ability to metastasize, they could still seed the surrounding tissues and proliferate, serving as a nidus for local recurrence.

As he sliced through the adhesions, gently pulling on the tumor with forceps, he slowly delivered the mass through the incision. Removing the last connections tethering the outer wall of the tumor to the soft tissues of the neck, he lifted the cyst, still intact, from the boy's neck and handed it to Mrs. Bagley.

"Nicely done," the English nurse said.

Callahan closed and dressed the incision. He then lifted the boy from the table and carried him to the recovery room. The boy's mother was waiting. Through an interpreter, Callahan explained the surgery had gone well. Her boy would be fine.

Walking from the recovery room, Callahan sat and opened the boy's chart. As he stared down at the blank paper, his thoughts turned to Bryce.

The previous day, the relief team members had checked every route for Bryce's egress from the tent city. Flyers hung from every other tent and had been distributed throughout Ulücuk and Izmir. In a few hours, Turkish authorities would officially list Bryce as missing.

Bryce . . . *Missing.* He still couldn't wrap his mind around it.

He slipped off his sweat-soaked cap and ran his hands through his hair. He needed to focus. Another case would soon be starting. Picking up a pen, he began writing.

The rain continued. Its steady beat was joined by the distant sound of women's voices. The voices became louder. They insinuated their way into his consciousness, their melodic rise and fall melding together into an odd singsong intonation. He'd grown accustomed to the habitual, guttural call to worship, but it was too early for the midday prayer, and the sound was different.

He set down his pen and walked to the recovery room. The boy was resting peacefully. The mother, sitting quietly at the bedside, smiled at Callahan and then tilted her head toward the voices. Following her gaze, Callahan walked to the tent opening and pushed back the flap.

In the rain, an old man sat at the front of a wooden cart pulled by a donkey. Callahan had seen the old man and his donkey on an almost daily basis throughout the tent city, performing a variety of odd jobs or carrying knickknacks, clothes, or food for sale.

Several veiled women, the source of the cry, filed behind the cart.

With a flick of his reins, the old man brought the donkey to a stop. He turned and looked back at the cart's rain-splattered tarp.

Callahan's gut wrenched. Pushing past the tent flap, he sprinted through the rain, splashing through puddles in the well-worn grass. He stopped at the back of the cart.

Shouts came from adjacent tents. Others poured outside.

Time slowing, his chest pounding, Callahan squinted into the cloud-filled sky. He felt the rain on his face, wishing it could wash away this moment.

Callahan's gaze dropped to Safiye, Brooke, Alin, and a dozen others who now surrounded the cart. He then looked down at the familiar pair of running shoes that jutted from beneath the rain-splattered canvas. As the women's voices resonated, growing louder, he reached out and pulled back the tarp.

What had they done to him?

Mehmet set down the phone after his conversation with Enver.

"Who was it?" Ayla asked. She'd returned to washing dishes.

"One of the lab techs," he lied.

"Calling the director on a Sunday morning? He must be trying to make an impression. Someone new?"

Mehmet didn't respond. He stared blankly out the patio door. *Nata.* That was the name of the little girl in the tent city. She'd been only eight years old.

Before he'd taken the job in Izmir, Ayla had tried to warn him. She told him that Tunç was a spoiled child, that he was ethically bereft, and that working for him would be a nightmare. He wouldn't listen to her. He told her it would be his lab with his name on the outside of the building. He would be the one making decisions. He couldn't have been more wrong.

The house phone rang again. Mehmet reached for it. "Hello."

"I'm at the hospital. I thought you should know what happened." It was Yalçin. "The farmer's daughter was supposed to be discharged today. She was getting better on Zagam but had a reaction to the antibiotic. She died early this morning."

The news knifed through Mehmet.

"I want your opinion," Yalçin continued. "Do you think I should let Iskender know what happened or wait to tell him at the Friday morning meeting? I'd prefer not bothering him today—"

Mehmet bent over, placing a supporting hand on the counter, Yalçin's voice fading. With barely a grunt, he hung up the phone.

"Mehmet, are you okay?" Ayla stood at his side, drying her hands. "Who was it?"

"Yalçin."

"What did he want?"

"He was at the hospital. He—"

Ayla's phone rang. She pulled it from a hip pocket and checked the caller ID. "It's Safiye."

After taking the call, Ayla raised her hand to her mouth. "Oh my God. *How*?"

Over the next minute, Ayla spoke intermittently but mostly listened, wiping away a flood of tears. "It's so sad . . . No, Safiye, it was the least we could do . . . Please, keep in touch . . . I'm so sorry."

Ayla ended the call. She was shaking. "Bryce's body was found on the side of the road south of Ulücuk. He's dead."

Mehmet embraced Ayla. Holding her, he stared down at the missing persons flyer and the smiling face of the Oxford physician. Safiye said Bryce was the most dedicated physician she'd ever worked with. How many children had the pediatrician saved? How many more would he have saved?

The little girl in the tent city, the farmer's daughter, and now Bryce Jones took their places alongside the busload of Tel Aviv passengers. All were innocent. All were victims of Little Tortona. It was no longer Tunç's Little Tortona, however. More than ever, it was his.

Callahan lifted the white coat from the cot. He folded the coat and set it inside Bryce's duffel bag. Earlier, he'd called Bryce's parents and told them of their son's death. It was the hardest thing he'd ever had to do.

There were a few photos in the bottom of the duffel bag. He picked one out. In the photo, Bryce stood arm in arm with his parents and his younger brother and sister.

"I'm sure they adored him."

Safiye had entered the tent and stood beside him. She removed another photo from the bag. "Who's this?"

Bryce was smiling in the photo, his arm wrapped around a beautiful dark-haired woman.

"Alanya, his late fiancée."

"Bryce was *engaged*?"

Callahan nodded. "She was a colleague of his at Oxford. She was working for Doctors Without Borders when she was killed in a small-plane crash in South America."

"That's awful. Did you know her?"

"No. It happened before Bryce joined the relief team. I found out about it after the excursion in Israel when I spent a few days with Bryce in London. One night, we were having dinner with his parents. Bryce was called to the hospital for an emergency, and I finished the dinner with his family. They told me about Alanya. She was from Ankara. Bryce joined the relief team as a way of honoring her."

"That's why Bryce knew so much about Turkey," Safiye said. "And the language."

Callahan nodded.

"Did he ever talk about Alanya?"

"No. I figured if it was something he wanted to talk about, he would have."

Callahan and Safiye stared at the photo, mesmerized by the smiling faces.

Alin and Adams entered the tent. Adams had come from University Hospital after hearing the news. Alin gave a solemn nod. "It's time."

Safiye returned the photo to the duffel bag. Callahan lifted the bag and carried it outside, setting it in the wooden cart.

The rain had stopped. The sun was out. The relief team members were congregating around the cart. Each had somberly taken their turn at Bryce's side, saying their goodbyes.

The old man sat at the front of the cart. He made a clicking noise with his tongue and flicked the reins. As the donkey pulled the cart forward, the team members followed.

Alin had informed WHO officials of Bryce's death. Officials would be arriving in a few days to investigate.

"Michael, Scott, Eric," Alin had said. "I beg you. Don't try anything heroic. The issue is *officially* out of our hands."

The old man and his donkey led the procession from the field hospital and across the tent city. At the bus stop, the procession came to a halt. Turkish officials were waiting with a truck. They lifted Bryce's body from the cart. As Bryce was unceremoniously placed into a plywood box, Callahan turned away.

The field near the bus stop was full. Hundreds of residents had joined the procession. The looks of trepidation they'd had when the relief team members first entered the tent city were gone. Many wiped away tears.

A girl broke from the crowd and ran toward the truck, holding a fistful of wildflowers. She set the bouquet on Bryce's casket and then scurried back to her mother's side.

"Allahu Akbar," a man called out, his voice ringing over the field.

"Allahu Akbar," the tent city chanted.

"Adhhab mae allah," the man called out.

The crowd chanted in reply.

The officials lifted the casket and set it in the back of the truck. As the truck pulled away, the Turks raised their fists in tribute. The relief team members did likewise.

"Yes, my friend," Callahan said. "Go with God."

35

Mehmet sat in his Land Cruiser outside Turkish Sky's administration building. He stared up at the redbrick façade. The fragile nature of life's routine was all too apparent. So easily, it had slipped away.

At the Monday morning meeting, the PhDs would be sitting around the conference table and sipping their coffees, listening as Tanik gave his article review. After today, they'd go their separate ways, but they would continue the work. He could only hope their accomplishments would overshadow Little Tortona.

After the previous day's bone-jarring sequence of phone calls from Enver, Yalçin, and then Safiye, he had spent the afternoon telling Ayla everything. From the distant lunch when Tunç had planted the seed of Little Tortona until his phone conversation with Yalçin, he'd unshouldered his burden. Any relief from finally doing so, however, was quickly replaced by shame. As Ayla listened, staring in disbelief, her incredulity had given way to looks of sickened disapproval. When he'd left this morning, that same look had been there.

Mehmet walked into the building.

Two of Tunç's bodyguards stood against the far wall beneath Atatürk's mural. The men wore T-shirts and shorts that were dirty and stained with sweat.

Mehmet walked past them and down the hallway. After a knock on the corner door, he entered the office.

Tunç sat behind his desk, typing a message on his cell phone. He looked up.

Mehmet set an envelope on the desk. He remained standing

as Tunç removed a letter from the envelope and began reading. After finishing, Tunç looked up. "I understand resigning from Little Tortona, but from your *own* laboratory?"

"If I had known the truth about Little Tortona—the real truth, from the beginning—I never would have . . ." He shook his head. "Iskender, I'm a scientist. My nature is to save lives, not destroy them. I'm not Josef Mengele or Shirō Ishii."

He'd researched Ishii. During World War II, Ishii had been the director of Japan's biowarfare program. Ishii and his men had experimented on and killed over 30,000 Chinese prisoners by feeding, spraying, or injecting them with plague, glanders, anthrax, dengue, or cholera. They'd given anthrax-filled chocolate to children. Ishii's bioweapons were used to attack eleven Chinese cities, killing over a half-million people.

Tunç flipped the letter aside and pushed back from his desk. "Come with me."

Mehmet walked with Tunç from the office and out of the building. The bodyguards followed.

"Those who enter the real world, *my world*, with the hope of following your antiquated code of ethics have already lost," Tunç said. "Only when people like me are successful is your world of academia even possible. In times of stability, you're a luxury. In times of crisis, intellectuals such as yourself become irrelevant."

They walked across the parking lot and along the road that led over the bridge. At the gate, Tunç came to a stop. A bodyguard pulled a ring of keys from his pocket. He opened a rusting padlock and pushed the gate aside.

Mehmet watched, shocked. The motor that previously opened the gate, along with the keypad, had disappeared. He looked toward the nearby hangar. The camera was gone.

Tunç walked ahead. Mehmet and the bodyguards followed him past the first two hangars. Tunç entered the third hangar through an open side door. Mehmet followed. Once inside the hangar, he stopped and stared.

Bright rays of light shone through vents near the peaked roofline. The black-painted ceiling had been removed. The tables of petri dishes, the stainless steel cabinets, and the guard station had disappeared. Little Tortona had vanished.

"*Where?*"

"Another place, another time," Tunç said. "You win, Mehmet.

No more Little Tortona." He walked farther into the building and raised his arms. "Now would you still like to resign from *Koba Laboratories?*"

When Mehmet had called Tunç's secretary that morning to meet with him, she'd said Tunç was at Turkish Sky. This was why. This was why the bodyguards were dirty and dressed the way they were. In the time since the Friday morning meeting, they'd disassembled Little Tortona. It would have taken them and a small army.

"You've been with us almost from the beginning," Tunç said. "Now is the time to take what is ours."

"*Ours?*"

"The heart, the soul of Turkey, the whole of Islam," Tunç said, clenching his fists. "Together, we'll watch my father's vision unfold."

Mehmet recalled Savon's words.

I only regret I won't be alive to see it.

"Are the Janissaries part of your father's vision?" Mehmet asked.

Tunç laughed. He looked toward the bodyguards and then back at Mehmet. "You surprise me. Not many people can do that. That's why I have faith in you. Yes, the Janissaries are part of my father's vision. Because of them, Turkey will once again be a beacon for Islam." He stepped toward Mehmet. "Soon, you'll control ten Koba Laboratories and have free rein with a nation of resources. Technology is what will make us strong again, and you can lead that. Trust me. Now isn't the time to leave. Think of your work. Forget Little Tortona. For you, *this* never happened."

Mehmet had confronted Tunç, believing he had a chance of making everything right. And he had. Their unholy pact had been dissolved. Little Tortona was gone. Funding for Koba Laboratories would remain the same.

"One month," Tunç said, extending his hand. "That's all I ask. After one month, if you still want to resign from Koba Laboratories, I'll let you go. But if you continue your work there, I'll maintain funding at its current level."

Mehmet looked toward Tunç's two thick-necked bodyguards, who'd inched closer.

Ayla had said he shouldn't risk a face-to-face confrontation, telling him he'd never survive it. But he told her he had to go. Deep down, he knew Tunç wasn't responsible for his involvement in Little Tortona. Tunç had only dangled the bait. He was the one who'd taken it—choosing the success of Koba Laboratories over everything.

Mehmet's gaze dropped to Tunç's extended hand.

In the lab, they could test their hypotheses by changing a single variable and measuring the difference in outcome. Here, there were too many variables—a myriad of possible outcomes. There was, however, one given. If he didn't shake Tunç's hand right now, Ayla's prediction would come true. He'd never leave here alive.

36

Mehmet brought the Land Cruiser to a stop and stared at the intersection. To the right, the road led home. To the left was Ankara.

If he turned right and drove home, he would return to a life without Little Tortona. If he turned left and drove to Ankara, his name would be disgraced, forever linked with Little Tortona.

Why was this so hard?

His mind spiraled out of control. He held out his hand, the one he'd used to shake hands with Tunç. Would one month eliminate the possibility of another Tel Aviv? Would it bring back the twenty-nine passengers in the bus, the two little girls, Bryce Jones?

Another place, another time . . . soon, you'll control ten Koba Laboratories.

Little Tortona wasn't gone. It had simply moved. Instead of ten Koba Laboratories, he envisioned ten Little Tortonas feeding bioweapons to lunatics like Hamid Sumay.

He thought of the look in Ayla's eyes when he'd left that morning, the look that would be there when he returned, and the look that would be there tomorrow and the next day. He hit a number on his phone. "The meeting is over," he said when she answered.

"Thank goodness. You're on your way?"

The relief in Ayla's voice meant the world to him. Maybe it was possible she could still love him. Maybe it was possible the look of disapproval wouldn't always be there.

"I'm on my way."

He reached beneath his seat and pulled out a manila envelope. He'd spent the previous evening chronicling his activities in the third hangar. This morning, he'd printed three copies of the document and placed them in separate envelopes, giving one to Ayla. If he didn't continue to call her once an hour, she was to take the envelope to Izmir's city hall and give it to the mayor. Earlier this morning, he'd passed by Koba Laboratories and placed the second envelope in Tanik's desk. He now set the third envelope on the seat next to him.

"Be careful," she said.

"I will. I love you."

"I love you too."

Ending the call, Mehmet looked toward the intersection. Releasing the brake, he turned left and accelerated, realizing life would never be the same.

37

At the dawn of the twentieth century, Ankara was a sleepy provincial town in north central Anatolia. During the War of Independence, it served as Atatürk's headquarters. After the war and the formation of the republic, Ankara became Turkey's capital. It had since grown to be the country's second-largest city.

Six hours after Mehmet left Turkish Sky, he passed into Ankara's downtown region. During his last call to Ayla, he'd promised another call once he entered the ministry of justice.

He parked and slipped on a suitcoat and tie. After a short walk, he stood at an intersection, waiting to cross into the courtyard of government buildings. Relief washed over him. He'd finally exceeded Iskender Tunç's considerable grasp.

Once the lights changed, he and a dozen others crossed the street. As he stepped onto the courtyard, a car skidded to a stop. Its rear door swung open. Enver Pasha stepped out.

Mehmet wasn't surprised Tunç had presumed his intentions. Of all Tunç's potential responses, however, Mehmet never imagined the elderly physician would be doing his bidding.

"Can we talk?" Enver said, walking toward Mehmet. Behind him, the car merged back into traffic.

"There's not much to talk about."

"How about the mistake you're about to make?"

Mehmet continued walking.

"Hold on."

Mehmet looked back. Enver stood with arms wide, smiling. "Could it hurt to humor an old man for a few minutes?"

The image reminded Mehmet of Tunç's pose only a few hours earlier.

Around them, the courtyard teemed with smartly dressed government workers hurrying between lunchtime appointments.

When Mehmet gave a reluctant nod, the two men sat at a nearby bench.

"I understand what you're going through," Enver said.

"You're a doctor. How can you condone Turkish Sky?"

"You're no longer in America, my friend. The Middle East is a dirty neighborhood. If you intend to play, you will get your hands dirty."

"But bioweapons production, rebellion, terrorism?" Mehmet asked.

"For years, the country has been run by infidels who outlaw the simple act of showing *deen* to Allah." Enver motioned at the passing workers. "Look at them. Look into their selfish, godless eyes. The AKP, a supposed Islamic party, has ruled for over a decade. It has restored some balance but not enough. Cebici points to the fact women can wear the hijab in government buildings as progress while sharia remains a distant dream. How can one not speak of rebellion?"

"My faith is between Allah and myself," Mehmet said. "I'm content with that. So are most. The majority decry the extremists and oppose sharia. I agree there are inadequacies in the current system, but Iskender's path will lead to ruin. Tel Aviv. Two dead young girls. The dead British physician. A trail of death follows Iskender. Do you think the West will stand by and watch?"

"The Americans are still reeling from Afghanistan and Iraq and ISIS. They didn't want to get involved in Ukraine, Syria, or Iran. They won't go to war with Turkey. If we know anything about the Americans, as long as they or their sacred dollar aren't threatened, they'll stand by and watch."

"And what will catapult Iskender to this exalted position? The armies of his dead father? The *Janissaries*?"

Enver's eyes flashed with anger. "Iskender thought you'd become more vested in our cause. He thought his contributions to Koba Laboratories might buy him some time—at least a month."

"They've bought him my last five years."

Enver took a calming breath. He sat back and scanned the courtyard. "Personally, I hoped you'd be able to look beyond the more distasteful aspects of our movement to the good that'll be done."

"I'm no longer for sale," Mehmet said. "I can no longer look the other way."

"Have you thought of your research?" Enver asked. "Are you willing to give up everything you've accomplished?"

"The others will continue the work."

"Are you sure about that?"

Mehmet turned. "What do you mean?"

"Does Tanik know about Turkish Sky?"

"He knows nothing."

"Maybe you should have thought of him and the other PhDs before you came here," Enver said.

"Tanik knows nothing. None of them do. The last thing I would do is involve them in this mess."

"And Ayla?"

Mehmet grabbed Enver by the collar. "She knows nothing."

Mehmet released the old man after a few passersby directed looks toward them.

"You should be thankful Iskender sent me," Enver said, straightening his shirt. "There are others whose actions would have been *less* negotiable." He leaned toward Mehmet. "I hope you also realize if you inform the authorities about Turkish Sky, your reputation will be ruined. You were a big part of Little Tortona. When you took over, you began with an empty slate. You're the one who built it into what it is today, personally bioengineering its most virulent organisms."

Mehmet nodded. "I'm aware of that. And I'm willing to pay the price for what I did—whatever it might be."

"But that's just it," Enver said. "You won't pay a price. By pointing a finger at Iskender, you'll be absolved." His eyes narrowed. "I'm here to make you realize you can't do this. We won't let you."

Mehmet followed Enver's gaze.

The car that had delivered the old doctor was now parked on the other side of the road. Tunç's bodyguards sat in the front.

"You need to come with us," Enver said. He pulled a handkerchief from his pocket and dabbed at his brow. "We'll take you back to Izmir. You belong there with your beautiful wife."

Mehmet shook his head.

"I don't think you understand the position you're putting me in," Enver said. "I beg you. Come back with us."

"I can't."

"Are you sure? And again, please consider your answer very carefully."

Mehmet looked toward the car and the figures of the two bodyguards. "I am," he said.

Enver nodded. "Then we have nothing more to discuss. I respect that, and I respect you, Mehmet Koba. I truly do. I wish you the best of luck."

The men stood. Enver extended his hand. As Mehmet shook it, the old doctor squeezed hard. Leaning forward, their faces inches apart, Enver punctuated the handshake by slapping his left hand onto Mehmet's right forearm. "Compliments of Turkish Sky," he rasped.

As Enver walked away, Mehmet watched and waited, bracing for the screech of another car or a sniper's bullet. But there was only the memory of the intense look in the old man's eyes and the lingering reek of his breath.

Enver stopped at the intersection and waited patiently for the light to change. It was hard to believe the frail old man was the same one with whom he'd just shaken hands. When the light turned, Enver crossed the street with the others.

Mehmet resumed his path toward the ministry, shaking his throbbing right hand. The old man had quite a grip. What did he say?

Compliments of Turkish Sky.

In the midday sun, Mehmet's eye was caught by a flash of light. He stopped. With his left hand, he removed a metallic object from his right coat sleeve. Between thumb and forefinger, he held up the object.

It was a miniature tack—its end tipped with blood.

The spot on his coat sleeve was where Enver had slapped him. In the old man's left hand had been a handkerchief.

Mehmet pulled back the sleeve. A small trickle of blood ran along his forearm. The tack had punctured his skin.

The puncturing device, a small dart, is coated with the concentrated cyanide.

As part of Mehmet's safety procedures, he and the technicians had been vaccinated against many of Little Tortona's organisms. They also had antidotes for most toxins, including cyanide. But the antidotes were in the lab—over six hours away.

Mehmet flipped the tack to the sidewalk. He sucked the blood from his forearm and spat.

We estimate incapacitation in minutes.

He looked down the corridor of the courtyard. The ministry of justice was still out of sight. If he started running, he might make it to the steps of the building—but that would only disseminate the toxin faster.

He looked toward Enver, who stood by the car, watching him. Tunç's bodyguards had left the car and were at the intersection, waiting to cross the street.

Mehmet ran to a nearby mailbox. He looked back. Enver and the bodyguards were blocked from view by a courtyard building.

He pulled the envelope from his coat along with a pen. From his phone, he copied down an address. Removing stamps from his wallet, he placed them on the envelope and sealed the envelope before sliding it into the mailbox.

Dialing Ayla's number, he walked to a bench and sat.

"I was getting worried," Ayla said.

"Have I told you?"

The bodyguards emerged from around the corner of the building. Spotting him, they came to a stop.

"*Told me?*" she said.

"How much I've taken you for granted?"

"Not recently."

He knew she was smiling.

"Ayla Koba, you mean more to me than the earth and stars," he said.

"Is everything okay?"

"Once and for all, yes."

His voice tremored. He extended his hand, feeling a tingling sensation in his fingertips. The cyanide was blocking production of ATP—the energy required to fuel his cells. The cells of his nervous system, those most dependent on cellular respiration, would be the first to be affected.

The bodyguards loitered near the corner of the building. They were waiting to see what would happen, knowing he didn't have much time.

"Mehmet, where are you?" Ayla asked. "You sound out of breath."

"I'm in the courtyard near the ministry. Do you remember when we were here? That first summer back in Turkey. You were wearing a tan dress. You were so beautiful."

"Why aren't you at the ministry?"

He took a breath, gasping for air.

The respiratory drive will be paralyzed, and death by suffocation will occur soon thereafter.

"Do as we planned," he said. "Leave for city hall. Pretend I didn't make this call."

"But you *are* making this call."

"Darling, I love you."

The cyanide was acting faster than he'd thought. He flexed his fingers, no longer sure if he was even holding the phone.

"Mehmet, what's happening?"

It mimics a heart attack.

"You've given me so much," he said. "You deserve so much more."

"What's happening?"

"I love you." Starry points of light entered his vision. He fought to maintain the image of Ayla in her dress. "*I lo—*"

Losing his balance, he fell to his side.

"Mehmet!"

"Call an ambulance," someone yelled as people circled around him. All the while, Mehmet knew the phone was nearby because he could hear Ayla screaming.

"Mehmet. Mehmet!"

He would give anything to hold her one more time. He tried to push himself up but couldn't. He tried to speak, but there was no sound.

As he lay frozen, Ayla's screams faded.

Part
3

"A revolution is a struggle to
the death between the future
and the past."

— Fidel Castro

38

Ankara

The crosshairs of the Turkish JNG-90 rifle moved slowly from the black Renault limousine to the side entrance of the old house. Beyir imagined the weather-beaten door opening, the bodyguards passing, and the tall, familiar silhouette. He glanced at his watch.

Four minutes.

His gaze returned to the scope, his thoughts focusing on his target. Acquiring the requisite information had not been easy. General Abdülaziz Volkan was not only the country's most powerful figure but also its most secretive.

From a young age, Volkan—the son of a general—possessed an uncommon devotion to the military. In Turkey that meant maintaining an absolute veneration for the flag, a secular state, and the teachings of Atatürk. At the Aliştirmak, Istanbul's elite military academy, he earned honors as top cadet. Following his graduation, his early assignments were mostly administrative, designed to provide him with an understanding of the army's inner workings. As did many young officers, however, Volkan yearned to show his mettle on the battlefield. For a Turkish soldier in the 1980s, that occurred in the southeast, where his father had been killed two years earlier and where the decades-long struggle for an independent Kurdistan, spearheaded by the Kurdish Worker's Party (PKK), had escalated to outright war.

After Volkan received his transfer to the southeast, his fervent desire for swift retribution for his father's death was thwarted. Instead, he learned the futility of conventional warfare against an unconventional enemy. But the young officer didn't give up. Meeting with local leaders, he demanded they form militias to watch their own and act as informants against the PKK. Those who didn't cooperate were publicly executed.

Quickly acquiring promotions, Volkan rose to the position of commander of the southeastern forces. Using a brutality forged by defeat and his father's death, he expanded his efforts, employing a combination of death squads, blackmail, and torture. It wasn't long before the PKK's hidden mountain strongholds began to fall. Over the next several years, 2500 Kurdish villages were stormed. Hopes of an independent Kurdistan were crushed.

Beyir saw the side door of the old house open. A bodyguard appeared. He nodded to another bodyguard by the limousine before closing the door.

Three minutes.

After Volkan's decade in the southeast, he returned to Ankara as a lieutenant general and commander of the famed First Corps. But the Ankara he returned to was much different from the one he'd left. Economic changes instituted in the early 1980s had taken effect. Deregulation, privatization, and floating of the lira had brought rapid economic growth that pushed the country from its old state-centered economy. People were flocking to the cities in search of opportunity. The rapid urbanization resulted in construction of makeshift *gecekondus* on the outskirts of Turkey's largest cities. Most residents of these hastily assembled slums were uneducated Muslim fundamentalists. Many were the same displaced Kurds whom Volkan had spent the last decade fighting.

In the elections of 1995, the fundamentalists' discontent proved to be fodder for the religious left. The Islamist Refah party won by capturing 21 percent of the fragmented popular vote. The new prime minister, Necmettin Erbakan, strengthened ties with regional Muslim countries and sponsored an Islamic economic bloc. The son of an Ottoman judge, Erbakan lifted bans on wearing religious clothing in public, changed the nation's work hours to accommodate Ramadan, and made plans to bring back sharia. Once banned by Atatürk, Sufi brotherhoods and other fundamental religious organizations re-formed. Soon, an Islamic media was flourishing.

Volkan became a fervent opponent of the new government. Accumulating information against Refah leadership, he began to document their Islamic and Kurdish allegiances and contempt for the secular state. Volkan's now famous "Fifteen Points" outlined a plan to halt the permeation of society by Islamic values. Accepted by the Military High Command and later adopted by the National Security Council, the Fifteen Points were submitted as recommendations to Prime Minister Erbakan in February 1997.

Erbaken ignored the recommendations. As the military's confidence in Erbakan dissipated, his government came to a standstill. In June 1997, Prime Minister Erbakan resigned, bringing an end to his democratically elected government. As a reward for his bloodless coup, Volkan was promoted to the army's top post.

Beyir's hands cramped. He loosened his grip on the rifle and ran his fingertips over the cool steel of its stock. In the woods east of Istanbul, he'd spent days practicing, calibrating, and recalibrating the gun, all in preparation for this single shot: seventy-six meters, −six degrees. Again, he glanced at his watch.

Two minutes.

Six months earlier, he'd assembled a team to tail Volkan. The men on the team, however, were inexperienced. Knowing it was only a matter of time before they were spotted by Volkan's security detail, Beyir ordered them to take up a myriad of inconspicuous observation points and simply document the general's arrivals and departures. After ten weeks of surveillance, they'd laid out their patchwork data.

If there was a point of vulnerability in Volkan's routine, it wasn't readily apparent. On Monday through Saturday, he left his ultrasecure condominium in downtown Ankara at 7 a.m. and drove to the ministry of defense. At noon, he'd leave the ministry for his office at the army base north of the capital, where he worked late into the evening. On two of the ten Mondays, however, Volkan didn't arrive at the army base until after 2 p.m. The two Mondays had fallen in the third weeks of the month.

The chance that Volkan's missing hour or two would turn into something important seemed tenuous at best. Thus, it had been with some skepticism that Beyir waited outside the ministry, three months earlier, at noon on the third Monday of the month.

Volkan's limousine had emerged from the underground garage at noon, preceded by a black four-door sedan. Beyir followed from afar, excited when the limousine didn't turn toward the army base but continued west into the Altindăg district in Ankara's old quarter. In the shadow of the Kale, a ninth-century hilltop fortress, the limousine stopped at an old but respectable-looking house.

Beyir drove by the house, wondering what was inside that was worthy of Volkan's monthly visit. Later, he'd learn the name of the person residing at 96 Esat Caddesi.

Yusuf Refet.

With the exception of Kemal Atatürk and his successor as president, Ismet Inönü, Refet possessed the most storied name in modern Turkish history. Refet had served as the military's commander in chief, its *başkomutan*, for thirty years. As the republic's chief preserver of Atatürk's reforms, most prominently the secular state, he'd routinely used his power, often belligerently, to shape Turkish policy. Eight years earlier, Refet had retired and moved into his childhood home in old Ankara. Volkan had subsequently been promoted from head of the army to *başkomutan*.

Beyir heard the turn of the ignition and the hum of the limousine's V8. His pulse quickened.

One minute.

Volkan's promotion had been applauded by Atatürk's followers. They'd hoped Volkan would reenact his bloodless coup and overthrow President Cebici and the upstart AKP. But times had changed. In a nod to the Islamic fundamentalism sweeping the country, Volkan granted concessions to the Islamists. He condensed his Fifteen Points. Men could have their beards; women could wear scarves in public; a religious media could exist. But there would be no allotment for an independent Kurdistan, no mandated religious education, no theocracy or caliphate, and no sharia. Atatürk's secular state would remain. In the last eight years, President Cebici had pushed Volkan's line on these issues but had not crossed them. He never would.

Beyir looked up from the scope as the side door remained closed. The minute had passed slowly, too slowly. The bodyguards should have taken their positions in the alleyway.

There was a creaking sound from deep within the rented house. Suppressing the urge to investigate, Beyir maintained his attention on the side door of the old house. His thoughts turned to the electronic device in his pocket. If necessary, he would use it. He would not allow himself to be captured.

The oval doorknob on the side door of Refet's house suddenly glimmered. It was turning. The door opened.

Instead of the bodyguards filing outside and taking their usual positions in the alleyway, Volkan stepped into view. The general scanned the nearby houses, aware of his sudden vulnerability. With head down, he strode toward the limousine.

Beyir set his finger against the trigger.

For you, Savon.

He squeezed the trigger.

Feeling the gun's familiar kick, Beyir was struck by the irreversibility of it all. Photos of Volkan—a smiling boy, a promising young cadet, and a proud father with his children and grandchildren—flashed before him.

The images were replaced by the unfolding scene in the alley. Half of Volkan's head was gone. In its place was a pumping mass of red flesh.

The bodyguards followed Volkan through the doorway. They lifted the general's limp body and carried him to the limousine.

Beyir set the gun aside. A rocket launcher laid on the floor next to him. Lifting it, he stuck it through the open window. Without hesitation, he pulled its trigger. In a fiery spit, a missile hissed forward.

The explosion consumed the old house and everyone in the alley.

Beyir slipped on a baseball cap and picked up the rifle. He walked from the room, down the stairs, and out the front door to his car.

After driving a short distance, he reached into his pocket. His fingers settled on the electronic device. He pushed its button.

Behind him, the rented two-story house erupted in a ball of flames.

39

Four weeks earlier
Istanbul, Turkey

Petrovich peeked through the blinds. It was 9 p.m. Across the street, EMİN's headquarters office had darkened. He slipped off his headphones. Swiveling in his seat, he looked at the wall.

During their two weeks of surveillance, he and Tatiana had photographed thirty of the thirty-two EMİN employees based at the headquarters office. They'd identified them using online information. The thirty photos with their corresponding names were taped to the wall. The names of the employees without photos—two of EMİN's five managers—were written on blank sheets of paper.

Savon Ali, Manager of International Operations

Beyir Abdullah, Manager of West Anatolian Operations

"Staring at them won't make them come back," Tatiana said, walking up behind Petrovich.

"At the law firm, when the five men were coming up the escalator, I was looking at all five managers," Petrovich said. "One of our two missing managers is the blue-eyed assassin. He was thinner than he was in Grozny. He was gaunt, almost sickly. But it was him. I'm sure of it."

"The other managers talk as if this Savon and Beyir aren't coming back," Tatiana said.

In addition to listening to the phone conversations of the

three EMİN managers, Petrovich and Tatiana had followed them to their homes. The three managers were single and lived alone in efficiency apartments within a few blocks of the headquarters. They packed their own lunches and walked to work, each wearing the same suit to work every day.

"You were right," Petrovich said. "In Grozny, they were doing someone else's work. They don't have the plutonium."

"And if they sold it, they're certainly not the ones reaping the benefits," Tatiana said.

According to the online organizational charts, EMİN was a subsidiary of Tunç Corporation, which was headquartered in Izmir. The five EMİN managers did not report to a low-level manager at Tunç Corporation, as would be expected, but directly to Iskender Tunç—the company's owner and CEO.

"I've resisted the urge to chase Savon and Beyir to Izmir, thinking they might come back," Petrovich said. "But it doesn't appear they are."

"The others talk as if none of them will be here for long, as if something is about to happen, something important."

"Whatever's happening," Petrovich said, nodding. "It's not happening here."

40

"Let them worship as they will; every man can follow his own conscience, provided it does not interfere with sane reason or bid him against the liberty of his fellow men."

—**Mustafa Kemal Atatürk**

Day 29

Callahan and Safiye sat alone in the University Hospital cafeteria. They'd spent most of their break in silence, their thoughts with Bryce.

"I'd better get going," Safiye said.

"Not that I have much of an appetite, but any plans for dinner?" Callahan asked.

"Mehmet and Ayla like to go out on Monday nights. Should I check with them?"

"Sure."

Safiye tapped a number on her phone. Moments later, the phone to her ear, a troubled look crossed her face. "No. It's Safiye. What's the matter? . . . What's he doing there? Ayla, slow down."

Safiye listened for several moments, her face pale. "Okay," she said. She slipped the phone into her pocket and stood. "I need to go."

"What is it?"

"Something's happened to Mehmet. Ayla's stopping to pick me up. She's only a few blocks away."

"I'll go with you."

At the main entrance, Ayla was waiting in a red Lexus sedan. Her eyes, swollen from crying, were a matching red. "Thanks for coming," she said as they climbed inside.

Ayla pulled away from the hospital. As she drove, heading farther downtown, she recounted what Mehmet had told her the day before.

Callahan and Safiye listened, stunned.

Turkish Sky was a biowarfare facility. It was the source of the trichothecenes that had killed Nata. It was the source of the antibiotic-resistant *Yersinia* that had afflicted the farmer and his family. Most inconceivably, Mehmet was the director of the facility.

"Why would Mehmet get involved in this?" Safiye asked.

"He agreed to run the bioweapons lab because he thought it had government backing," Ayla said. "When he realized it didn't, he tried to resign, but Iskender wouldn't let him. Iskender has blackmailed him into running it ever since."

"Did you know about this?" Safiye asked.

"I found out about it for the first time yesterday," Ayla said. She looked into the rearview mirror at Callahan. "I'm sorry. I'm so sorry."

"None of this is your fault," he said.

"And I'll never believe it's Mehmet's either," Safiye said.

Ayla swung the car into a parking space in front of a multistory white building at the edge of Konak Square. There was a sign: Büyükşehir Belediyesi.

"City hall," Ayla said. She lifted a shoulder bag from the front seat and led them from the car.

The building bustled with activity. Policemen and people in suits scurried in and out as street people loitered on the sidewalk. Inside, they stopped at a central desk. Ayla spoke with a receptionist. The receptionist shook her head and pointed.

"The mayor isn't in," Safiye interpreted for Callahan. "She's saying we can meet with the deputy mayor, but we'll have to check with his office about his schedule."

"Dr. Özmen?"

They turned toward the voice.

City Councilman Ançak Barhal stood behind them. "Yes," Barhal said. "I thought that was you." With the help of his cane, he made his way toward them.

Safiye introduced Callahan and Ayla, then turned toward the councilman. "Listen, Ançak. I'm sorry for being so blunt, but could you help us? We're in the middle of an emergency. Ayla's husband, Mehmet Koba, is in trouble."

"Mehmet Koba?" Barhal asked. "Of Koba Laboratories?"

"Yes," Ayla said. "He—"

Barhal raised a hand. "Of course. Come, please. Let's talk in my office."

Leaning heavily on his cane, the overweight councilman tried to hurry, but he moved slowly as he led them down a hall, through a reception area, and into a conference room. Out of breath, he fell into a chair at the head of a table. As the others sat, the councilman removed a handkerchief from his pocket and wiped the sweat from his forehead. "Now, what can I do for you?"

Safiye explained the reasons for Mehmet traveling to Ankara.

"And when he was in the courtyard, something happened?" Barhal asked.

"Yes," Ayla said. "Before the connection ended, he began slurring his words."

Barhal nodded thoughtfully. "This information you're describing—the information he was bringing to the minister. Could I see it?"

Ayla lifted her shoulder bag to the table. She pulled out a manila envelope and slid it across the table.

Barhal unhooked the envelope's clasp. Removing Mehmet's letter, he started reading.

With each line, the councilman's eyes grew larger. He finally looked up at Ayla. "Could this be a misunderstanding?"

"Misunderstanding?"

"Yes," Barhal said. "Iskender Tunç is a pillar of our community. And Turkish Sky is a symbol of—"

"There's no *room* for misunderstanding," Ayla snapped. She pointed at the papers. "Because of this biowarfare facility, people are dying."

"Yes, of course," Barhal said. "We need to alert someone in Ankara your husband is in trouble." He slipped the papers back into the envelope and slid it toward Ayla. "I'll get the mayor involved in this."

"He's out of town," Ayla said. "The receptionist said he isn't in. But the deputy mayor is."

"In that case, I'll see what he can do," Barhal said. "I'll be right back." Standing, he gave a curt nod before leaving the room.

Ayla threw a concerned look toward Safiye.

"The deputy mayor will have connections in Ankara," Safiye said, setting a consoling hand on Ayla's shoulder. "This could be resolved in a matter of minutes."

Ayla nodded. As she sat back, her shoulder bag fell over. A laptop slid out onto the table.

"You brought your laptop?" Safiye asked.

"It contains a detailed description of Little Tortona," Ayla said.

"Mind if I take a look?" Callahan asked.

"No," Ayla said, looking toward the door. "I have a feeling we may be here for a while."

"Vandegut, Tanik, Loy," Callahan said as he read from the laptop. "Who are these guys? The work they're doing is incredible."

After finishing Mehmet's description of Little Tortona, he'd begun reading Mehmet's weekly research summaries from Koba Laboratories.

"All were protégés of famous researchers," Ayla said. "Most were on the verge of making their own names, but Mehmet enticed them to come to Izmir."

"Why haven't they published? They could fill a small library with their research."

"Mehmet envisioned a grand presentation eventually, but he despises the complacency that comes with recognition along with the time and work that's required to publish. For Mehmet, pushing ahead has always been more important than reporting where they've been."

"How could they do it?" Callahan asked. "Just give up everything—the opportunity to run their own labs, their homes, recognition?"

"Mehmet made them believers in the consortium," Ayla said. "Working together, they could achieve more than they could on their own. And, there was the money. With Tunç's backing, Mehmet doubled their salaries. Add in nice homes and beautiful vacation cottages. It seemed like the perfect arrangement."

Barhal entered the conference room, dabbing at his forehead with his handkerchief. "I'm sorry that took so long. I've arranged a meeting with the deputy mayor."

They followed Barhal from the room. As the city councilman turned toward the rear of the building, Ayla pointed in the opposite direction. "I thought his office was that way."

"He's not there," Barhal said. "I'll take you to him."

Barhal led them through a maze of hallways to a set of swinging doors. They pushed through the doors into a hallway lined by tarps. The air was heavy with dust. In the distance, they heard the whine of a saw.

"You'll have to excuse the mess," Barhal said. "The area is under renovation."

They walked down the hallway and pushed through another set of swinging doors, emerging onto a loading dock. Like the hallway, the area was lined by tarps.

A brown windowless van was parked on the dock, its sliding side door open. The rear of the van was empty. A driver sat in the front.

The city councilman held his handkerchief to his brow and waved them toward the van. "The deputy mayor is off-site today. The van will take you to him."

"You want us to get into that?" Ayla asked.

"It's less than optimal," Barhal said, leaning on his cane. "But in emergency situations, this is done quite often."

"Are you coming?" Safiye asked.

Barhal shook his head.

"Why can't we just contact the Ankara police?" Callahan asked.

"We could," Barhal said. "But trust me, the request would be buried in our bureaucracy. If you want something done fast in Turkey, it must come from the top. The deputy mayor will know what to do." He pointed toward Ayla's shoulder bag. "Make sure you show him your information."

"Where is the deputy?" Safiye asked. "We'll drive there."

Ayla stepped toward the van. "I'll ask the driver where he plans on taking us."

Barhal pushed up from his cane. "If you want to help your husband, get in."

"We're *not* getting in there," Ayla said.

A short, wiry man appeared from behind a tarp. He had a shaved head and close-set eyes. He made a theatrical sweep with his arm toward the van. "Please, step inside." He spoke in broken English, his voice gravelly.

The driver now stood by the side door. He slid it fully open. Another man appeared from behind the tarp.

Callahan motioned Safiye and Ayla back to the double doors. "Let's go."

The wiry man blocked their path. "I don't think so." He reached around to his back and removed a gun.

Safiye and Ayla gasped.

The man grinned, showing off a large gap between yellowing front teeth. The other two men also removed guns.

"If you don't get in the van, these men have instructions to kill you," Barhal said.

The wiry man stepped toward Callahan and raised his gun. "We should kill this one now."

"Basil, those are not our instructions," Barhal said.

The man waved his gun toward the ground. "On your knees," he said to Callahan.

When Callahan didn't obey, Basil swung the gun toward Safiye. "On your knees," he said. "Or I'll shoot her."

Callahan knelt. Stepping forward, Basil smacked the gun's butt against Callahan's head.

"Michael," Safiye screamed.

"Shut them up," Basil said, pressing the gun to Callahan's temple.

The two other men grabbed Safiye and Ayla and pushed them toward the van.

Callahan watched, his head throbbing, as the men bound and gagged Safiye and Ayla.

After the two men finished with Safiye and Ayla, they stepped toward Callahan. Basil grabbed a handful of Callahan's hair and pulled him to his feet.

Callahan staggered, seemingly overwhelmed by the impending confrontation.

"Coward," Basil said.

When Basil momentarily relaxed his grip, Callahan recoiled. With the butt of his right palm, he struck Basil squarely on the nose.

Basil's nose gushed blood. He doubled over, his gun falling to the floor.

Callahan swung his knee toward Basil, but the driver leaped forward and blocked the blow. With all his force, Callahan drove his palm into the driver's temple. The man crumpled to the ground.

Callahan stepped toward Basil and again drove his knee toward him. This time, Basil was ready. He slipped to the side.

Missing Basil, Callahan was thrown off-balance.

The third man, now standing in front of Callahan with raised fist, struck him in the gut.

Callahan doubled over in pain.

Basil grabbed Callahan's scalp and lifted his head. Basil's face was flushed with a combination of embarassment and rage. Giving a guttural grunt, he struck Callahan squarely in the nose.

A numbing sensation split Callahan's head. Hundreds of tiny points flashed before him before everything went black.

41

Beyir stared above the truck's jostling hood. From Turkey's fertile west coast across the arid central plateau, the scenic panorama scrolling before him went largely unnoticed. His mind's eye was elsewhere, fixed firmly on the northern woodlands as they appeared from the Saltuk Tepesi—a mountain in Turkey's Pontic Range.

As boys, he and Savon sojourned almost daily to the ridge, where Greek monks once monitored traders venturing inland from the Black Sea. They would climb the tallest of the Aleppo pines and pretend to be bandits robbing imagined passing caravans. When they were older, they spent hours in the highest of the great pine's branches, mapping out futures that extended far beyond the rolling green of the distant horizon.

Savon's voice now came to him. As they'd sat in the tree, he recalled Savon reading from a book.

> "For three days, Atatürk's body lay in Istanbul's Dolmabahçe Palace while hundreds of thousands paid their respects. The fallen leader was placed into a horse-drawn caisson, carried across the Galata Bridge to the wharf below the Old Seraglio, and then transferred to the Yavûz. The battleship ferried him from the Bosporus into the Sea of Marmara, where an international phalanx of ships waited in quiet memorial.
>
> Afterward, Atatürk's body was transferred to the presidential train. As the train ventured east, carrying the father of the Turks to his final resting place, the people lined the railways, lighting the night sky with their meager rations of gas."

On Savon's own final eastward journey, there would be no solemn procession across the Galata Bridge or passage across the Sea of Marmara. There would be no tribute of international ships, train rides, or funeral pyres. In the back of the produce truck, hidden unceremoniously among boxes of olives and figs, Savon lay in a simple wooden casket, his body cleaned and prepared for burial.

Three months earlier, Beyir first noticed something wrong. Savon appeared pale. When Beyir mentioned it, Savon claimed he hadn't slept well. Two days later, incapacitated by abdominal pain, Savon was unable to get out of bed.

From that day on, what Beyir now recognized as the reek of death hovered over Savon. As Savon's body and once-invincible bravado decayed, the lives they envisioned from the top of the Aleppo pine blurred and gradually disappeared. With startling brevity, the optimism of their youth had come full circle, culminating with the reality of Savon's premature death. It was a tragic ending to what had been a brilliant beginning.

On the day of their graduation, surrounded by past graduates, Beyir and Savon and the three others in their class stood in a wooded field, listening as Iskender Tunç spoke.

"In 1826, Sultan Mahmud II attacked and defeated the Janissaries. It wasn't until over a century later, when my father rushed into a burning mosque and rescued a crying baby boy, that the Janissaries were reborn."

Everyone in the field clapped.

"On my father's next tour of duty, he saved four boys. During his remaining tours, he returned with as many as ten. Besides saving the boys from senseless destruction, he wanted to raise them to be good soldiers and devout Muslims, hoping to imbue them with the same values as the Janissaries of old."

Tunç paused, his gaze narrowing. "The Ottoman sultans sent the Janissaries into battle to sway the outcome at the most vital juncture. My father believed his Janissaries would be no different. They too would be educated in an Enderun and learn the art of warfare and the lessons of the Quran. They too would form an elite corps and be an instrument for change—swaying the battle's course at its most vital juncture. When that day came, they would strike to unite Islam and to consolidate the Middle East into one great nation."

Tunç looked toward those circling the field. "For fifty-seven years, we've asked our graduates to remember where you've come from . . . and you haven't forgotten. We've asked you to share your successes . . . and there have been many. We've asked you to send the best of your sons . . . and you have. In all of these endeavors, you've performed extraordinarily."

Beyir and his classmates clapped, acknowledging the past graduates—many of whom were their own fathers and brothers.

"For fifty-seven years, my father or I has stood before the new graduates and congratulated them." Tunç looked toward Beyir and his classmates. "I now congratulate you. No one sits where you are now without demonstrating exceptional intelligence, discipline, and diligence."

There was a round of applause from the past graduates.

Tunç turned to their class banner. It was a large copper pot. "The kazan was the most valued of the Janissaries' possessions. Not only did they cook their rations in it, but it also served as a rallying point during battle. To tip over the kazan was a sign of mutiny. If the kazan was lost, the battalion was disgraced. When the kazan passed in parade, every Janissary stood."

Again, there was a round of applause.

"For fifty-seven years, we've encouraged our graduating class to go into the world, to assimilate and prosper, to take what we've taught you and prepare for the day of reckoning," Tunç said. "On this day of commemoration, however, we ask something different from our graduates, something more. We ask that you stay with the Enderun. We ask that you devote your every life's breath to the day of the reckoning, to the day of the Sayişma."

A buzz filled the field. The word *sayişma* meant nothing to those listening other than its literal meaning—to settle accounts. None had heard the word used in reference to the day of reckoning. The fact Tunç used it, and so emphatically, indicated the day no longer lingered as some distant point.

"Signs of Atatürk's failing experiment are everywhere," Tunç said. "The economy is in ruins. Unrest and discontent reign. It will be the Kazans' task to ignite the fuse. Once those in power fall, the people will reach for the one rope binding us together—Islam." He raised a fist. "To those who will lead us to the Sayişma. To the Kazans. May you prosper more than any before."

Long after darkness had settled over the produce truck, Beyir flipped off his headlights. He was on a narrow gravel road. After a short distance, he turned onto a grassy path and drove slowly as the truck passed through a gauntlet of low-hanging branches. He stopped in front of a barn.

He opened the barn door and drove the truck inside. He locked the door behind him and walked to the back wall of the barn. In the darkness, his hands searched the wall before settling on a button, which he pushed twice in rapid succession.

The quiet rolling of ball bearings was accompanied by the appearance of an opening in the floor, unveiling a dimly lit stairwell.

Beyir stepped into the opening and walked down the stairs. The moist, dank smell of the passageway hit him. When he reached the bottom of the stairs, the opening above him closed.

He was in a small room. The walls were covered by iron panels. He entered a five-digit sequence on a keypad.

A thin metallic voice sounded from a speaker. "It's been six years since that code was used."

Beyir silently added the years. After their graduation from the Enderun, the Kazans had apprenticed for a year at Tunç Corporation before moving to Istanbul to run the EMİN Corporation. If the Kazans were going to lead the Sayişma and what would follow, working at the courier service would allow them to become familiar with the Şebeke—the international network of Enderun graduates. They'd worked in Istanbul for the past five years.

With a loud clang, one of the iron panels slid back. Beyir slipped through the opening and ran down a passage, his legs stiff from the hours of driving. Ahead, an opening at the end of the passage was closing. He slid through it seconds before it shut.

"Barely made it," the voice said, this time minus the electronic timbre.

Beyir bent over and stretched his hamstrings. "I'm getting too old for this."

No objection came from the boy who sat at a desk in front of several glowing screens.

Beyir walked behind the boy and looked at the screen displaying the inside of the barn. In the darkness, the outline of the produce truck was visible.

You're home, Savon.

Beyir walked down a long sloping tunnel that opened into a room. On the opposite wall was a portrait of Muhammed Tunç. Gleaming Ottoman sabers—the preferred weapon of the early Janissaries—hung on each side of the portrait. The remaining walls contained glass cabinets filled with banners and photos from each graduating class.

Beyir remembered the many years of passing through the trophy room and being in awe of those who'd gone before. He looked toward their banner. In addition to the copper cooking pot was a stitched figure of a hawk in flight. The symbol had been added in honor of their role in the Sayişma. Fierce and deadly, the bird was in perpetual flight—frozen in the eternal hunt. For six years, the Kazans had circled, waiting for the day of reckoning. Finally, it had come.

Beyir walked from the room. Above the doorway leading from the trophy room was the İmam-ı Azam, the universal banner of the Janissaries. Made of white silk, it carried an inscription embroidered in red:

WE GIVE YOU VICTORY AND A SPARKLING VICTORY. IT IS GOD WHO HELPS US AND HIS HELP IS EFFECTIVE. OH MUHAMMAD, YOU HAVE BROUGHT JOYFUL NEWS TO TRUE BELIEVERS.

Beyir passed into the sleeping quarters. It was pitch-black. Since the Sayişma had begun, many past graduates had returned. The room would be full.

Beyir listened. There were no sounds of men breathing, no snoring—only the familiar hum of fans pumping fresh air into the room. He reached toward the nearest bunk and then the next. They were empty, their sheets cool and taut.

The lights flashed on. Dozens of Janissaries, young and old, converged through open doorways into the room. They clapped

Beyir on the back, laughing and smiling. Somebody shoved a newspaper into his hands, its headlines bold.

VOLKAN, REFET KATILEYT!

The Janissaries parted as the Enderun's three teachers approached, led by Edirne Kavas—the *kapı ağasi* or chief eunuch. Wearing his familiar turban, Kavas grinned broadly. In the last six years, the belly of the school's longtime headmaster had somehow become larger. His long beard had thinned and turned mostly gray.

Kavas grabbed Beyir's hand and thrust it into the air. "The Sayişma has begun," he shouted.

"Allahu akbar," the Janissaries began chanting.

Beyir held the newspaper high and pumped his hand in the air, letting the euphoria of the moment wash over him.

"You've proven yourself worthy of the Enderun and your teachers," Kavas said to Beyir when the chanting ended.

Kavas and the whole room bowed, their heels clicking in unison.

With his own deep bow and heel click, Beyir returned the gesture. He then looked into the gleaming eyes of his fellow Janissaries. Once again, he thrust the newspaper skyward.

As none had done before, a deafening roar echoed through the Enderun's corridors.

42

Callahan woke. He tried to move but couldn't. Waiting for his eyes to adjust to the persisting darkness, he realized a hood covered his head, his mouth was gagged, and his hands and feet were bound tightly behind him. Overwhelmed by the sensation of impending suffocation, he pulled against his bonds but soon became fatigued and blacked out.

When he returned to consciousness, a buzz filled the air. The ground vibrated. He recognized the sensations. He was in the van.

He recalled the events in city hall. Safiye and Ayla couldn't be far away. He listened for them but heard only the constant drone of tires.

His nose broken, his head pounded. Air, thick and wet, wheezed through his distorted nasal passages—his only source of oxygen. He took long, slow breaths but felt his airway—progressively filling with secretions—choking off. As panic squeezed in, he once again writhed against his bonds and passed out.

Callahan continued to fall in and out of consciousness. Moments of lucidity were spent fighting the creeping sensation of asphyxia.

As the van ride continued, they stopped three of four times for fuel. Each time, his nostrils would fill with the sweet, dizzying scent of gas, and he'd drift back into the void.

He jolted awake. A hollow, clunking noise sounded beneath him—the sound of stones kicking up into the wheel wells. They were on a gravel road.

How long had it been since they were in city hall? Ten hours? Twenty?

They continued on the gravel road for several minutes before the van turned onto a smooth, rolling surface. Tree branches grated against the van's side panels.

The van came to a stop. Instead of the rattle of the nozzle into the spout, the splash of liquid into the tank, and the aromatic scent of gas, a key fumbled into a lock. The door screeched open. Unseen hands grabbed him and pulled him from the van, dropping him to the ground. A pole was slipped between the ties binding his arms and legs. He was picked up and carried away.

Is this what it had been like for Bryce? Did he die a quick death? Or was it slow and painful?

The men talked quietly to one another in Turkish as Callahan swung back and forth, wisps of grass brushing against his back. After a few minutes, he heard the men's shoes scuffing against stone. They came to a stop. A lock turned. A door creaked open. He was dropped on the stone surface. The pole was slipped from between his arms and legs.

Someone said something and the men laughed.

The door closed and the lock turned. The sound of retreating footsteps was followed by silence.

43

One day earlier
Izmir, Turkey

"He's probably not even coming in this week," Tatiana said to Petrovich, lifting an earpiece on her headphones.

They'd spent the past three weeks in Izmir, conducting surveillance on Iskender Tunç. The CEO was their only connection with EMİN's two missing managers—Savon Ali and Beyir Abdullah. The blue-eyed assassin had not made an appearance. Three days earlier, unsatisfied with their progress, Petrovich had broken into Tunç Corporation's headquarters offices and bugged the CEO's office and phone. They'd spent their time since listening to the silence coming from the taps.

"It's only Monday morning," Petrovich said. "Give him a chance."

"Someone else must do the day-to-day managing. He likely just shows up for board meetings."

"Maybe he went on a business trip. Or—"

Tatiana raised a hand. She turned on the speaker and slipped off the headphones. A man's voice sounded from the speaker.

"That's Tunç," Petrovich said. "I recognize his voice from an online interview. He's on his cell phone."

As Tunç spoke, Tatiana interpreted.

"Yes, Enver. He had to be stopped . . . . We sent men over to their house. She wasn't there . . . . I agree. We have to find her as soon as possible. Our teams are sweeping the city . . . . Yes, we have to presume the others at the lab know."

There was a ringing noise.

"His office phone," Petrovich said.

Tunç answered the call.

Tatiana turned on the speaker that contained the feed from the office's hard line. A man's voice sounded. Speaking in Turkish, he was out of breath. "It's Ançak. She's here."

"City hall?"

"Yes," Ançak said. "She's with Safiye Özmen and one of the WHO doctors—an American. They want to meet with the mayor."

"Have they met with anyone?"

"No. I spotted them in the lobby and directed them to my office."

"Did anyone see you?"

Ançak paused. "The receptionist."

"We need to get them out."

"I'll bring them to the loading dock."

After the call ended, Tunç made a series of other calls, arranging for the forceful pickup of the three individuals from city hall.

"We need to see what's happening," Petrovich said.

As they walked outside to the silver BMW, Tatiana located city hall on her smartphone. They made the short drive to the downtown building and parked near the rear.

The building was under construction. A newly poured concrete foundation was surmounted by a budding skeleton of two-by-fours. Much of the area was covered by tarps. From within came the pounding of air hammers.

As Petrovich and Tatiana waited, deliberating whether they should go inside or not, a brown windowless van emerged through a break in the tarps.

"That's it," Tatiana said. "The van they were talking about."

"Shall we?"

She turned toward him. "I doubt your assassin or the plutonium is inside that van."

"I'm sure they're not," Petrovich said. "But right now, this is all we have."

Over the next several hours, Petrovich and Tatiana followed the van into central Turkey. They passed Ankara and then headed north. It was almost 3 a.m. when the van turned off the highway near Havza, a small town south of the Black Sea port of Samsun.

The van, the only other vehicle in sight, led them along progressively narrower roads to a single-lane gravel road. When the van turned its lights off, Petrovich did the same. Finally, the van's brake lights appeared, and it veered from the road.

Petrovich continued slowly through the darkness, their way lit by the moonlight's dull gray reflection from the gravel. When he neared the spot where the van had disappeared, he stopped near a small break in the trees.

"I don't feel good about this," Tatiana said.

"We'll take a quick look."

Petrovich turned into the darkened corridor. They passed along a grass-covered path, slipping beneath a canopy of low-lying branches. After fifty meters, he brought the car to a stop in front of a shadowed building. "Wait here," he said.

He walked to the front of the car and looked up at the building. It appeared to be a barn. He put his ear to the door. He heard nothing. Bending down, he ran his hand over the grass before returning to the BMW.

"We have to get out of here," Tatiana said.

Putting the car in reverse, Petrovich backed slowly away.

44

"Those who use religion for their own benefit are detestable. We are against such a situation and will not allow it. Those who use religion in such a manner have fooled our people; it is against just such people that we have fought and will continue to fight."

—**Mustafa Kemal Atatürk**

Tanik Goya speed-dialed Mehmet's cell phone for the third time that day. Mehmet had missed work on Monday without a word. It was now Tuesday, and his office still sat empty.

A man appeared in Tanik's office doorway. He wore the white coat of a university physician. When Mehmet's voicemail clicked on, Tanik set down the phone.

The man stepped forward. "Tanik," he said, a note of familiarity in his voice.

Tanik glanced at the stitched name on the white coat—Dr. Suley Zubak. Recalling the blurry image of a distant classmate, he added a crown of thick hair and subtracted thirty pounds from the man in front of him. "Suley," he said. "It's been a long time."

"The last time I remember seeing you was at one of your talks at the old technology seminar," Zubak said, as they shook hands. "I was disappointed when I heard we lost you to the US. It's good to see you're back."

"How long have you been on staff?" Tanik asked.

"Ten years."

Both men shook their heads.

"Time flies," Tanik said.

"It sure does."

Zubak glanced nervously at the door. "Listen, I don't want to keep you. I had some business with Mehmet Koba."

"He's not in."

"Do you know when he'll be back?"

"I'm not sure." Tanik looked at the stitching beneath Zubak's name—Staff Pathologist. "Do you have autopsy results?"

Before the words left his mouth, Tanik regretted his question. The young man they'd treated may have died by now.

"I do," Zubak said. "Do you know the decedent? A young man with pancreatic cancer?"

"No," Tanik said, a sharp pain stabbing at his forehead. "I don't."

Zubak looked down at the briefcase that he clutched in his right hand. "In many respects, this is one of the strangest cases I've been involved with."

"What do you mean?"

"Let's just say it was far from protocol." Zubak again glanced at the door before stepping forward. "Sunday, an elderly doctor brought the body to the morgue. His patient failed chemotherapy and radiation treatments and decided to forego hospice care and die at home. The doctor refused to fill out any paperwork and paid cash—twice the normal rate."

"How was Mehmet involved?"

"He wasn't. The doctor said I should give Mehmet the tissue blocks, said he might find them useful for his research." Zubak held up his briefcase. "Histology just finished preparing the slides. They're incredible."

Tanik nodded toward a double-headed microscope next to his desk. "We could take a look."

"You're not familiar with the patient?" Zubak asked.

"No. But if the slides are incredible, as you say, it'd be nice to see them."

Zubak considered this for a moment and then nodded. As Zubak sat by the microscope, Tanik closed the office door and sat across from him.

The pathologist opened his briefcase and removed a tray of slides. "Because of the findings—" He shook his head. "As I said, they're amazing."

Zubak picked out a glass slide from the tray and set it onto the microscope stage. As they each looked through their oculars, the pathologist brought the slide into focus.

"The old doctor gave me a slide from the original pancreatic biopsy," Zubak said. "It gives us a baseline of what the tumor looked like before therapy. As you can see, the biopsy shows a typical adenocarcinoma. It's relatively monotonous. The tumor has well-formed glands, pleomorphic nuclei, desmoplastic stroma."

Tanik nodded.

"The entire biopsy looked just like this," Zubak said. He set the slide into the tray and removed another slide, which he set on the stage. "This is the pancreatic tumor I removed during the autopsy. It looks the same, right?"

"Yes."

"But look at this." Zubak moved to another part of the slide. "The adenocarcinoma is gone. This looks like normal brain tissue. See the neurons and glia?"

"This is from the pancreatic tumor?" Tanik asked.

"Yes—after therapy. When I opened the abdomen, I saw the tumor had replaced the pancreas. The surrounding tissues were studded with metastases." Zubak moved to another area on the slide. "Look at this. Here's normal-appearing bone." He slipped another slide onto the stage. "This area of the tumor contains skin. Here's normal lung . . . and muscle."

The pathologist sat back and motioned toward the tray of slides. "In other areas of the tumor, I can tell you there's normal-appearing mammary tissue and prostate, testicular *and* ovarian tissue. It's a jumble of normal tissues that shouldn't be in the same person, male or female, much less a single pancreatic tumor."

"Almost like a teratoma," Tanik said.

At the NIH, he and Mehmet had studied teratomas. Teratomas were misguided germ cell tumors that were attempting to form a living organism. Unable to do so, they still managed to differentiate into a striking hodgepodge of tissues.

"Exactly," Zubak said. "But the problem with the diagnosis of teratoma is the original tumor contained only adenocarcinoma. Adenocarcinomas maintain lineage fidelity. In other words, they remain adenocarcinomas even after treatment. They might advance to a higher grade, but they don't do this. They don't become normal."

Tanik recalled Mehmet's words.

Blocking Primidin will force another form of selectin to be activated. But we don't know which one.

"This tumor acts as though it's not sure what it wants to be," Zubak said. "I've never seen anything like it."

Tanik could barely control his excitement. The autopsy results, ironically, were a confirmation of their success. They'd blocked Primidin. Another selectin had been activated. As Mehmet worried, however, they couldn't control which selectin was activated or the resulting path of cell differentiation. The random nature of selectin activation was reflected in the myriad of tissue types in the post-treatment tumor.

"I have to wonder if this isn't some type of treatment effect," Zubak said. "But it's unlike any I've seen." He eyed Tanik. "You wouldn't happen to know if the patient received something experimental?"

"If you're asking if we had something to do with this, the answer is no," Tanik said. "We're not authorized to treat patients."

"Why would this old doctor want me to give the slides to Mehmet?"

Tanik shrugged. "I'd ask the old doctor."

"Like I said, he refused to fill out paperwork," Zubak said. "I have no way of contacting him. I don't even know the decedent's name. After the autopsy, the doctor took the body away. All I have left are these tissue blocks and slides for Mehmet."

"I can have Mehmet give you a call when he comes in. Maybe he knows more. In the meantime, if you want to leave the slides with me, I can make sure he gets them."

Zubak pushed the tray of slides across the table. From his briefcase, he pulled out a plastic bag containing several tissue blocks and set them on the tray. Closing the briefcase, he paused and looked pensively at the blocks. "It's almost as if the tumor cells were reprogrammed, brought back to the stem-cell level and then let go, allowing them to differentiate however they wanted."

Tanik didn't respond.

"Off the record, whatever happened to that tumor is incredible," Zubak said. "If this is something experimental, whatever you or someone else did almost worked."

"Like I said, we're not—"

"Authorized to treat patients," Zubak finished. Smiling, he stood. "If Mehmet wants to talk, tell him to give me a call."

Tanik walked his old classmate out of the lab. After the two said their goodbyes, Tanik returned to his office and sat behind his desk. He looked toward the microscope.

This tumor acts as though it's not sure what it wants to be.

The pathologist's assessment had been exactly right. The post-treatment tumor contained a myriad of tissue types that shouldn't be near the pancreas.

Tanik felt the warm glow of accomplishment. They had unlocked the secrets of cancer. In their first try at a therapy, they'd redirected the course of a malignancy and found a potential cure for cancer—one applicable to every form of neoplasia.

His eye was caught by the corner of an envelope protruding from his top desk drawer. He removed the envelope. His name, in Mehmet's handwriting, was on the front. He tore it open. Inside were several papers and a red flash drive. The front sheet contained a handwritten letter.

> My dear Tanik,
>
> Enclosed please find the information I'm taking to Ankara on Monday to share with the Minister of Justice. I haven't told you many things. I apologize. What I've done is abhorrent. I alone am responsible, and I alone am accountable. I'm truly sorry for any injuries to our friendship or research.
>
> Forever your friend and colleague, Mehmet

Tanik became furious as he read the next few typewritten pages. While they were at the NIH and Mehmet had told him of the proposed laboratory in Izmir, he'd told Mehmet it sounded too good to be true. Nobody paid what Tunç was paying without strings attached. Those strings were finally apparent. Tunç had been pulling them for the past five years, blackmailing Mehmet into running his biowarfare lab.

Tanik looked toward the tissue blocks. Without Tunç's Little Tortona, however, they would have only half their current number of PhDs and technicians. The intimate details of cancer biology they'd unlocked would still be conceptual drawings buried in Mehmet's spiral notebooks.

Tanik walked to the microscope. He picked up the bag containing the blocks of tumor. He held it up. Despite his anger, he felt his euphoria from only a few minutes earlier return. Zubak was right. This was revolutionary. The adenocarcinoma had been transformed into something benign.

As he looked at the tissue blocks, he realized that he too would have done anything to make this possible. He too would have endured Tunç's Little Tortona.

A shrill scream pierced the air.

Tanik stepped to his doorway.

A figure wearing a ski mask ran toward him.

"What's going on?" Tanik demanded.

The figure, coming to a stop, reached up and pulled back the mask, revealing a pockmarked face.

"Farrat?" Tanik said. "What are you doing?"

Farrat raised his right arm. In his trembling hand, he held a gun.

45

Callahan regained consciousness. Still hooded and gagged, he fought against his bonds. The more he struggled, the deeper the ties tore into his already raw flesh.

Approaching footsteps on the stone floor were followed by the sound of a key in a lock and a door swinging open. Hands grabbed him and held him down. An arm locked around his forehead. He froze as the cold sensation of metal, a knife, slid along his throat. The knife turned, its edge cutting into his skin.

A few inches from his ear, a man hissed unintelligibly in Turkish.

Callahan tried to move away, but a sharp jerking motion tore at his neck. He was surprised there was no pain. Instead of the sensation of his jugular opening, warm blood running down his neck, and a descent back into darkness, he felt the hood coming off, the tape over his mouth being torn away, and his gag being removed.

He blinked, his eyes burning as blurred figures moved above him.

He was in a cell. Safiye was in a similar cell a dozen feet away. She lay curled on the ground, unconscious. They were in a circular room, some type of cave, its walls made of chiseled gray stone. Light shone through a small window in the back of the room.

A figure bent down, filling his vision. It was Basil. His nose was bandaged. The skin beneath his eyes was a purplish-black.

"If you try to escape, *ölü, ölmüş, ölmüş*," Basil growled, making a slashing motion across his neck.

Three others stood behind Basil, holding guns. One of them

was the man who had appeared with Basil from behind the tarp at city hall. The other two weren't men but boys. Not more than fourteen, they wore oversize bandoliers that crisscrossed their chests.

Basil untied Callahan and then pulled him to his feet. Callahan's arms and legs shook uncontrollably. Basil pushed him from the cell and down a corridor. At the end of the corridor, Callahan stopped in front of a wall of vines. From behind, Basil shoved him forward, propelling him through the vines.

Emerging into sunlight, Callahan tumbled down a sloping dirt pathway. When he came to rest, he looked back.

A stark gray cliff rose above him. An ancient ruin was carved into its façade. Intricate latticework, columns, and statues, eroded by time, framed several stories of porticos and walkways overgrown by moss and vines. Shadowed passages, including the ground-floor corridor from which he'd emerged, disappeared into the depths of the ruin.

Basil and the other man walked past him, beckoning him on.

Callahan followed the two men along a trail through woods. When they came to a stream, Basil pointed. "Clean yourself."

Callahan walked to the water's edge. He bent to untie a shoe. Basil again pushed him from behind, knocking him into the water. The two men then dragged him to the middle of the waist-high river and held him underwater.

Callahan tried to resist, but the men's combined strength was too much. As the last of the oxygen seeped from his lungs, he flailed wildly. The men released him and he burst from the water, coughing and choking.

When Callahan finally regained his breath, the men were sitting on rocks on the riverbank. Basil motioned to where clothes and a towel had been stacked on a large rock. "When you're done, put those on."

Callahan stretched his limbs. He let water flow over his open wounds. Clearing his nostrils of blood and mucus, he ran his fingers over the bridge of his broken nose. He set his feet wide apart. Clamping his hands on opposite sides of his nose, he jammed his palms together. In one sharp crunching motion, he set the bone and cartilage. Seeing stars, he lost consciousness.

He emerged from the river, flailing again, coughing up water.

The two men remained on the rocks, watching. They turned toward each other and continued talking.

Several minutes later, the two men were walking Callahan, dressed in a white T-shirt and shorts, back to the cliff.

The bandolier-wearing boys sat on the walkway over the vine-covered passage. Callahan passed beneath them and through the hanging tendrils.

Safiye was conscious. She sat in her cell, her ties removed.

"Are you okay?" he asked.

"Silence," Basil yelled, punching him in the kidney and pushing him into his cell.

As Callahan crumpled to the stone floor, Basil locked the cell door behind him and then entered Safiye's cell.

"Michael!" she screamed, retreating.

"Quiet," Basil yelled. With a vicious blow, he struck Safiye, knocking her unconscious. He lifted her and threw her over his shoulder. Setting his hand over her buttock, he directed a gap-toothed grin at Callahan before carrying her down the corridor.

Ayla slowly woke. She sat up. She wore a plush white bathrobe and was in a Victorian-style bed. The blinds on a window were drawn, but enough sunlight seeped past them to make out the details of the room.

A small vanity table and chair were against the far wall. A wingback chair and nightstand with a lamp were to her right. A dresser and cabinet were to her left. A door to the right was closed. A door to the left opened into what appeared to be a bathroom.

She jumped in surprise. A wraithlike figure rose from the wingback chair. The figure walked across the room and flipped a wall switch. A ceiling light came on.

The figure, a woman, was covered from head to toe with a black cloak. Through a thin slit above a face veil, the woman peered at Ayla through dark sedate eyes. The skin around her eyes was thin and wrinkled. She was bent at the neck and waist.

"Who are you?" Ayla asked.

"Betül."

"Where am I?"

"You're at Iskender's estate" the old woman replied, her voice thready and hoarse.

"Where are Michael and Safiye?"

"They're fine."

"And Mehmet?" Ayla asked.

"Who?"

"My husband, Mehmet."

"I don't know."

Neither spoke for a few moments.

"Why am I here?" Ayla asked.

"You're Iskender's guest. He said to do everything I could to make your stay here as comfortable as possible." The old woman opened the door to the right, which led into a hallway. She picked up a tray of food and carried it to the bedside.

"I was kidnapped," Ayla said.

"But you're fine," the woman said, her voice eerily calm. "And so are your friends." She extended the tray.

"What if I don't want to be here? What if I don't want to be Iskender's guest?"

The woman's head tilted. "I'm afraid you don't have a choice."

Ayla knocked the tray to the floor. As Ayla stepped toward the woman, she was pulled to a jolting stop. She looked down. A bracelet around her left ankle was connected to a wire. The wire disappeared under the bed.

"Your stay here can be a pleasant one but only if you cooperate," the woman said, standing in the open doorway. She motioned down the hallway.

A man appeared wearing rubber gloves and holding a bunched cloth in his fist. It was the man who'd driven the brown van. His left temple was bruised and swollen.

At city hall, as she and Safiye were bound and gagged, she'd heard the men fighting. Michael must have given him the bruise.

The driver stepped toward her. She tried to push him away, but he grabbed her by the back of the neck and clamped the cloth to her face.

"Don't leave a mark," the woman said.

Ayla struggled to break free, but the driver's grip was too tight. After a few breaths of the ammonia-scented cloth, she lapsed into unconsciousness.

Callahan lay on his side on the stone floor. He sat up as Safiye and Basil appeared at the end of the corridor. Safiye was walking under her own power, her hair wet from the river. Barefoot, she was dressed in a white T-shirt and shorts.

"Guards will be posted just outside," Basil said, locking Safiye into her cell. If they hear anything . . . from either of you, we'll take you back to the river. And it won't be to clean yourself.

The two bandolier-wearing boys appeared at the end of the corridor. They were carrying blankets and pillows, which they dropped into the cells.

Basil and the boys walked away, disappearing through the wall of vines.

Callahan and Safiye lay quietly for several moments before Safiye covered her face and began crying.

The room was spinning when Ayla woke again. Clamping her eyes shut, she fought the nausea. It took several minutes before the spinning stopped. She opened her eyes.

The old woman rose from the bedside chair and walked to the vanity table. She lifted another tray of food. "Can we try this again? Kaya, our cook, fixed another plate of food." She set the tray at the end of the bed.

Ayla pushed up onto her elbow. "We're at Iskender's estate?"

"Yes."

"Do you live here?"

The old woman nodded.

"Where's Mehmet?"

"That's enough questions for now." The woman walked to the doorway, where she turned. "I also recommend not talking too much about your husband."

"Why not?"

"Take it from me. Some advice from someone who's been here a lot longer than you."

Extending her foot, Ayla nudged the tray. It crashed to the floor.

The woman nodded down the hallway.

The driver appeared again. Within moments, he was on her, clamping the cloth to her face.

46

In the center of Ankara's Kocatepe business district, a monument commemorates the great pashas who helped guide the country through the early years of the republic. On a stone pulpit, the fez-topped brass figures of two men, Generals Seyddi Alištirmak and Muhammed Tunç, stand back-to-back, facing the borders they once protected.

From a nearby building, Iskender Tunç looked down on the monument, knowing his father would be pleased. Foremost in his father's eternal eastward gaze was the grand mosque—the Kocatepe Camii. The business district surrounded it. With its contemporary buildings, the district was a symbol of modern Turkey and served as headquarters for the country's most influential businesses.

"Your father made all of this possible."

Tunç turned. He was in the offices of Turkey's Yeni political party. Ulus Beyram, the Yeni's chairman, had entered the conference room.

The men shook hands.

Beyram, a balding, overweight man in his late sixties, motioned him toward a table. "How was your flight in?" he asked as they sat.

Tunç had arrived that morning from Izmir on his company's private jet. "Excellent," he replied.

"Good," Beyram said. "First, let me say on behalf of the Yeni party, we're grateful for your donations. The money was instrumental in helping us gain several seats in the last election."

"After my father's death, I wanted to ensure his legacy,"

Tunç said. "With his business enjoying unprecedented success, I decided it was time to give to an organization that's fighting for his ideals."

The Yeni appealed to Tunç for a number of reasons. Turkey was flooded with a mélange of political parties. Many were reconstructed versions of parties that had failed, thinly veiled by a new name or motto, but still laden with the same political baggage. The Yeni had arisen from a need for competent, forward-thinking leadership. They advocated a strong military to block regional aggression and to protect interests in the Mediterranean and Caspian Seas. They favored a peaceful coexistence with the Kurds, allowing them fair representation and increased autonomy. Neither a senseless uprising of the impoverished nor a puppet of the military, the Yeni were pragmatic businessmen unbiased by the sheltered idealism of the universities or the mosques, yet still capable of working with both.

In the last election, the Yeni had won nine more seats in the 600-member Grand National Assembly, increasing their number to seventy-nine. Despite their modest success, they possessed far less than a majority. But the Yeni were stronger than their numbers indicated. Designed to function within the cauldron of the National Assembly, they were a party that other minority parties would rally behind after hopes of advancing their own agenda and electing their own speaker deteriorated.

"In addition to thanking you for your donations," Beyram said, "I thought it was important, particularly with the approaching elections, that we have a face-to-face discussion on whether or not you have any political aspirations."

When large donations with the respected Tunç name on the bottom line had begun pouring into the Yeni party coffers, the leadership took notice. Conjuring images of a better time, the Tunç name held a special place in the hearts of the Turkish people. The deeds of the father were legendary, and the name brought instant credibility to the son.

"I hope Turkey may once again stand in the forefront of nations," Tunç said. "That we're recognized by the international community as a—"

"No," Beyram interrupted. "I mean *personal* aspirations."

Tunç sat back. As if considering the question for the first time, he nodded thoughtfully. "I've always been interested in serving my country in an effective capacity."

"Could you be more specific? Before my executive council meeting tonight, I thought it important we define those aspirations."

Tunç knew Beyram had something in mind. So did he. But the first thing that could kill his budding political career was to come across as too eager. As businessmen, the Yeni looked unfavorably upon career politicians. It had to appear as though he were doing the Yeni a favor, not the other way around. "Please, Ulus. You're much more aware of the Yeni's needs. Could I ask you to be more specific?"

The Janissaries assembled in a grassy field at the base of a tertiary branch of the Pontic Range's Saltuk Tepesi. Headmaster Kavas read from the Quran while Savon's linen-covered body was lowered into a grave.

After the trip from Izmir, Beyir had spent the remainder of the night talking with the others. At dawn, he and the Kazans had removed Savon's casket from the produce truck. They'd wrapped his cleansed body in white linens and carried him to the burial site, which the boys had prepared.

Once Kavas concluded the prayers, the Janissaries formed a line. Each grabbed a handful of earth and walked past Savon, sprinkling the dirt over the grave.

Beyir was the last in line. He extended his hand, palm skyward, and let the dirt sift between his fingers. His gaze wasn't directed toward Savon—as he lay on his right side facing Mecca—but toward the tallest of the pines on the nearby mountain ridge, where two boys sat in the highest of the great pine's branches.

Beyir wanted to tell the boys to turn away, to not be concerned with cancer and death and pain. He wanted to tell them that no matter how bad this appeared, no matter how hard life's obstacles, they should continue to imagine a better, more glorious life. They should continue looking well beyond the horizon.

47

A silver shaft of moonlight shone through the narrow window in the back wall of the cave, falling on the stone floor between the two cells.

"Michael, I'm sorry," Safiye said, her voice penetrating the darkness.

"For what?"

"For doubting you. For doubting Bryce and Scott. I should have known Iskender could do something like this. If I had raised a flag, Bryce might be alive. And we—we wouldn't be here."

"You haven't seen him in over a decade. It was reasonable to presume he'd changed."

"Men like Iskender don't change."

Neither spoke for a few moments.

"I hate to ask this," he said. "But he did something terrible to you, didn't he? I mean, it's why you broke your engagement."

Safiye didn't reply.

"Does it have something to do with your friend's death?"

"Rabia?" Safiye said. "Mehmet told you about her."

"He said her death was traumatic for you and Ayla."

"It was."

"What happened?"

His question hung in the air. Deciding not to press her, he wrapped his blanket around himself and rolled over.

"It was the night before a party at Iskender's house—the summer after we graduated from high school," Safiye said, her soft voice filling the room. "Iskender wanted me to try the recipes their cook was planning for the party. I drove to his home. His father was away. The servants had already left. We walked onto his back porch, where the food was set out."

She paused. He could hear her breathing, gathering herself. "That's all I remember. When I came to, I was on a reclining chair on his porch. I felt nauseous. My whole body ached. Iskender was next to me. When I asked what happened, he said that after eating I'd closed my eyes and drifted off.

"It was late. I drove home. I was tired. I slipped into a nightgown and fell asleep. In the morning, I realized the aches I was feeling were—were more localized." Her voice trembled. "I was bleeding vaginally. I was raw, but not just there."

Callahan heard a sharp intake of breath.

"I was eighteen years old," Safiye continued. "I was naive, very naive. I'd been a virgin, but I realized what Iskender had done to me. He'd drugged me. He'd raped and sodomized me and then pretended it didn't happen. I didn't know what to do. I—I was humiliated beyond anything I could imagine. I spent the day in a haze. That night, Ayla called and told me she and Rabia were coming to pick me up for the party. I said I was sick. Ayla said the three of us should skip the party and stay overnight at my house. But I said no. I didn't want to see anybody or do anything.

"That night, while I sat at home by myself, I realized I had to break off the engagement. I drove to Iskender's house. When I arrived at the party, I couldn't find him. Someone said he might be on the beach. I went looking for him. In the darkness, I almost stumbled over a couple in the sand. That's when I saw them: Iskender and Rabia.

"My first thought was he'd also drugged her. But she was awake. I could hear her. She was enjoying it. Rabia was a wonderful girl but not the type boys paid attention to. In an innocent way, she'd always been infatuated with Iskender. I thought—well, I thought the worst. I left the party.

"The next morning, I went to Ayla's house. Rabia was there. I confronted her with what I'd seen. She denied everything. Rabia said she'd had too much to drink and had passed out in a bedroom. When she woke, she was tied down to the bed. Several boys we didn't know were taking advantage of her. I told Rabia she was lying, but she stuck to her story. I told her I hoped she and Iskender would be happy together and I never wanted to see her again."

Safiye took a deep breath. "That night, they found Rabia in

her bathtub. Her body was scrubbed raw with a washcloth and bleach. Her wrists were slit."

"Safiye, don't—"

"I don't know everything that happened that night," she said. "Maybe Iskender drugged her. Maybe Rabia couldn't remember being with him. All I know is she didn't deserve to die. With time, I've come to realize that whatever happened, it happened *to* Rabia, not because of her. But the part I can't bear, the part that still keeps me up, is that Rabia didn't kill herself because of what Iskender did to her. She slit her wrists because of me, because of what I said."

"Don't do this to yourself."

"I survived what Iskender did to me," Safiye said, her voice firm. "Rabia would have too. She committed suicide because of me. That was the difference. I was there, pointing my finger, calling her a whore."

Ayla sat in the wingback chair next to the bed. Her left leg was extended, the cord taut around her ankle. The room was dark. Closing her eyes, she let her thoughts drift.

"This all started five years ago?" she asked Mehmet.

He grimly nodded. It was Sunday. Mehmet had just finished telling her about his involvement in the biowarfare lab at Turkish Sky.

"Just quit," she said.

"It's not that easy."

"We'll move. You can find another lab. We'll start over."

"I tried to resign once," he said. "It's not an option."

"We don't have to ask. We'll just leave. Pack up our belongings and go."

"You don't understand. He was furious. He said he would kill us, our families: brothers and sisters. He said he would kill the other PhDs. I believe him."

"Not if we go directly to city hall."

Mehmet shook his head. "He has connections everywhere. I wouldn't know who to trust."

"We'll go directly to the mayor or to Ankara. He doesn't control Ankara. This Little Tortona, it's despicable. You can't keep doing this."

The bedroom door swung open. Betül appeared, holding another tray of food.

"Where's my husband?" Ayla screamed. She lunged from the chair. "Where are Michael and Safiye?"

Sprawled on the floor, straining against the cord, she reached for the chair by the vanity table. She curled a finger around its leg and dragged it across the hardwood floor. Standing, she picked up the chair and threw it.

Betül stepped back, avoiding the chair as it clattered through the doorway.

Ayla grabbed the pillows from the bed and threw them into the hallway, screaming obscenities. As Ayla tore the sheets from the mattress, she was knocked flat to the bed.

The driver was on her, pressing the white cloth over her face. She tried not to breathe. When it felt as though her head would split from lack of oxygen, she acquiesced and sucked in a mouthful of air.

Her nostrils, however, were not assaulted by ammonia. The darkness did not come. Instead, her arms and legs went limp. Her rage dissipated.

The driver rolled her over.

Ayla stared up at him, immobile.

He lifted her into a sitting position. Picking up the pillows from the hallway, he wedged them at her sides, propping her up. He worked efficiently, his head down, not meeting her eyes. Setting the chair by the vanity table, he left the room.

Betül entered with the tray of food. "How are you?"

Ayla blinked as she tried to focus on the old woman's face.

"I—I'm fine," Ayla said. And she was, she thought. Only a few moments ago, she'd been angry about something. She'd felt terrible—furious and sad—wanting to scream and punch and kick all at the same time. But she couldn't remember why.

"Would you like some food?" Betül asked.

"Yes, I'm *starving.*"

Betül set the tray on her lap.

Ayla looked down at her inert arms. "I'm sorry. But I can't move them."

Betül picked up a spoon. She dipped it into the soup and raised it to Ayla's lips.

The old woman patiently fed Ayla the bowl of soup. When the soup was gone, Betül held a glass filled with clear liquid to Ayla's lips. "Drink this."

As Ayla finished the glass, another elderly woman entered the room. She was dressed in the same black cloak and veil as Betül, but she was rotund, her eyes bright and friendly. "I'm Kaya."

"The cook," Ayla said. "Your soup was good. What was it?"

Kaya laughed. "Chicken broth. You haven't eaten in a while. Your stomach couldn't take much more."

The women helped Ayla into the bathroom. They undressed her and gave her a bath. Afterward, they toweled her dry and dressed her in red satin undergarments.

"This red looks nice," Ayla said, seeing herself in the mirror.

"You're a beautiful woman," Kaya said.

The women led Ayla to the bedroom and sat her in the chair at the vanity table.

Ayla stared dreamily into the table's small oval mirror as the cloaked women went to work over her. They dried her hair and combed it out. They then applied lipstick, rouge, and eyeliner.

The women took Ayla's arms and helped her stand, directing her to the bed, where they propped her back into her sitting position.

Betül brushed a few strands of Ayla's hair into place. Stepping back, the women admired their handiwork.

"I once looked like that, didn't I?" Kaya asked.

"I don't think so," Betül said.

"You forget. We both did."

"Maybe, a long time ago."

As the old women stared at Ayla, lost in their thoughts, there was a tap at the door. Tunç entered.

"Iskender," Ayla said.

"Hello, Ayla."

The women slipped from the room. Tunç closed and locked the door behind them.

"Are they treating you well?" he asked.

"Yes, very. Everyone here is so nice."

"You had something to eat?"

She nodded.

Tunç walked to the bedside. He turned the wingback chair to face her and then sat. "While you're here, you're my guest. More than anything, I want you to enjoy yourself. If there's something you want, just let Betül or Kaya know."

"Thank you, Iskender."

He steepled his hands in front of him.

"What is it?" she asked.

"What are you wearing?"

"You should see it." In better control of her motor functions, she pushed back the covers and stepped from the bed. Teetering slightly, she held out her arms and modeled her satin nightie and panties.

"Turn around," he said.

She spun. Losing her balance, she fell face-first onto the bed. "I don't know what they gave me," she said, trying to push herself up, "but I feel great."

Tunç's hand was suddenly on her back, holding her in place. "Stay there." He ran his other hand along her bare hip. "Your skin—it's so smooth."

"Thank you."

Tunç's fingers fumbled at her back, unfastening her nightie.

"What are you doing back there?"

"Just relax." He pressed against her. At her hip, he slipped his fingers beneath the elastic band of her panties. He moved his hand to the front.

In the deep recesses of her mind, Ayla knew something wasn't right. Something wasn't right about the women giving her a bath, dressing her, combing out her hair, and putting on her makeup. Something wasn't right, but she wasn't sure what it was. And this, what Iskender was doing to her, wasn't right—but it felt so good, way too good to ask him to stop.

She closed her eyes and breathed deeply. "Oh Iskender," she moaned.

Tunç sat back on the chair. "Take off your clothes."

Ayla pushed up from the bed. She removed the nightie and slipped out of her panties.

Tunç motioned for her to do a pirouette. She did so but again lost her balance. This time, she fell into his lap, laughing.

"This isn't fair," he said.

"Why not?"

Tunç reached out and ran his thumb along her bottom lip. "I still have my clothes on."

48

Tunç stood at Ulus Beyram's office window, once again looking down at his father's statue. His gaze traveled from the statue to the outline of the citadel on the hill overlooking the city. On the day of the statue's dedication, his father had set a hand on his shoulder and pointed to the citadel.

"Its foundation has been traced to the masonry of the Galatians in the third century BC. After the Gauls, the Romans, Byzantines, Seljuks, and then Ottomans inhabited the hill. It's been ruled by Alexander the Great, Tamerlane, and Caesar along with Suleiman and the other great sultans. Since the Ottoman downfall, Kemal Atatürk and his ideology have ruled over the hill, Ankara, and all of Anatolia. As those before have fallen, my son, the time for Atatürk and his disciples has also come and gone."

Tunç turned from the window and scanned the office. After driving from the northern estate that morning, he'd spent the day at his corporate offices in Ankara. In the early afternoon, Beyram had called and set up the meeting.

"Something came up about your father during our council meeting last night," Beyram said.

"My father?"

"He was a member of the Muqaddim?"

"He was, but I'm not."

"The Yeni are devout, but we're far from extremists," Beyram said. "We believe in a secular state. Our women shun the head scarf. We oppose sharia. We—"

"Like my father," Tunç said, interrupting, "I too am

devout. But my religion is a source of internal strength—not a blueprint for governing."

The Yeni were a close but not perfect fit. He'd told Beyram what he wanted to hear. He'd have to make allowances, at least for the present.

"Good answer" Beyram said, laughing. "We'll make a politician out of you yet."

"Besides, these days, the Muqaddim are far from extremists."

"I agree. But since you're not a member, that's not a point you would have to make."

"You're right," Tunç said. "It's not."

Tunç turned back to the window, his thoughts drifting to the night before and his late-night visit with Ayla. They'd given her a cocktail of Rohypnol and gamma-hydroxybutyric acid (GHB). Rohypnol was a benzodiazepine that caused dissociation and amnesia; GHB was a central nervous system depressant. The combination had been perfect. More than just compliant, she'd been a willing participant. The look in her eyes had said it all. They were doing something taboo, something terribly wrong. Still, she wanted him. She enjoyed it.

The office door clicked open. Beyram entered. "Iskender, it's good to see you again."

"It's nice to be back," Tunç said. "I confess I never get tired of looking at my father's statue. Seeing his likeness, I feel as though I'm home."

"That's good. I hope Ankara will soon be your new home."

Tunç threw an inquisitive look toward the Yeni chairman, who motioned him toward a table.

As they sat, Beyram smiled. "I'm not good at beating around the bush." Clearing his throat, he continued, a formal ring to his voice. "As you know, our executive council met. The Yeni would like to extend to you a nomination for—"

The door burst open. Several smartly dressed men entered. "We can't let Ulus have all the fun," the man in front said. It was Eren Agman, CEO of Anatolian Airlines. Behind Agman were the remaining Yeni council members, a veritable who's who of Turkish industry. Tunç had met most and knew the others by reputation.

"Has he accepted?" Agman asked.

"I haven't asked him yet," Beyram replied.

"Then, please," Agman said. "Go ahead."

With the council members standing behind him, Beyram spoke. "At our upcoming convention, the Yeni would like to extend to you a nomination for . . . " He straightened in his chair. "For the presidency of the Turkish Republic."

Tunç's eyes widened in surprise. "The presidency?"

The council members nodded.

Tunç sat back. "I'm honored and humbled and flabbergasted all at once."

"Don't believe him for a second," Agman said. "It takes more than that to humble a Tunç."

"Do you accept?" one of the men asked.

Tunç pursed his fingers in front of him. He had to make this look good. After a deep, pensive breath, he nodded, bowing his head in acknowledgment. "I do."

The council applauded. Tuxedoed waiters entered the office carrying bottles of champagne. Once they all had a glass, they turned to Agman, the most senior of the councilmen.

"Turkey is at a crossroads," Agman said. "With Cebici retiring, a vacuum has been created. This *was* an opportunity for the military to regain some of what they've lost, but with Volkan's assassination, the military is in turmoil." Agman smiled slyly. "The next administration will have an unprecedented opportunity to press its agenda and fill the impending void." He raised his glass toward Tunç. "Let's hope it'll be the Yeni. To a long and fruitful relationship. *Yaşa.*"

"Yaşasin," the others chimed in.

Tunç felt the mens' gaze. They knew he was devout, undoubtedly viewing it as a weakness. This moment would give them an indication of just how devout. He raised the glass and then downed the champagne.

The others glanced at one another. Not too devout, their eyes said before they tossed back their own glasses.

"Since I've made a rather abrupt transition from businessman to politician, I too should make a speech," Tunç said as the glasses were refilled. "But I know the Yeni are not about speeches. You, or should I say *we*, are about action. I hope my acts will be worthy of your nomination." He met the eyes of each of the men and raised his glass. "To the Yeni."

"To the Yeni," the others repeated.

Spirits were high as champagne and wine flowed freely.

Hors d'oeuvres and then dinner were brought into the adjacent conference room, followed by cigars and brandy. After the last of the toasts had been made, each of the Yeni councilmen stopped to shake Tunç's hand before leaving. Finally, only Beyram and Tunç remained.

"That's an impressive group," Tunç said.

Beyram took a pull on his cigar. "It is." He jabbed the cigar toward the distant backs of the Yeni councilmen. "Those men have more connections and pull than I think even they're aware of."

"I'm honored to be included in their company."

"For better or worse, you are," Beyram said. He leaned forward. "Tell me, Iskender. Do you wonder how I'm associated with a group like that?"

Tunç shook his head.

"Why not? I'm not a business tycoon. I have no previous political appointments."

"Ulus, I remember my father talking about you when I was a boy. You've been in Ankara for a long time. You know the machinery of government, how it works."

"Precisely," Beyram said, again jabbing with his cigar, ashes flying. "I do the things they can't or won't. If you want something done, Iskender, you come to me. Do you understand?"

Beyram's jowls sagged as his eyes bore down on Tunç. "Your association with the Yeni can be long and fruitful. But you must understand, you are where you are because of me." He raised his glass in salute and finished his brandy.

"In a way," Tunç said.

Beyram set down the glass. "What do you mean?"

"I'm aware of plans for a coalition of the conservative minority parties . . . and of the recent deals that have been brokered."

There was a moment of unease in the Yeni chairman's eyes. "Good," he said. "Then you also know if you accept the nomination, the presidency is yours."

"Yes," Tunç said. "But at a price. An expensive one."

"You'll soon learn deals are necessary in politics, Iskender. To gain power, concessions must be made. Without them, minority parties remain in the minority—no matter how impressive the membership."

"I chose your party because I believe in your ideals," Tunç said. "I accept your nomination but only under my terms."

Beyram's brow furrowed.

"If you're so willing to make compromises, let me make *you* an offer," Tunç said. "Call back your colleagues. Tell them I refuse the concessions. I'll still guarantee a Yeni victory."

"*How*?"

"Let's just say I've made my own deals—under my own terms."

Beyram shook his head. "That's not how this will work," he growled, snuffing his cigar in the bottom of his glass. "If you want this party's nomination, it will be on *my* terms."

"You haven't heard my conditions."

"And I don't want to," Beyram snapped. "The question is, do you want the Yeni nomination?"

Tunç was quiet for a few moments. He then stood and extended his hand. "It's been nice doing business with you."

Beyram ignored the proffered hand.

Withdrawing his hand, Tunç lifted his suit coat from the back of his chair.

"Where are you going?" Beyram asked.

"Home. I have a corporation to run."

Tunç walked from the room, leaving the door open behind him.

Beyram followed him to the door. "You have one week to reply to the offer of the nomination," he shouted. "After that, it's gone."

49

Caria Mahid went about her receptionist duties at city hall's central desk. She did her best to ignore the faces on the opposing wall. The faces were on a flyer posted to a bulletin board along with the usual hodgepodge of advertisements and announcements. The faces belonged to the two physicians who'd come to her desk on Monday with a woman who requested to meet with the mayor. In the days since, they'd stared at her not only at work but from dozens of similar flyers posted around town along with television newscasts, internet posts, and newspapers. Her gaze was drawn to the flyer. She wished she could forget the faces, but she could think of nothing else.

"Good morning."

Caria turned. Ançak Barhal stood behind her, leaning forward on his cane. After she'd directed the physicians and woman toward the deputy mayor's office, they'd struck up a conversation with the city councilman.

During Caria's four years of employment at city hall, Barhal had hobbled by her desk without so much as a nod in her direction. In the three days since he'd led the physicians back toward his office, he'd made it a point of saying hello. Their conversations were uncomfortably long. His eyes, as they did now, bore into her.

"Are you okay?" he asked.

"I'm fine," she replied. "Thank you."

"You look a little peaked."

Barhal was responsible for city land appropriations. Although his position was historically filled by mayoral appointment, with the appointee changing with each shift in the city's governance, he'd become a fixture in city hall. His generosities with city land had endeared him to Izmir's most influential people. As a result, Barhal was reportedly untouchable.

Trying to be convincing, knowing her job and perhaps more depended on it, she smiled. "I'm fine," she repeated.

Barhal raised an eyebrow. "You should think about leaving early today."

"I'll consider that, Mr. Barhal."

Barhal threw a concerned glance toward the flyer before nodding and hobbling away. After he disappeared down the hallway, she looked toward the flyer.

If you have information on the missing WHO physicians, please contact the Task Force Search Committee located in the exhibition hall at the Aegean University.

She stared at the photocopied faces, a slurry of anger and resolve building within her. Did Barhal think if he was nice to her, she'd forget he'd met with them? Was he trying to intimidate her?

She stood and walked down the hallway and out of city hall. In Konak Square, she passed Yalı Mosque and then the Clock Tower. She looked south of the square toward the Aegean University's exhibition hall. The missing persons flyers along with the internet posts and newscasts would eventually go away. If she did nothing, however, the faces of the two physicians would never disappear.

From the oncoming pedestrians, an elderly man veered from his path. Unbalanced, he was about to fall. She grabbed him.

"Are you okay?" she asked.

The man blinked. He shook his head, his eyes slowly focusing. Well dressed and trim, he carried a cane and had a full head of gray hair combed perfectly back. As he regained his composure, he smiled kindly. "Yes, yes, I'm fine." He pushed up on the cane, locking an elbow. "Allah'a şükür."

"Amin."

The man, without the support of the cane, stepped back and bowed. He surprised her as he spryly clicked his heels together before returning to the flow of pedestrians.

Caria resumed her path across the square. She glanced back toward the elderly man. His gait was steady as he swung the cane at his side.

That was quite a recovery.

As Caria walked, she noticed a pain in her right calf. She glanced down. A circle of blood—several centimeters in diameter—had formed on her pant leg.

She pressed her finger to the spot. It was numb.

During her collision with the old man, the end of his cane had hit her. The blow had seemed mild. The large plume of blood on her pant leg, however, suggested otherwise.

She cast a look of regret in the direction of the exhibition hall. She couldn't go anywhere like this. Her plans would have to wait. She turned back toward city hall but came to an abrupt stop.

Ançak Barhal stood at the entrance to city hall. He was talking to the man who she'd run into.

Caria spun and continued toward the exhibition hall. As she did, she swore to herself. By panicking, she'd confirmed her guilt.

She looked ahead. The roofline of the exhibition hall was within sight. With each step, however, the numbness in her calf worsened. Her leg began to stiffen. Fixing her gaze on the exhibition hall, she walked faster. When she reached it, everything would be all right.

Ten meters from the hall's front entrance, the toe of her shoe struck the pavement. As she fell, she tried to catch herself, but her arms moved too slowly. Her jaw hit the pavement with a sickening crunch.

As she lay immobile, tasting blood and concrete, a man rolled her over. He winced when he saw her face.

She tried to speak, but her lips and tongue wouldn't comply. Instead, her neck muscles spasmed. Her head began whipping back and forth. She tried to stop but couldn't.

Starry points of light entered her vision. The points multiplied and expanded, consuming her vision, consuming everything.

50

Ayla jumped from bed. She rushed into the bathroom and fell to her knees, vomiting into the toilet.

It was morning. The night before, Tunç had made his second late-night visit to her room. Naked, she glanced toward her ankle. The cord was gone. Vaguely, she remembered Tunç unlocking it after it had become wrapped around his own leg. As visions of the variety of positions he'd put her through came to her, she vomited again.

Huddled over the bowl, catching her breath, she stared down into the swirling contents. Mehmet was dead. She was sure of it. Tunç wouldn't be doing this to her if he was alive. With thoughts of Mehmet, she recalled their last conversation.

She sat at her kitchen table, her cell phone in front of her.

"I was getting worried," she said when Mehmet finally called.

"Have I told you?"

She smiled, his tone putting her at ease. "*Told me*?"

"How much I've taken you for granted?"

"Not recently."

"Ayla Koba, you mean more to me than the earth and stars," Mehmet said, his voice breaking.

"Is everything okay?"

"Once and for all, yes."

"Mehmet, where are you? You sound out of breath."

"I'm in the courtyard near the ministry. Do you remember when we were here? That first summer back in Turkey. You were wearing a tan dress. You were so beautiful."

When Mehmet made his confessions the day before, they both knew it would be a long road back to her good graces. The road would be filled with uncertainty, but it was one she was sure they'd travel together. She also knew there would be a time for apologies. Now wasn't that time.

"Why aren't you at the ministry?" she asked.

"Do as we planned. Leave for city hall. Pretend I didn't make this call."

She stood. "But you are making this call."

"Darling, I love you."

"Mehmet, what's happening?"

"You've given me so much. You deserve so much more."

"*What's happening?*"

"I love you," he said. "*I lo—*"

She heard a loud thud.

"Mehmet. *Mehmet!*"

Ayla pressed her palms against her temples, her head pounding. When the pounding and nausea subsided, she reached for a tissue and wiped her face.

The women's toiletries sat on a nearby counter. Among them was an old-fashioned razor. She picked up the razor and removed the blade. She held up the glistening blade and then set it against her wrist. With one swipe, there would be no more nights like last night. Tunç would never touch her again.

She thought of Rabia and realized how much courage it must have taken her to do it. To cut one wrist and then the other. To slice deep through skin and sinew and watch as the blood pumped from her wrists.

Ayla pressed the blade deep into her skin and sliced. She drew a thin line of blood before pulling the blade away.

No. It was too easy an out. For her. For Iskender.

The young men who'd raped Rabia had gone unpunished. And the event had taken place in Iskender's house. If he wasn't one of the rapists, he must have at least condoned it. Now he was doing this to her.

She curled her fingers around the blade. The next time Tunç came into her room, she would find the courage. One slice, furious and deep.

With renewed purpose, she pushed herself up from the bowl.

The door to the adjoining bedroom was open. She stepped into it. Twin beds were separated by a nightstand. In the corner was a desk. She walked to the desk and looked through the drawers. They were stuffed with a variety of sewing items: swatches of cloth, colored ribbons, and needles and thread. In the bottom drawer was a stack of money.

A bulletin board cluttered with faded photos of flowers and yellowing recipe cards hung above the desk. The only thing that appeared to be from this decade was a map—white and crisp. The words *Otobüs hatlari* were typed at the top. It was a bus schedule.

Her thoughts turned to Michael and Safiye. They too had endured that terrible van ride. They were here because of her. Opening her hand, Ayla looked down at the razor blade. Before she did anything, she needed to make sure they were safe.

The morning air in the cave was cool. Callahan lay on his side, his head propped up on his hand. "Mehmet said your father was friends with Muhammed Tunç?"

Safiye sat in the shadows of her cell, her back against the rear wall of the cave. "*Friend* isn't the right word. Fan maybe. My father worshipped him."

"Even after the broken engagement?"

"I never told my father what happened. I was too humiliated. In a way, however, I don't blame him." She paused. "I'm actually very grateful to my father. He let me go with him to Washington. He paid for me to go to college and then medical school. He didn't live to see me become a doctor, but I remember when I showed him my acceptance letter to med school. He didn't say anything. He just looked at me, smiling unabashedly as tears streamed down his cheeks. He never brought up the engagement or Iskender Tunç again."

"Did you ever tell Ayla?"

"I never did," she said.

"Did you two ever talk about the confrontation between you and Rabia?"

"You mean did I ask her if she believed my story or Rabia's? No. After Rabia committed suicide, Ayla and I never talked about that morning at her house or about the party. It was a time to come together, not to let the circumstances pull us apart. Besides,

I felt so guilty. I was just glad Ayla didn't hold me responsible for Rabia's death, that she still wanted to be my friend."

"And Ayla was fine with Mehmet going back to Izmir?" he asked.

"We *have* talked about that. Ayla didn't learn Tunç Corporation was involved until after Mehmet came back from his first interview. She tried to dissuade Mehmet. By then, however, Iskender had already charmed him, giving him carte blanche to pursue his research. In the end, Ayla said she couldn't ruin Mehmet's chance to run his own lab."

Neither spoke for several moments.

Callahan rolled onto his back and looked up at the ceiling. "Ayla said your brother was younger?"

"Six years," Safiye said.

"Do you keep in touch?"

"Not since our father passed away. At the funeral, my brother tried to get me to stay in Turkey. He told me Iskender and I still had a chance, that I was passing up the opportunity of a lifetime."

"Why would it make a difference to him?" Callahan asked.

"My father's adoration of the Tunç family extended to my brother. But while my father was able to put the broken engagement behind him, my brother couldn't."

"Did you always plan on coming back to Istanbul?"

"No, but when I finished my training, it felt right," she said. "Turkey's my home."

"Do you have other family here?"

"Just my brother," Safiye said. She was quiet for a moment. "When we were younger, if somebody would have told me my brother and I wouldn't be close, I wouldn't have believed them. I was the nearest thing he had to a mother. But when he was eight, he went away to school. After that, I only saw him during breaks. When my father and I went to the US, my brother stayed at the school. My father said it was for the best. And my brother was happy to stay. Still, I always felt as though we abandoned him."

"What does he do now?"

"I don't know. The funeral was the last time we spoke. But I know one thing. Whatever my brother does, he's good at it. He's smart, off-the-charts smart. He's also driven."

Voices came from the end of the corridor. Four young guards

appeared. They walked down the corridor and unlocked Safiye's door.

It was their third day in the cells. They knew the routine. A morning trip to the river to bathe. Two meals a day. Three times a day, the guards would take them into the woods to relieve themselves. Otherwise, they were largely left alone.

Safiye walked across the cell, pulling her hair back into a ponytail. Her features transformed from the calm person Callahan was talking with moments earlier to something approaching a caged animal. Her eyes ablaze, her arms glistened, jutting defiantly as she stalked from the cell.

The guards—two of them armed—stepped back as she passed. They followed her down the corridor and outside.

Callahan wondered how he could have been on four previous excursions with Safiye and hardly noticed her. Pacing the cell, he tried not to think about Safiye's trips to the river and her increasing entourage of ogling young guards. Instead, he occupied his mind with thoughts of escape.

When they were removed, at least two of the guards stood back, their guns leveled. Taking the guards down would entail a headlong rush across the room. He didn't stand a chance. And if he or Safiye did manage to elude the guards, there were video monitors everywhere. How far would they get? And where would they go? They had no idea where they were or what lay beyond the surrounding woods.

But the most unsettling aspect of an escape was the calm in the eyes of their young captors, the lack of reaction when he walked too far ahead in the woods or swam too far in the river. It was as if the possibility of their escape wasn't a concern.

51

Tunç lay on Ayla's bed. "That was incredible," he said. It was his third straight late-night visit to her room. Rolling from bed, he began dressing.

"You can't stay?" Ayla asked.

"Important visitors are coming to the estate. We have to be ready for them. I'll be back tomorrow night."

Ayla stood and pressed against him. "I'm not sure I can wait that long."

He reached for her breast, but she deftly caught his hand.

She placed his thumb in her mouth and fondled it with her tongue. With her other hand, she reached down and wrapped her fingers around him. "And it feels to me, as if you can't either."

He tossed his shirt aside and lifted her by her hips. She wrapped her arms and legs around him. They fell together to the bed. As he thrust into her, Ayla smiled back.

Afterward, he rolled from bed. "I have to go. We have meetings tonight."

When he finished dressing, he looked down at her.

The sheet had fallen away from her, exposing her upper torso. He couldn't help but stare. Her body was exquisite.

He again reached for her breast. This time, she let him take it.

Bending down, he ran his tongue over her nipple. He moved his palm down her stomach to her groin. As he began massaging her, she lay back and spread her legs.

"Don't stop," she said. She shut her eyes, her breaths coming faster. "Harder."

After her back arced and body shuddered, she looked dreamily up at him. "After your meetings tonight, you might want to make another visit."

He smiled. "I will."

Leaving the room, he closed the door behind him. He walked down the hallway to the back stairwell.

Betül was running up the stairs. "Are you okay?" she asked, her eyes wide.

"Yes. Why?"

"I'm sorry," the old woman said. "I—I was just doing the dishes, and I saw Ayla's iced tea."

"*And?*"

"It—it was untouched."

"She didn't drink it?" he asked.

"None of it."

Ayla hadn't had the cocktail of Rohypnol and GHB; yet, she'd been compliant. Her eyes had been lucid, her speech crisp, her movements fluid. She'd been perfect. "Are you sure?"

"Yes," Betül said. "When I went to pick up her tray, I didn't notice the glass was still full. I'm sorry. I won't let it happen again."

He looked back down the hallway toward Ayla's bedroom. He shook his head. "From now on give her whatever she wants to drink . . . but without the cocktail."

"With nothing?" Betul asked.

"Yes. With nothing."

52

Day 33

Alin sat next to Adams in the barren mess tent. He looked at the members of the WHO and UN joint-inquiry panel, who sat at the only remaining table. The panel members and a team of investigators had begun arriving on Tuesday. It was now Friday.

The panel chair, a German attorney, was presenting the results of their investigation. "We've conducted interviews with people in the area. They report nothing unusual." He spoke English with a thick German accent. "Officials at Tunç Corporation have been most cooperative. Thus far, we've found no evidence of weapons bioengineering at the Ulücuk facility."

In his day, Alin had listened to the ramblings of more than one politically appointed ad hoc committee. Their agendas were often far from their supposed intentions.

"What about the detection of an elevated trichothecene level in the girl's blood?" Adams asked. "And the cultures we sent to Paris, the ones confirmed as *Yersinia*?"

An older, bespectacled British physician leaned forward. "The possibility the single elevated trichothecene level resulted from exposure to a naturally occurring fungus in the river cannot be excluded. And *Yersinia* infections do occur. The unfortunate incident with the family in Ulücuk may simply represent a natural sporadic infection."

"And the bacteria's antibiotic resistance?" Adams asked.

"Perplexing, we agree," the physician said. "But we've found no link between the *Yersinia* and Turkish Sky." He cast a stern look at Adams. "In my opinion, to take such circumstantial evidence—the detection of trace fungal toxins, positive cultures for *Yersinia*, and the antibiotic resistance—and postulate it's the result of a biowarfare facility, well, it's not unlike finding a gold coin on the ground and presuming a leprechaun dropped it there."

Adams looked imploringly toward the panel members. "Can't you see something is going on here? A doctor was killed. Two others are missing." He held up a sheet of paper. "What about the neurotoxins you found at Turkish Sky?"

"Turkish Sky Manufacturing once used toxin-containing paints and glues—acceptable byproducts of airplane fabrication," the German attorney said. "If similar searches were conducted on facilities in the United States or Europe, more than half would be cited for such violations."

"What do you need?" Adams asked. "A factory with 'Biowarfare Plant' stenciled on the side?"

"With the fiasco in Iraq, I think you can appreciate the difficulties in proving the existence of weapons of mass destruction," the attorney said. "This panel will not jump to conclusions. At this point, we feel there's not sufficient evidence to proceed with a formal investigation."

"What about Bryce?" Alin asked. "The cuts on his face, his broken bone. There was no blood, no erythema. Many of his injuries were inflicted after he was dead. Someone murdered him and then tried to hide it."

The British physician held up a stapled set of papers. "The forensic pathologists examining Dr. Jones could not exclude the possibility his injuries weren't the result of a multistage car accident."

"Could not exclude?" Alin said.

The attorney sat forward. "Considering the fact Dr. Jones was found on the side of the road, a car accident is a reasonable conclusion. There could have been multiple points of impact. He might have been dragged. He might—" The attorney paused and looked down at his paperwork. "Dr. Jones's death is unfortunate. From the information before us, however, this task force must conclude there was no definitive evidence of foul play."

"What about Drs. Callahan and Özmen?" Adams said. "Doesn't their disappearance indicate foul play?"

THE OTTOMAN EXCURSION 277

"Determining their whereabouts is beyond the scope of this panel," the attorney said. "A search committee has been convened by local authorities to investigate their disappearance."

Alin could see what was happening. The West couldn't afford an incident that might push away the Islamic, yet Western-leaning country. Turkey was an important NATO ally that had checked southern expansion of the former Soviet Union for decades. It was an important player in the Middle East. Despite Turkey's history of Kurdish persecution and being a consistent offender of human rights, the West had always looked the other way. It was unlikely things would change now.

The WHO's status as a relief organization had allowed Alin unencumbered access to foreign countries for over three decades. Year after year, he'd seen the true ills afflicting their host nations: religious and racial discrimination, oppressive governments, and economic injustice. He'd fought them all. He'd come to realize, however, the socioeconomic currents of even the smallest of nations couldn't be redirected in a few weeks' time. He was adept at healing the body, but the mind-set of men was well beyond his grasp. For him, the only route to men's souls was through the compassion he showed as a healer. To color that relationship with anything else would only make it less. *One patient at a time.* He'd said it more times than he cared to remember.

Alin looked at Adams, who flipped the paper with the lab results into the air. The young physician was furious, and rightly so. Adams's behavior, along with that of Michael and Bryce, reminded him of his own younger days. He'd survived them, perhaps because someone wiser had done what he was about to do.

"Thank you, gentlemen," Alin said, standing. "If there's any further assistance we can provide, you know where to reach us."

As expected, given a moment's reprieve, the panel members began to leave. It was hard to figure out who was worse: those who'd killed Bryce and kidnapped Michael and Safiye or these indifferent bureaucrats determined to do nothing about it.

Adams rose to speak, but Alin squeezed his shoulder. "Hold on. I have something important to tell you."

The panel members' exit was followed by the entrance of several Turks. Adams and Alin helped the men carry the remaining table and chairs from the mess tent and load them into a waiting truck. They then turned and watched as the supporting ropes of the mess tent were let loose. The tent collapsed—the last one standing in the field hospital.

Day thirty-three of the excursion would be its last.

Alin and Adams joined Brooke and Haas and the other relief team members around the fire pit. Recalling better times, they said silent farewells to Bryce and prayed they hadn't seen the last of Michael and Safiye.

As the team walked through the near-empty tent city, the remaining inhabitants sat quietly outside their tents. Kids were nowhere in sight.

When the team members reached the bus stop and the waiting buses, Adams turned to Alin. "What was it you wanted to tell me?"

Alin knew there was nothing they could have said to change the panel's verdict. Likewise, there was nothing the panel members could have said to calm Adams. Alin didn't know how far the panel members would go to discredit dissent. He didn't want to find out. He'd done his job simply by getting Adams out of harm's way.

"I was wondering how Lil is doing with her pregnancy," Alin said.

Adams looked toward the road as the van with the panel members drove away.

"I'm sure you're anxious to get back to her," Alin said.

"I am," Adams said. "Lil is doing fine. She's still a couple months from her due date."

"What do you think you'll do when you get back?"

Adams turned toward the spot where the truck had carried Bryce away a few days earlier. "I'm going to hug Lil and my girls." He shook his head. "Seeing Bryce in the back of that cart—it could have been me. I could have been the one in that casket. Lil would have been without a husband. The girls would be without a father."

Alin set a hand on Adams's shoulder. "Can you do me a favor?"

"Sure."

"Tell Lil and the girls I said thank you for sharing their husband and father with us. Tell them they should be proud of what he's done, that he's made a difference."

53

Callahan ran. Branches blocked his way, cutting his outstretched hands. Safiye and Ayla were at his side. The sounds of men shouting and dogs barking came from behind.

They stopped at a dirt wall. The wall resembled the rift on the road near Turkish Sky—only much larger. The wall, teeming with roots and vines, was over ten feet high. It extended in both directions as far as they could see.

"We'll have to climb it," Callahan said, grabbing a large dangling root.

The root slid smoothly from the wall. He grabbed another, which also slid easily away. He furiously pulled at the roots. One after another slid effortlessly from the dirt.

Safiye and Ayla joined him. As they extracted the roots, tossing them onto a growing pile, Safiye came to a halt. "Are those—?"

A pair of feet jutted from the wall. On the feet were Bryce's running shoes. As the three of them stared, incredulous, a high-pitched howling filled the air. They looked up.

Basil sat on top of the wall, watching and laughing.

Callahan jolted awake, breathing hard.

He was in the cave. Safiye lay on her side in her dimly lit cell, her head resting on her open palm. Accustomed to each other's nightmares, she was watching him. "You said your parents live on Green Bay. Is that where you grew up?"

Their time in the cave had melded into a continuous mosaic of restless sleep and talk. "No," he said. "It's where they retired. I grew up in a suburb of Detroit."

"Was your childhood like *8 Mile*?"

"The movie?"

"Yes," she said.

"You mean was I frequently involved in rap battles? No."

"How about *The Virgin Suicides*?" she asked.

"That was about a different suburb of Detroit, but yes, you're getting warmer."

"*Gran Torino*?"

"Colder. The movie gives an accurate description of much of Detroit but not where I grew up." He laughed. "You've seen a lot of movies about Detroit."

"I spent much of my downtime in the US watching movies."

"Did you read *Middlesex*?"

"Yes," she said. "It's about Izmir and Detroit. I loved it."

"The author also wrote *The Virgin Suicides*. He grew up in Detroit. In both books, his descriptions of the city were accurate. Combine the suburbs from *Middlesex* and *The Virgin Suicides* and you have my childhood, of course minus the hermaphrodite and suicide parts."

Safiye looked thoughtfully toward him.

"What is it?" he asked.

"You know almost every detail of my life, but I have yet to learn one intimate thing about you. It's like what Brooke says about Eric. He's always deflecting, turning everything into a joke."

"I told you about Jenna."

"I already knew about her." Safiye sat up. "Tell me why you became a doctor?"

"That's a boring story."

Safiye slid with her back to the wall and looked expectantly toward him.

He took a breath. "When my sister Kate was five and I was nine, she was diagnosed with leukemia. She didn't respond to the first course of chemotherapy or the second."

"I'm sorry," Safiye said, covering her mouth. "I didn't—"

"It's okay," he said. "It ends happily. Kate eventually had a bone marrow transplant. Her leukemia went into remission. She's been fine since. She lives in Colorado with her husband and two adopted kids."

"I'm glad to hear that."

Callahan nodded. "I was going to be an engineer, like my dad. I thought he knew everything. But seeing what Kate's illness did to him—his helplessness and frustration—becoming a doctor became more appealing, at least from the perspective of a nine-year-old boy."

"You realized your father wasn't invincible."

"I didn't know yet that neither were doctors."

Safiye smiled. "If you were so impressed by your sister's doctors, why didn't you become a pediatrician?"

"To be honest, even now when I see a sick child, I get queasy. And then, there's what happened in med school."

"What?"

"During my pediatric rotation, I was discouraged from going into pediatrics," he said.

"Why?"

"My pockets weren't big enough."

"Your *pockets*?" she said.

"I couldn't hold enough suckers."

Safiye groaned. "See, you are like Eric. You're worse. Was your sister even sick?"

"She was. But maybe I should have gone with a shorter version of why I became a doctor. Like I wanted to cure cancer or save the world."

"Or you wanted to forget your fiancé."

Neither spoke for a few moments.

"No," Callahan said. "I don't think so."

"You don't think what?"

"You may have gone to Washington to get away from Tunç. You may have even started taking classes to forget about Rabia's death. But you didn't go to medical school and finish a residency simply to forget. You had a thousand pathways in front of you. But you chose college and medical school. Then pediatrics. I've seen you with kids. You're a natural.

"I imagine you wanted to be a doctor for the same reason many do, me included," he said. "You wanted to immerse yourself in something meaningful." He shook his head. "You shouldn't give Tunç credit for you becoming a doctor. You chose to be a doctor because of who you are: your intelligence and abilities, your work ethic, your heart. Despite growing up in Turkey with all its misogyny, despite Iskender Tunç and everything he did to you, you became exactly the person you were meant to be."

Tunç sat at his desk in his office at the Samsun estate. He was trying to work, but his thoughts were of Ayla. The first two nights with her had been incredible. But the past two nights, with her being drug-free, had been even better. She'd not only been compliant, she'd been an active participant. She was enjoying it.

Unable to concentrate on his work, he walked to the second floor and tapped at Ayla's door.

"Come in."

He stepped inside and closed the door.

Ayla slipped from beneath the sheets. She wore only panties and a bra. "I didn't expect to see you this early," she said, giving him a kiss.

"I needed a break."

"You do look tense. Here, sit."

He sat on the edge of the bed. She knelt behind him and rubbed his shoulders. He rolled his head back and forth as she moved up his neck.

"Can you stay?" she asked.

"For a little bit. I'll be driving to Ankara later, but I should be back late tonight."

She leaned against him. Reaching around him, she undid his belt. "Raise your arms."

When he obliged, she pulled his shirt over his head. She then moved in front of him. After tugging off his shoes and socks, she grabbed the front of his pants and pulled him to a standing position. She dropped to her knees and unzipped his pants. As his pants fell to the floor, he stood before her, wearing only boxers.

Seeing his excited state, Ayla smiled. She pulled down his boxers and wrapped her hands around him, taking him into her mouth. Her hand began pistoning back and forth, her head moving in rhythm. When he groaned, nearing orgasm, she pushed him back onto the bed. Slipping off her panties, she climbed on top of him and placed him inside her.

They moved as one. As his orgasm welled within him, she moved her hips faster. His orgasm was long and deep. Expanding, it extended as she ground her hips against him.

When it was over, she collapsed to the bed. Side by side, they stared at the ceiling.

"That was great," he said.

"It was," she said, a touch of melancholy in her voice.

He turned. "Is everything okay?"

"Pretty much."

"What is it? The food? The room? I want to make you happy."

"You do, Iskender. I love your visits. I love this: talking, being together, but—"

"But what?"

"You never stay overnight," she said. "And the rest of the time, staying in this room by myself, it's getting to me." She lifted her leg and curled a finger beneath the cord around her ankle. The skin beneath the cord was red and irritated. "I want to make the best of this. I do, Iskender. I'm trying. But it would be nice to get out, to get some exercise, to have different clothes to wear."

He waved a hand toward the room. "This is only temporary. Trust me. Soon, everything will change."

"I do trust you. But I'm not asking to go out to dinner or to go shopping. I'd just like to get out of this room, get some fresh air." She pushed up onto an elbow. "You know what would be nice?"

"What?"

"When Betül was cleaning yesterday, she opened the window. I saw your gardens. They're beautiful. It would be nice to spend some time on the lawn, helping out with the gardening, walking with Betül."

He gave a thoughtful nod.

She reached out and ran her forefinger along his bottom lip. "I would find it rejuvenating, very rejuvenating." She kissed him, running the tip of her tongue slowly over his lip. "It's something you won't regret."

54

Ulus Beyram emerged from his office, chewing furiously on the stub of a cigar. It was Saturday night. The Yeni chairman had spent the day developing campaign strategies with five candidates for parliament. Tomorrow, he'd work with five more. With the elections approaching, a seven-day work week had become a necessity.

He passed the conference room and recalled the night of the celebration with Tunç. Although Tunç's week to accept their offer was not up, the Izmir businessman would not be receiving the Yeni's nomination. At the next council meeting, Beyram would persuade Agman and the others that Tunç wasn't ready for the presidency. It wouldn't be difficult.

Beyram stepped into the elevator. He'd seen too many men like Tunç. They didn't know the art of politics. They might make good generals, but they didn't make good governors. Every situation was all or nothing. They didn't understand compromise or negotiation and didn't know the importance of not making enemies. After elections, when their black-and-white worlds turned gray, the cracks in their rigid façades appeared.

At this point, there was no way to be sure what lay beneath Tunç's outer façade. But the other night in the conference room, he'd glimpsed it. It wasn't good. The agency they'd hired to vet Tunç had not found evidence of gross misconduct. Aristocrats like Tunç, however, always had their eccentricities. And when men like Tunç fell, after they'd wrought their havoc on the world, it was always up to men like himself to clean up the mess.

He emerged from the elevator onto the first floor and walked to the entrance. As he stepped outside, a fine blanket of mist washed over him.

A janitor was on a ladder, washing the windows above the door.

Snorting and spitting, the mist burning his nose, Beyram pulled a handkerchief from his pocket and wiped his face. "Thanks a lot," he yelled.

The janitor wore goggles and a mask along with a pair of headphones resonating with music. Oblivious to what he'd done, he continued squirting liquid onto the windows, his head bobbing in rhythm with the music.

Beyram climbed into his car and drove from the building, making a note to have the janitor fired on Monday. After two blocks, he stopped at a light.

The burning in his nose persisted. He opened the window, but the fresh air only made the burning worse. Cursing, he flicked his cigar through the open window.

"Samandarin."

A sleek, black four-door Mercedes had stopped next to him. Its rear window was rolled down. Iskender Tunç sat in the back, smirking. The bastard was supposed to be in Izmir.

"Samandarin," Tunç called out.

"*What*?"

"It's a neurotoxin produced by the fire salamander," Tunç said. "After the salamander is eaten, it secretes the toxin from its skin and kills its attacker."

Beyram shrugged. "Who cares?"

"You will, very shortly," Tunç said. "Like those who prey on the salamander, Ulus, you should be careful whom you try to devour. That sensation you're feeling is the neurotoxin. You were exposed to a lethal dose of it when you left your building. It's affecting your airway. The muscles in your throat are contracting, cutting off the flow of air into your lungs."

Beyram rolled up his window, more confident than ever in his decision to rescind the Yenis' nomination. The cracks in Tunç's façade were wide enough to drive his car through.

When the light turned green, Beyram accelerated ahead. In his rearview mirror, he saw Tunç's car pull to the side of the road. He would have smiled, taking consolation at the thought of Tunç having car trouble, but the burning in his nose had spread to his throat and chest. As he brought the car to a stop at the next intersection, he recalled Tunç's words.

Neurotoxin . . . lethal dose . . . airway.

He took a deep breath that was cut short by a sharp chest pain. The pain radiated to his shoulder.

He didn't know what was happening, but he couldn't just sit here. Başkent Hospital was only a block away.

Turning the wheel, he drove up onto the sidewalk. Pedestrians jumped aside, yelling as he passed. Avoiding a fire hydrant and then a street sign, he turned onto the intersecting road.

Başkent Hospital appeared in front of him. He jammed his foot down on the accelerator.

He was panting now, his breathing reduced to a high-pitched whistling.

The muscles in your throat are contracting, cutting off the flow of air into your lungs.

He tried to focus on the hospital, but the image began to blur. Unable to breathe, his chest pain unbearable, he slumped forward.

The Yeni chairman never saw the oncoming truck, never heard the horns, and never felt the impact.

55

Safiye paced in her cell. The morning trips to the river were wearing on her. But she couldn't show it. She couldn't show her humiliation, fatigue, or fear. They would only be taken as signs of weakness. And men like Basil preyed on weakness.

Michael appeared at the end of the corridor. He was followed by Basil and a young guard. Michael wore a clean T-shirt and shorts, his hair wet from the river. The bruising beneath his eyes had turned a greenish yellow. He briefly met her gaze before stepping into his cell.

When Basil opened her door, she walked briskly down the corridor and through the hanging vines. Six young guards waited outside. She walked past the guards onto the path.

At the river, she stepped into the cool, slow-moving water. With bare feet, she moved gingerly over the pebbled bottom. When the water was waist high, she immersed herself.

Basil and four of the young guards stood at the river's edge. As usual, they pretended to talk but mostly watched. She never met their gazes. Direct eye contact would be taken as a challenge or invitation, and she didn't want to extend either.

When she finished washing, she stepped onto the riverbank. She glanced at the camera mounted on the side of a nearby tree, wondering who was watching. Feeling the camera's and the guards' eyes on her, she focused on what was in front of her.

Fresh clothes and a towel had been set on the rock. She wrapped the towel around her waist. Beneath it, she slipped off her wet shorts and put on the clean pair. Draping the towel over her shoulders, she contorted her torso back and forth and removed her wet shirt, all the while covering herself with the towel. She slipped on the clean shirt over the towel, dropped the towel on the rock, and walked back along the path.

Basil stepped in front of her. Like Michael, the bruising beneath his eyes had faded. "Today, you and I are headed that way," he said, nodding in the opposite direction.

Safiye felt a stab of panic as she looked toward the others. They were returning to the cliff. She and Basil were being left alone. She tried to step around him, but he blocked her path. "This is nonnegotiable," he said. "I'll carry you if I have to."

She grudgingly turned and walked.

Basil pointed her past the river's bend onto a well-worn trail. "I don't know how you get out of your clothes like that," he said. "But it's impressive."

She didn't respond.

"It's not like I haven't seen what's beneath your towel," he continued. "But the boys haven't. When you get undressed next time, do it without the towel."

The trail intersected with another. Basil directed her ahead. "You're a beautiful woman. Your breasts are firm and succulent. I'd like to taste them, to taste you."

She wondered if he thought he was doing anything but making her sick. Making a loud hawking sound, she cleared her throat and spat on the trail.

Basil laughed. "Maybe I'll visit you tonight," he said, undeterred. "Your American friend can watch. He'll want to see how a Turkish man treats a woman."

They came to a break in the woods. There was a well-manicured lawn. Across the lawn, snuggled in the shadows of a wooded mountain, was a three-story house. The house, dark and Gothic, peered broodingly over the lawn.

They stepped onto the grass and walked toward the house. They passed a garden. Two women, cloaked in abayas, worked under the hot sun. The women straightened and looked toward them.

Safiye's attention, however, wasn't on the women. Her gaze was directed toward the house.

A young man sat on the back porch. As they approached, the man stood.

"Selamünaleyküm," Basil said. He placed his hand over his heart and bowed.

The man returned the gesture. "Aleykümselam," he responded.

Basil walked into the house, leaving her and the man alone.

A sheepish smile creased the man's face.

The last time she'd seen her brother, he'd been a skinny eighteen-year-old. His arms and shoulders now rippled with muscles.

"Beyir, what are you doing here?"

He motioned to the patio table, where plates of food had been set out. "Let me explain."

She didn't move.

"I know you're angry," he said. "You have a right to be, but I'm here to help you. I see a way out of this—for you and the American. Just listen to me. It'll help you understand what's happened. It will also help you understand me and Babasi."

"*Father*?"

Beyir pulled out a chair.

Safiye looked back across the lawn. Above the line of trees, the top of the stone cliff was visible. She walked to the table and sat.

"To be honest, I'm a little nervous," Beyir said, sitting in an adjacent chair. "I've been rehearsing this conversation for most of my life."

Beyir unfolded his cloth napkin and set it on his lap. He took a breath. "This is where I was sent when I was a boy. This is where I went to school and where our father went to school."

"This house?"

"There's a school beneath it—the Enderun. It's a school with a headmaster and teachers and classrooms."

Beyir told her the story of how the Janissaries had been reborn in a Kurdish village in southeastern Turkey. He told her how Muhammed Tunç had saved the orphans, educated them, and given them a purpose.

"Babası was one of these boys," she said. "A Kurdish orphan?"

"He was in the third class to graduate from the Enderun."

"And you've been here, at this Enderun, all this time?"

"I graduated six years ago. I've been in Istanbul for the past five years."

"That's where I've been. Why didn't you contact me?"

"It's complicated," he said. "The members of my graduating class were chosen for a great honor—to lead the Sayişma." As she stared back, he continued. "In the years since World War I, Islam has been carved into a myriad of fiefdoms—ineffectual bands of rogue nations left behind by the West. In the ancient struggle between Islam and Christianity, we've lost. The Sayişma is the Janissaries' attempt at reversing that. We hope to unify the Middle East into one Islamic state."

"An ISIL?"

Beyir shook his head. "Our movement will appeal to the common man. We're not terrorists. We're not extremists. We'll *unite* nations."

"And you think that's possible? Uniting Sunni and Shia. Uniting Persians and Arabs, Turks and Kurds?"

"If Islam is to succeed, we must. Think of it, Safiye. Atatürk exiled the sultan. He abolished the caliphate. The Islamic world has been without a leader for almost a century. Someone needs to take that back. Someone needs to lead."

When she didn't respond, Beyir clenched his fist. "This may not happen in my lifetime. But with all my heart, I believe it must."

"And what does your heart tell you about Turkish Sky? Is that part of your new state? You say you're not extremists, but I can't think of anything more extreme."

Beyir glanced at the house and spoke quietly. "Every movement has its less enviable aspects."

"And who is going to lead this Islamic state? Who is going to be this new caliph?"

As if in reply, the patio door slid open. Iskender Tunç stepped outside, a broad grin on his face. "Brother and sister reunited," he said. "It's heartwarming."

Beyir stood and bowed, clicking his heels together.

Safiye started forward, but Beyir stepped in front of her.

"How could you do this?" she yelled as her brother held her back. "Where are Mehmet and Ayla?"

Tunç ignored her questions. He instead patted Beyir on the shoulder. "Did your brother tell you? He's a hero—the sharp edge of the Sayişma's sword. He's the assassin of Generals Volkan and Refet."

Safiye looked up at her brother. "You *killed* them?"

"It was necessary," Beyir said.

"Is this also part of your Sayişma?"

Before Beyir could reply, she knocked his hand away and stepped toward Tunç. She froze when Tunç extended his hand. Between the tips of his right forefinger and thumb, he held an object—a ring containing a familiar princess-cut diamond.

"I kept it," Tunç said.

"*Why?*"

"Your brother said he knew a way for you to get out of this. This is it, Safiye. Marry me. Be my wife. Accept me as your husband."

"I once told you I'd rather die than marry you. After Kólpos Kallonís, I tried to tell you again. Nothing's changed."

Tunç motioned back toward the house. "Ayla will be here. She has already accepted my offer."

"Offer?"

"To marry me."

"She's already married."

A pained look crossed Tunç's face. "I'm sorry to be the one to deliver the bad news, but Mehmet had a heart attack. He died in Ankara."

Safiye looked at her brother, who nodded.

"It's very sad," Tunç said. "Ayla is in mourning, but she's recovering."

Safiye shook her head. "She'd never marry you."

"Oh, but she will," Tunç said.

"What makes you think I would marry you? That we both would?"

Tunç walked to the other side of the patio. He looked up into the sky, his hands behind his back. "The Quran says, 'Marry of the women that please you, two, three, or four, but if you fear you will not be able to deal justly with them, then only one.'" He turned. "Monogamy is a new and impractical construction of the West. Many of the companions of the Prophet practiced polygamy. Our greatest leader, Suleiman, had a harem with over 300 wives."

"You're sick."

"Think of your choices," Tunç said. "As your brother said, this is your only way out. I'll let your American doctor go back to Ann Arbor. You and Ayla can stay here. You'll live in luxury. You'll have servants. You'll want for nothing." Stepping toward her, he extended the ring.

Safiye stared back. She looked up at the house and then across the lawn before her gaze returned to Tunç. With a look of resignation, she extended her hand.

"Stay with me," Tunç said, setting the ring in her palm. "Give me time. Give us time. Our world is changing. Soon, everything will be possible."

She curled her fingers around the ring. It was still infused with the warmth of Tunç's hand. Raising her hand, she threw the ring as far as she could over the lawn.

Tunç stepped toward her but stopped when she grabbed a knife from the table. "You pig," she screamed. "*Marry you*? So you can drug me again, like you drugged Rabia? So you can rape and sodomize me again?"

She swung the knife at Tunç, but Beyir grabbed her wrist. He gave a quick twist and the knife popped into the air and clattered across the stone tiles.

The patio door opened. Two men ran outside and grabbed her. She thrashed wildly as they pinned her down.

Tunç stood over her, leering as she struggled beneath him.

"How can you follow this maniac?" she yelled at her brother.

Basil appeared in the doorway. He wore rubber gloves and held a bunched cloth in his fist. He walked toward her, but Beyir stepped in front of him.

Basil looked toward Tunç, who waved him off. "Tomorrow," Tunç said. "For now, take her back to her cell."

That evening, Ayla sat in her bedside chair, reading. Earlier, Edirne Kavas had given her a tour of the Enderun. While walking through the library, he'd given her a book—Ahmet Tanpınar's *A Mind at Peace.*

Ayla closed the book. She now understood why the headmaster had been so excited for her to read it. *A Mind at Peace* was about the turmoil caused by Atatürk's rapid transformation of Ottoman Turkey. Mümtaz, the protagonist, struggles to adapt as Atatürk's government pushes aside centuries of Ottoman culture. As Mümtaz falls apart in the new society, his mind is anything but at peace. For a man like Kavas, who'd chosen a life immersed in Ottoman culture, who'd chosen to become a eunuch and teach a new generation of Janissaries, the novel would be an anthem. The plight of Tanpınar's Mümtaz was justification for Kavas's decision to root himself in the past.

There was a knock at the door. Tunç stuck his head inside. "Ready?"

Ayla's stomach clenched as she wondered what Tunç had in store for her. She stood and held out her arms. "Do you like?" She wore a tight-fitting tank top and yoga pants, which he'd bought for her during his recent trip to Ankara. "And look." She lifted her foot. "No wire."

Tunç had given her permission to leave the room as long as she let Betül or Kaya know what she was doing.

"Let's go," he said. "There's not much light."

Outside, the sun was near the horizon. They walked across the lawn and then stepped onto a well-worn pathway that led into the woods.

"Your Enderun was impressive," Ayla said.

"I'm glad you were able to see it," Tunç said.

"The headmaster said many of the boys were at an offsite facility?"

"Yes, several kilometers from here. About fifteen years ago, we built a highly private school with dorms. We previously had to send the boys away for the last two years of secondary school so they could build the academic record needed to get into a military academy or university. Now, we don't have to."

They walked past a winding river and continued through the woods along the trail. The trail ended in a clearing in front of a stone cliff. Coming to a stop, Ayla stared up, stunned.

The yellow-red rays of light from the setting sun illuminated the side of the cliff. The cliff's façade was intricately carved into six stories—an ancient monastery.

"I wanted you to see it in the dusk," Tunç said. "The sun catches it at the perfect angle."

She'd visited similar monasteries cut from the soft rock of Cappadocia in central Turkey: the churches of Göreme and the Selime monastery. But this had more in common with the mountain monastery of Sumela in Trabzon—carved by Greek Orthodox monks in the fourth century AD.

"It's beautiful," she said.

"When I was a boy, I knew its passageways like the back of my hand." He looked into the woods. "I spent most of my summers here. They were magical. We used to run through the woods like a pack of wolves." He pointed to the monastery. "Would you like to see inside?"

"I'd love to."

He led her forward. At the cliff's base, she was startled to see two young men on a second-floor ledge. They sat motionless, watching them.

"No matter what you hear or who you see from this point on, you have to promise to be quiet," Tunç said.

She raised her hand. "Promise."

Beneath the young men was a vine-covered opening. Tunç led her through it. The vines fell into place behind them, blocking the light.

They walked slowly through the darkness, eventually coming to a stop.

Ahead, a faint ray of light shone through a round hole on the far side of a room. Hearing voices, Ayla recognized them—Michael and Safiye.

As Ayla's vision adjusted to the dark, she made out two inky-black shadows huddled on opposite sides of the room.

Tunç's hands were suddenly on her.

"What are you doing?" she whispered.

In reply, he pulled her tank top over her head.

"What about—"

"They're in cells," he whispered. "And the boys will stay outside unless I call them."

"We can go back to the bedroom. It'll be more comfortable."

He grabbed her hand and set it on his erection—his pants already down. "Put it in your mouth."

Ayla looked toward the two shadows. She knew what she had to do. Like Mehmet, she had to endure.

Leaning over, she did as Tunç commanded. After a couple minutes, he began tugging at her pants. "Lie down," he whispered.

She pulled off her pants and underwear and lay down on the stone floor.

Tunç entered her, groaning quietly with pleasure.

Unaware of what was happening, Michael and Safiye continued with their conversation, oblivious to Tunç's noises, oblivious to her shame.

When Tunç finished, he and Ayla dressed and walked down the darkened corridor.

Ayla listened to Michael's and Safiye's voices, cherishing them until they were gone.

56

The sun dipped below the horizon as Beyir sat in a dark-blue Zafer coupe outside a fast-food restaurant north of Ankara. Looking every bit the young executive unwinding after a long day, he'd unfastened the top button of his white cotton shirt and loosened his tie. With the car's windows down, he sipped cola from a plastic cup and listened to the news on the radio.

The assassinations in old Ankara and the subsequent fallout had dominated the recent news. In retaliation, President Cebici had attacked the culpable but innocent political left—the traditional enemies of the military. Fortuitously for Cebici, the left were also the most vocal critics of his burgeoning autocracy. At Cebici's order, dozens of members of leftist parties had been detained and questioned. Several had been jailed.

"It's been one week since the two doctors from the World Health Organization left University Hospital and didn't return," the newscaster said. "The leader of the city's search team reports there have been no leads regarding the doctors' whereabouts. In other news—"

Beyir turned off the radio. Yesterday had been a disaster. He'd heard rumors of what Basil and some older Enderun students had done to Rabia at the night of the party in Teos. Had Tunç also drugged Safiye? Had he raped and sodomized her? Given Tunç's lack of denial, he had to believe his sister was telling the truth. It would explain the broken engagement and Safiye's years of unrelenting hatred.

He picked up a palm-size walkie-talkie from the passenger seat and tapped the power light. The light remained on, unblinking.

After the Janissaries walked in slow procession from Savon's burial back into the Enderun, Edirne Kavas had given the Kazans their next assignment. Their target was Volkan's replacement as *başkomutan*, General Hamza Kayseri.

That very night, Beyir and the Kazans had driven to Ankara. Knowing they had days instead of months to strike, they threw themselves into an intense but abbreviated study of their subject, hoping what they lacked in preparation would be offset by the inexperience of their target. Despite the risks, they placed a continuous tail on Kayseri.

Almost immediately, the tail paid off. In the early evening of their first day of surveillance, Kayseri's limousine left the command center and traveled to the Yükselen—the general's old military prep school north of Ankara. As the Kazans circled the facility with binoculars, they spotted Kayseri jogging around the track in the school's stadium. The general had returned every night since.

On the passenger seat of the coupe, the walkie-talkie crackled to life. "Merhaba."

The call meant Kayseri had left the command center and was on his way to the Yükselen.

"Burada," Beyir responded. He threw his uneaten food into a garbage can and drove from the restaurant.

Instead of relief the call had finally come, he was filled with apprehension, his mind teeming with a myriad of variables. With longing, he recalled his confidence while sitting in the second-floor room of the rented house in old Ankara, certain of the sequence of events and the outcome. Now, as if he were launching himself into the first act of an unrehearsed play, his vision of the finale was more wish than foregone conclusion.

Two minutes later, he pulled the coupe off the road. He drove deep into the woods and parked at the base of a hill.

It was dark now. Exchanging his leather shoes for a pair of black tennis shoes, he slipped on a black pullover and jogged to the top of the hill. He came to an abrupt stop as the open end of the Yükselen's horseshoe-shaped stadium came into view.

The stadium lights were on. The stands were full. Athletes dressed in blue or gold jerseys swarmed the pitch. It was a soccer match.

They'd been too focused on Kayseri's comings and goings. They'd forgotten to check the Yükselen's schedule.

"One," Beyir said to himself, counting the first unforeseen variable.

Beyir scanned his surroundings. He was well hidden by the trees and darkness. They would have to try another time, but there would be no harm in waiting.

He reached underneath a fallen tree and pulled out a leather case. He removed the Turkish JNG-90 rifle. It was the same rifle he'd used in old Ankara but without the silencer. The silencer had added too much scatter to his shot plots. The inconsistency had been tolerable for old Ankara but not here. This shot was longer: 1,200 meters, -0.8 degrees. He wanted to be closer. At the open end of the horseshoe-shaped stadium, however, a fence swung widely around a grassy field. From every other direction, the track was surrounded by stands. A shot from another location would be impossible.

Beyir settled in behind the rifle, resting the barrel on a fallen tree. He took several deep breaths. Feeling his heart slow, his hand steady, he curled his finger around the trigger. He'd decided to take the shot when Kayseri was jogging on the track's straightaway, approaching the nearest turn. The general would be running directly at him, motionless in two dimensions.

He pulled the trigger. The rifle's hammer clicked into an empty chamber.

After a few more practice shots, he swiveled the rifle toward the stands—a swarming sea of blue and yellow banners.

To Beyir's surprise, Kayseri came immediately into view. The general stood in the first row to the right, leaning forward and clapping.

Of course. The newly appointed *başkomutan* would be front and center, the guest of honor at his old military school.

Beyir snapped a bullet into the chamber. By the time he looked back through the scope, however, Kayseri had sunk into the row of spectators.

The first row of stands ran a few degrees from parallel with the barrel of the gun. With the general sitting midway down the straightaway, the shot would be longer than planned. Beyir turned the adjustment on the scope. When Kayseri appeared again, he would fire.

Beyond cheers from the stadium, he heard the ambient sounds of the woods. A soft wind blew through the trees. Squirrels ran across beds of dry leaves. His senses, as they had in old Ankara, were coming alive as the moment drew nearer. He tried to block out the noises. But when he heard the distinct snap of a twig, he turned.

Someone was walking from the hill's crest toward him. It must be one of the Kazans. They'd know about the soccer match by now and would be wondering what he was doing. When the figure stepped into the stadium light, however, Beyir saw it wasn't a Kazan. It was one of the cadets.

"Two," he whispered, tallying another unforeseen variable.

The boy stopped several feet away, his cherubic face directed toward the stadium. A harness crisscrossed his uniformed chest. The butt of a flare gun protruded from his holster.

The boy stood, looking toward the stadium. His walkie-talkie suddenly crackled. "Cadet Yakup, I see your motorbike, but it's unoccupied."

"Three," Beyir mouthed.

The boy, hands shaking, pulled the walkie-talkie from his harness. "Captain, I found an unoccupied car in the woods. I decided to search the hill."

"I don't see a car."

"It's there, sir. Behind the underbrush. Dark blue."

"Are you watching the match?"

"No, Captain."

"If you see something unusual during your rounds—anything causing you to leave your designated route—you're required to report it," the captain said. "Otherwise, we'll have to list you as being truant. I believe you know what that means."

A roar came from the stadium.

Beyir looked through the scope. Gold banners were waving. The Yükselen had scored. From the first row of bleachers, Kayseri stepped forward, fist raised—the crosshairs on his chest.

Realizing he didn't have a choice, that it had to be now, Beyir pulled the trigger.

The sound from the unmuffled shot blasted through the trees. With an average muzzle velocity of 1,200 meters per second, the bullet would take just over a second to travel the distance to the target. But Beyir didn't have a second. He hopped to his feet.

The cadet had dropped his walkie-talkie. He was fumbling for his flare gun.

"I'm sorry, my friend," Beyir said, before striking the cadet in the nose.

The boy fell back, unconscious.

"Cadet Yakup," the walkie-talkie crackled. "That sounded like a gunshot."

Beyir strode to the hill's crest. He snapped another bullet into the rifle's chamber. Leaning against a tree, he raised the rifle.

A military police car was parked on the side of the road next to a motorbike. A uniformed man crouched behind the driver's side door. His face, as well as his raised pistol, intermittently appeared as he peeked up toward the hill, his voice sounding from the cadet's distant walkie-talkie.

"Cadet Yakup . . . *Cadet Yakup.*"

Beyir assessed the distance and adjusted the scope. Taking a deep breath, he curled his finger around the trigger and waited for the captain to reappear.

57

London

Jonathan Fontaine, an intelligence analyst in the CIA's Piccadilly office, turned on his office computer. It was Monday evening. He'd spent most of the day in meetings, last checking his messages at noon. He input the week's passwords and activated the encryption programs, rubbing his eyes as his messages downloaded. The night before, he'd been out late with friends—a pub crawl through Leicester Square.

Three unread reports appeared in his inbox. He read the first two reports, which were from case officers overseeing operatives in Jerusalem and Tehran. He moved the reports into working files. The third message was a report from Paul Aurelius—the CIA station chief in Istanbul.

To: europeanop@cia.london
From: paurelius@cia.istanbul
Re: 245. Op Bin 39902. Director's eyes only.
Ankara/Embassy_BD.
London,
Was contacted by SVR Istanbul chief regarding their surveillance of Iskender Tunç, CEO of Izmir's Tunç Corporation. Surveillance was initiated after managers from one of Tunç Corporation's subsidiaries, EMİN Corporation, were linked to the disappearance of 300 kilograms of stolen

```
weapons-grade  plutonium  (see  attachment  #1).
The SVR turned over progress reports and photos
obtained  during  surveillance  (see  attachment
#2). They believe we have a common objective.
```

Fontaine highlighted the name of Iskender Tunç and hit a function key. The screen went blank except for the flashing words: "Accessing data files."

He sat back and waited while the computer made a transatlantic link, submitting the name into the CIA's voluminous Langley database. Seconds later, the screen began scrolling down with entries, ending with the message: "283 items found."

Fontaine looked at his watch. "Damn."

Tonight, there'd be no visits to Leicester Square.

58

Ayla sat in the chair by the corner vanity table. She stared at herself in the oval mirror. Everything that had happened—to Rabia, to Mehmet, to Michael and Safiye, and to her—originated from a single mistake. That single mistake, that single moment had shaped everything since, turning into thirteen years of lies.

"Why isn't Safiye coming?" Rabia asked. "I can't imagine her missing *this* party."

Ayla was driving her car. Rabia sat in the passenger seat, talking at her usual frenetic pace. They were on their way to Iskender's graduation party.

"She said she's not feeling well," Ayla said.

"Does Iskender know she isn't coming? Are they fighting?"

"Not as far as I know."

Cars were spilling out onto the street by the time they arrived at Tunç's sprawling two-story beach house. They parked and walked up the estate's long winding driveway.

"Can you imagine living in this place?" Rabia asked.

"No, but I wouldn't mind trying," Ayla said.

The party had a Mongolian theme. The young men wore warrior outfits. The young women wore silk robes.

Iskender greeted them at the front door with a tray of drinks. "Where's Safiye?" he asked.

"She's not feeling well," Rabia said.

"You saw her last night, didn't you?" Ayla said. "How was she?"

Iskender shrugged, extending the tray. "Fine."

The girls each took cups of a white glistening liquid. "What is it?" Rabia asked.

"*Airag* or mare's milk," Iskender said.

They sipped the drinks.

"It tastes funny," Rabia said.

Iskender grinned. "It's *fermented* mare's milk."

Ayla took another sip. The strong, metallic-tasting drink made her feel warm inside.

In the estate's main hall, a dance floor had been set up. Ayla and Rabia mixed with friends. Iskender eventually came by with another tray of drinks. "I didn't think you drank," he said when Ayla took a second cup.

"I do," she lied.

They turned toward Rabia. Also holding her second cup, she was in the middle of a small circle of young men. Not accustomed to the alcohol and even less to the attention, Rabia was glowing under the influence of both. She looked over at them and raised her drink, contorting her face into a silly smile.

"Who are they?" Ayla asked.

Iskender shook his head. "Nobody."

The stereo grew louder. As the crowded room began to pulsate, everyone began dancing. Iskender set down the tray and pointed to the dance floor. "Do you want to?"

Ayla took a drink and then nodded.

They joined in. The volume increased. Everyone raised their arms and jumped in rhythm with the music. The lights went off, but the music and dancing continued. When the music finally ended and the jumping stopped, the room remained dark.

Ayla felt Iskender's arms encircle her. She didn't move, her heart thudding. "Would you like to take a walk?" he whispered.

Feeling the warmth of his breath in her ear, she couldn't remember something ever feeling so good. "I don't think Safiye would approve."

"She doesn't have to know."

When Ayla turned to protest, their lips met.

"Let's go," he said, taking her hand.

It was still dark. No one could see them. No one would know.

She let him pull her from the hall and out of the house. On the beach, they walked hand in hand. Once the house had disappeared behind a dune, they fell onto the sand and kissed. Soon, he was moving down her body, his fingers touching, probing.

"We shouldn't," she said.

Iskender lifted her robe and slid off her panties. She wanted to object. Instead, she lay on the sand, her head back, Iskender's tongue flickering and hot. She stared at the stars, unable to stop him, not wanting to.

An unfamiliar sensation began working its way through her body. The sensation built, encompassing her until it felt as though he'd pushed her over the side of a cliff. Overcome, she fell, tumbling, landing softly. "Iskender," she said, out of breath. She reached for him, but he was over her, inside her.

Drained of energy, she looked skyward again. But the stars that should have been visible beyond Iskender's shoulder were blocked from view. As she blinked, trying to focus, she saw a shadowed figure standing over them.

"*Iskender?*"

It was a female voice. No, it couldn't be.

"Iskender."

It was Safiye.

He turned. "What?"

Safiye shrieked. She stumbled back, falling into the sand. Climbing to her feet, she ran toward the house.

Meanwhile, Iskender continued, his body pistoning.

"Iskender," Ayla said. "That was Safiye."

He didn't stop.

"That was Safiye," she repeated. She pushed back at him but to no avail.

When he finished, he rolled off her. "That makes it easier."

"Easier? *For what?*"

"For us."

"There is no *us*," she said. "Safiye's your fiancée."

"And your best friend." He laughed. "At least, she was."

Ayla slipped on her panties. She ran to the house, where she searched for Safiye and Rabia. Not finding them, she drove home.

That night, she lay awake, wracked with guilt. In the morning, there was a knock at her bedroom window. It was Rabia.

The three girls, who lived only a few blocks apart, often visited one another in this way. As Ayla opened the window, however, she could see this visit was far from routine.

Rabia crawled through the window, still wearing her robe from the night before. Almost hysterical, Rabia told her what had happened. She hadn't left the party with Safiye. She hadn't left the party at all. During the night, she'd passed out. When she woke, she was strapped to a bed. A boy was on top of her. After he finished, another took his place and then another—all boys she didn't know.

"Where were you?" Rabia asked, breaking down. "Why did you leave me?"

Ayla hugged her. "I thought you'd gone home with Safiye."

"She was there?"

"Yes, she—"

The bedroom door swung open. Safiye appeared. She began yelling.

To Ayla's relief, Safiye's contempt wasn't directed at her. It was directed at Rabia. Safiye accused Rabia of being with Iskender.

"I didn't do that," Rabia said, horrified. "I—I wouldn't."

"I saw you," Safiye screamed.

Rabia tried to explain what had happened, but Safiye wouldn't listen.

"You weren't tied down," Safiye said. "You were on the beach. You were enjoying it. You called out his name."

For thirteen years, Ayla had pushed aside the guilt of Rabia's death. The guilt had remained dormant, a small rotting nidus walled off into a remote corner of her subconscious. Now, the guilt spread, overwhelming her.

Still in front of the mirror, Ayla stared at the reflection of the bed's rumpled sheets. She deserved these nights with Tunç. She deserved the humiliation, the—

"Dear, it's time for our walk." Betül stood behind her, tapping her shoulder.

Ayla tried to focus on the old woman's reflection.

"If you want, we can stay here," Betül said.

Ayla had endured too much for this. "I—I'm okay," she said.

"You don't look well," Betül said. "Maybe—"

"I'm fine."

Ayla stood and together they walked from the room, down the stairs, and out onto the patio.

Men had arrived at the estate the day before. They were the men everyone had been preparing for. Mostly elderly, they wore turbans and robes and sat on the lawn in varying states of meditation and prayer. A few broke from their thoughts long enough to glare unapprovingly at Ayla's yellow silk dress—another one of Iskender's recent purchases.

"Who are they?" Ayla asked.

"I don't know," Betül replied.

"I don't like them," Ayla said. "And I don't think Iskender cares for them either."

"No. He doesn't."

When they reached the gardens, Betül picked a dandelion from a clump of acanthus.

"Iskender said he spent his summers here as a child," Ayla said.

"Yes," Betül said, straightening. "Whatever childhood he had, it was here."

"What happened to his mother?"

The old woman directed a forlorn look toward the house. "She died giving birth to Iskender."

"That's terrible. Did you know her?"

Betül nodded. "Her name was Adelina. Iskender was her first and only child."

During Ayla's tour of the Enderun, Kavas had told her Betül and Kaya were brought here to be Muhammed's wives. Presumably, it was the same with Adelina.

"Did you have children?" Ayla asked.

Betül opened her palm and stared at the crumpled dandelion. For a moment, Ayla thought she'd pushed the old woman too far, but then Betül spoke, her tone unexpectedly light. "I had five children. Four girls and a boy."

"Where do they live?"

Betül shrugged.

"Do you see them?"

"They're all grown. The girls went away when they were babies."

"You were separated?" Ayla asked.

"It was for the best." Betül looked toward the men on the lawn. "This isn't a good place for girls."

"And the boy?"

"The youngest," Betül said, suddenly beaming. "He went to school here but left a long time ago. His name is Cemil. They tell me he's in the military now."

Ayla looked toward the house. "What was it like?"

"What do you mean?"

"Being married to Muhammed . . . living in a harem?"

Betül tossed the dandelion aside. "You have to understand, I was from Dohuk, a small town in Iraq. When I was a little girl, my family was killed during a bombing. For almost a decade, I lived in an orphanage before I was brought here with Kaya. We were Muhammed's fourth and fifth wives. Adelina came later."

"How old were you?"

"Fourteen," Betül said. "Considering the alternatives, I was fortunate."

"And you stayed after Muhammed's death?" Ayla asked.

"This is my home. It's where I've always lived. It's where I'm needed."

The women finished their walk through the gardens before returning to the patio. Kaya had breakfast waiting.

"Thank you for my time outside," Ayla said. "It means so much."

"I'm glad things are working out for you," Betül said. She looked toward the house. "For both of you."

Ayla followed the old woman's gaze to a third-floor window. Iskender stood framed in the window, staring down with pride.

"I've never seen him happier," Betül said. "You're a big part of that."

59

unç stood at his study window. He watched as Ayla walked with Betül toward the house. His thoughts were of the night before.

He and Ayla were in her bedroom, undressing. Ayla slipped off her wedding ring—a simple gold band—and set it on the nightstand. "Considering everything," she said. "The past few nights. Us. It seems right."

He reached into his shirt pocket. He'd been planning on doing this later, but the timing was an omen. He set Safiye's ring on the nightstand. His men had found it after she'd thrown it onto the lawn.

"It's beautiful," Ayla said. "But I *am* still married."

Thirteen years earlier, after their time on the beach, he thought they'd be together. But Ayla had spent the summer studying in Istanbul. In the fall, he'd left for two years of school in Paris. He'd always been attracted to Ayla, but something had always stood between them: Safiye, school, and then Mehmet.

"I'm sorry," he said. "But something happened . . . in Ankara."

Over the past several days, a myriad of unspoken truths had passed between them. This was one of them.

Ayla looked down at the gold band. "What?"

"They found him on a park bench. The cause of death was listed as a heart attack."

Ayla pressed her eyes closed, but tears squeezed through. They were understandable. Mehmet was her husband.

It was a few moments before Ayla spoke. "When he went to Ankara, I thought something might happen."

"You knew he was going?"

She nodded.

"Do you know why?"

"Little Tortona," she said. "I encouraged him to meet with you. I told him he should try to work it out with you, that you'd be reasonable."

"I thought we had worked everything out. We got rid of Little Tortona. I told him to forget it existed. He said he would, but he still went to Ankara."

Ayla glared up at him. "You did what?"

"We got rid of Little Tortona."

"*How?*"

"Does it matter? It's gone," he said.

"I wish I had known. I would have told him not to go. I wouldn't have gone."

"To city hall?"

"Yes," she said.

"Mehmet wanted you to turn over his information packet. Did you know what was in it?"

She met his gaze. "Yes."

"Does it bother you? The information about me?"

"It does. But with everything that's going on in the world, it seems trivial. I told Mehmet to meet with you, to try to work it out. But he was so—"

"Idealistic."

"Yes," she said. "He couldn't see our lives were perfect. We had the house, the cottage, money, security. He had his research. And it was all because of you." She looked at him, her eyes questioning. "You got *rid* of Little Tortona?"

"By the time Mehmet showed up on Monday morning, it was gone. I told him he could keep his lab. He could continue his research."

"And he still went to Ankara?" she asked.

"All he had to do was forget Little Tortona existed."

Ayla stood on the patio. Her dress, yellow and flowing, caught the morning sun, giving an ethereal glow. Beyond the glow, Tunç saw contentment—here and with him.

Ayla waved. When he'd left her room this morning, the diamond ring had been on the dresser next to the gold band. As she now moved her fingers back and forth, the diamond sparkled, catching the morning sun.

He smiled.

Ayla knew exactly what had led them to this place and time. Despite everything, they'd been able to share the last week. The look in her eyes told him she was prepared to share much more.

As Ayla and Betül disappeared into the house, his gaze moved across the lawn. Kavas was leading the men toward the Enderun's entrance. The pieces of the puzzle were falling into place.

He returned to his desk and continued working. A few minutes later, his phone rang. "They're in the room," Kavas said.

Tunç took the back stairs down into the Enderun. He walked through the hallways to a closed door. After a quick knock, he stepped inside.

The twelve robed men were seated around a table.

"Hello, Iskender," said Ali Gazi, the eldest.

"Ali," Tunç said, bowing. "I hope you and your council are enjoying your stay."

"Everything has been perfect, Iskender, more than perfect," Gazi said.

The others nodded.

"As I said when you arrived, I'm honored this year's meeting of the Muqaddim council is being held at my estate," Tunç said. "My staff and I are at your service."

"Thank you," Gazi said. "It's nice to finally see your father's Enderun. He guarded its location as if lives depended on it. From the many young men we've seen roaming the hallways, I see why."

"The Enderun held a special place in my father's heart," Tunç said.

"And it's because of respect for your father and appreciation of our shared goals that we turned over our electronic devices," Gazi said.

"I apologize for any inconvenience," Tunç said. "But it's imperative we do everything we can to maintain the privacy of the Enderun."

"These steps were unnecessary," Gazi said. "But the brief

sabbatical from a twenty-four-seven news cycle has been rejuvenating." The council members nodded their agreement.

Once again, Tunç bowed his head in appreciation.

"Before I forget," Gazi said. "I'd like to remind you of our meeting's keynote address. Omër will be speaking tonight on the state of the theocracy in Iran."

Tunç turned toward Omër Gazi, Ali's oldest son. "In the auditorium. I look forward to it."

Omër stared back through a perpetual glaze of serenity.

"I'm glad you're here," the elder Gazi said. "We would be interested in knowing your opinion regarding an idle question we were discussing."

Tunç raised an eyebrow. There was nothing idle about the Muqaddim leader.

"With regard to the great Ottoman Empire, who contributed more to its success, the caliph or the sultan?" Gazi asked. "The caliph, as the successor of Muhammad and leader of Islam? Or the sultan, as a member of the dynastic House of Osman and ruler of the Ottoman Empire?"

Tunç smiled. "You're right. It does seem idle."

The council members laughed.

From the time Sultan Selim Khan assumed the caliphate in the early sixteenth century until the collapse of the Ottoman Empire four centuries later, the two positions were incarnate within one being.

"Amuse me," Gazi said. "Which posting raised the empire to a higher position?"

"From the viewpoint of the soldier or the cleric?" Tunç asked. "Between them, the question could be endlessly debated."

"From *your* viewpoint."

Tunç considered the question for a moment and then spoke. "The positions were synergistic. They served each other to raise the Exalted, and thereby the empire, to greater deeds and higher esteem."

Gazi smiled. "That's why you'll make such a good politician. But since this is a purely academic exercise, I beg you—pick one."

All eyes turned to Tunç. "The sultanate," he said.

"The sultanate," Gazi repeated, nodding reassuringly to the others.

Tunç had stepped into the cleric's trap but only with the intention of biting his captor. "Any sway the caliph exerted came from the pulpit of the sultan," he said. "One only has to look to when Sultan Selim Khan took the caliphate from the Mamluks in Cairo and ended their line. Religious fervor, although admirable, amounts to nothing in the face of superior military force."

"Don't forget," Omër said from the other end of the table, his voice emotionless and flat. "There is no greater force than God. All power comes from him. The power men and governments hold is only temporal. Selim Khan and his line are no more, while Allah's followers live on."

"Yes, but your father asked about the days of the *great* Ottoman Empire," Tunç said. "They were great because the Ottomans used their power to do incredible things. Without the power of the Ottomans and the sultanate, the caliphate no longer exists. Atatürk stripped the sultanate from Abdülmecid II and left him with the caliphate. Abdülmecid's subsequent twenty-year exile from Turkey shows the utility of the caliphate without the sultanate. Abdülmecid died in obscurity."

"We should know not to engage a Tunç in debate," Gazi said. "Like your father, you're very stubborn."

"I'll take that as a compliment," Tunç said.

Gazi continued. "The sultanate was man's creation, not God's. It is written Allah will place his caliph among us. Proper *deen* must be shown to Allah by recognizing his chosen one."

"And I'm the stubborn one?" Tunç said. "I ask you, are we arguing over the way things should be . . . or the way they are? Religious dogma is impotent without the power to enforce it. History has taught us that."

Gazi, unaccustomed to being challenged, cleared his throat. "Let me ask you, Iskender. If, or should I say *when*, a new caliph is appointed, should it be someone who has devoted his life to the Quran and the teachings of Abraham?"

All eyes moved to Omër. Gazi's son had spent the last six years studying under the ayatollahs in Iran. Since arriving at the estate, he'd dressed too extravagantly, wearing iridescent pearl-white robes when plainer ones would do. Tunç now understood why.

The Muqaddim had provided Tunç with access to the inner sanctums of Turkey's leading Islamic political parties. It had been here where he'd cut his deals to consolidate the religious vote in the upcoming election. He knew Ali Gazi would have a price for his services. That price was finally clear.

"The caliph should be someone who shows deen to God and the values of Islam," Tunç said. "But I'm sure you're aware of my opinion regarding the caliphate. Decisions with respect to the caliphate will come *after* the Sayişma."

By appointing a caliph without first establishing a power base, the Muqaddim were trying to reverse the natural order of things. Tunç would be the leader of the Sayişma and what came afterward. If the caliphate were to exist again, it would be his right to assume it.

"Yes," Gazi said. "We can wait to announce the new caliph. When that time comes, however, the decision will be mine. As the Yeni nominee, you'll become Turkey's next president. But Omër will be caliph. As a man of God, as a Sunni who has the blessing of the Shia ayatollahs, Omër is in best position to establish a Middle Eastern coalition and unite Islam's 1.6 billion worshippers."

Ayla walked quickly up the stairs. In her room, she slipped from the yellow dress and picked up her tank top. She turned it inside out, exposing a hidden pocket she'd sewn using the supplies from the women's desk.

She removed an envelope from beneath her mattress and slipped it into the pocket. Putting on the tank top and the pair of yoga pants, she checked her profile in the mirror. The bump in the small of her back was hardly noticeable.

Ayla walked from the room and down the back stairs. In the empty kitchen, she grabbed a key from a nail by the rear door.

Two days earlier, as she worked in the kitchen, one of the young men took the key before leaving the house. She'd asked Kaya what he was doing. "Visiting your friends," the cook said. "Letting them out for a while."

Ayla palmed the key and stepped onto the patio. Betül and Kaya had taken off their face veils and were eating breakfast. "Where did they go?" she asked.

The lawn was empty. The robed men were gone.

"They've disappeared into the Enderun," Kaya said.

"That's a good thing," Betül said. "I don't think Iskender would approve of your wearing your outfit with all those men around."

"She'll only be young once," Kaya said. "And with a figure like that, I wouldn't hide it either."

Ayla gave the cook a kiss on the forehead. "Thank you." She looked back and forth at the old women. "You should consider going without your veils more often. You're both very pretty."

Kaya winked. "With all these young men around, they'd never leave us alone."

The two old women looked at one another and giggled.

With a shake of her head, Ayla retreated from the patio, hiding the bump in the small of her back.

As the old women's attention returned to their plates, Ayla turned and jogged across the lawn. She listened for shouts of protest but heard none.

She ran onto a trail. Once the trail had brought her even with the far end of the lawn, she glanced back.

The old women remained at the table. Fooling Iskender had been difficult. Fooling the women had been even harder. Both possessed a profound maternal instinct toward Iskender. Despite her attempts to appear friendly, they'd maintained a scrutinizing eye.

Ayla continued along the path, aware of the tree-mounted cameras looking down at her. The trail led her deep into the woods. At the branch point, she ran straight ahead along the same path she'd taken during her previous morning's run. In a break between the cameras, she removed the envelope from the small of her back. She dropped the key into it.

From the envelope, Ayla removed a tan ribbon—another item from the old women's desk. She picked up a softball-sized rock from the ground. Folding the envelope over the rock, she tied the ribbon around them and then sprinted ahead.

The trail opened after a few hundred meters in front of an uncut portion of the cliff. Without breaking stride, she flipped the assembly through a round hole carved from the rock. Continuing along the cliff's curving façade, she stopped in front of the monastery.

Two guards sat on the ledge above the vine-covered opening. They were different from those who'd been here the previous two days but were still perfect. Each looked like he was about nineteen.

"Hi," she gasped, her chest heaving as she tried to catch her breath.

The guards dropped to the ground.

"Just passing by," Ayla said. She raised her arms above her head and stretched, forcing herself to smile as the young guards' eyes passed boldly over her. "The monastery is so fascinating." She looked at the façade. "Have you been up there?"

Without waiting for a response, Ayla grabbed one of the guards by the hand and tugged him toward a ladder. Skipping ahead, she began climbing.

On the second floor, she walked along the narrow ledge to the next ladder and continued her way up the façade. She moved nimbly from one floor to the next. When she reached the highest ledge, she glanced back.

The guards, a few floors beneath her, were following.

She walked down a dark corridor. At the end of the corridor, she turned into a room. It was surprisingly well lit. Shafts of light shone through vent holes in the ceiling.

In the middle of the room was a stone table. Walking to it, she turned and waited.

60

allahan and Safiye stood by their cell doors. Three minutes earlier, an object had flown through the rear window of the cave and clattered across the floor into Safiye's cell. She unraveled a tan ribbon from the object to find an envelope folded over a rock. The envelope contained a stack of Turkish lira, a key, and a note from Ayla.

Michael and Safiye, after you receive this, wait exactly three minutes and then leave.

"Go ahead," Callahan said, looking at his watch.

Safiye reached through the bars and slid the key into the lock. As she turned the key, the door swung open.

Safiye opened Callahan's cell door. They ran to the end of the corridor and peered through the vines.

The clearing was empty. The guards, their legs dangling from their usual position on the second-floor ledge, were gone.

You have to hurry. There are cameras everywhere. Once you're out, they'll know. They won't be far behind.

They ran to their right along the cliff's curving façade. Spotting a trail, they turned into the woods. When the trail ended, they continued, weaving in and out of the trees.

Keep the sun behind you.

As they ran, they glanced back frequently, hoping Ayla would join them. With each passing tree, however, that hope diminished.

Twenty minutes later, they emerged from the woods, gasping for air. In front of them was a gravel road.

Travel along the road to the right to a bus stop. A bus is scheduled to stop at 9:07 and every half hour after. Be careful. By now, they'll know you're gone.

Ayla lay on the stone table, staring up into the dust-flecked shafts of sunlight. She was surprised at how removed she was from the room and the two sweat-slicked guards taking their turns above her.

Shouts from the clearing echoed down the corridor. In a panic, the young guards backed away and ran from the room.

Ayla allowed herself a smile. Her plans, conceived only days earlier as she stood in the old women's room, had worked. She would disappear into the woods and head in the opposite direction from which she'd sent Michael and Safiye, toward a different bus stop. She'd fooled the old women. She'd fooled Tunç. She'd won.

She looked at her watch. The next bus would stop in twenty-five minutes. As she sat up, however, she realized she'd never make that stop.

Basil stood above her. His hand raised, he swung.

When Ayla regained consciousness, Basil was on her. He reached for her breast and ran his forefinger over her nipple. The skin on his fingers—calloused, cracked, and dry—felt like sandpaper. She wanted to push him off her, to scream, but she lay paralyzed, her head throbbing.

"There you are," he said, seeing she was conscious. "I was hoping you'd be awake for this." He lingered over her, his breath foul. "You didn't think your friends would escape, did you? They were spotted by our cameras once they stepped into the clearing. I'm sure they've been caught by now."

She shoved weakly at his chest. As Basil thrust into her, he looked down at her hand and laughed. She pulled it away, realizing her resistance was only exciting him more.

"Even your friend put up more of a fight, and she was drugged," Basil said. "What was her name? *Rabia*?" He grinned, his tongue pulsing through the gap between his yellowing teeth. "Yes, I was there that night. I fucked her. We were too young for your party, but we were in the shadows, seven of my classmates and me, watching and waiting."

He pressed his lips against her cheek, his weight crushing. "Rabia was the first. The first for all of us. She was a whore." He licked her cheek. "Like you."

There was a snapping sound—her rib breaking. Her scream, however, only served to increase the intensity of his thrusts.

She looked up into the shafts of sunlight and tried to let her mind drift. But this time, her thoughts remained fixed on the room and the beast moving within her.

Just when she thought it would never end, Basil's eyes rolled into the back of his head. Grunting, he gave several more uncoordinated thrusts into her before climbing from the table.

Summoning her energy, Ayla rolled from the table and dropped to the stone floor. She landed hard on her shoulder. Ignoring the pain coursing through her side, her head, her entire body, she grabbed her tank top and stood.

"I'll tell the boys you're waiting for them," Basil said, pulling up his pants. "Like Rabia, you'll be the first for a whole new generation."

"I'm next."

The driver stood in the hallway, watching and smiling. "You didn't think I was going to let you have all the fun," he said.

"Hurry up," Basil said, leaving the room. "I'm heading back."

Ayla held her tank top in front of her.

"It's a little late for modesty," the driver said.

Ayla, accepting her fate, let her arms drop. The tank top fell to the floor.

"That's good," the driver said, his eyes fixing on her breasts. "Let's make this as enjoyable as possible."

As he reached for her, Ayla swung—the old women's razor blade pinched between her fingers. The blade cut deep.

A wave of blood poured from the driver's neck. He fell to his knees, clutching his throat.

Ayla ran from the room. In the corridor, Basil was just stepping onto the ledge—his frame silhouetted by the carved stone columns of the portico.

"Have I told you?"

Mehmet's voice came to her.

"You mean more to me than the earth and stars."

She took a step forward and then another and began running down the corridor.

"I love you."

Hearing her approach, Basil turned, but it was too late.

Ayla let the blade fall from her hand. Looking beyond Basil's silhouette, she took it all in: the trees, the sky, the sun.

"I love you. I lo—"

Beyir jolted awake. He was in the Enderun's bunk room. He'd heard something. The only sound, however, was the ever-present hum from the ventilation system.

Last night, after he'd taken down Kayseri, he and his fellow Kazans had driven from the Yükselen back to the estate. After arriving in the early-morning hours, they'd gone immediately to the bunk room and fallen asleep.

Beyir looked around the room. The Kazans were still sleeping. The other beds had emptied.

He heard the noise again and recognized the squeak of tennis shoes. One of the boys sprinted into the room. "Your sister," he said, breathless. "She escaped."

Wearing sweatpants and a T-shirt, Beyir pulled on tennis shoes and ran from the room.

Edirne Kavas stood outside a conference room. He motioned for Beyir to stop, holding a finger to his lips. "Iskender is meeting with the Muqaddim."

The conference room door opened. Tunç exited, closing the the door behind him.

Kavas stepped forward and spoke quietly. "The American doctor and Safiye have escaped."

"How?" Tunç asked.

"Ayla *distracted* the guards," Kavas replied.

"Where is she?" Tunç asked.

Kavas looked toward Beyir. "I think she's still at the monastery."

Beyir began running. He ran through the trophy room, past the guard station, and down the passageway. Sliding past the iron slat, which was kept open during the day, he took the stairs three at a time up into the barn. As he ran from the barn toward the monastery, a gunshot sounded. Moments later, he emerged into the clearing.

A recent Enderun graduate sat at the base of the monastery, his back to the cliff's façade. Beyir couldn't remember his name. The young man leaned forward, holding the butt of a rifle between his legs. The barrel of the rifle, the sound of its report still echoing, protruded through the back of his head.

Two entangled bodies lay next to the young man.

Beyir came to a stop. He looked up at the façade and then down at the bodies.

Basil appeared to have taken the brunt of the fall, his legs broken—jagged pearly white bone jutting through muscle and sinew. Ayla clung to his back. Naked, she stared into the sky, her eyes open.

"'When the soul is taken, the eyesight follows,'" Beyir recited from the Quran, pushing Ayla's eyelids closed.

Beyir separated the bodies and carried Ayla to the river. As he cleaned her—rinsing away blood and dirt and semen—he remembered the radiant girl who'd always been at their house when he was a boy. He could almost hear her squeals of laughter as she played with Safiye and Rabia.

On the riverbank, he took off his shirt and slipped it over her. He carried her along the wooded trail and across the rear lawn of the estate.

The two old women stood on the patio. They watched as Beyir carried Ayla past them and into the house. Tunç and Kavas were waiting.

Beyir saw sadness in Tunç's eyes. But the sadness quickly faded, replaced by an overwhelming fury. As Tunç stormed away, his eyes flashing red, Beyir looked down.

His hand clamped Ayla's left elbow to her side, causing her forearm to jut skyward. Her wrist bent, the fingers of her hand drooped like the petals of a withering flower.

The only adornment on the fingers of her left hand was a ring. On her ring finger, the site where Tunç had been glaring before he left the room, was a simple gold band.

61

allahan and Safiye stood in a dusty alley next to a bus depot. Freshly shaven, Callahan wore a black sports shirt, khaki shorts, and a pair of sandals. Safiye wore sunglasses and a black head scarf along with a tan tunic shirt, blue flared pants, and a pair of canvas slip-on shoes.

After emerging from the woods, wearing their soiled white T-shirts and shorts, they'd run barefoot along the side of the gravel road to the bus stop. Despite looking like escapees from an asylum, they'd made it onto the bus, paying the driver with money from Ayla's envelope. The bus had then taken them on a circuitous route before coming to its terminal stop at a depot in the town of Bafra.

They'd bought a phone card and two tickets for the next bus to Ankara. Callahan had placed a call to the American Embassy. When no one answered, he was directed into a phone tree, where he'd left a message, saying they would be arriving in a few hours. With a half-hour of free time before their bus left, they walked into town and purchased toiletries and clothes, cleaning up and changing in the store's bathroom before returning to the depot.

"There it is," Safiye said, pointing across a street to a bus-filled parking lot. "Bus thirty-four. It leaves at ten-thirty."

As Safiye stepped forward, Callahan held her back. A guard from the monastery stood in the depot entrance.

They'll send men to Bafra. Try to be inconspicuous.

Callahan and Safiye remained in the alley. They hid behind a stack of wooden crates and watched as a steady stream of passengers filed in and out of the depot. All the while, the guard remained by the entrance.

When a wave of passengers exited, Callahan looked at his watch. "Go ahead. We'll have a better chance if we're separate." When Safiye hesitated, he waved her forward. "I'll be there in a minute."

Safiye walked across the street. She looked indistinguishable from a handful of other women making their way across the parking lot. As she disappeared inside bus 34, the guard remained at the entrance, continuing to scan the passersby.

Callahan slipped on his own pair of sunglasses. From a back pocket, he pulled out the black baseball cap he'd purchased and placed it tightly over his head.

He stepped from the alley. His back crawled with thoughts of the guard watching him as he crossed the street and stepped onto the parking lot. Hearing the bus's engine start, he jogged ahead and waved at the driver, who held the door. He handed his ticket to the driver and walked down the aisle, sitting a few rows behind Safiye.

The driver put the transmission in gear and drove across the parking lot. He made a sweeping turn past the depot. As they accelerated through downtown Bafra, Callahan moved next to Safiye and extended his hand. She wrapped her fingers in his and they squeezed each other's hand, the euphoria of the moment washing over them. Two hours earlier, they'd been in Tunç's stone prison. Now, they were on their way to Ankara.

They looked outside and savored the sight of Bafra's passing buildings. A guard from the monastery suddenly appeared. He stood not more than ten feet away, staring directly at them.

When the guard disappeared from view, Callahan stood and looked back through the rear window of the bus.

"Did he see us?" Safiye asked when Callahan settled back in his seat.

"He was running toward the depot."

They looked ahead.

"The next stop is in Samsun—fifty kilometers from here," Safiye said. "But we can't wait that long, can we?"

Callahan shook his head. "They'll be waiting."

62

London

Fontaine walked from his office, his hair mussed. He filled his coffee mug. His tie hung loosely around his neck, and his shirttail was out. He'd worked through the night, poring over the 283 items on Iskender Tunç.

Other CIA workers filed into the Piccadilly office for another day of work. "Nothing bad, I hope," someone said.

Fontaine shrugged. "Not sure yet."

Back at his desk, Fontaine sipped his coffee and sifted through his notes. Not surprisingly for one of Turkey's richest men, Tunç owned a large estate in Teos, condominiums in Istanbul and Ankara, a vacation cottage on the northern Aegean coast, and a gaudy assortment of boats and cars. Single, he devoted his free time to his expensive toys and dutifully paid his sizable taxes. He'd made donations to a local mosque, but there appeared to be nothing radical in his devotion.

The profile before Fontaine hardly seemed to be that of someone who might steal 300 kilograms of weapons-grade plutonium. The closest thing to dirt was an MI5 file, which the British had initiated when Tunç's deceased father, a retired Turkish general, was linked to the Muqaddim, an Islamic group. By today's standards, however, the once-militant Muqaddim were tame. Their last known act of terrorism was the bombing of a London hotel in the mid-1980s. Since then, their most egregious activities had been limited to generous donations to several Middle Eastern universities. Since Muhammed Tunç's death, the MI5 file had been closed. There was no evidence that Iskender Tunç had continued his father's affiliation.

Fontaine clicked on a downloaded video. It was of a speech by the leader of the Muqaddim, Ali Gazi, at a meeting of the Organization of Islamic Cooperation in London. It was made on September 20, 2001—nine days after the terrorist attacks on the World Trade Center. In the video, the Muslim cleric wore a white robe and turban. He spoke in Arabic. Fontaine was fluent in the language.

"During the Abbasid Caliphate in the eighth century, a House of Wisdom was built in Baghdad," Gazi said. "For 500 years, it served as the world's intellectual center. It was where the first observatory was built, where algebra was developed, and where the great works of Hippocrates, Archimedes, Aristotle, Euclid, Galen, and Plato were translated and preserved. The work of the Baghdad scholars became the foundation for modern medicine, mathematics, philosophy, astronomy, and physics. The first university, the University of al-Karaouine, was an Islamic institution. The man credited with being the world's first scientist, Ibn al-Haytham, was a man of Islam."

The Muqaddim leader paused. "Arabic was once the language of the world's most learned. That ended in the thirteenth century when the Mongol hordes marched across the Islamic world. They destroyed our great cities: Samarkand, Nishapur, Bukhara, Derbent, Tabriz, and Merv. When they overthrew Baghdad, they not only destroyed our House of Wisdom and the greatest libraries the world had ever known, but they also killed our scholars. They killed our intellectualism."

Gazi scanned his audience. "I've seen the source of power—the great cities, their skyscrapers, and their sidewalks teeming with people. I have toured the NASA space center in Houston, Volkswagen's Wolfsburg plant, and the Newport News dry docks, along with the Smithsonian, Hermitage, and Louvre. I have walked among the campuses of Oxford, Harvard, and Yale. If the Middle East—if Islam—is to have a role as anything more than terrorists at the international table, we must rebuild our House of Wisdom. The first brick of this new house cannot be a bullet or a bomb. It must be . . . a book."

Gazi's gaze narrowed. "I'm an old man. I don't delude myself to think that things will change significantly in my lifetime. But it's a journey we must start now. We must begin by rebuilding our intellectual infrastructure. Only through education will our future generations have a chance at competing with the rest of the world. Only through innovation and industry will our children have a chance of a return to our former golden age."

As the audience stood and applauded, the video ended.

Fontaine closed the file. A flashing icon was at the bottom of the screen. An "Immediate read" email had arrived. He clicked on the icon. It was another message from Aurelius, the station chief in Istanbul.

Aurelius 307-287-88. Security Level High.

Received call from contact at the US Embassy in Ankara, informing me of a telephone recording left at the embassy from a man claiming to be Dr. Michael Callahan (see attachment #1).

In the message, Callahan said he and two women: Dr. Safiye Özmen, a fellow physician (see attachment #2), and Ayla Koba, a local woman, were kidnapped while in Izmir's city hall by a city councilman, Ançak Barhal, and two other men. The men were working for Iskender Tunç.

Dr. Callahan reported he and Safiye Özmen escaped from their kidnapper to Bafra. He claimed Tunç is part of a plot to overthrow the Turkish government, and that Tunç had a hand in the deaths of Gens. Volkan and Refet. Dr. Callahan stated he and Dr. Özmen would be traveling by bus to Ankara. Additional details were not forthcoming.

63

On the Enderun's auditorium stage, a single spotlight shone onto an empty podium. The spotlight found Iskender Tunç as he walked across the stage and took the podium.

"I regret to inform you your scheduled speaker, the good imam Omër Gazi, was beckoned to Tehran on important matters," Tunç said. "In his absence, I hope I will suffice."

There was a murmur of disapproval from the Muqaddim council members, who sat among the first few rows of the auditorium.

Tunç unfolded a piece of paper and placed it on the podium.

Once the auditorium grew silent, Tunç's voice rang strong and clear. "Gentlemen, sovereignty and sultanate are not given to anyone by anyone because scholarship proves that they should be, or through discussion and debate. Sovereignty and sultanate are taken by strength, by power, and by force."

He looked up from the paper. "These were the words of Atatürk as he addressed the Turkish National Assembly in 1922. These are the words that led to the establishment of a secular state and the exile of the beloved Caliph Abdülmecid II—the Sovereign of the Imperial House of Osman, the Commander of the Faithful on Earth, and the Servant of Mecca and Medina."

Tunç recited a passage from the Quran. "'And when your Lord said unto the angels: *Verily I will place my Khalifa on Earth.*'"

Tunç's eyes narrowed. "For almost a century, Islam has been without a leader. It was by the will of God the caliphate was created. It was by the will of man it was abolished. Turkey has become a nation without an identity. As we've tried to model ourselves after others, we've forgotten who we are. Uniformly, we believe

Muhammad is the true prophet. Yet Atatürk's secularism remains. Almost a century ago, Atatürk planted his evil seed. It has yet to bear fruit."

Tunç stared into the spotlight and again recited from the Quran. "'The judgment is for none but Allah. He has commanded you worship none but Him; that is the straight religion, but most men know not.'" His gaze dropped, his pious tone taking a note of urgency. "For true believers, the worship of Allah is all-encompassing. It must extend beyond the mosque. It must encompass Sunni and Shia and envelop the Middle East. It must become *more* than what it's become."

A few of the council members nodded their approval.

The subtle nod of affirmation had been decades in the making. Forty years earlier, his father had successfully campaigned for the Janissaries and Muqaddim to work together, convincing them of the need for action, of the need for a Sayişma. The Muqaddim's tentacles were spread too far and wide throughout the Muslim world. If the Muqaddim opposed the Sayişma, then they would have the power to strangle it.

Over the past forty years, as the Sayişma had taken shape, the Muqaddim had transitioned from militants to politicians and financiers. A dozen years earlier, they withdrew their support from the Sayişma, telling his father they were directing their funds elsewhere. His father pleaded for them to change their minds. Ali Gazi subsequently informed his father they would not participate in the Sayişma, but also they would not impede it. This had been a victory for his father. But the campaigning had taken its toll. A week after his father reached an agreement with the Muqaddim, his blood pressure had spiraled out of control, and he died of a cerebral hemorrhage.

"'But if they violate their oaths after their covenant and taunt you for your faith; *qatilu*, fight the leaders of Kufr, fight the leaders of disbelief, for their oaths are nothing to them,'" Tunç said, again reciting from the book. He shook his fist. "If the Prophet were alive, he would fight. He would fight the leaders of Kufr. He would fight the leaders of disbelief."

His voice booming, Tunç paused, listening for a response.

The only sound, however, was his own voice echoing back. As firmly as the Muqaddim believed in anything, they presumed they were Allah's true messengers. By declaring God's will, Tunç had torn that away from them.

"Who among the warriors of Allah will join me?" he asked.

As the question dissipated in silence, his father's words came to mind.

"The Janissaries have maintained an unwavering commitment to the hardships necessary to reach our goals, never straying from our core principles. Meanwhile, the Muqaddim have grown complacent and old, rich and comfortable. They will not fuel the revolution. Instead, it will be the poor and destitute, the true believers. These are our people."

After withdrawing their funding for the Sayişma, the Muqaddim were now preparing to vault to its forefront.

Gazi stood from his front-row seat and walked toward the central stairway. "War will not push us forward, but back. I'm sure of that. You are to be commended for your bravery, but we've had enough."

Tunç stepped from behind the podium. "In the ancient battle between Christianity and Islam, we have lost," he said. "Until that is reversed, nothing will change. We must remember the words of our great poet Ziya Gökalp. 'Let the mosques be our barracks, the minarets our bayonets, the domes our helmets, and the faithful our soldiers.'" He stopped at the top of the stairs and looked at Gazi, his thoughts once again turning to his father.

"They have become entrenched in the status quo. They are the ones we fight against."

Gazi stood midway up the stairs. He held out his arms and smiled benevolently. "Iskender, you're young and strong and filled with emotion, but violence is not the way."

"Violence is the *only* way," Tunç said. He planted his foot in the middle of Gazi's chest and kicked him back.

Gazi backpedaled down the first two stairs and then tripped. His bodyguard caught him before he hit the floor.

With the council members assembling around him, the old cleric pointed a shaking finger at Tunç. "How dare you?" he bellowed.

Tunç smiled. Unperturbed, he swept a hand toward the auditorium's curtain, which began to rise.

A lone figure was unveiled. The figure, suspended in midair, was shrouded in the white silken robes of a holy man.

Gazi's creased mouth slowly opened. He emitted a low-pitched moan. Omër, his son and Islam's future caliph, hovered above the stage, a rope around his neck.

As shouts of anguish filled the auditorium, Tunç raised a fist.

Enderun students stood sentinel at the auditorium's rear doors. The boys stepped out into the hallway, slamming the doors behind them.

The Muqaddim turned toward the noise. As they did, a dozen boys materialized on the stage. Forming a line, they each held Lugers at their sides.

"Silah omza," Tunç commanded, stepping behind the row of boys, who raised their pistols.

The heads of the Muqaddim swiveled back toward the stage.

"At!"

It was dark as Callahan and Safiye stood outside a small town. Several dim lights illuminated a post office, a gas station, and a store. Only the store was still open.

Earlier that day, Callahan and Safiye stood in the bus's exhaust, watching as their newfound freedom accelerated away. Hearing an approaching car, they hid as a car containing the two young guards sped past. Knowing Bafra would soon be crawling with Tunç's men after the car caught up with the bus, Callahan and Safiye spent the day walking along Bafra's southern outskirts, staying within the cover of the woods. Southwest of Bafra, they came upon a two-lane road and a marker indicating the next town, Sinop, was ninety-eight kilometers away.

"It seems peaceful," Safiye said. "Should we try it?"

"How do you feel?" Callahan asked.

"My feet hurt and I'm hungry, but otherwise I feel okay. We should probably keep going."

They'd decided to continue to Sinop, hoping Tunç's men wouldn't be searching for them that far away.

"We could run in and make another call to the embassy," Callahan said. "Let them know we're headed toward Sinop."

Safiye shrugged. "It couldn't hurt."

As they stepped from the woods, a pair of headlights appeared. They crouched.

The car stopped at the store. The two young men from Bafra climbed out.

64

Northern Turkey

Petrovich and Tatiana sat on the balcony of their second-floor hotel room. The trail of the missing plutonium had led them from Grozny to Hamburg, from Istanbul to Izmir, and now to a small town in northern Turkey.

After their all-night, cross-country trek into the northern woodlands, they'd driven to the nearest town. Once they were in a hotel, they'd submitted the barn's GPS coordinates to their SVR control.

Satellite images revealed the barn was on a large wooded estate. After exploiting the SVR's Turkish contacts, their control informed them the estate had been given to Iskender Tunç's father seventy years earlier. In the time since, there'd been no record of Turkish utilities supplying electricity, water, or gas to the area. Building permits had not been issued. Taxes had not been paid. The land was Tunç's domain, an off-the-grid, tax-free gift for exemplary duty.

During their subsequent reconnaissance, Petrovich and Tatiana discovered groups of young men regularly patrolling the woods around the barn. The woods were also heavily populated by cameras. Realizing further incursions onto the estate would be too dangerous, they looked for phone lines to tap. If lines existed, however, they were unmarked and buried. With no other means to surveil the estate, they'd spent much of their time parked in the nearby woods, unsuccessfully monitoring random radio frequencies in an attempt to intercept cell phone calls.

"How are you feeling?" Petrovich asked.

"Frustrated," Tatiana said.

If the estate wasn't the final destination for the plutonium, they'd concluded it would at least contain information that would lead them to its whereabouts. But their request for the necessary backup for a raid on the estate had fallen on deaf ears. Before sanctioning a raid, the SVR hierarchy needed more proof of wrongdoing, preferably evidence the plutonium was at the estate.

"Maybe we should take the day off," Petrovich said.

Neither looked forward to another day of monitoring random radio frequencies.

"I'll be fine," Tatiana said.

"We'll at least go out tonight." Petrovich sat back and scanned their surroundings. "Bafra must have at least one good place to eat."

Next to the hotel, a sidewalk café was filling. Among the patrons was a young man. A coffee, untouched, sat in front of him. Unlike the others leisurely enjoying their meals and talking, the young man sat alone. He wore an earpiece, and his hand was cupped over his mouth. His lips moved almost imperceptibly as his head swiveled back and forth. It took a moment for Petrovich to see whom he was talking to—a similarly dressed young man standing a few blocks away.

In any part of the world, surveillance was a complicated task reserved for experienced members of intelligence agencies and police staff. But these two were hardly old enough to be out of secondary school.

"The young man in the gray T-shirt and khakis," Petrovich said, nodding toward the café. "What do you think?"

After watching for a few seconds, Tatiana looked up the street. She smiled when she saw the second man. "At least their shirts are different colors."

Petrovich stepped into the hotel room. He grabbed the radio receiver and carried it back to the balcony table. Slipping on the headphones, he turned on the receiver and adjusted the reception frequency.

The receiver's static was broken by a male voice, speaking in Turkish. Petrovich handed the headphones to Tatiana, who slipped them on.

"I don't mind so much what happened to Basil, he was a pig,"

Tatiana said, quietly interpreting. "But he didn't deserve this . . . . It's the woman's fault. She was a whore."

Petrovich waved. Tatiana lifted her earpiece. "Sounds like important police work," he said. She rolled her eyes and let the earpiece fall back into place.

"Why did they let her stay in the house?" Tatiana continued. "She should have been with the other two. I wish they would have let Basil take care of them in Izmir."

Tatiana looked toward Petrovich, her eyes widening. "Killing them at city hall would have been better than this."

65

"I have no religion, and at times I wish all religions at the bottom of the sea."

—**Mustafa Kemal Atatürk**

A li Gazi's mind crept slowly from the fog of sleep. A uniformed man was bent over him in a pool of light, gently tapping his shoulder. The man wore captain's stripes on a faded blue jacket with a matching cap.

"Mr. Tunç wanted you to see this," the man said.

Gazi rubbed his eyes and looked around. It was dark. He sat in the front row of an airplane. The window seat next to him was empty.

The man lifted the shade. The sun filled the window. Gazi winced, raising a hand to block the glare.

The man turned Gazi's reading light off and then walked into the cockpit, closing the door behind him.

Gazi peered outside. He recognized Ankara's skyline.

Prior to the Muqaddim's meeting, the council members had flown separately into Istanbul. Together, they took a charter flight to an airfield outside Samsun and were then driven to Tunç's estate. The plan was to leave by the same route.

Gazi looked back over the darkened passenger compartment. Shadowed figures filled the seats around him. "Why are we landing in Ankara?"

No one replied.

The morning sun glimmered off a pool in Gençlik Parki. They were flying through the heart of the city. They passed over the capital's opera house and concert hall.

The airport was north of the city, but they were heading west.

Gazi reached across the aisle and prodded the adjacent figure. "Why are we landing in Ankara?"

When the figure didn't respond, Gazi turned his reading light back on. As the light fell on his fellow traveler, he shrieked.

His bodyguard sat in the adjacent seat, his face bloodied. Memories of the events in Tunç's auditorium returned.

Gazi stood and pulled at the cockpit door. It was locked.

The pilot's words rang in his ears.

Mr. Tunç wanted you to see this.

He looked outside. In moments, they'd be over Beştepe. The day before, he'd been discussing the upcoming election with Tunç and a Turkish council member.

"I hear rumors Cebici may run for a fifth term," the Turkish council member said.

Tunç smiled. "He's said repeatedly he won't. He's seventy-nine."

"Yes, but he also said he wouldn't run for a third term or a fourth," the council member said. "The assassinations have revived him."

"In what way?" Gazi asked.

"Cebici is using them to attack his opponents and further consolidate power," the council member said. "And, by breaking up several terrorist cells and sending more troops to fight the Kurds, he's tapped into a nationalistic fervor. His approval ratings are higher than ever."

Gazi turned to the Turkish council member after Tunç walked away. "Will Cebici run?"

"He's not acting like he's ready to step aside."

"If he did run, what would happen?" Gazi asked.

"It would change *everything.*"

There were many aspects to Tunç's Sayişma but being elected president was an essential one. Without the presidency, his Sayişma would collapse.

"As long as Cebici wants it," the council member said, "the presidency is his."

The Beştepe neighborhood contained Cebici's newly constructed presidential palace. They were approaching the palace from the east—straight out of the rising sun.

Gazi pounded on the cockpit door. The cockpits of the new jets were protected from terrorists breaking into them but not from terrorists once they were already inside.

He looked toward the window. The ground was near. Knowing he only had seconds, he hurried down the aisle, hitting each of the reading lights.

The council members, bloodied and dead, were tied to the seats. He continued until he came to the figure he was looking for.

Ömer.

His son sat in the window seat. His eyes were closed, his head tilted toward the open window as if listening for something in the distance. Even in death, a light shone through him.

The engines roared as the plane swung back and forth. The pilot was making his final adjustments.

Gazi sat and embraced Ömer.

Outside, the passing trees melded together.

"I'm sorry we failed you," Ali Gazi said. "You were the perfect son. You would have made the perfect caliph."

66

Istanbul

A fter a night flight from London, Fontaine stood at Aurelius's office window. It was just after dawn as he looked across the shimmering Bosporus.

The Hagia Sophia, the massive domed mosque with its four minarets, rose from the other side of the waterway. Built in the sixth century on the orders of Emperor Justinian to surpass all previous constructions, the Hagia Sophia was the supreme achievement of Byzantine architecture. It had since served as the seat of the Eastern Orthodox church, a Roman Catholic cathedral, a mosque, and, for most of the last century, as a museum. Little did the building's architects, Anthemius of Tralles and Isidore of Miletus, know it would still stand fifteen centuries later as the most magnificent structure in the city.

"They should have arrived at the embassy yesterday afternoon," Aurelius said.

Fontaine turned from the window toward the CIA's Istanbul station chief.

"Ayla Koba's car was found outside the lab, but her body hasn't been identified," Aurelius said. He slid a newspaper across his desk. The paper was a week old.

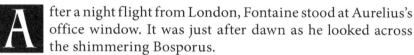

KOBA LABORATORIES DESTROYED BY FIRE
Izmir—Explosions tore through Koba Laboratories in downtown Izmir on Tuesday morning. Firefighters

343

watched helplessly as the research laboratory burned to the ground. This occurred the day after Mehmet Koba, the lab's director, was found dead of natural causes in downtown Ankara. None of the lab's employees survived. Investigators have not identified a link between Mehmet Koba's death and the . . .

"Forensic analysis indicates the explosion and fire were a cover-up," Aurelius said. "Each of the victims was badly burned but also had fatal gunshot wounds."

The office door swung open. An aide stuck her head inside. Her face was chalk white. "You'll want to see this," she said. "Both of you."

They followed her to a media room.

Over a dozen people stood in the room, staring wide-eyed at one of several flat-screen monitors. The monitors showed the same image—an aerial view of a smoking building.

"Ak Saray," she said.

The camera panned back. A black scar traveled from a large building, across a lawn, and through a row of small evergreens, where it ended in numerous small brush fires.

"Ak Saray?" Fontaine said.

"The White Palace," Aurelius said. "Home of the Turkish president."

"That's what's left of the living quarters," the aide said. "The plane must have been loaded with explosives and fuel."

"And Cebici?" Aurelius asked.

The camera focused on a section of burning fuselage.

"Dead," the aide said.

"Jesus," Aurelius said. "Do we know who's responsible?"

"Turkish intelligence has identified the plane," the aide said. She looked down at a notepad. "A charter from Samsun-Çarşamba Airport in northern Turkey. The flight report indicates thirteen were aboard. Only one name cross-checks with anything in the database. Ali Gazi. He's head of the—"

"Muqaddim," Fontaine said, his eyes locked on the screen. "An Islamic group. Low priority. Their last known activity was in the eighties when they claimed credit for the bombing of a London hotel."

"That's right," the aide said. "They're code green—intermittent surveillance only."

67

tthhhew, ttthhhew, ttthhhew . . .

The sound reverberated through Callahan's subconscious. It was the sound of his father chopping wood when he was a boy. The sound grew louder, transitioning to the flat tire on his first car. As the noise continued, his frustration built.

Why won't it stop?

When he opened his eyes, neither his father nor the gold Firebird of his youth were anywhere in sight. It was daytime. He was on the ground. Safiye lay next to him, sleeping.

Early that morning, they'd come to the grassy clearing and lay down to rest. Around them, the grass was bent, the sound deafening.

Ttthhhew, ttthhhew, TTTHHHEW . . .

"Safiye, here," Callahan yelled.

They slid beneath a large pine tree. Through the branches, they caught glimpses of a helicopter. It had an unmarked blue fuselage. Two men were inside. The passenger, leaning through his open doorway, held a rifle. He aimed it toward them.

There was a loud crack. The bullet hit the ground inches from Safiye's leg, kicking up a handful of pine needles.

They shuffled around the tree, putting the tree's base between them and the helicopter.

There were more shots. A bullet tore into the ground. Another peeled off a strip of bark.

Ttthhwacckkk.

The resonating noise was followed by a shower of pine needles. The helicopter's engine coughed. The pilot opened the throttle.

With a roar, the engine caught, spewing large chunks of black smoke.

The helicopter's rotor had hit the tree. The helicopter flew away. After a few moments, it stopped and hovered as the pilot intermittently gunned the engine.

Once the engine had stabilized, the pilot directed the helicopter back toward the tree.

In seconds, they'd once again be sitting targets.

Callahan turned and looked toward a thick patch of woods. If they were going to make a run for it, it had to be now, and it had to be in that direction.

Tunç sat alone on the back porch of his Samsun estate, eating breakfast.

Edirne Kavas approached. "A helicopter spotted them."

"Where?"

"Between Bafra and Sinop," Kavas said. "They fired and may have hit one of them but weren't able to confirm."

"They didn't land?"

"They tried but almost crashed. The area was too wooded. They're flying back to refuel. Two search teams are headed to the area along with the other helicopter."

"I want them dead," Tunç said.

"The men are under orders to kill, if necessary."

"If necessary? It's imperative. If they escape, it's over. The Sayişma. *Everything.*"

68

Istanbul

Fontaine stood with Aurelius at the front of a full conference room. "Please," Aurelius said. "Quiet."

Aurelius had called an emergency meeting of his team leaders. He'd hoped the incident at Refet's house was an isolated event. With Kayseri's assassination and that morning's attack on the presidential palace, however, it was clear that someone had declared war.

"As many of you know, we have our first credible lead," Aurelius said. "It's come from an unexpected source—the Russians." He turned toward Fontaine, who'd moved to a podium. "Jon will give us an update."

As the lights went off, the screen behind Fontaine filled with an image of Iskender Tunç. The image was momentarily obscured by a flash of light as the conference room door opened. Through the projector's glare, Fontaine saw a shadowed figure slide into a seat along the back wall. Fontaine looked toward Aurelius, who nodded for him to proceed.

"Nineteen months ago, while the Russians were collecting plutonium from decommissioned warheads, 300 kilograms of weapons-grade plutonium was stolen from a convoy in Grozny," Fontaine began. "The Russians have linked the disappearance to this man, Iskender Tunç, the CEO and owner of Tunç Corporation."

A snort of laughter came from Sidney Pomfoy, a National

Security Council adviser. Two years earlier, Pomfoy had lost his seat in the House of Representatives. Luckily for him, his party had retained the presidency, and he'd been able to find employment as a congressional liaison to the CIA. Two terms of voting the party line had paid off.

"Turkey is a democratic country and a NATO ally," Pomfoy said. "An unstable Turkey benefits Russia. Are you going to trust anything the Russians have to say?"

"Not without verification," Fontaine said. "But we have it from another source that Tunç had a hand in the assassinations of Volkan and Refet."

"Another *Russian* source?" Pomfoy said. "What are they proposing he's trying to do? Overthrow the government? Maybe the plutonium was never stolen, maybe—"

"Sid," Aurelius interrupted. "Please hold your questions until the end of Jon's presentation."

A grinning Pomfoy, showing off a mouthful of overly whitened veneers, sat back.

Fontaine provided a brief biography on Tunç. He summarized Russian information connecting Tunç with the events in Grozny and told them about the missing physicians and the phone call from Callahan. He then turned toward the screen. "These are surveillance photos provided by the SVR." He advanced through the images, providing commentary as needed.

"Go back two photos."

The request was made by the late arrival. He had a thick Russian accent.

Fontaine flipped back two images to a photo from Kólpos Kallonís. Tunç stood on the Kobas' schooner.

"As I said, this is Tunç talking with the Kobas along with Drs. Callahan and Özmen," Fontaine said, directing his laser pointer to the screen. "This is—"

"Yes," the man said impatiently. "But who is this?"

Another laser dot appeared on the screen, erratically circling a figure on Tunç's yacht.

In the photo, light passed through the opening at the top of a stairwell. A man's head was visible as he ascended from below deck. The man wore wire-rimmed spectacles and had tousled, receding blond hair. His face was blurred.

Fontaine swore at himself for the oversight. "We can have the picture sent to Langley for analysis, but I'm not sure if there's enough for a match," he said. "If I recall, he's not in the other photos."

"He's not," the man declared. "Think back, fifteen months ago. A blond-haired male. *The most sought-after face on the globe.*"

The CIA agents responded in chorus. Fontaine mouthed the words himself.

"Max Göttingen."

"Who?" Pomfoy asked.

"Dr. Maxwell Göttingen," Fontaine said. "He's a German physicist. His lineage of training extends back to Heisenberg."

Pomfoy stared back without recognition.

"Dr. Werner Heisenberg led the Nazis' program to build an atomic bomb during World War II," Fontaine said. "Thankfully, he acquired a distaste for the Nazi way of life. Heisenberg abhorred the idea of Hitler possessing such a weapon and never seriously pursued making a bomb, believing the Nazi regime would collapse within a year or two. By his inaction, he likely influenced the results of the war more than anyone."

"Unfortunately," Aurelius said, standing, "Heisenberg's morality hasn't carried over to all of his protégés." He stepped toward the screen and eyed the image. "A couple years ago, while Göttingen was at Leipzig University, he developed a compact nuclear accelerator that allowed the development of a briefcase-size hydrogen bomb. A year and a half ago, it came to our attention he was interested in selling his knowledge to the highest bidder. While under surveillance, Göttingen disappeared."

"We thought he'd gone with the North Koreans," Fontaine said. "It helped explain many of their recent advances."

Aurelius turned toward the shadowed figure in the back of the room. "Do you think we've found Göttingen's employer?"

"I think so," the man said.

Fontaine looked anew at the image of Iskender Tunç. After a moment, he turned off the projector. "That's all I have."

As the lights came back on, everyone turned to the back of the room. The seat belonging to the meeting's latecomer, however, was empty. The nearby conference room door was closing.

"Who was that?" Pomfoy asked.

"Anyone want to hazard a guess?" Aurelius asked, a smile crossing his lips.

"Alexei Petrinko," Fontaine said.

Aurelius nodded.

"Who?" Pomfoy asked.

"The head of the SVR's Near Eastern intelligence unit," Aurelius said. "He wanted to make sure we gave Tunç top billing." He looked toward the others. "When it comes to nuclear terrorism, it appears the Russians have drawn a line. I believe them when they say they're willing to work with us."

"You let a *Russian* agent sit in on a high-level CIA meeting?" Pomfoy asked.

"I don't trust the Russians any more than you do," Aurelius said. "But Petrinko is the one who gave us the photos along with most of the information on Tunç. He could have given Jon's presentation."

"You let us speak in front of a Russian agent? You let him know our thoughts?"

"Sid, if I could stop you from thinking the crazy shit you do, I would," Aurelius said. "But your thoughts are probably only dangerous to you."

Pomfoy stood and walked from the room, slamming the door behind him.

"That probably wasn't the smartest thing to say," someone said.

"It wasn't," Aurelius said. "But right now, Sidney Pomfoy is the least of my worries."

69

"**I** swear upon my honor and repute before the great Turkish nation and before history to safeguard the existence and independence of the state, the indivisible integrity of country and nation, and the sovereignty of the nation; to abide by the Constitution, the principles and reforms of Atatürk, and—"

Tunç muted the television in his third-floor study. On the screen, Imar Yerbaten, the vice president, was taking the oath of president.

"'The principles and reforms of Atatürk,'" Tunç said. "If that alone isn't a reason for revolt, I don't know what is."

Edirne Kavas and Enver Pasha sat on a couch. Enver had arrived that morning from Izmir.

The image on the screen switched to an aerial view of the decimated presidential residence. When a passport photo of Ali Gazi appeared, Tunç hit the volume.

"Over the past twenty years, the Muqaddim leader has been a confidante of top Middle Eastern leaders, an adviser for both respected statesmen and terrorists," the commentator said. "His influence has transcended borders, extending to the highest reaches of Abidjan, Karachi, Riyadh, Tehran, and Cairo. In this photo from 1993, he's seen walking with Osama bin Laden. He's known to have met regularly with former Egyptian president Anwar Sadat, former PLO leader Yasser Arafat, and the Ayatollah Khomeini. Based in Egypt, he's a frequent visitor in Tehran, where he's maintained ties with Iranian leadership."

A photo of Omër Gazi appeared on the screen.

"Ali Gazi's son, Omër Gazi, has spent the last six years in what has been described as the strictest of Tehran's madrassas."

351

Tunç grinned. Not only were the Muqaddim receiving the blame for the attack, but with Cebici gone, the Muslim vote would be his. And with it, undoubtedly, the presidency.

"The identity of the pilot is unknown," the commentator said. "The name he used is false, and the photo he provided is a stock photo from an online database."

"Juvan will be enjoying his rewards in heaven," Enver said. He'd been an Enderun classmate with the former commercial airline pilot.

Tunç walked to the coffee table where the two men sat. They looked down at the map sprawled over the table. Kavas had been updating Enver on the search for the two physicians.

"We spotted them here, southeast of Sinop," the headmaster said, pointing. "We then moved fifty of our men into the surrounding towns of Dağköy, Durağan, Boyabat, Dereköy, Yaykin, and Alaçam. Another thirty are in Sinop, Bafra, and the northern coastal towns in between, while twenty more are combing the countryside. We have two helicopters scouring the area."

Enver nodded his approval.

"The region is heavily wooded," Kavas said. "They may be able to hide for a while, but they'll eventually have to come out. When they do, we'll be waiting."

Callahan and Safiye emerged from a patch of woods onto a promontory. In front of them, a red-tinted river was surrounded by a rich panorama of steep gray-black cliffs interrupted by green tufts of forest.

After the helicopter had spotted them the day before, they knew Sinop and their trek toward it were no longer safe. Altering course, they'd spent the remainder of the previous day and night traveling blindly to the south.

"The Kızılırmak," Safiye said. "It's also known as the Red River."

They walked down the hill to the river. Safiye removed the canvas shoes she'd purchased in Bafra. Callahan grimaced when he saw the backs of her heels. "Are you okay?"

"I'll be fine," Safiye said. She pulled up her pant legs and stepped into the river. Sitting on a large rock, she took a deep breath and exhaled. "Better."

Callahan removed his sandals and sat on the rock next to

her. Together, they looked over the river, their feet dangling in the water.

Callahan held out Safiye's head scarf, which they'd fastened into a sack. Several oranges were inside. They each picked one out. Earlier, they'd passed an orchard. By trial and error, they found the apples weren't ripe and the olives tasted terrible off the vine. The orange trees, however, carried a mix of flower blossoms, young green fruit, and ripe oranges.

"The river's color comes from red sandstone in the Ihlara Valley," Safiye said as they ate. "In antiquity, the river was known as the Halys. Croesus, the last king of Lydia, crossed it to attack Cyrus the Great and the Persians after an oracle informed him he'd destroy a large empire if he did so. That empire ended up being his own."

"One of Ayla's history lessons?"

Safiye nodded. She lifted her foot and watched the water drip from it. "Running through the woods, at the bus stop in Bafra, I kept thinking she'd join us."

"She had our escape orchestrated so well. It only made sense she'd be a part of it."

They sat quietly, the river massaging their feet, lost in their thoughts. The soothing, babbling sound of the running water was interrupted by a distant but familiar sound.

Ttthhhew, ttthhhew, ttthhhew . . .

Pulling their feet from the water, they ran toward the woods.

70

Northern Turkey

Petrovich stood outside a tobacco shop in the small town of Durağan. Sweat beaded on his forehead as he looked through the front window at a collection of hand-rolled cigars. At Burdenko, they'd successfully treated his nicotine addiction with patches. But now, as the sweet scent of dried tobacco leaves wafted through the shop's door, his craving returned, hitting him hard.

His eye was caught by a reflection in the window. The two young men from Bafra emerged from the hotel across the street. Petrovich and Tatiana had begun surveilling them after their overheard conversation had linked them to the events at Izmir's city hall. The young men had traveled from Bafra to the small town of Alaçam, thirty kilometers to the west. After staying for only a few hours in Alaçam, they'd headed southwest to Durağan.

Last night, their SVR control informed them about the kidnapping of the WHO physicians and the physicians' escape from Tunç's estate. The young men's surveillance suddenly made sense. They were pawns in Tunç's search. Petrovich had no idea how many players Tunç had on the board, but the frequent movements meant they were closing on their target.

Petrovich watched the reflections. The young men were walking toward their car, carrying duffel bags. For the third time in two days, they were on the move.

Petrovich slipped into an alley and sprinted to their hotel. He ran through the lobby and up the stairs, coming to a stop outside their second-floor room.

The door was ajar. Men's voices came from inside. Removing a handgun, he pushed the door open.

Tatiana stood in the middle of the room—surrounded by four men. One of them spotted Petrovich. "Hey—"

The others turned. One went for a gun, but Tatiana grabbed the man's wrist. "It's Vlad." She looked toward him. "These are the Americans."

Their control had said that with respect to Iskender Tunç, they were on the same team as the Americans. Petrovich hadn't taken him literally until their control informed them the CIA agents would be joining them.

"We've got to go," Petrovich said, lowering his gun. "They're moving again."

71

"We do not consider our principles as dogmas contained in books that are said to come from heaven. We derive our inspiration, not from heaven, or from an unseen world, but directly from life."

—**Mustafa Kemal Atatürk**

Callahan and Safiye followed the Kızılırmak to the east. Safiye knew the river would eventually lead them north to the Black Sea. They'd have to circle back near Bafra and closer to their stone prison, but of all the paths before them, it seemed the least likely Tunç would expect.

They traveled for the next three days and nights, sleeping during the heat of the day and walking through the night. In the middle of the third night, they passed Bafra, spotting its lights to the east. The following morning, as the horizon glowed with the dawn, an infinite number of reflections rippled to the north. They'd reached the Black Sea coast.

After finding a bridge and crossing the river, they spent the day hiking east along a trail, which paralleled the coastline. In the late afternoon, they came upon a lone house perched majestically in the hills.

The house, with a burgundy-tiled roof and whitewashed walls, overlooked a sleepy fishing village. With the exception of the telephone and electrical wires leading inside, the house appeared untouched by the last hundred years.

"Shall we?" Safiye asked.

At each sign of civilization, Callahan had been tempted to try to contact the embassy again. The more isolated the outpost, the greater his urge. When he felt himself resigning to these temptations, his thoughts turned to Bryce's contorted body in the back of the cart, and he'd be reminded of the consequences of underestimating Tunç's resolve. But Safiye's limp, caused by the growing ulcers on her heels, had worsened. She'd willed herself this far, but he wasn't sure how much farther she could go.

"Let's give it a try," he said.

Safiye knocked at the front door of the house while Callahan remained in the woods. When no one answered, they walked to the back. Using a rock, Callahan broke through a windowpane in a rear door.

Wandering the house, they found old mail and a map indicating they were in Özören, a small town west of Samsun. The house had not recently been occupied. It was without running water or electricity, and the phone was dead.

They took separate turns washing in a rainwater collection barrel. Afterward, they made a meal of stale crackers and peanuts they found in the pantry along with fruit from their last trip into an orchard. Sitting side-by-side at the kitchen table, they looked out a picture window onto the Black Sea.

"It's beautiful," Safiye said.

Callahan handed her a peeled orange. She tore it in half and handed a half back. "Promise me someday we can come back and do nothing but sit on the porch and look out onto the water."

"I'll promise to find a porch that looks over water but not the Black Sea."

"That's fair," Safiye said. She slipped a wedge of orange into her mouth and looked thoughtfully toward him.

"What is it?" he asked.

"During the excursion, what happened between us?"

Callahan shrugged. "It's like you said that morning on the bus. You thought we had something. So did I. By the time we straightened everything out, however, the end of the excursion was nearing—"

"Which puts a damper on most relationships," she said, finishing his sentence.

"No matter how torrid."

She smiled. "We were rather torrid, weren't we? I mean, we weren't *you and Jenna* torrid."

"Ugh," he said. "You're not going to let me forget that."

"Probably not."

"I can see I'm going to have to make you forget I was ever interested in Jenna." As he leaned toward her, she backed away. When he went to kiss her, she stuffed an orange slice into his mouth. "I'm a mess," she said.

"And I'm not?" Undeterred, he turned her chin toward him.

"Mmmm," she said as their lips met. "I don't remember you being so citrusy."

A second kiss was soft and lingering. As they stared into each other's eyes, they heard a snickering.

Three small boys peered through the rear door's broken windowpane. Their eyes going wide, the boys turned and ran away.

72

In a grassy field in a corner of the sprawling military complex north of Ankara, Colonel Cemil Kura stood alone. Cupping a hand against the wind, he lit a cigarette. He took a drag and slowly exhaled. With dark, intense eyes, he looked through the smoke, wondering if the charade that had been his life was over.

Eighteen years earlier, as a twenty-two-year-old company commander in southeastern Turkey, Cemil stood at attention in a divisional meeting. He reported Kani Shekhir, the head of the Kurdish Gazani tribal confederation, would be in the town of Siirt the following day.

The division commander stood and walked across the silent room.

In the late eighties and early nineties, the success of the PKK had been attributed to their recruitment of Shekhir. Until then, the Kurds had been nothing more than disparate mountain tribes, as likely to fight one another as the Turks. The PKK and Shekhir had worked together to unite the tribes, giving them two clear objectives: a free Kurdistan and death to anyone opposing them.

"Captain Kura," General Abdülaziz Volkan said, stopping in front of Cemil. "Do you know what Kani Shekhir might be doing in Siirt?" Despite Volkan's success against the PKK, Shekhir had eluded him.

"Attending his niece's wedding, sir," Cemil said.

"And the location of this wedding?"

Cemil extended a piece of paper. "I request the privilege of leading my men in apprehending Shekhir."

Volkan took the paper. "What's your source?"

Cemil was quiet.

The general stared deep into Cemil's eyes. "Why should I risk the lives of *my* men and trust you?"

When Cemil didn't reply, Volkan turned. "Thank you, gentlemen," he said. "That will be all."

The meeting began to break up.

"Sir," Cemil said, stepping toward Volkan. "Let me take a squad to Siirt."

"That will be all, Captain."

"But General, I—"

"This meeting *is* adjourned," Volkan said.

The following night, in a community center in Siirt, the wedding festivities of Kani Shekhir's niece were abruptly ended by a single gunshot. The startled wedding party ran outside to find the bride's uncle dead, a bullet hole in the back of his skull.

The next morning, forty kilometers to the northeast, on the slopes of the Doğruyol Daği, Volkan sat behind his desk. Cemil sat across from him.

"As I'm sure you're aware, Captain Afyon's foray into Siirt last night was successful," Volkan said. "I'll ask you again. What was your source?"

Cemil didn't respond.

"I understand not wanting to provide the source of your information during the meeting," Volkan said. "In fact, I commend you for it. Spies are everywhere. Not in my command, of course, but we really didn't know until last night, did we?"

Volkan walked to a cart and lifted a decanter of brandy. He poured a glass and then tipped the decanter over a second glass. "Drink?" he asked.

"No, thank you, sir."

Volkan opened a box of cigars and extended it. "The finest northern tobacco."

Cemil raised a hand. "No, thank you, sir."

"This is a victory," Volkan said. "Kani Shekhir is dead. We deserve to celebrate." He removed a cigar from the box and picked up the glass of brandy, extending both.

"No, thank you, sir."

Volkan returned to his chair. He put his feet up on the desk and lit the cigar. "By not telling me your source, by not drinking my brandy or smoking my cigars, I'm not sure if you're being insolent or stupid, Captain Kura. Since you're a top graduate of my beloved Aliştirmak, I can only presume the former. Which begs the question—*why*?"

Sitting back in his chair, Volkan exhaled a column of smoke. "I believe men are at their best when they're insolent, Captain Kura. But despite my respect for your impudence, before you leave this tent, you *will* tell me the source of your information."

Cemil met Volkan's stare.

Volkan set down his cigar. Walking around the desk, he unbuttoned the flap of his waist holster and removed his pistol. "Do you know what happens to those who refuse my direct order?" He pressed the gun to Cemil's temple. "Insolence can lead to martyrdom, Captain Kura. This isn't Istanbul or Ankara. It's southeast Turkey. The vaunted Kurdistan. We're at war."

Cemil stared ahead, his heart pounding.

"What did you think would happen if you took down Shekhir?" Volkan asked. "Did you think it would buy you influence? A *promotion*?"

Cemil took a deep breath and closed his eyes, awaiting his fate.

After several moments, Volkan backed away. "Get out of here."

Cemil stood. On shaky legs, he walked from the tent.

"Just a minute," Volkan called out.

When Cemil turned, a small box was flying through the air. He caught it and snapped it open. Inside were gold clusters. For a naive moment, he thought they were his.

"You should have the privilege of pinning these on Captain Afyon," Volkan said. "Let the major know his promotion was for excellence displayed in eliminating key enemy leadership." He pointed. "And Captain Kura, if you ever choose to share more gems like this *and* their source, I may choose to forget what happened here today."

There were no more gems. And it was a decade before Volkan forgot. While Volkan soon returned to Ankara, Cemil remained mired in the southeast being passed over in favor of less capable officers. After Cemil eventually fell beneath Volkan's contempt, his request for transfer was finally approved.

It had been eight years ago when Cemil began his career anew, steadily accumulating promotions and respect. He was now a colonel and aide to General Fätäh, commander of the First Division. Following Fätäh's impending retirement, Cemil would take over command of the First Division and receive his first star. His life would be his own. Or so he thought.

Three days earlier, he received a telephone call from Edirne Kavas—his former teacher at the Enderun. The call came as unexpectedly as Kavas's previous call eighteen years earlier informing him of Kani Shekhir's location.

Cemil always wondered what he'd do if the Enderun called again. Thoughts of defiance were tempered by the steadying image of Muhammed Tunç. While his recollections of the Enderun were nothing more than a few clouded snapshots, his memories of Muhammed Tunç were strong and clear. When Muhammed sent him to the Alištirmak, he told him to excel, to not forget the Enderun, and to be patient. Cemil, only fifteen years old at the time, swore he'd do all those things. He'd kept his promise for the last quarter-century. Against his better judgment, he continued to do so.

He agreed to meet with Kavas in a secluded park east of Ankara. His former teacher told him of an upcoming secret meeting of the Turkish High Command and provided him with a briefcase and instructions. As they were about to part, Cemil asked Kavas a question that had tormented him for the past eighteen years.

"Why did you give me the information on Kani Shekhir?"

"We hoped to advance your career," Kavas said. "But we did the exact opposite. I apologize."

"But why did you want Shekhir dead? The Enderun should have been on the side of the Kurds."

"Kani Shekhir was in Siirt that day for a reason other than his niece's wedding," the old eunuch said. "For almost a century, the Kurdish people have been squeezed between Turkey, Syria, Iraq, and Iran. They've maintained a tenuous hold on their unofficial Kurdistan by playing the different countries and different religious factions against one another as it suited them."

"Shekhir wanted to make peace?"

Kavas nodded. "At the time, Volkan and his forces were crushing the PKK. To stop Volkan's onslaught, Shekhir was prepared to shift the PKK's efforts away from Turkey—toward the Shia against Iran and Iraq."

"And Muhammed didn't want that?"

"He realized the PKK and Shekhir—by playing nation against nation and Sunni against Shia—were keeping the Middle East in a state of flux. Muhammed wanted to end the cycle. He believed if the Middle East was to find peace, mercenaries like Shekhir had to be stopped."

Remorse crossed Kavas's face. "I'm sorry. A mistake was made—a mistake you've spent the last eighteen years paying for."

Cemil remained in the grassy field, looking up into the sky. He took another drag on the cigarette. His gaze traveled across the field to the entrance leading down into the bunker.

He'd been at General Fätäh's side, one of two dozen sitting around a table, when the meeting of the Turkish High Command was about to start. General Nuri Yata, a young man with ambitions of his own, asked why Cemil was allowed into the meeting while the other aides waited outside. Before Fätäh could defend his presence, Cemil acknowledged Yata's astute observation and excused himself. No one noticed the briefcase he left behind.

"Don't pay attention to Nuri," General Izzet Pazar had said, following Cemil to the door. "In a few years, you'll be running this meeting."

Cemil had taken the stairs up from the bunker and walked across the grassy field to the spot where he now stood. He slid his hand into his pocket. As he ran his fingers over the disc Kavas had given him, the faces of those in the bunker flashed before him: the fatherly Fätäh, the smiling Pazar, even the ambitious Yata.

He pulled his hand from his pocket. He couldn't do it. He was no longer the fifteen year old who'd left the Enderun. For twenty-five years, he'd searched for an identity. He'd finally found it. The men in that bunker were everything to him. They meant more than a fading allegiance to the Enderun or the long-dead Muhammed Tunç. They certainly meant more than an alliance with Iskender, Muhammed's petulant son.

Staff members and drivers stood in small groups in a covered parking lot next to the bunker's entrance. A rotund man in a chauffeur's outfit with a billed cap broke from the others. His head down, he walked across the field toward Cemil. Stopping at Cemil's side, he raised an unlit cigarette to his lips. "Hello, Colonel," he said, looking up.

Cemil jumped back. It was Edirne Kavas—his beard gone.

"Is the briefcase in the room?" Kavas asked.

Cemil nodded as he lit the cigarette.

Kavas took a drag, surveying Cemil from beneath the brim of his cap. Exhaling, he looked into the sky in the direction Cemil had been staring. "Well, are you going to do it?"

Cemil became aware of the disc in his pocket.

Kavas gave a knowing smile. "We thought this might happen. It's been a long time, Cemil. You actually did very well." He winked. "Just be thankful I waited for you to come up."

Kavas raised his hand. In his palm, he held a disc—identical to the one he'd given Cemil.

Cemil lunged forward, but it was too late. Kavas's thumb was already planted deep into the disc's button.

Cemil felt a brief rumbling. The sensation quickly passed.

In the parking lot, the staff members and drivers continued talking. For several moments, nothing appeared different. Then he saw it.

Outlets from the bunker's ventilation system were distributed throughout the field. Numerous columns of black smoke plumed into the air. Men began shouting as smoke billowed up from the stairs.

Cemil took a step toward the bunker, but Kavas grabbed his arm. "You and Iskender will soon be in positions of great power. Stay vigilant. In the next general election, everything will become self-evident."

73

Callahan woke on his back. He lay at the base of a flowering bush, its branches radiating over him. In the morning sun, the yellow flowers glowed. For several seconds, he lost himself in the beauty and the scent before he sat up and looked out onto the mountain steppes.

It was morning but already hot and humid. The surrounding hills were sprinkled with workers bent over the summer's crop of tea leaves.

After a hurried exit from the mountain home in Özören, he and Safiye had resumed their journey. Using a map they'd taken from the home, they'd traveled through the day and into the night. Turning inland, they passed south of Samsun. Late last night, as Safiye's limp worsened, Callahan insisted they stop.

Safiye's head rested on her rolled-up scarf, her back toward him. She was shivering. At the mountain home, she'd found antibiotic ointment and gauze and applied it to the ulcers on the backs of her heels, holding the gauze in place with a pair of white tube socks. Her socks and shoes were now off. The gauze, soaked with blood, lay by her feet.

The edges of the ulcers had turned a grayish yellow. The surrounding tissue was red and swollen. He pinched one of her toes. After her skin blanched, he was comforted to see a small degree of pink return, albeit slowly.

"Are you flirting with me?" Safiye asked. She sat up and pulled her feet toward her.

"I have a thing for feverish women." He put his hand to her forehead.

"Thank you for your concern, but I'm fine," she said, gently brushing his hand away. She plucked one of the flowers and held it to her nose. "Where to today?"

They'd traveled an incredible distance. Going farther, however, was no longer possible. Safiye needed antibiotics and rest, or she could lose one or both feet.

"We're just west of Terme," he said, looking at the map. "I think it's time to catch that bus."

"Terme?" She looked between the branches to the north. "Then those must be the plains of Themiscyra. It's the site of the ancient city of Thermodon—the land of the Amazons."

"An Ayla lecture?"

Nodding, Safiye looked down at the flower. She once again held it to her nose and inhaled before setting it aside and sliding out from beneath the bush.

Iskender Tunç sat in his third-floor office. His phone rang. "Hello."

"I'm on a secure line." It was Kavas. He sounded out of breath.

"And?"

"Cemil came through. He planted the briefcase. The entire High Command was in the bunker when it went off."

"Excellent," Tunç said.

"Is there anything on our missing doctors?" Kavas asked.

"I just received word they were sighted by a crew near Terme."

The day before, fieldworkers had sighted two people south of Özören who fit the descriptions of the American doctor and Safiye. Safiye and her friend had been industrious, traveling much farther east than anyone expected.

"We have four men in Terme," Tunç said. "But I've alerted the others. Over twenty men will be there in the next half-hour."

Tunç ended the call. As soon as he did, the phone was ringing again.

It was Madrik Zara, the public relations director and temporary acting director for the Yeni party.

"Mr. Tunç, it's as you expected," Zara said. "The results of Ulus Beyram's autopsy indicate foul play. Ulus was dead before his car crashed."

Tunç smiled. Zara didn't know yet about the fate of the High Command. Once word spread, there would be chaos.

"Many oppose the Yeni's ascendancy," Tunç said. "We must show them we cannot be intimidated. Set up a press conference for tomorrow. That's when you'll introduce me as the Yenis' presidential candidate."

"The press surrounding Ulus's death will work to our advantage. But shouldn't we wait? Whoever did this to Ulus may come after you."

"Ulus warned me running for the presidency was not for the weak of heart. This is what he was talking about. We must make the announcement as soon as possible. He would want us to act decisively."

"Of course," Zara said. "I'll make the arrangements. I'll see you tomorrow at party headquarters."

Tunç reached for his computer mouse and clicked on a file labeled "Firstpressconf." He hit the Print button. The first in a series of speeches that had been years in the making began scrolling from the printer.

"Yes," Tunç said. "I look forward to it."

74

Safiye leaned on Callahan, a hollow look in her eyes. They made their way slowly from the hills to the outskirts of Terme. "Michael, where do you wish we were right now?"

"On the porch of Mehmet and Ayla's cottage, listening to the water lap onto the shore."

"And drinking wine," she added.

"How about you?" he asked.

"Watching the sunset and listening to music at the conservatory in Konak Square."

Safiye began humming Beethoven's "Moonlight Sonata." Near the edge of town, she dropped her shoes to the ground and slid her feet into them, pushing the backs down with her heels.

"Wait here," he said. "I'll find the bus depot and come back."

Safiye looked up, meeting his gaze. "I'll be fine. Besides you can't go by yourself. Amazons hate men. They would kill you."

"Right," Callahan said.

Wrapping her scarf over her head, Safiye took a tentative step forward and then another.

As Safiye continued resolutely ahead, Callahan realized he'd have to be content knowing their walk was almost over. He moved to her side.

Terme looked like the other half dozen small towns they'd passed in the last few days. A minaret was the tallest structure in town. There was a sprinkling of pedestrians.

They stopped in the shade of a peddler's canopy. A woman was selling clay pots. Safiye asked if there was a bus depot in town. After the woman gave directions, Safiye pointed to a cooler. "What's in there?" she asked in Turkish.

The woman cracked open the cooler. It was filled with bottles of water.

"How much for two bottles?" Safiye asked.

"Two lira."

When Safiye hesitated, the woman countered. "One lira."

A high-pitched wail filled the air as the muezzin blasted from a nearby loudspeaker. The woman unrolled her prayer mat and knelt, facing Kaaba.

Safiye pointed Callahan toward an open area on the sidewalk. "You should be in front."

While the morning sun beat down on them, Callahan moved through a sequence of prostrations—copying the motions of others on the sidewalk in front of him.

When the prayer concluded, Callahan turned.

Safiye was on one knee, struggling to stand. He helped her to her feet. With a stiff-legged gait, she stepped toward the peddler woman and extended an object.

Safiye had told Callahan about the meeting with Tunç and her brother. Safiye's engagement ring had somehow found its way from the lawn into Ayla's envelope.

I'm sure you recognize the ring, Safiye. If it helps, in any way, use it.

Safiye spoke to the woman in Turkish.

The woman looked toward their matted clothes and then down at Safiye's feet. She pulled two bottles of water from the cooler and held them out. When Safiye extended the ring, the woman made a clicking sound with her tongue, shaking her head.

"Lütfen," Safiye said. "Lütfen."

"Yok olmaz," the peddler woman replied, waving her hand.

Safiye pushed the ring into the woman's open palm. The ring fell to the ground.

The woman directed exasperated looks toward Callahan and Safiye and then swept up the ring, slipping it beneath a fold in her robe.

"She has no idea how much I hate that thing," Safiye said as they walked away. "Or how thirsty I am." She unscrewed the cap from a bottle and took a drink.

At the end of the street, they emerged onto what appeared to be the town's main avenue.

"The depot is down this street and just south of town," Safiye said.

They continued down the sidewalk. When Safiye finished the bottle, Callahan removed the cap on the second bottle and handed it to her. As she drank, he wrapped an arm around her and touched his lips to her forehead. She was on fire, her skin dry.

"What's that for?" she asked, her voice trembling.

"Perseverance," he said. "Just lean on me. Pretend we're going for a casual Sunday morning walk."

"Is it Sunday?"

"Let's say it is."

A man stood in front of them outside a coffee shop. A network of pink scars covered the right side of his face. He had salt-and-pepper hair, a military cut, and bushy eyebrows. The man, who appeared to be of East European descent, was watching them, smiling warmly as if the sight of the approaching couple, arm-in-arm, sparked a fond reminiscence.

Callahan considered asking him for help. But the man suddenly turned, uninterested, and looked into the shop window.

Callahan tightened his grip on Safiye, who was breathing heavily. "Hang on," he said. If necessary, he would carry her to the depot.

"*Michael.*"

Callahan turned.

The man still peered into the window, his hands cupped at his temples. "Don't look at me," he said with a thick Russian accent. "Walk into the shop. Act like you want a cappuccino. Tunç's men are here. They've spotted you."

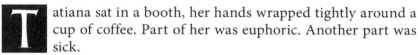

Tatiana sat in a booth, her hands wrapped tightly around a cup of coffee. Part of her was euphoric. Another part was sick.

Vlad stood outside the coffee shop, framed in the window. He was looking down the street, a smile on his face. The night before, he'd dropped to his knee, extended a diamond ring, and asked her to marry him.

"I was planning on waiting until we were back in Saint Petersburg, maybe a romantic dinner at the Taleon and a proposal while strolling alongside the Neva," he'd said. "But I couldn't wait that long."

Tatiana looked down at the ring. This is what she'd wanted. She had accepted, but why hadn't he waited until they were back in Saint Petersburg? Did he know this would be happening today? *Now*?

Five minutes earlier, one of the CIA agents had knocked at their hotel room door, his face flushed with excitement.

"Tunç's men just spotted the two doctors walking into town," the agent said.

The day before, they'd followed Tunç's men from Durağan to Terme. The two young men had been joined by two more. The four of them had spent the previous day and night patrolling the streets of Terme.

"We'll meet the doctors," Vlad said. "You bring the cars."

The CIA agent hurried away.

She and Vlad walked from the hotel and through a small courtyard before stepping out onto the main street.

They immediately spotted the two young men from Bafra at the outdoor café across the street.

Feeling the young men's glare, Tatiana calmly turned toward Vlad and smiled.

He returned her smile. "How about a little wake-me-up?" He nodded in the direction of the coffee shop up the street.

She melded into his side. "What did you think that was this morning?"

"That," he said. "That was unbelievable."

"Unbelievably noisy. I hope our CIA colleagues next door didn't mind."

Vlad laughed. "I hope they did."

Outside the coffee shop, Vlad peered into the window. Behind him, the doctors stepped into view, their clothes matted and dirty. The Turkish woman was on the verge of collapse.

"They're here," Tatiana said into her cell phone.

The doctors stepped through the shop's open front door and sat in a booth.

Tatiana slid into the seat next to the woman. "Drs. Callahan and Özmen, in a few moments, two sedans will pull up. The men inside are CIA agents."

The American looked skeptically back, yellow-green crescents beneath his eyes. "CIA?"

"I'm Tatiana." She pointed toward the window. "That's Vlad. We're with Russian intelligence. We're working with your CIA. They were alerted after you left a message at your embassy."

In the distance, there was the screech of tires.

"Get in the cars as fast as possible," Tatiana said. "Your lives depend on it."

At the window, Vlad waved.

"Go!"

The sedans skidded to a halt outside the coffee shop, their doors flying open. The agents, two inside each car, waved them forward.

The doctors ran from the shop. The woman moved surprisingly fast. As Tatiana followed, the morning's quiet was broken by gunfire.

Tatiana and the doctors dropped to the sidewalk. Bullets riddled the two sedans, their windows shattering. The CIA agents slumped over.

One of the young men from Bafra was on the sidewalk to Tatiana's right. The other was on the roof of the coffee shop. Both were holding automatics.

There were two more shots.

The man on the sidewalk collapsed. The other fell from the roof, landing with a sickening snap of bones.

The Turkish doctor inexplicably stood.

"Get down," Tatiana snapped.

Staring across the street toward the roof of a one-story building, the doctor instead stepped forward.

Above the parapet of the building, the upper torso of a young man was visible. He was one of the men who'd joined the two from Bafra. Holding a rifle, he yelled, "Leave, Safiye. More are coming."

Vlad sprinted across the street. He opened the BMW's rear door and waved the doctors forward.

Tatiana looked up and down the street. *Where was the fourth?*

She soon had her answer.

There was more gunfire. A spray of blood flew from Vlad's shoulder. The shock of the bullet spun him around. As their eyes met, a smile briefly crossed Vlad's face.

Each knew what came next. Each knew they were powerless to stop it.

There was another salvo.

Vlad's body jerked with each bullet. Tatiana felt each one.

The American doctor ran and caught Vlad. They fell into the back seat of the BMW. The Turkish doctor dove into the front.

Tatiana ran and slid over the car's hood. Inside, the keys in place, she turned the ignition. As the diesel engine coughed to life, there was another burst of gunfire. The windows shattered.

In the rearview mirror, Tatiana spotted the fourth young man down the street, his automatic raised. "Down!"

Tatiana ducked, expecting another barrage. But there was only a single echoing shot.

In the rearview mirror, she saw the young man crumple to the ground. She looked to the roof of the one-story building.

A rifle barrel, protruding from above the parapet, slipped from view.

76

"Lasting peace is sought; it is essential to adopt international measures to improve the lot of masses. People of the world must be taught to give up envy, avarice, and rancour."

—**Mustafa Kemal Atatürk**

T he F-18 swept from a cloudless blue sky, touching down on a NATO airfield east of Ankara. When the jet came to a stop, Fontaine climbed from the rear cockpit. Two men wearing flight suits with captain's bars waited in the front seat of an open-air jeep. Fontaine hopped into the back. The jeep pulled ahead.

"How was your flight, sir?" the captain in the passenger seat yelled.

"Good," Fontaine said. "And yours?"

The two captains were part of a squadron that had flown in from their NATO air base in southern Turkey's Incirlik.

"Outstanding, sir," the captain said. "Do we have clearance?"

"For whatever constitutes necessary force."

Turkey's new president, Imar Yerbaten, had met with NATO commanders. In a teleconference, Fontaine briefed Yerbaten and the commanders on recent events. After Fontaine presented evidence pointing toward Iskender Tunç as the culprit, Yerbaten granted permission for a NATO strike on Tunç's estate in northern Turkey.

During Fontaine's flight to the airfield, where he would brief the strike force, the CIA agents in northern Turkey reported they'd sighted the missing physicians. Moments earlier, when communications with the CIA agents had been lost, Fontaine's plans changed.

The jeep came to a stop. Two Black Hawks were waiting, their rotors spinning. The driver turned off the ignition and sprinted toward a helicoptor. The other captain waved Fontaine toward the second Black Hawk. They ran toward it, buffeted by the downdraft.

Inside the helicopter, the captain slammed the door shut behind them and went to the front. Fontaine buckled himself into a seat. Six helmeted Rangers sat in the back. A man with a medic insignia tossed him a helmet.

The Black Hawk lifted straight up at full throttle.

"Mr. Fontaine, can you hear me?" came the captain's voice in his headset.

"Yes, Captain," he said.

"Terme is 135 kilometers northwest. Projected time of arrival is twenty-four minutes."

In the back seat of the old-model BMW, Callahan tore away Vlad's shirt and assessed the damage. The Russian had at least three chest wounds.

"How is he?" Tatiana asked, glancing back as she drove.

"He needs surgery."

"There's a first aid kit," Tatiana said, pointing to the glove compartment.

Safiye removed the kit and handed it back.

"We're heading north from Terme toward the Cape of Hercules," Tatiana shouted into her cell phone. "We have the doctors. Vlad is injured, and your men are down . . . . Yes, I'm sorry . . . . I'll stay on the line." She glanced toward Safiye. "Our ride arrives in twenty-three minutes."

"Ride?"

"Helicopters. Courtesy of the United States of—"

Quieting, Tatiana took her foot off the gas. Ahead, three cars were parked in the middle of the road.

"Where did they come from?" Safiye asked.

Tatiana brought the BMW to a stop. "Tunç has men all over northern Turkey looking for you," she said. She tried to casually turn around, hoping not to draw attention, but they were the only other car on the road.

"They're following," Safiye said, watching out the busted rear window.

Tatiana jammed her foot on the accelerator and picked up the phone. "The cape is out," she said. "We're headed back to Terme."

Safiye pointed ahead. "Someone's coming."

Two cars raced toward them from Terme. One veered into the oncoming lane.

"Hold tight," Tatiana yelled. Jerking the wheel, she turned off the road.

The rolling landscape, sparsely covered with small bushes and grass, had been baked to a hard crust by the July heat. The BMW bucked wildly as it moved across the unforgiving terrain.

Callahan held Vlad in position as he peered out the back window. The cars speeding north from Terme swerved from the road. One continued over the plain. The other stopped. Three men exited.

"They have rifles," Callahan said.

The men fired.

A taillight shattered.

Tatiana swung the car around and brought it to a stop, facing their pursuers. She extended a pistol and bullet clip back toward Callahan. "When the clip is empty, eject it like this and snap the new one in place. Got it?"

He nodded.

"I'll do the long-range shooting," she said. "Wait until they're close. And don't waste shots."

Callahan took the pistol and clip.

Tatiana slipped outside. She disappeared behind the car and opened the trunk.

Callahan rolled from the car and crawled across the dusty ground. When he was twenty yards from the car, he looked back.

Safiye was tending to the injured Russian in the back of the BMW. The car's trunk was still open. A bullet punctured the trunk door.

Tatiana lay on a distant rise behind a rifle. Aiming, she fired twice in rapid succession. The approaching car's radiator burst in an explosion of steam. The doors flew open, and the passengers jumped out.

The cars from the roadblock were parked next to the second

car from Terme. Their passengers were already running across the plain.

Tatiana continued firing. Two of the men dropped, but the others continued forward in a rapid leapfrog advance. After Tatiana hit a third and then a fourth, the men took cover.

An eerie calm settled over the plain. Over the next several minutes, Tatiana and Callahan fired occasional shots, hoping to keep Tunç's men at bay. The men intermittently shouted out to one another but were surprisingly content to maintain their positions. When Callahan emptied his clip, he snapped in the one Tatiana had given him.

Ttthhhew, ttthhhew, ttthhhew . . .

Callahan scanned the horizon. He spotted a helicopter making its way across the plain. Tatiana had said US helicopters were coming. There was only one.

The helicopter approached. It came to a stop over Tatiana. As the helicopter began to turn, Callahan saw the fuselage—blue and unmarked. "It's one of theirs," he yelled. He began firing. Tatiana joined in.

The helicopter moved to a higher altitude. As it did, an object fell from the window.

Callahan's stomach sank as he watched the object fall. It landed near Tatiana and exploded, immersing her in a cloud of dust.

Another hand grenade fell. It disappeared into the dust and exploded.

Callahan hopped to his feet and ran toward Tatiana. A fusillade of bullets whistled by.

One of Tunç's men was on the ground, slinking forward near the front of the BMW. The man raised his rifle, but Callahan fired first, striking him in the neck.

Another of Tunç's men was on his knees, several yards behind the first, his pistol raised. Callahan swung his gun toward him, but the man fired first.

The bullet struck Callahan in the left shoulder. Falling, he fired his pistol.

Callahan hit the ground hard. He lay face down, his nose rebroken, paralyzed by the pain knifing through his shoulder and face. He spat out a mouthful of blood and dirt.

Hands rolled him over. Safiye. "Michael," she said, brushing the dirt from his face.

Callahan lifted his head. The man who'd shot him was slumped on the ground. Two other men were running toward the BMW.

Callahan raised the gun across his pain-racked body and fired twice. The men fell.

Callahan collapsed back, howling in pain. Raising his pistol toward the helicopter, he fired, repeatedly pulling the trigger until the bolt clicked against an empty chamber.

Safiye pressed her hand to his shoulder, his blood seeping between her fingers. Huddling together, defenseless, they looked up as the helicopter descended.

77

"We have airborne," crackled the captain's voice over Fontaine's headset.

"Friendly?" someone asked.

"We won't know until we make visual," the captain said.

"I hear gunfire," a voice said.

Fontaine unfastened his harness and made his way on hands and knees to the cockpit. The copilot was calling out greetings, turning a dial on the control panel.

In the distance, a helicopter came into view. Next to it was a rising cloud of dust.

"They're not responding," the copilot said, peering through binoculars. "There's a car beneath it."

"Four-thousand feet and closing," the captain said. He glanced back at Fontaine. "What shall we do, sir? It's not one of ours."

Fontaine hit autodial on his phone. Taking off his helmet, he listened to the phone ring. As the approaching helicopter loomed larger, another cloud of dust plumed from the ground.

"*Sir*?" the captain said.

With the seventh ring, Fontaine turned to the copilot. "Is it still over the car?"

"It moved."

"Take it," Fontaine said.

"Target acquired," the copilot said, flipping a switch.

"Launch," the captain said.

The Black Hawk bucked as a missile hissed away. The projectile disappeared into the helicopter's silhouette and exploded. The fiery heap of metal dropped, its spinning rotors digging deep furrows into the dirt.

"We're taking fire," came a voice in the headset.

The copilot pointed. The other Black Hawk hovered over a group of cars on the road. Men crouched behind the cars, firing at the helicopter.

"Sit tight," the captain said.

The fallen helicopter had come to rest a dozen yards from the car—a dust-covered BMW riddled with bullets. "I see a man and woman," the captain said, scanning the terrain. "Do we have more cargo?"

"We're looking for two men and two women," Fontaine said.

The captain moved the Black Hawk in a small circle above the BMW. "I see a man in the back."

"It's getting hot over here," the other pilot said as smoke poured from the tail of his helicopter. "Permission to fire?"

The captain looked to Fontaine, who grimly nodded.

"Permission granted," the captain said.

The other pilot adjusted the helicopter's pitch. As the tail moved skyward, it brought the men on the ground face-to-face with the Black Hawk's bottom-mounted thirty millimeter.

Some of the men continued firing. Others stared helplessly.

Thirty seconds and 300 rounds later, there was silence.

Part

4

"*The biggest battle is the war against ignorance.*"

—Mustafa Kemal Atatürk

78

Iskender Tunç sat in his study chair, staring at his father's portrait. He scoured the inanimate canvas, searching for answers to questions they hadn't foreseen.

There was a soft knock at the door. Edirne Kavas and Enver Pasha entered. Moving quietly across the room, they sat on the couch. It was a few moments before Enver spoke. "Edirne and I have been discussing the situation."

"And what is the solution to *our* situation?" Tunç asked.

"The Sayişma cannot proceed," Enver said. "The estate needs to be evacuated, its records destroyed."

"You never should have brought the doctors here," Kavas said. "They'll lead the authorities back to the estate."

"Let them come," Tunç said. "Let them make their inquiries. They made inquiries into Turkish Sky but found only an old, empty hangar. The same will happen here. They'll find a quiet estate with two elderly caretakers."

"They'll turn their attention to you," Enver said. "They undoubtedly already have."

"Then where are they?" Tunç asked, raising his arms. "Why haven't they come?"

"Perhaps they know about Little Tortona," Enver said. "Perhaps they know about the plutonium and Göttingen and fear the repercussions of a counterattack."

"That's right," Tunç said, his eyes growing wide. "That's exactly right. They're afraid."

"We cannot shepherd the Turkish people into the future with the threat of a bioweapons attack *or* at the point of a nuclear warhead," Enver said.

Ignoring the two men, Tunç continued, lost in his thoughts. "Tomorrow, when I speak to the Turkish people, I'll let them know the Yeni are under siege. Further attacks will appear as nothing more than a smear campaign by our enemies."

"We cannot proceed," Enver said, standing. "The campaign, your presidency, the Sayişma. The West won't allow them."

"Allow them?" Tunç laughed. "Soon, they won't be able to stop them. When I speak to the nation, when the people hear me, they'll flock to our cause. Interference by a weakened military or the Americans won't be tolerated."

"We must preserve our future," Enver said. "The estate is lost but not the Şebeke. The Şebeke is still intact."

Tunç looked back and forth at the old men. "We must have the courage to look at what is right with the Sayişma—not wrong. Think of it. Did either of you dream we'd be *this* successful? The High Command is in ruin. Cebici is dead. Tomorrow, when I announce my candidacy for the presidency, the Muslim faithful will fall in line. Now is the time for reckoning."

"As emissary for six decades of Enderun graduates, as proprietor of the Şebeke—the Şebeke that's provided you with everything," Enver roared. "I demand that you step down."

"I respectfully decline," Tunç said. He turned to the portrait. "I'm held to a higher obligation than my allegiance to the Şebeke. I'm held to the promise I made to my father."

"No, Iskender," Enver said, "You're not."

"*What?*"

"You owe him nothing," the old doctor said, his voice a low growl. He thrust a forefinger into his chest. "I was the boy Muhammed carried from the burning mosque. I was the first to come to this estate and the first to graduate from the Enderun. I also carry the promises I made to Muhammed Tunç. I owe him my life, but I've paid dearly."

"We all know you were the first," Tunç said, giving a dismissive wave. "We've all paid a price. We've all made sacrifices."

"Don't talk to me about sacrifices," Enver said. "I've given everything to the Enderun. I've worked my whole life toward the Sayişma. I've had to watch as Muhammed—"

Kavas placed a hand on the old doctor's shoulder.

Enver swatted the hand away. "I've had to watch as Muhammed raised my son . . . as his own."

Tunç's eyes widened.

"Yes, Iskender," Enver said. "You're the son of a Kurdish refugee. I release you from any obligations to Muhammed Tunç. I've paid both our debts."

"My father is dead," Tunç said.

Enver held his arms out wide. "I'm not. Regrettably, your mother is. Her name was Adelina."

"I know who my mother was," Tunç snapped. "Adelina Vata. She was an Albanian refugee. My father brought her to the estate to serve as his wife."

Enver nodded. "When Adelina came to the estate, I was practicing in Samsun. I made frequent visits to the Enderun to serve as a physician and to teach. I fell in love with your mother. When Adelina became pregnant, she wanted us to run away. I said no. I was too committed to Muhammed's cause. But as you grew within her, my love for her deepened. I decided after she gave birth, we would start a new life. We would be a family." His voice dropped. "During your delivery, however, she hemorrhaged. She lost too much blood and fell into a coma. I whispered my plans into her ear, but—" He shook his head. "It didn't matter. She never heard me. She died the day after you were born."

Tunç shook his head. "The others would know. Someone would have told me." He looked toward Kavas. "Tell me he's lying."

Kavas opened his mouth to speak but then lowered his gaze.

"Muhammed was in his seventies when you were born," Enver said. "He believed you were his miracle child. He gave you his name. He picked you to lead his businesses." He paused, his eyes glistening. "No matter how much I wanted to be a father to you, I couldn't take that away from you."

Tunç looked imploringly toward Kavas. This time, the headmaster met his gaze. "Most of Muhammed's sons had left the estate by the time you were born. Your sisters were sent away when they were young and raised by past graduates." Kavas paused, raising an eyebrow. "You must have known his other wives bore him children, that he had other sons."

"Father always said Adelina and I were special," Tunç said. "That's why he brought me home. It's why he didn't give the others his name."

Kavas shook his head. "Whether we were Kurdish orphans or his own, Muhammed thought of all of us as his sons. But like many great leaders, he fell short when it came time to make plans for his succession. After Cemil, his last biological son, was born,

Muhammed believed he'd have more sons. When he went several years without children, he made plans to take Cemil to Izmir, to give him his name, but then Adelina became pregnant with you."

Tunç wrapped his arms around his head. "No," he bellowed. "Cowards. *Liars.*" He looked up at the portrait into the patriarch's eyes. This time, finding answers, he strode from the room.

Kavas sat back on the couch, his breathing unsteady. He slipped a tin from his pocket. Fumbling to push back the lid, he removed a nitroglycerin tablet and placed it under his tongue.

Enver stood motionless in the center of the room. He stared down at a small revolver in his open palm.

"I can't blame you for not doing it," Kavas said.

"He's still my son," Enver said, setting the gun on the desk.

Leaving the study, they walked down the back staircase and outside. By the moonlight, they made their way onto the lawn.

The boys' howls filled the night. The younger students had been bused in from the outside facility. With their elders focused on the Sayişma, the boys had run wild.

"The estate is as vibrant as ever," Kavas said.

"A bit too vibrant," Enver said.

From behind, a group of boys swept past them. A few bumped into the old men before disappearing into the woods. Enver started forward, but Kavas grabbed his arm. "Let them go."

"We never would have done that," Enver said.

"We wouldn't have."

"We must try to teach them. We must speak our minds."

Kavas smiled. "As long as we have them."

Enver met the headmaster's gaze. "And maybe a bit longer."

The lifelong friends laughed.

"You have much more patience than me," Enver said. "That's why you've made such a great teacher. I've always admired you for staying here. We've all struggled to find a purpose. No one has found a greater one than you."

"Thank you," Kavas said. "Coming from you that means a lot."

"Looking back, would you do it again?"

"You mean become a eunuch?"

Enver nodded.

"My answer once would have been no. With time, however, I've seen the wisdom in it. It made me a better teacher. It eased a yearning, not just for physical pleasures but the desire to go out in the world, to get married, to have children. I respect and envy you and the others for doing what you did, but the envy is less, it's not crippling. Does that make sense?"

"It does."

"There are positives," Kavas said. "But there are certainly negatives."

"Iskender was right about one thing," Enver said. "We've all made sacrifices."

The two old men were on the trail leading to the barn. In a small clearing, they came to a stop. The men looked up, mouths agape, struggling to comprehend what was before them.

In a splash of light from the barn, the two instructors hung from ropes tied around their necks. Their eyes were bulging, their bodies twitching.

At the edge of the clearing, a ring of boys stood in the shadows.

The old men rushed forward and frantically pushed up on the eunuchs' legs. But the instructors, unable to support their own weight, were too far gone.

"Don't just stand there," Enver yelled at the boys.

"Help us," Kavas pleaded. "They're dying."

The boys each took a step forward into the light. "Headmaster, Doctor," the oldest of the boys said. "You've been charged with conspiracy against the Sayişma."

"Conspiracy?" Kavas said. "What are you talking about?"

The boys looked up into the tree. Shadowed figures scurried among the branches. From the main branch, two ropes descended— their ends fashioned into nooses.

79

Callahan walked from the hospital at the NATO airfield east of Ankara. He wore a flight suit, his arm in a sling, his shoulder throbbing. In a moment, he'd take a few pills from the bottle of Norco in his pocket and drift into oblivion. But not yet. He wanted to be alert for this.

Safiye shuffled at his side, her feet encased in bandages.

"We must make quite the sight," Safiye said.

The day before, after the Black Hawk had flown them back to the base, Callahan underwent surgeries to remove the bullet from his shoulder and repair his nose. The ulcers on Safiye's heels had been cleaned, and she'd been started on antibiotics.

They turned toward each other. There was a brief spark in Safiye's eyes. After everything, they'd survived. The spark, however, quickly faded.

Earlier, they'd met with Fontaine. The CIA agent informed them that Mehmet was dead. On the day he'd driven to Ankara, he was found on a bench near the ministry of justice. There was no word of Ayla.

Callahan and Safiye watched as soldiers carried a casket toward a waiting C-37 transport. Tatiana walked behind the casket. On the flight back from Terme, Vladimir Petrovich had succumbed to his wounds.

Tatiana had suffered a minor concussion but otherwise escaped unscathed from the firefight on the plains of Themiscyra. The Russian agent stepped toward them. She and Safiye embraced.

"I'm so sorry," Safiye said. "We owe our lives to you, to both of you."

"I'm sorry we couldn't save him," Callahan said. In the

helicopter, before passing out from lack of blood, he'd directed the medics taking care of the injured Russian agent.

"You did everything possible," Tatiana said. She looked at the casket, her eyes red and swollen. "He's been living with so much pain. He's finally at peace." She grabbed their forearms. "Please, whenever you do something good for your patients, when you save a life, think of Vlad."

"We'll think of both of you," Safiye said.

Tatiana gave each of them a hug and kissed their cheeks. She then walked away, disappearing into the rear of the transport.

A jeep approached and stopped near two F-18s. Fontaine hopped from the Jeep and waved, then climbed aboard one of the twin-seat fighters.

"How is it?" Safiye asked, looking at Callahan's shoulder.

"All right. Surprisingly, all right," he lied, moving his shoulder in a small circle. "Almost like new. How about you?"

She looked at her feet, her chin quivering. She tried to contort her face into a smile, but that was asking too much.

Callahan wrapped his good arm around her. She buried her face in his chest. They held each other for several moments until Safiye stepped back, wiping her eyes.

Callahan didn't like leaving her, not like this. But he had to go. And she had to stay. This was her home. He reached into his pocket. "Something to remember me by until—"

His last word hung in the air.

Until. *Until when?* Not seeing Safiye until the next excursion seemed inconceivable.

He placed the slug they'd removed from his shoulder into the palm of her hand.

Safiye rolled the distorted piece of metal back and forth in her palm and smiled. "No matter how terrible the circumstances, Michael Callahan, you can always make me feel better."

The C-37 lumbered down the runway and lifted into the air.

Callahan wrapped his arm around Safiye and kissed her forehead. "Take care of yourself."

"You too, Michael."

The ground crew helped Callahan up the ladder into the second F-18. Removing the Norco from his pocket, he slipped two pills into his mouth.

A ground crew member fastened Callahan's helmet and harness. The man patted him on the helmet and gave a thumbs-up sign. When Callahan nodded, the man leaped to the ground. The canopy closed.

Safiye stood by herself on the tarmac. She waved. He waved back.

For the past two weeks they'd been constant companions. Now, he wondered if he'd ever see her again.

As the jet taxied away from Safiye, an emptiness tore through him. The emptiness expanded until it felt as though the ground between them would give way.

Faster than he thought possible, however, the F-18 was roaring down the runway and lifting into the sky, leaving the airfield and Safiye far behind.

80

Callahan sat in front of a computer, sipping a coffee. Fontaine was at his side. After their transatlantic flight, they'd landed at CIA headquarters in Langley, Virginia.

"I'm going to show you a series of pictures," Fontaine said. "I want you to identify as many people as you can."

The first photo was of Iskender Tunç. It was followed by images of Yalçin Kaldırım and Ançak Barhal. Callahan identified the three men.

"After you left your message at the American Embassy, Turkish authorities went to city hall to question Barhal," Fontaine said. "They couldn't find him. He's disappeared."

A woman's photo appeared.

"I don't know her name," Callahan said. "But it looks like the receptionist from city hall."

Fontaine nodded. "Her name is Caria Mahid. Did Barhal see you talking to her?"

"We were standing by her desk when he approached us," Callahan said. "Why?"

"A few days after your visit to city hall, Caria Mahid was outside the entrance to the Aegean University exhibition hall when she collapsed and died. The hall housed your search committee. We believe Barhal may have stopped her before she could provide evidence against him."

"She died because she talked with us?" Callahan asked.

"We can't prove anything at this point, but forensic analysis of her cause of death is ongoing," Fontaine said. He advanced to the next image.

In a photo, Callahan was with Safiye, Mehmet, and Ayla on the Kobas' boat. They were talking with Tunç.

"This is from Kólpos Kallonís," Callahan said.

"Yes. What did you talk about with Tunç?"

"It was small talk, mostly. He asked us to have lunch with him, but we declined. Safiye made it obvious she didn't want to be around him." Callahan pointed at the photo. "Did Tatiana and Vlad take it?"

Fontaine gave a nod. "Tatiana told you they were following Tunç. Did she tell you why?"

"Because of what his men did to Vlad."

"Then, you know about Grozny?"

Callahan nodded. "And the stolen plutonium."

"I recommend keeping that to yourself," Fontaine said. "It's classified."

"Who would I tell? A Russian agent?"

"You've got a point." Fontaine advanced to the next screen.

A split-screen image appeared. The photo on the left was another photo of the Kobas' schooner. On the right, a higher-power view of the same image spotlighted a space next to Mehmet. Mehmet was still partially in the photo, but it was centered on a blurred figure in the stairwell of Tunç's yacht. The person wore glasses and had tousled, receding blond hair.

"Do you remember this man?" Fontaine asked.

Callahan squinted. "It's not a good picture, but I do. While we were talking, he walked up from below deck."

"Did you speak with him?"

"No," Callahan said. "He seemed surprised to see us, but then he abruptly disappeared below. I presumed he was a deckhand or cook."

"Could you identify him?"

"Not sure."

Fontaine clicked on a folder. Dozens of photos filled the screen. "This is a photo lineup. Look through it. Take your time."

Callahan spent the next few minutes scrolling through the photos. When he finished, he moved back several screens and pointed.

The photo was of a fair-haired man with wire-rimmed glasses. His thinning blond hair was combed neatly back and he had a prominent brow.

"On the boat, his hair was longer," Callahan said. "He also had a beard, but I'm pretty sure that's him."

"Are you positive?"

"The eyes are identical, the brow. I'm fairly sure. You could ask Safiye, but I doubt she saw him. When Tunç came onto the boat, she never looked up. She just stared into the water."

"A colleague at the air base showed her the same set of photos an hour ago," Fontaine said. "She didn't remember seeing him."

"Who is he?" Callahan asked.

"Hopefully not the man who starts World War III."

When Callahan gave him an inquisitive look, Fontaine stood. "Come on. You already know too much."

They walked from the room and down a hallway.

"Secretary Hawthorne wanted me to extend an invitation to you for dinner," Fontaine said. He stopped at a door.

"*Who?*"

"Secretary Kevin Hawthorne."

"The secretary of state?" Callahan asked.

"Yes," Fontaine said. "The invitation is for you and friends and family." Smiling, he pointed at the door.

Callahan opened it. As he stepped into the room, there was a roar.

Callahan's parents were waiting. Next to them were his sister Kate and her husband. Beyond them were Alin, Haas, Brooke, Mrs. Bagley, and Thomas. Overwhelmed, crying or clapping and some both, everyone rushed toward him.

81

On the grounds of the US Naval Observatory in Washington, DC, in a small gathering in the dining room of a house at 1 Observatory Circle, Secretary of State Kevin Hawthorne stood. "Today, I read a report describing Dr. Michael Callahan's actions during a gun battle north of Terme," he said. "Because of that report, I'd like to preface our dinner with a presentation."

The Queen Anne-style house at 1 Observatory Circle was traditionally the residence of the vice president, who'd instead chosen to live in a condo in downtown Washington. With the house open, the secretary of state and his wife had moved in.

"Although this award is historically a military honor, President Kennedy opened its eligibility to civilians," Hawthorne said.

Callahan looked around the walnut dining table. Seated were Fontaine, members of Callahan's family, and the relief team members who'd greeted him at Langley. He and Safiye had spent the last week hiding in the woods of northern Turkey—sleeping on the ground and raiding orchards for food. Now, he was here.

Hawthorne unfolded a piece of paper. Peering through his spectacles, he read aloud. "'Whenever any singularly meritorious action is performed, the author of it shall be permitted to wear on his facing, over his left breast, the figure of a heart in purple cloth or silk edged with narrow lace or binding. Not only instances of unusual gallantry but also of extraordinary fidelity and essential service in any way shall meet with due reward.'" He folded the paper and looked up. "These words were written in 1782 by George Washington."

The secretary of state pulled a small metallic object from his breast pocket. "Before presenting a commendation, I believe thorough research is in order. For those doubting the severity of Dr. Callahan's injury, I direct you to this." Hawthorne held up the object. "You can see what his shoulder did to a perfectly good bullet."

As everyone laughed, Callahan stared in amazement. It was the slug he'd given to Safiye.

"Let me say it's clear Dr. Michael Jeffrey Callahan displayed uncommon courage under fire," the secretary of state said. "I've been provided with a vivid description of Dr. Callahan's activities, not only during the skirmish, but since he arrived in Izmir. His actions have been extraordinary."

Callahan followed Hawthorne's gaze.

Safiye stood in the entrance hallway outside the dining room. Next to her was Hawthorne's wife, Dr. Matti Carlyle.

"Safiye," the relief team members cried in unison.

The team members rushed forward. Each took their turn hugging Safiye. Callahan, the last in line, wrapped his good arm around her. "How are you?"

"All right . . . Surprisingly, all right," she said. Wearing a black pantsuit, she pulled up the legs, exposing her still bandaged feet. "Almost like new."

"When did you get here?"

"Forty-five minutes ago. They drove me straight from the airfield."

Callahan hugged her again and kissed her on the cheek. "It's great to see you."

Haas cleared his throat.

Everyone had returned to their seats. They were standing, watching them. Matti Carlyle waved Safiye toward a place setting next to her.

"In the true spirit of our Founding Fathers," Hawthorne said, stepping toward Callahan, "on behalf of the president of the United States, it's my honor to present you with the oldest military decoration in use and the first created for the common soldier. The Purple Heart." As he pinned the medal on Callahan's chest, a photographer appeared from a side door.

The moment turned into a photo shoot as everyone took a turn next to Callahan and the secretary of state. While posing, Callahan looked toward Fontaine. Earlier, the CIA agent had shown him news footage of Tunç announcing his candidacy for the Turkish presidency.

"How can this happen?" Callahan had asked.

"Turkey is in a precarious situation. With the recent assassinations, the usual checks and balances aren't in place."

"Can't we do anything?"

"With Tunç potentially having access to nuclear and biochemical weapons, the situation is a mess," Fontaine had said. "He's playing a high-stakes game. It's one he'll eventually lose. But right now, the answer is no. We can't do a damn thing."

Once the photo-taking concluded, Callahan walked to Alin and set a hand on his shoulder. He nodded toward the photographer. "This will make a nice addition to a certain office wall."

"It will," Alin said. "But this is for your wall."

Matti and Safiye approached. "When they told me a Turkish doctor was flying in, I never thought I'd be meeting a fellow Georgetown graduate," Matti said, her arm wrapped around Safiye. She extended a hand to Callahan. "Nice to meet you and welcome back."

"Thank you," Callahan said. "And thank you for letting us into your home."

"As I often tell our visitors, the house belongs to you as much as me," Matti said. "I just happen to be the current tenant." She turned toward Alin. "Good to see you again." They embraced.

"As director of the American Cancer Society, Matti is a fervent supporter of the WHO," Alin said to Callahan and Safiye. "More than a few times, she's twisted arms to make sure the relief team has funding."

"I should say thank you," Callahan said. "Your organization has also provided me with a few research grants over the years."

"I have no doubt it was money well spent," Matti said, her voice trailing off. Looking down at the table, she picked up a bottle of beer. A bottle sat at each place setting. "Iron City?" she said.

"Eric thought he'd add a 'Picksburg' flair to dinner," Brooke said, standing on the other side of the table. She nodded toward Haas, who was holding his cell phone in the air.

"What are you doing?" Callahan asked.

"FaceTiming," Haas said. "It's Adams."

Haas extended the phone to Callahan. Safiye moved to his side.

"Mike. Safiye," Adams said, his face filling the screen. "It's great to see you."

"Scott, hello," they replied.

Adams was wearing scrubs. He was unshaven, his hair disheveled.

"Are you on call?" Safiye asked.

"No, I just look like it," Adams said. "Which brings me to the reason I couldn't make it. I wanted to see everyone, but Lil went into labor last night—a little sooner than expected. She delivered a few hours ago."

A blonde-haired woman appeared, sitting up in a bed. Her hair was also disheveled, but she was smiling. "Scott has told me so much about you," she said, speaking with the same southern drawl as her husband. "We wept tears of joy after hearing you were safe."

"Thank you," Callahan and Safiye said.

Lil's eyes were suddenly searching. "Where's Alin?"

Callahan swung the camera toward Alin, who smiled. "Did your husband deliver my message?" he asked.

"He did," Lil said. "The girls and I would like to say you're welcome. And that, yes, we're proud of him." She pulled Scott toward her and kissed him on the cheek. "We missed him, terribly, but we know y'all were doing something very important over there."

"Hey," Adams said. "Lil and I were just talking. We have an announcement we'd like to make."

A baby bundled in a crib filled the screen. The baby rested peacefully, wearing a light-blue cap.

"Scott had a boy," Callahan said.

As Callahan held the phone in the air, the relief team members clamored around him. "Congratulations," everyone called out.

"Thank you," Adams said.

"He looks perfect," Safiye said.

"He takes after his mother," Adams said, reappearing on the screen. "Can you hear me okay?"

"Sure," they all called out.

Adams clenched his jaw, his eyes suddenly glistening. "Lil and I've decided on a name." He swung the camera to the baby. "I'd like everyone to officially meet our son. His name is Bryce Michael Adams."

The baby boy's eyes cracked open as he looked toward the camera.

"I couldn't think of two better guys to name him after," Adams said.

"Welcome to the world," Brooke said. "Mr. Bryce . . . Michael . . . Adams."

Callahan stared at the baby boy. Unable to speak, he buried his face in Safiye's shoulder.

Callahan and Safiye held each other tight.

The other relief team members wrapped their arms around them in a group hug.

When the team members finally looked up, their eyes wet with tears, Callahan raised his fist. "To Bryce," he said.

The others set their hands over his. "To Bryce."

82

B eyir sat alone in the Enderun's trophy room. He closed his eyes and enjoyed a moment of peace.

The last several days had been a sleepless, frenetic blur. He'd moved from Sinop to the towns of Boyabat, Özören, and then Terme in search of Safiye. From his rooftop perch in Terme, binoculars raised, he'd watched the skirmish on the plains of Themiscyra. Twenty Janissaries were dead. Safiye was free. As simple as that, the Sayişma was over. Or that's what he'd thought.

This morning, he and the others watched a national television broadcast of Tunç announcing his candidacy for the presidency. On the steps of the National Assembly, Tunç outlined his platform, speaking frankly of a desire for a return to Muslim values.

"Turkey is a nation rich in military, religious, and cultural tradition. We are of one mind, one heart. Our people must remember what we have in common: our history, our faith." Tunç paused, scanning the crowd. "Today, as I announce my candidacy for the presidency, I extend my hand to the soldiers and clerics. I extend my hand to the academics in our great universities, to the workers, and to the poor. I extend my hand to all Muslims: Sunni and Shia. We are one nation under Allah. Long live Islam. Long live the Turkish people."

As Tunç spoke, the tranquil applause of the Yeni faithful grew into the impassioned chanting of many. Drawn to Tunç's booming voice and mesmerized by a piercing glare reminiscent of Atatürk himself, casual passersby transformed into believers. The camera panned the crowd, stopping to frame shouting, tear-streaked faces. When it was over, Tunç had stood with arms raised, nodding as the crowd chanted his name.

Beyir stood from the high-backed leather chair and walked across the dimly lit room. At the trophy case, he looked at the Kazans' class picture. His eyes passed over their hopeful faces and settled on Tunç, who stood with the graduates.

The calm, confident look Tunç possessed in the picture was now gone. In its place was the same unbridled glare that had passed to the boys doing his bidding. They would do anything for him. What was most unconscionable, however, was there was no limit to what Tunç asked of them.

After returning from Terme late the previous night, Beyir came upon the bodies of Kavas, Enver, and the two instructors hanging from a tree near the barn. Kavas and the instructors were dead, but Enver was alive. The old doctor's blue fingertips were locked around the rope, his neck veins bulging, his legs bicycling as he tried to slip from the noose.

Beyir lifted Enver enough for him to slide the rope from around his neck. The old doctor fell to the ground, choking and gasping for air.

"Who did this?" Beyir asked.

"The boys," Enver rasped.

"We need to tell Iskender."

"*He* sent them."

They heard laughing and shouting. A group of boys was approaching.

"Go down to the Enderun," Enver said. "Pretend you didn't see this."

Beyir looked up at the three hanging figures. "We have to get them down."

Enver shook his head. "We don't have time." Jumping to his feet, he ran into the night.

Beyir stepped back from the trophy case and looked over the class portraits. How many ways were the graduates in debt to Headmaster Kavas, Enver Pasha, and the two instructors?

A siren pierced the air.

Beyir instinctively ran from the room. It had been six years since he'd participated in a drill. This, however, was not a drill.

The back halls were filling with Janissaries queuing up to ascend the ladders. Beyir climbed a ladder and joined several others in a bunker—one of a dozen circling the rear lawn of the estate. He grabbed a rifle hanging from a rack and moved to an open spot along the wall.

A boy stood next to him. The boy tried to put on a brave face, but his hands gave him away. His rifle was shaking.

Beyir grabbed the barrel of the boy's rifle and set it on the bunker's ledge. "Rest it here," he said. "Only use your hands when you want to redirect the gun. And breathe. Remember to breathe."

The boy wore the traditional hat of the Janissaries. A polished spoon was displayed on the front of the hat. The spoon was a symbol of the brotherhood of the Janissaries—soldiers who ate, fought, and lived and died together.

A flare arced above the rear lawn of the estate, lighting up the night.

Lifting his rifle to the bunker's ledge, Beyir peered into the night sky, wondering if it was now time to die.

83

President Thomas Herald stepped into the White House's situation room followed by Secretary Hawthorne, who'd been called away from his dinner with the relief team members.

The situation room teemed with members of the National Security Council and their subordinates. General Stacey Lippincott, chief of Central Command, addressed them. "Mr. President, four of the five strike teams have reported. Tunç Corporation's headquarters, Tunç's home, Turkish Sky, and his yacht on Kólpos Kallonís have been secured."

"And the fifth?" President Herald asked.

"The Samsun estate, sir."

"What happened?"

"During the drop, we received a transmission indicating the platoon was under fire," the general said. "In the hour since, we've heard nothing. We assume they were taken."

"How many?" Herald asked.

"Thirty, sir."

Herald grimaced. "Do we have Tunç?"

"No."

"How about Göttingen?" Secretary Hawthorne asked.

Lippincott shook his head.

President Herald ran his hands through his hair.

"We have the resources and clearance to take out the estate," Lippincott said. "A squadron of F-35s are within five minutes of the estate, but if you'd like my opinion . . . "

"Speak freely," the president said.

"There's a drop zone four miles away," Lippincott said.

"Paratroopers can be on the ground in thirty minutes and at Tunç's estate in less than an hour."

Herald looked around the room. Staff members were fielding reports from the various strike teams. Amid the chaos, he forced himself to think. Not only had Tunç been warned, he'd also had time to mobilize his resources. And the question remained: What were those resources?

The national security adviser held up the receiver on a speakerphone, his hand over the mouthpiece. "President Yerbaten is on the line, sir."

"Hit the intercom," Herald said. "We can all listen to this."

The national security adviser tapped a button on the speakerphone and nodded toward the president.

Herald leaned over the phone. "President Yerbaten," he said. "How are you?"

"I've been better, Mr. President," Yerbaten said. "Thank you. I just received a communication from Iskender Tunç. Do you mind if I read it?"

"Go ahead," Herald said.

The Turkish president cleared his throat. "'President Yerbaten, we have met the aggressions of the Americans and prevailed. Ten US soldiers remain alive. Captain Adam Candor, Second Lieutenant Peter—'"

One of General Lippincott's aides checked the names against a list, silently nodding when Yerbaten finished.

"'If the United States continues to show aggression, these brave soldiers will be the first casualties of another attack,'" Yerbaten continued. "'We hope this is entirely clear. We're also prepared to unleash biological and nuclear weapons on select European and Russian sites. It's my deepest regret the enemies of Turkey and the Yeni party have forced this upon us. My only hope is, as a representative of the Turkish people, you'll join me in denouncing this attack on our beloved homeland. Long live the Turkish people, Iskender Tunç.'"

When Yerbaten finished, there was silence.

"Mr. President, are you there?" came Yerbaten's voice.

"Yes," Herald said.

"We're sending a second message from Tunç," Yerbaten said. "It regards Drs. Özmen and Callahan."

An aide handed the president a piece of paper.

Herald read the message, which condemned the use of 'the

American spies.' Tunç promised, in his words, 'Allah's justice would descend on Drs. Callahan and Özmen.'

"It seems Mr. Tunç isn't fond of our mutual physicians," Herald said.

"No, he's not," Yerbaten said. "Do you have recommendations?"

"Can you give me a minute?"

"Yes, Mr. President."

Herald hit the phone's mute button and sat. He'd made it through the first six years of his two-term presidency without a major terrorist incident. Although a promise made during his first campaign that America would never be held hostage to terrorism now seemed little more than distant rhetoric, he knew the public and possibly history's perception of his presidency could depend on the vagaries of such an event. As a former prosecuting attorney, he also knew the necessity of thorough preparation. Over the years, he and his National Security Council had spent countless hours developing strategies for a multitude of terrorist scenarios. Circumstances similar to those in Turkey had been considered.

Herald turned toward Lippincott. "Do you think the men are alive?"

"You mean, do I believe ten US Army Rangers voluntarily gave up their tags?" Lippincott said. "No. They're dead. I'm sure of it."

Herald looked toward Hawthorne. "Would you consider Tunç a terrorist?"

"I would," he said.

"Why didn't we know about this guy?" Herald asked. "Stolen plutonium, biologic weapons. It's not like he's hiding in some cave. He's the CEO of a major corporation. *Christ.* He's a presidential candidate."

No one responded.

Herald closed his eyes. Kneading his temples, he appraised the events in light of his council's previous conclusions. Like many decisions during his presidency, it came swiftly and with conviction. He would hold true to his campaign promise. If he was wrong, God help him. God help all of them.

84

Captain Antonio Rodriguez stared at the darkened jump light above the rear door of the transport. His heart pounded. From Bravo Company's earlier drop onto the estate, he recalled the radio operator's description of the ground "erupting in fire." Quelling echoes of small-arms fire and the screams of the radio operator, he prayed and said a silent farewell to his wife and three children. When the jump light turned red and then green, the rear door of the transport lowered. Rodriguez stood. His men—members of the US Army's 101st Airborne Recon Unit—did likewise.

Rodriguez looked into the yawning black space and let the adrenaline take over. He sprinted into the abyss. Swept up in the rush of air, he was swallowed by the thick gray-blue of the predawn sky. The sensation of falling was followed by the upward jolt from the parachute and the roar of air on silk.

The captain watched as his men dropped one by one from the platform, their parachutes opening. As the transport retreated toward the horizon, he braced for what lay below. A veteran of Afghanistan and Iraq, he realized this time there were no detailed position photos or head counts of an enemy bombarded into submission.

Without event, however, they landed safely on the ground. After stowing their parachutes, they spread out and began running.

Thirty minutes and six klicks later, Rodriguez led his men between rocky bluffs—a break in a southern tributary of the Pontic Range. They continued for several more minutes through thickly wooded terrain until they came to a freshly cut lawn.

By now, the sun peeked over the horizon. At the far end of the lawn was the house, a shadowed structure nestled among trees. In the center of the lawn was the garden. Just west of the garden, a fire burned, its column of smoke curling skyward.

The paratroopers moved along the lawn's western perimeter. When they were parallel with the garden, Rodriguez signaled for them to stop. He continued forward on hands and knees to the edge of the lawn.

The fire, which had almost burned out, was a smoldering heap of blackened computer consoles and partially burned banners, photos, and books.

Rodriguez looked toward the three-story stone house, his gaze passing from one arched window to the next. He sensed movement to his right. Through a patch of trees, he spotted a figure. As if on guard duty, the man was facing a barnlike structure.

Rodriguez crawled toward the figure. The man, who wore a robe covering a protuberant belly, wasn't a member of Bravo Company. When the man came into range, Rodriguez raised to his knees. Aiming his silenced pistol, he fired twice.

The man jerked as the bullets entered his upper back. Miraculously, he remained standing.

Rodriguez fired a third time. The man shuddered but again didn't fall. Instead, he spun.

When Rodriguez saw the rope and the angle of the man's neck, he dropped to the ground, hoping he hadn't given their position away. He found himself face-to-face with the muzzle of a machine gun. Rolling away, he extended his pistol.

The gun, which hadn't moved, jutted from the opening of an almost imperceptible bunker. He slid toward the bunker and peered inside. It was empty.

Magazine casings littered the ground around him.

Rodriguez picked up a casing and lifted it to his nose, smelling the fresh scent of gunpowder. Following the gun's barrel skyward, he imagined thirty paratroopers descending.

The men of Bravo Company would have been easy targets.

A few hours earlier, Tunç stood on the Enderun's stage, holding up a fistful of dog tags. He howled, reveling in the victory. The boys did likewise.

Tunç read the names on the dog tags and threw them one-by-one from the stage. The boys fought over the tags until the victor slipped it over his head—his first spoil of war.

Beyir stood with Aras and the other Enderun graduates in the back of the auditorium. A collection of senior military officials, police officers, businessmen, politicians, doctors, and lawyers, they talked quietly, shaking their heads and clicking their tongues in disapproval.

The men eventually filed from the auditorium. Beyir went with them. Outside the barn, Beyir watched as the men climbed into their cars and drove away, returning to the comfort of the lives they'd created.

In the swirl of headlights, a car swung toward Beyir and stopped. Aras climbed out.

"Come with me," the oncologist said.

Beyir had dedicated his life to the Sayişma. All too willing to step to the forefront during its success, he must now have the honor to do so in its failure.

"There's no point in staying with him," Aras said, motioning toward the barn. "If you do, at best, you'll spend the rest of your life behind bars."

"I was a manager at EMİN," Beyir said. "They'll be looking for me. I can't do anything that might compromise you or the others in the network."

"Then go with the boys," Aras said. "They need someone who can guide them."

Beyir looked back toward the house and shook his head, an unyielding look in his eyes.

Aras nodded. "You're a good man." He set a hand on Beyir's shoulder. "The best the Enderun has to offer."

The oncologist climbed into his car. Pausing, he looked back. "I'm sorry we couldn't save Savon."

"I don't think it was possible."

"No," Aras said, looking down. "It wasn't." After a nod goodbye, he drove away.

Beyir watched the taillights of the car disappear down the grassy path.

The woods were suddenly still and dark.

Beyir stood by himself for a couple of minutes before he walked back to the barn and down into the Enderun.

In the auditorium, Tunç and the boys were still celebrating. Tunç had worked them into a frenzy.

After the paratroopers had stopped descending and the shooting ceased, the Janissaries had carried the bodies of the dead American soldiers below. One of the boys now stood over a dead American and was slashing him with a knife.

"They're soldiers," Beyir yelled, pulling the boy away.

The boy spun with knife raised, a feral look in his eyes.

Beyir sent him reeling with a single swat of his hand. He then stepped toward another boy, who was kicking a soldier. Tunç appeared in front of him, blocking his path. "Come with me."

Beyir looked into his eyes. Tunç's gaze was calm and steady. Surprised by Tunç's rapid transition to apparent sanity, Beyir followed him. They walked through the Enderun's hallways and up the back stairs to the house.

In the third-floor study, Ançak Barhal was waiting. "I came once I received your call," Barhal said, pushing himself up with his cane.

"Did you bring the buses?" Tunç asked.

"And the truck," Barhal said. "The arrangements have been made." He paused. "Are you sure you want to do this?"

"We don't have a choice. More men will come. They'll come until we're all dead or captured." Tunç placed a hand on Barhal's shoulder. "You're now the chief executor of the Şebeke. The network along with the Enderun and the boys are in your hands."

"What about Enver Pasha . . . and Kavas?"

"They've betrayed us," Tunç said. "They've betrayed the Sayişma. Edirne and the instructors paid with their lives."

"And Enver?"

"He escaped."

Beyir uneasily recalled the events of the previous night, wondering if Tunç knew of his role in Enver's escape. Tunç, however, quickly moved on. Grabbing an empty box, he began tossing in books and anything else he could remove from his desk. He picked up his computer and threw it to the floor.

Less than twenty-four hours earlier, Tunç stood on the steps of the National Assembly surrounded by a crowd chanting his name. Now, his world was turned upside down, his life in ruins.

"Go," Tunç snapped, seeing the looks on their faces. "Tell the others to collect everything they can from the Enderun and carry it to the lawn. Then burn it. Burn it all."

As the two men walked from the room, Beyir paused at the door.

Tunç stood motionless—staring at his father's portrait. Although Tunç didn't say it, his eyes did for him.

The Sayişma has failed.

Common sense had told Beyir the same thing, but he didn't believe it until now. Everything Tunç had promised was bluster and lies. It was over. And it had all been for nothing. The Sayişma, the Enderun, EMİN . . . their lives.

After a frenzied hour of running through the halls of the Enderun, Beyir, the three other Kazans, and Tunç, along with several recent graduates, watched as the buses containing Barhal and the boys pulled away. The group somberly turned and climbed into the waiting truck.

Beyir sat in the rear. As the truck pulled away from the estate, he held back the flap and looked outside.

The horizon was pink with the first hint of dawn. On the distant mountain ridge, he could make out the tallest of the Aleppo pines.

"What do you want to do when we leave here?" he asked Savon.

The two sat in the upper branches of the tree.

"Everything," Savon replied.

"You might need to be more specific."

"Why?" Savon asked. "Atatürk had an unwavering belief in himself. Without it, he never would have achieved what he did. We don't agree with what he did, but he shaped an entire country. With Islam on our side, we should be able to do even more."

Beyir didn't respond.

Savon clenched his fist. "Look at us. Look at the other Kazans. Is there anything we can't do?"

Beyir looked toward the horizon. After a few seconds, he shook his head. "No, there's not."

Beyir continued peering past the truck's rear flap. He watched until the great pine and the lives he and Savon once envisioned dissipated in the blur of passing trees.

85

"This beats the hell out of the mess tent," Haas said. "We should talk to the chef—ask if he might be interested in volunteer work."

Following the previous night's dinner at 1 Observatory Circle, Callahan and his family, Safiye, and the other relief team members had been chauffeured to the Willard Hotel in downtown Washington. After spending the night, they were now enjoying the Willard's breakfast buffet.

"Even the world's best cook can't do much with frozen sausages, powdered eggs, and bulk oatmeal," Alin said.

Fontaine entered the restaurant and walked toward them. The CIA agent was followed by two men in blue suits. "Good morning," Fontaine said, stopping behind Callahan and Safiye. "Sorry to interrupt, but could I speak with you two?"

"Is it something they can hear?"Callahan asked, motioning toward the others at the table.

They were out of earshot of anyone else in the restaurant. Fontaine nodded and pulled up a chair. The two agents took positions behind him.

"Last night, Tunç's businesses and estates were secured, but he escaped," Fontaine said. "He's since sent a letter to President Herald. In the letter, he threatened both of you, accusing you of being spies."

Callahan's mother gasped.

"He's crazy," Fontaine said. "But we don't want to take risks. The CIA would like to place both of you in protective custody until he's apprehended."

"Where would they go?" Callahan's father asked.

"I don't know," Fontaine said. "Neither can you. That's part of the process. To protect them. To protect you."

"When?" Safiye asked.

"It's recommended you leave immediately," Fontaine said. "If Tunç is going to try anything, it'll be sooner rather than later."

Callahan looked at Safiye. "What do you think?"

"Would we be together?" Safiye asked.

"We were planning on housing you at the same facility," Fontaine said, "unless you have an objection."

Callahan and Safiye shook their heads.

"Okay, then," Fontaine said. "I recommend saying your goodbyes, and then we'll go." He motioned to the men behind him. "They're here to escort you to your destination."

"Now?" Callahan's mom asked.

Fontaine nodded. "I'm afraid so."

One of the blue-suited men stepped forward. "We'll send men to collect your belongings from your hotel rooms. Whatever else you request, from your homes or elsewhere, will be brought to you."

"When will we see them again?" Callahan's mom asked.

"When Tunç is caught," Fontaine said. "I'll be heading to Ankara to direct an international team of investigators who'll be searching for him. I can't make any promises when you'll see your son again, but I hope it's very soon."

86

Callahan and Safiye were taken from the Willard to Andrews Air Force Base and flown to Newark, New Jersey. They were then driven to a high-security facility and placed into a two-bedroom suite.

The facility was a two-story building with a dozen living units. The first floor contained a small grocery store, workout facility, movie theater, cafeteria, and library. The roof had an outdoor sun deck, sauna, and pool.

During Callahan and Safiye's first week in the facility, their mornings were spent reading while drinking coffee in the library. In the afternoon, they exercised and swam and lounged on the deck. After dinner, they spent their evenings watching movies.

Fontaine called from Ankara every couple days with updates on his team's progress. Investigators sent to Turkish Sky, much to the embarrassment of the officials who'd previously inspected the facility, found dozens of partially unearthed barrels in a muddy field near the river. Exhumed and analyzed, the barrels contained a cornucopia of biowarfare agents of such variety and quantity it surpassed anything seen since the Cold War.

Among the barrels' contents was an antibiotic-resistant strain of *Yersenia pestis*. Yalçin Kaldırım was questioned about the hospital's reporting of test results regarding the farmer and his family. He maintained his lab had correctly identified the organisms as *Pasteurella*. The interview was considered unproductive. But Kaldırım didn't show up to work the following day, or the next. Three days after the interview, Kaldırım's cleaning woman found the microbiologist and his wife dead. Kaldırım had shot Berna before placing the gun in his mouth and pulling the trigger.

After Callahan and Safiye had spent a week in the facility, Fontaine sent five driver's license photos of unshaven young men. Safiye identified her brother in one of the photos. As Beyir said, he'd been in Istanbul. He and the others in the photos had been working for the past five years as managers at a subsidiary of Tunç Corporation and living under false names.

In Ankara, UN-appointed forensic experts performed a second autopsy on Mehmet. There was no evidence of a heart attack. His coronary arteries were clean. Laboratory analysis of his tissues detected toxic levels of cyanide metabolites in his liver. Similar studies detected the same metabolites in the liver of Caria Mahid, the receptionist at city hall.

It was after Callahan and Safiye had spent a month in the facility that Fontaine called with word of Ayla's death. Her body was found buried in the hills near Tunç's northern estate.

Callahan found Safiye standing by a window after the call. She was staring outside, her eyes red.

"You opened it?"

Safiye held a crinkled slip of paper. She handed it to him.

The paper had been among the items in the envelope Ayla had thrown into their cell. It had been encased in tape and labeled with a message: "Safiye, only open when you are free and if I cannot be with you. Love, Ayla."

Callahan sat and read.

Safiye,
If you're reading this, it means you're free. That thought brings me great happiness. It also means I could not be with you to hold your hand and confess the truth I should have so many years ago. My silence has tormented me. The fact I've never told you, and to do it this way, is cowardly. But you must know the truth.
Rabia was never with Iskender on the night of the graduation party. I was the one you saw with him on the beach. I was young and foolish and had too much to drink. I realize now I was probably drugged. I'm not making excuses and do not seek your forgiveness. From the depths of my heart, however, I apologize.
You feel guilty about Rabia's death. You shouldn't. I alone am responsible. If I had told the truth the following morning, Rabia would still be alive. I realize now I didn't

do it because I couldn't bear the thought of no longer being your friend. Again, I'm sorry.

You deserve happiness. I hope you find it.

With the greatest love, Ayla

Callahan looked at Safiye. She was in tears.

"What was worse?" she asked. "My false accusations or Ayla's silence?"

"If Ayla had told the truth, you never would have made your accusations."

"But I did make them. And because of it, Rabia is dead."

87

As the days turned into weeks and weeks into months in the New Jersey facility, Callahan regained a full range of motion in his shoulder while Safiye's ulcers disappeared. But their other wounds didn't heal so easily.

Safiye experienced the pain of Rabia's death all over again with the heightened guilt of knowing she'd wrongfully accused her friend. When Safiye's thoughts weren't consumed with Rabia, they were with Mehmet, Bryce, and Ayla. As if it would keep the four of them alive, she was determined to relive her memories of them and her guilt on a daily basis.

Callahan talked to Safiye about current events. He urged her to watch movies. They listened to Beethoven and Green Day. His attempts to elevate her mood, however, were to no avail. No longer interested in morning coffee, leisurely meals in the restaurant, exercise, or movies, she gradually retreated into herself.

After their second month in the facility, Fontaine called.

"Any leads?" Callahan asked.

"No. I'd hoped to have this resolved by now. To be honest, I feel we're no closer to finding Tunç than when we started." Fontaine paused. "How are you two doing?"

It was late September. Callahan stood at his bedroom window. Outside, beyond the facility's barbed-wire fence, lay the gray barren expanse of an abandoned railway station. He couldn't help but think they'd exchanged one stone prison for another. "Let's just say neither of us is looking forward to winter in New Jersey."

"Which brings me to the reason for my call," Fontaine said. "Our secretary of state insists we make you as comfortable as possible. I checked into whether we had a more scenic location. We have an opening in a secluded one-bedroom beach house on Saint John for a Mr. and Mrs. Joseph Lambert."

"Saint John?" Callahan said. "The Virgin Islands?"

"Yes."

"Sounds great. But one bedroom might be awkward."

Callahan had come to realize Safiye needed a friend more than anything. He'd promised himself he wouldn't initiate anything romantic between them. Thus far, he'd stuck to his promise. "Do you have something with two bedrooms?"

"Hold on," Fontaine said. He typed on a keyboard before speaking again. "How about two rooms in the Caymans? They're in a hotel but not quite as picturesque."

"We'll take the beach house," Safiye's voice boomed over the line.

Callahan hadn't heard her pick up.

Fontaine laughed. "Are you sure?"

"I am," she said.

"It's being booked as we speak," Fontaine said, hitting a key. "By the way, when this is over, you're invited back to Secretary Hawthorne's house for dinner and a movie. You two made quite an impression on the secretary and his wife."

After the call, Callahan and Safiye met in the hallway. As they high-fived, Safiye locked her fingers in his. "A beach house sounded better than a hotel room."

He nodded. "It does."

"So, Mr. Lambert. Was I being too presumptuous? Will pretending to be a couple be a problem?"

Callahan shook his head. "We'll make it work." He turned to walk away, but Safiye, still holding his hand, pulled him back. "If it's a problem, tell me. I'm not as fragile as you think."

Under the circumstances, she'd been stronger than he could have imagined. Unfortunately, he wasn't.

"I'm sure I won't have to pretend," he said.

Safiye smiled. It'd been a long time since she'd done so.

She lifted their hands, their fingers still entwined, and pressed her lips to the back of his hand. "No," she said. "I don't think we'll have to."

88

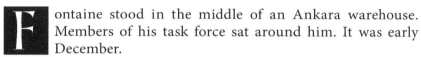

F ontaine stood in the middle of an Ankara warehouse. Members of his task force sat around him. It was early December.

Fontaine stared at a bulletin board containing photos of the Samsun estate. The men of the 101st Airborne had found the estate uninhabited except for the corpses of two elderly women in an upstairs bedroom. The two women were found to have ingested toxic doses of GHB.

The paratroopers had taken a back stairway into a basement, which opened into an elaborate underground facility. Room by room, they'd secured the facility without resistance—passing through sleeping quarters, a gymnasium, classrooms, and a cafeteria. In what appeared to have been a trophy room were empty glass cabinets and naked nails bent from the strain of supporting something no longer there. In an auditorium, they came upon the mutilated bodies of the men of Bravo Company.

Fontaine turned away from the now too-familiar photos and scanned the warehouse. Tunç's offices and homes, along with EMİN Corporation, had been gutted. Every piece of evidence had been sent here. As his team poured through the material, it had become clear the EMİN Corporation had been the right arm of Tunç's illicit operations. Prior to the assassinations of Generals Volkan and Refet, EMİN's five managers had simply stopped coming to work. They hadn't been seen since, leaving behind nondescript apartments and offices.

In the days following the raid on Tunç's northern estate, the equivalent of $10 million had been wired from the EMİN accounts to a dizzying array of other accounts. The further Fontaine's team followed the money-laundering trail, the larger it grew, ballooning electronically to $80 million as it was incrementally fed from over a dozen conduits. Fontaine knew they'd eventually have to trace the conduits back to their sources, but for the present, they pushed ahead, searching for the money's ultimate destination.

"The money trails end here," Fontaine said, pointing to a list of fifteen banks on the bulletin board. "From Marrakesh to Munich, Lisbon to Tokyo, Tunç's men simply entered the banks and cashed out their accounts."

Tatiana Andropovna walked to the board. After two weeks of grieving for Vladimir Petrovich, she'd joined the team. She'd proven to be invaluable. Not only fluent in the affairs of Tunç's enterprises, the Russian agent had also spent the majority of her SVR career following money-laundering schemes throughout Europe and Asia.

"Most of these make sense," Tatiana said, looking at the list of banks. "Istanbul, Morocco, Paris, Zurich, Bern. If I wanted to cash out millions, this is where I'd do it—large banks with large reserves. The banks would go through a rigorous identification process, matching fingerprints and verifying records, but within a few hours, these men would likely walk out, cash in hand." She pointed at one of the banks. "But this doesn't make sense. North Sulawesi in Indonesia. What's there? And for such a large amount—6 *million*?"

In the last four months, Tatiana had worked feverishly to avenge her fiancé's death. Her frustration was palpable. She needed a break. At a minimum, she needed to get out of this warehouse.

"Do you think it's worth a look?" Fontaine asked.

Tatiana nodded. "I think it is."

Fontaine and Tatiana flew to Indonesia and met with an official from North Sulawesi's Bank Panin. They discovered the bank hadn't cashed out the $6 million account as its records indicated. Instead, the money was electronically transferred to a different account and then to a larger bank in Borneo. From there, the money had been split between banks in Papua New Guinea and the Phillipines, where the accounts were then liquidated.

Not to be deterred, Fontaine and Tatiana traveled to Papua New Guinea's Port Moresby and met with Tako Yashito, the president of the Fifth Bank of Japan.

"Is it possible someone with the correct identification and paperwork could walk into your bank and cash out 3 million US dollars?" Fontaine asked Yashito.

"We can handle such a transaction," the bank president said, nodding proudly.

As he'd done at every other bank marking the end of a money trail, Fontaine asked if any subsequent large deposits had been made into the bank's other accounts.

"The Fifth Bank of Japan would like to cooperate with authorities on this matter," Yashito said. "However, I'm only authorized to provide information on the activities of"—he looked down at a piece of paper—"the N698923 account."

"Let me remind you, Mr. Yashito, we're hunting men who have threatened the use of nuclear weapons," Fontaine said.

Papua New Guinea was among the 187 countries that had signed United Nations Resolution 54/109—a treaty designed to stop the international financing of terrorism by providing avenues of communication between banking institutions and governments. By threatening nuclear retaliation, Tunç paved the way for the fast-tracking of UN sanctions against the Tunç and EMİN Corporations.

"What size transfers are you looking for?" Yashito asked.

"Deposits of anything over 400,000 US dollars."

"That will take *some* time."

"How much?" Fontaine asked.

"A few hours."

Fontaine couldn't help but smile. He enjoyed operating in places like New Guinea. The same request in New York, London, or Tokyo—even with the weight of the UN behind it—would be buried in a mountain of red tape. He didn't like playing hardball, but the EMİN accounts were all they had. And $80 million didn't just disappear.

Later that afternoon, Fontaine and Tatiana reentered Yashito's office.

Yashito slid a piece of paper toward Fontaine. It was a list with three names. "All are respected customers of the Fifth Bank of Japan," the banker said.

"Do you have amounts for the transfers?" Fontaine asked. "And account balances over the past two years?"

Yashito's eyes narrowed. Opening the top drawer of his desk, he pulled out more papers. He slid the top sheet across the desk.

"Hideki Takamuso is a respected businessman, an executive with Sony. He's banked with us for twenty years." He slid a second sheet toward Fontaine. "Dr. Shigeru Kyushi is a retired physician from Japan. His lawyer recently opened this account, informing me Dr. Kyushi plans to spend his summers here." He slid the last sheet of paper across the desk. "The third account is with Amit Singh, a businessman from Mumbai."

The bank president placed his hands, palms down, on the desk. "We're thankful for our customers' business, Mr. Fontaine. We hope you'll handle further interactions with the *utmost* discretion."

"Mr. Yashito," Tatiana said, looking at one of the balance sheets. "You said Dr. Kyushi was planning on vacationing here?"

"Yes."

Tatiana handed the sheet to Fontaine. The Kyushi account had recently been opened with a deposit of $3 million. The deposit had been made the day after the raid on the Enderun.

"Doesn't $3 million seem a bit exorbitant?" Fontaine asked.

"Perhaps he plans on purchasing real estate," Yashito said.

"What interest rate do you provide on savings accounts?" Tatiana asked.

"It's complicated," Yashito said.

"Just ballpark figures—a half percent, 1 percent?" she asked.

Yashito crossed his arms. "For our more select customers, we provide 2 percent."

"That's impressive," Tatiana said.

"Don't worry." The edge of Yashito's mouth curled into a smile. "If we invest properly, we can still turn a profit."

"I'm sure you do," Tatiana said. "Let me ask you, Mr. Yashito, is Dr. Kyushi a *select* customer?"

"He is."

"It appears he's not accruing interest," Fontaine said, sliding the balance sheet back across the desk.

Yashito ignored the paper. "Perhaps he lives off the interest." He grinned, showing off a mouthful of stubby, yellowing teeth. "The *great* American dream."

"Would it be possible to obtain documentation on where that money goes?" Fontaine asked. "Two percent yearly interest on 3 million dollars. That's a lot of money."

"The Fifth Bank of Japan has been most cooperative," Yashito said. "As a banking professional, I feel I've compromised some of my most esteemed customers."

Fontaine enjoyed Yashito's discomfort. Perhaps it was because Yashito had made them wait a half hour before their meeting, perhaps it was his condescending tone, or perhaps it was simply because he was a banker.

"We need to know where that money is going," Fontaine said. "We won't stop—"

Yashito again pulled open his top drawer. He removed a single sheet of paper and extended it. "I believe this concludes our business, Mr. Fontaine."

The paper listed monthly transfers of the accumulating interest from Dr. Kyushi's account. There was only one destination for the money—an entity called Jogai Transports.

"Is this one of your accounts?" Fontaine asked.

"A *smaller* one."

"What can you tell—"

Yashito jabbed a narrow finger forward. "Everything we know about Jogai Transports—their contact information, withdrawals, and deposits—is on that piece of paper."

89

As they'd done faithfully once a week for the last five months, Beyir and his fellow Kazans began their trek through the jungle. Leading with his machete, Beyir sliced through the occasional vine blocking the well-worn trail.

Except for Tunç, the nine others who'd been in the truck that had left the Samsun estate were either Kazans or more recent Enderun graduates. Without a Sayişma, they had no purpose in life. Without the EMİN Corporation or the Enderun, they had nowhere to go. As always, they went where Tunç led them.

From the estate, they'd traveled east and crossed the border into northern Iran. Driving along Iran's western border, they made their way to the Persian Gulf, where they continued by boat, journeying east through the Arabian Sea and Bay of Bengal to the Strait of Malacca and the South China Sea. After five days on the boat, they arrived on a small, uninhabited island in the South Pacific, where they'd since lived.

The unnamed island, along with the surrounding smaller islands, were known simply as the 5°-180° group, based on their latitude and longitude. The ten men stayed in decrepit World War II–era tin shacks and slept on beds of leaves. To avoid the mosquitoes and heat, they spent their days beneath netting in the shade of a central compound, where Tunç paced, fabricating ever-more farfetched plans for his return and a second Sayişma. At night, the nine of them swam, fished, and wandered the island, enjoying the freedom that came with the darkness. The nights, cool and pleasant and free from Tunç's rants, were never long enough.

That morning, after a typical night of diving and fishing, the nine of them had lain in their hammocks, fighting sleep. As Tunç began his daily oration, Kabul, one of the Kazans and a manager at EMİN Corporation, climbed from his hammock and walked across the compound.

"Where are you going?" Tunç asked.

Afraid a wandering fisherman or airplane might see them, Tunç didn't permit them to leave the central compound during the day. The Kazans' weekly trek to collect supplies was the only exception to this rule.

"To find quiet," Kabul yelled.

"The rules I make are for your own good," Tunç said. "After everything, we're still alive and free."

Kabul spun and raised his arms. "You call *this* living? You call this freedom?" He turned and continued walking.

Tunç ran and locked an arm around Kabul's neck. Kabul tried to pry him off, but Tunç maintained his hold. When Kabul began choking, the others leaped from their hammocks and pulled Tunç away. But no one thought to restrain Kabul. After catching his breath, he rushed and tackled Tunç.

Too surprised to react, the others watched, at first in amazement and then in sublime enjoyment, as Kabul pummeled Tunç. It was almost a minute before they pulled Kabul away.

Tunç stood. Unsteady, his face bloodied, he glared at each of them before marching into his shack.

Because of that morning's events, Beyir was more thankful than ever for the trek to the other side of the island. He savored the strain of the supplies on his shoulders, the sweat pouring from his skin, and the long drink of cool water when they returned. Despite the smothering heat and humidity, the walks were a time of peace and quiet. And contrary to Tunç's demands, the Kazans did little to hurry them along.

They emerged from the jungle trail, enveloped by the roar of the Beechcraft. The twin-engine plane was flying overhead, a large package sliding from its rear door. A parachute billowed open, and the package fell, landing softly in the distant sand.

The four Kazans walked across the beach and partitioned the supplies. Lifting them to their shoulders, they looked toward the distant plane.

The Beechcraft landed offshore once a month. From the time the plane first creased the bay's languid waters, the Kazans fantasized about boarding it. While Tunç's return to civilization was impossible—he was and always would be a hunted man—

the nine others were largely unknown to the world's intelligence agencies. With new identities, their reassimilation back into society, somewhere, was possible.

After the plane landed, however, the pilot always stayed far offshore with the engine running. The copilot would row an inflatable dinghy to shore, where he would pick up the previous weeks' worth of parachutes and containers and exchange communications between Barhal and Tunç. Tunç had informed them the pilot had instructions to leave if anything unusual happened, even if it meant leaving the copilot behind.

With the Beechcraft's routine essentially unassailable, the Kazans' conversations regarding the plane wandered to the pilots and what awaited them when they returned. Maybe they had girlfriends and would go out for dinner that night. Maybe they were married and would go home to a wife and kids. Whatever it was, however mundane, it was something far beyond the four young men's realm of possibilities.

The Kazans watched the plane, which was now little more than a dot on the horizon.

"It lands in two weeks," Kabul said. "Next time it leaves, we'll be on it."

90

After flying from Port Moresby back to Ankara, Fontaine and Tatiana returned to the warehouse. Tatiana went immediately to the bin of material collected from Tunç's home in Teos and began searching through a stack of books. When she'd seen Shigeru Kyushi's bank statement, his name had seemed familiar. On the flight back, she realized why.

She pulled a dog-eared soft-cover book from the bin. "The book describes the proceedings of a post–World War II tribunal investigating the affairs of Dr. Shirō Ishii, the head of Japan's biowarfare program," Tatiana said as she paged through the book. "If I recall, one of the most vivid descriptions of Ishii's activities was provided by someone named Shigeru Kyushi. In the tribunal, Ishii and his colleagues were granted immunity by your General MacArthur in return for their research data."

"Research?" Fontaine said.

"The Japanese used bioweapons to attack eleven Chinese cities, killing over a half-million Chinese. The groundwork for their program lay in their experimentation on Chinese POWs. Ishii's men performed thousands of experimental surgeries. To simulate battlefield conditions, prisoners were shot and then operated on in an attempt to improve surgical techniques. Limbs were amputated and then reattached. Organs were removed to monitor the effects. Prisoners were injected with bioagents, put in centrifuges, and given animal blood. They were exposed to extreme temperatures and pressures, flamethrowers, bomb blasts."

"That's sick. It's beyond sick."

Tatiana nodded. "What Ishii and his colleagues did makes Josef Mengele and the Nazis look tame." She looked up. "And your government knew about this. They not only didn't punish Ishii, they employed him as a consultant at your Fort Detrick. During the Korean War, Ishii worked on your own bioweapons program, which deployed pathogens against North Korea and China."

Fontaine stared silently back.

"You Americans wonder why some countries hate you," Tatiana said. "This is why. You think you're not capable of evil deeds, but you are."

"Ishii was a poster boy for Tunç?"

"It appears so." Tatiana held out the book. "Here's the part that talks about the testimony of a Second Lieutenant Shigeru Kyushi. Near the war's end, US troops landed on a South Pacific island and found the remains of one-hundred badly decomposed Chinese soldiers shackled to trees. The men were thought to have been starved to death until US soldiers started getting sick. A diagnosis of the plague was eventually made, but not before a few soldiers died. In the postwar tribunal, Kyushi reported the Chinese prisoners had been taken to the island and tied to trees. A bomb containing plague-infected fleas was dropped on the island to observe its effects on the prisoners. Some lasted as long as three weeks."

One of the CIA analysts approached and extended a paper to Tatiana. "As you requested, I made inquiries with the Japanese government," he said. "Their records indicate a Shigeru Kyushi served as a medic under Shirō Ishii. After the war, Kyushi went to medical school and practiced in Tokyo until his retirement in 1994."

"Is that where he is now?" Tatiana asked.

The analyst shook his head. "Three years after his retirement, Dr. Shigeru Kyushi died."

"The same Kyushi?"

The analyst nodded. "The biographical data matches." He handed a second paper to Tatiana. "Langley also found records of the recent purchase by Jogai Transports of a twin-engine Beechcraft. Subash Jogai, the owner of Jogai Transports, paid $3 million for the plane."

"Combined with the 3 million in the Kyushi account, that adds up to 6 million—the amount transferred from Borneo," Tatiana said.

"Jogai purchased the Beechcraft in Manila," the analyst said. "After the 3 million was transferred from Borneo to the Phillipines bank and then liquidated, the same amount appeared in a new account Jogai had opened with the bank."

"Which he then used to purchase the Beechcraft," Fontaine said.

The analyst nodded.

Tatiana turned toward Fontaine. "If half of the 6 million from Borneo went for Jogai's plane, what do you think the interest from the other half in Dr. Kyushi's account is buying?"

"I don't know," he said. "But that's a good question for Mr. Jogai."

91

The Kazans made their trek across the island to collect supplies. Kabul and Tunç's fight had been one week earlier. In the time since, Tunç had been content to stay in his tin shack. The others had spent the time wondering how and when he'd retaliate.

The Kazans emerged from the jungle. The supply package was already sitting in the sand, the parachute flopping lazily in the breeze. They'd heard the plane fly overhead several minutes earlier. Beyir pointed. In the distance, the Beechcraft was still visible.

The Kazans partitioned the supplies. They lifted the supplies to their shoulders and dragged the parachutes and containers to the jungle's edge, where they stuffed them into the storage box. Pausing, they looked across the bay, their brows dripping with sweat.

The Kazans had spent the last week coming up with a failsafe plan to board the Beechcraft. In one week, when the plane lifted from the bay, they would be on it.

They watched the Beechcraft until it disappeared from view. As the others returned to the trail, Beyir remained on the beach, taking a last lingering look toward the horizon.

In one week, for the first time in his life, there'd be no Iskender Tunç or Enderun. There'd be no Sayişma, Şebeke, or EMİN. He would disappear into the world and start again. A different continent. A different country. A different name.

His thoughts turned to his sister. The image of her writhing on the patio had haunted him. He wondered if he'd have the chance to tell her he was sorry. He wondered if she could forgive him.

He turned and walked back along the trail. As he did, he heard a faint click. Although subtle, it was the distinct sound of metal on metal. The noise didn't belong here—on an empty beach, on a deserted island.

In one fluid motion, he dropped his supplies and flipped the gun from his shoulder. As the stock landed squarely in his palm, he turned, ready to fire.

Fontaine and members of a Navy SEAL team hid in the underbrush at the jungle's edge. Well camouflaged, they were spread out around the trail as it opened onto an expansive white beach and aqua-blue bay.

Fontaine and Tatiana had returned to Port Moresby and visited Jogai Transports. The Beechcraft had been a welcome addition to the company's aging fleet of two forty-year-old German transports. The Beechcraft's Australian pilot, under the threat of his license being revoked, revealed that once a week he delivered 150 kilograms of supplies to the largest of a group of small unnamed islands in the South Pacific.

The islands, located at 5 degrees latitude by 180 degrees longitude, were where Shirō Ishii had dropped his plague-infested bombs. In January 1944, the islands had been sprayed and cleared of their population of plague-infested fleas. No one had lived on the islands in the decades since. Even today, inhabitants of the surrounding South Pacific islands believed the islands were *tupuqa*—inhabited by spirits of the dead.

Fontaine watched as four men emerged from the jungle. Carrying guns, they wore tattered clothes and had beards. Fontaine recognized them as four of the five managers of EMİN. The largest of the men was Beyir Özmen, Safiye's brother.

The men divided the supplies and carried them across the beach. After stuffing the parachute and crates into a container, the quartet stopped and looked across the water. They exuded looks of determination, their backs straight under the weight of their loads.

While the other three returned to the trail, Beyir remained on the beach. He stood for several moments before he turned and began walking back along the trail. That's when Fontaine heard the noise. So did Beyir.

Fontaine was surprised by the large man's agility. Beyir

dropped the supplies, flipped the gun from his shoulder, and spun.

In an act of self-preservation, the SEAL who'd made the noise fired a short burst from his silenced automatic. The burst struck Beyir in the chest. As Beyir flew back, he fired his gun into the sky, filling the air with a harsh staccato.

The three others also went for their guns. They too were cut down.

"What was that?" rang Tatiana's voice in Fontaine's earpiece.

Tatiana was on a US Navy vessel moored in a small cove on the far side of the nearest island. The vessel had brought them to the island the night before. Early this morning, Fontaine and the SEALs had taken electric-powered rubber boats to the main island, where they'd dug in and waited.

"They're down," Fontaine said. "All four."

Fontaine and the SEALs rose from their hiding places and began sprinting along the jungle trail.

Satellite reconnaissance over the past week revealed that the largest island of the 5°-180° group was inhabited by more than just the spirits of the dead. Ten men lived on the island. They spent their days in a central compound.

After a couple minutes of running along the trail, Fontaine heard gunfire. Through the sea of jungle green, he caught a glimpse of the clearing marking the edge of the central compound. He and the SEALs dove to the ground and lobbed gas canisters into the air. They slipped pressurized oxygen cylinders over their mouths and waited.

The odorless anesthetic soon had the desired effect. The firing from the compound tapered and then stopped.

Fontaine and the SEALs advanced into the compound.

Four young men were unconscious on the ground. These four plus the four on the beach made eight.

A SEAL pulled a coughing young man from a shack.

Nine.

"We're missing one," Fontaine yelled.

"Do you have Tunç?" Tatiana asked.

"I don't see him," Fontaine said.

"Now's probably not the best time to tell you this," she said, "but we're also missing one."

"Who?"

"Cemil."

Like Tatiana, Cemil Kura had been a highly motivated addition to the Ankara task force. The recently promoted general, who'd witnessed the bombing of the Turkish High Command, had functioned as a liaison with Turkish intelligence. He'd worked tirelessly to find Tunç and avenge his fallen comrades.

"How can he be missing?" Fontaine asked.

"He's not onboard."

92

Tunç ran from the central compound. Veering from the trail, he plowed through the jungle thicket. To his right were the gravesites of the Chinese POWs. His attention, however, wasn't focused on the one-hundred moss-covered, crumbling posts but the approaching mangroves and the reflection from a small pool of water.

He leaped into the waist-high pool. Reaching down, he grabbed a mesh bag and removed a small oxygen canister along with a mask and flippers. After slipping into the gear, he paused to listen.

The shooting had stopped. But there was the stomp of boots. They were getting closer.

He slipped the mouthpiece of the canister into his mouth and sank beneath the water. Setting his feet against the roots of the mangroves, he pushed off and swam through a narrow channel connecting the inland pool with the open sea. He was soon skimming the ocean floor.

Over the next several minutes, the sea bottom turned from sand to leafy grass and back to sand again as he approached the nearby island. When the island's rippling tree line came into view, he followed the shoreline to the south side, where he swam into a deep-bottomed cove. Near the shore, the hull of a resting motorboat broke the waterline.

He climbed onboard. He'd ordered Barhal to make arrangements with Jogai to place the boat on the island in the event they needed to make a quick exit. The boat was large enough for all ten of them. The others, however, could rot in hell. He'd endured their insubordination and finally their insurrection. They were now paying the price.

He removed a bag of clothes from a stern hatch. A satellite phone was in the bag. He activated the phone, establishing a link between its transmitter on the bow of the boat and a New Guinea call station. He dialed the number that was written on a piece of tape on the phone's handle. As he waited for a reply, he noticed a handgun was in the bag. He checked the clip. It was loaded.

"Hello," a voice answered.

"Who is this?"

"Subash Jogai."

"My plans have changed," Tunç said. "I need you to be at the rendezvous point tomorrow morning."

"Tomorrow is short notice. Tomorrow will be complicated."

"You'll be well paid for your troubles."

"If you're calling, that means you're on the boat," Jogai said. "And, they've found you."

"They don't know I'm here and don't know about the boat," Tunç said. "From your perspective, the rendezvous point is safe."

There was a moment of silence.

"I'll see you tomorrow," Tunç said.

"Yes," Jogai said. "At dawn."

Tunç ended the call. He would spend the night traveling to the rendezvous point on the island of Nauru, but he would be here until nightfall. He set the phone into the bag. As he did, he froze.

A man stood motionless on the shoreline. Wearing a camouflaged uniform and beret, he blended almost imperceptibly with the jungle. When the man smiled, Tunç felt the blood drain from his face.

"Iskender," the man said. "You look like you've seen a ghost."

Standing on the shoreline was a younger version of his father.

The man removed his beret. His dark hair was dusted with gray at the temples.

Tunç squinted, recognition passing through him. "*Cemil?* How did you get here?"

Cemil Kura grinned. "It wasn't hard for a grieving soldier wanting to avenge the deaths of his superiors to gain a position on the task force."

Tunç stepped forward. He stopped as Cemil raised a pistol.

Tunç forced a smile. "Those of us at the Enderun were very appreciative for what you did at the bunker. We've also been impressed by your progress through the army's ranks."

"Your Enderun is now spread over the floor of an Ankara warehouse."

"Yes, but the Şebeke's in place," Tunç said. "When we return, we'll take what is ours."

"We?" Cemil said. "*Ours*?"

"Yes, you and me."

Cemil shook his head. "Thanks to you, the Tunç name is now a disgrace. But that shouldn't concern you. From what I understand, you never were a Tunç."

Tunç clenched a fist. "Everything can still be as my father envisioned. We'll organize another Sayişma. With your growing influence in the military and my Şebeke, we'll—"

"Your Şebeke? Your Şebeke belongs to your father, your real father."

Tunç's mouth fell open.

"Yes," Cemil said. "Enver Pasha has assumed his old position. For the last few months, we've all been under his direction, including Barhal."

A noise came from the jungle. Not hearing it, Cemil continued. "The information Barhal provided was accurate," he said. "The island next to the largest; a small inlet on the south shore. We would have picked you up earlier, but we chose to sit back and watch until now." He smiled. "You're right, Iskender. The Şebeke is in place. Plans are being made for a new Sayişma. But you won't be alive to see it."

"How can Enver question *my* dedication?"

"He knew you'd eventually be caught. And when that happened, he was sure you'd do whatever you could to save your own skin. He didn't mind if you told the authorities about the Enderun or the Sayişma. Neither exists—not as you knew them. But he didn't want you talking about the Şebeke. That's why I'm here—to make sure the secrets of the Şebeke remain secret."

Tunç stared silently back.

"Not exactly ringing words of endorsement from your own father," Cemil said. "But it does beg the question: Where are our colleagues? Did you even tell them about the boat?"

"We were friends once," Tunç said. "Don't you remember? The summers at the Enderun? Running through the woods? The monastery?"

Cemil laughed. "Do you really think we wanted to include you? You were small and weak—an outsider. Muhammed told us to make you feel like you belonged."

"I did nothing to you, to any of you."

"Oh, but you have, Iskender. You've served as a constant reminder of what could have been. You were Muhammed's chosen one. The one he took home with him." Cemil paused. "Just once, put yourself in someone else's shoes. I was fifteen years old when Muhammed sent me from the Enderun. Now, I learn that I was his last son, that he was planning to give me his name."

"It's not true," Tunç said. "None of it."

Cemil smiled. "When you first saw me, who did you think I was?" he asked. "Trust me, you wouldn't be the first to notice a resemblance."

There was another noise. This time, Cemil heard it. He turned.

Tunç thrust his arm into the bag and grabbed the gun. He ran along the port walkway and dove from the boat, pulling the trigger. His first bullet struck Cemil in the abdomen. The second hit him in the sternum.

Tunç landed in shallow water and rolled onto a narrow strip of sand. Standing, he watched triumphantly as Cemil fell backward. His celebration was short-lived, however, as the source of the noise became apparent.

A woman was crouched in the jungle. Like Cemil, she wore a camouflaged uniform and beret.

Tunç raised his gun, but the woman fired first.

Lifted off his feet, Tunç found himself staring up at a canopy of leaves. He was in the sand. The waves lapping onto the shore crested against his cheek.

The woman was above him. She'd taken off her beret. Her hair brushed against his face. Long and dark, it sucked the oxygen from the air. "That was for Vlad," she said.

He tried to sit up but couldn't.

"Where is Göttingen?" she asked.

"The Şebeke," he said, his voice barely a whisper.

"Where's the Şebeke?"

"Everywhere."

"Where's Savon Ali?" she asked.

"Savon . . . is dead."

The woman continued talking, but her words were inaudible. He looked past her and past the canopy of leaves to a small patch of sky.

The sky was a brilliant blue. He wondered why he hadn't noticed until now.

"Where's the plutonium?"

"Enver," he answered.

"Who is Enver?"

"He—he's my father."

"Where's the physicist?"

He was panting now. He looked into the woman's eyes. "I—I'm dying?"

"Where's the plutonium?" she asked.

"S—save me," he pleaded.

He tried to look toward the patch of sky, but she blocked his view. He opened his mouth to speak, but no words came.

As she leaned closer, her eyes filled with hatred, everything darkened.

93

The morning after Fontaine's call to the New Jersey safe house, Callahan woke at Safiye's side. For the next three bliss-filled months, he woke in that same position.

When it seemed as if Safiye had been ready to break, that she could bear no more guilt and had no more tears left to shed, an inner resilience shone through. Her smiles came easier and more frequently. After placing the weight of the world on her shoulders, piece by piece, she let it slip off. As lovers, they could have happily survived the time in New Jersey. Saint John was icing on the cake.

The house was situated on a white sandy beach, a stone's throw from the water and a dock harboring a small wooden sailboat. They spent their days swimming, fishing, and sailing. They were soon able to spot the schools of fish running beneath the bow of the boat. In one cast, they could net enough fish for dinner. With a few dives, they could collect enough conch for a midday salad. They became expert at blending their catch with the variety of spices, onions, lemons, and limes they gathered during their daily sojourns to the island grocery.

Each day on the island brought a greater appreciation for its brilliant aqua-blue bays and unbroken sea of jungle green. Neither tired of the sensation of the water gliding over their backs, the heat of the sun as they lay on the beach, or the glow of the horizon after sunset. Opening themselves to the island and to each other, they settled comfortably into the rhythms of both.

The morning Fontaine knocked on the beach house door was an unwelcome intrusion. He told them Iskender Tunç was dead. They hadn't spoken of him since arriving on the island. News of his demise now served only as inadequate retribution for the deaths of Rabia, Mehmet, Bryce, and Ayla. Thoughts of their deaths had faded, replaced by sweet, enduring memories of when they were alive. Together, Callahan and Safiye had embraced those memories.

"Two tickets to fly out of Saint Thomas," Fontaine said, handing them an envelope. "You can finally return to your normal lives."

Normal was going for a morning jog along the Reef Bay trail past Mongoose Junction, followed by a swim and a walk to Cruz Bay for breakfast. It was sailing to Tortola for a late lunch and back to their cove to cast their net, swim, and make love. It was dropping the sail and anchoring on a secluded beach, sunbathing on the deck, and having a late dinner of grilled mahi while drinking sangria and watching the waves lap onto the shore.

"And Beyir?" Callahan asked.

Fontaine turned a sympathetic eye toward Safiye. "There was a gunfight," he said. "I'm sorry."

Back in Washington, DC, Kevin Hawthorne and Matti Carlyle came through on their promise and invited them for dinner and a movie. After the dinner at the house on 1 Observatory Circle, Callahan and Safiye walked the grounds of the Naval Observatory. They stopped and wrapped their arms around each other.

"It feels as though we're still on the boat, swaying with the waves," Safiye said.

"Only colder," Callahan said.

Safiye burrowed into him, shivering.

It was late December, a few days before Christmas. They wore jackets and gloves.

"Not exactly the best time to come back from the Caribbean," he said.

"I'm not sure if there is."

He looked into the night sky. It was clear, the stars bright. "It *is* the same sky."

As their breaths condensed around them, they held each other for several moments before Safiye glanced at the house. "We should get back. Matti was anxious to start the movie."

Callahan nodded but didn't move. He didn't think it would be like this. He didn't think he'd be nervous. But he was.

"Are you okay?" Safiye asked.

He had to do it now.

He dropped to a knee and pulled off his glove. He extended a diamond ring. "Safiye Özmen, will you marry me?"

On the island, as their feelings of guilt for not only surviving but living had faded, Callahan's thoughts had turned to the future. He'd come to believe they would spend it together.

Her eyes filled with tears. "Yes," she said. "I will."

Safiye slipped off her glove. He placed the ring on her finger.

"It's beautiful," Safiye said. "Where'd you get it?"

"On the island. I was going to ask you the night Fontaine arrived."

"Part of me wishes he never came," Safiye said. "It would have meant they never caught Iskender, but also that my brother would still be alive. It's a trade I'd gladly make."

In Terme, Beyir had come through for Safiye. They owed him their lives.

Safiye looked thoughtfully at him.

"What is it?" he asked.

"When we were in the cave, did you think we'd make it back?"

"No," he said. "Did you?"

She shook her head. "Whatever expectations I had for the future, I erased them. If I didn't have expectations for the future, I couldn't feel as bad if I didn't have one."

"That's a normal reaction."

"The problem is, I haven't been able to envision one since," she said. "Saint John was great. But when I look forward, I still only see a future without Mehmet and Ayla, without Bryce, and now one without my brother. He wasn't a part of my life, but I always thought he would be."

"I hope you can envision a future with me."

"I want to," she said. "I mean, I can. I love you. I have no doubt about that. But right now, thinking ahead is so hard."

"I'm here for you. I always will be." He touched the ring. "If that complicates things, I can take it back. There's no need to rush into this."

"I think I'm ready. I want to be."

Back in the house, a Secret Service agent escorted them to the theater room. Matti was inside, flipping through channels, a concerned look on her face. "Kevin was just called in for an emergency," she said, settling on a news channel.

"What happened?" Callahan asked.

Matti looked at Safiye. "I'm sorry to be the one to tell you this, but there's been another earthquake. It was in Istanbul."

They watched as film crews documented the damage nature had once again inflicted. Images of men scurrying over rubble and pulling bodies from collapsed buildings filled the screen. A British reporter stood outside a downtown hospital, providing estimates of the number of injured.

It was the same gruesome telecast they'd watched several months earlier.

"Why does this have to happen?" Matti asked.

Safiye stared at the screen, her face white. "The epicenter is a few blocks from my clinic."

"Do you think Alin is organizing your team?" Matti asked.

"It doesn't matter," Callahan said. "They'll need doctors. We'll go. We can work in your clinic. If not there then for one of the aid agencies."

Safiye nodded.

"If you'd like, I can have someone arrange your flights," Matti said. "You can stay here tonight and leave in the morning."

Callahan woke to a darkened room. Someone was knocking at the door. The door cracked open.

In the light from the hallway, he saw Safiye talking to a Secret Service agent. The agent stepped inside. He picked up Safiye's bags and carried them from the room.

Already dressed, Safiye turned toward him. "My taxi is waiting."

Callahan turned on the bedside lamp and looked toward the clock. The alarm wasn't supposed to ring for another half hour. "We still have three hours before we fly out."

"I'm leaving now," she said.

He slipped from the bed. "I'll get ready. It'll take just—"

"I moved up my flight," Safiye said. "I'm leaving by myself."

"By yourself. Why?"

"It's Christmas, Michael. Your family needs to see you."

"They'll understand."

Safiye shook her head. "Your life is in Ann Arbor. It's time for you to go back."

He followed her gaze to the dresser. The engagement ring sat on an envelope.

"The time we've spent together has been precious," she said. "But it's all happening too fast."

"You don't mean that."

"I do," she said. "Saint John was incredible. But it wasn't . . . real."

"But the way we feel for each other. That is real. We're engaged, Safiye. I'll go with you. I love you."

"And I love you," she said. "I always will. But I'm sorry, Michael. I have to go. Alone."

Ann Arbor
The following summer

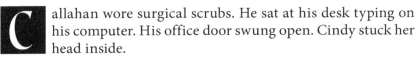

Callahan wore surgical scrubs. He sat at his desk typing on his computer. His office door swung open. Cindy stuck her head inside.

"It's eight a.m.," the nurse said. "Dr. Fisher is here. You can go home."

Callahan looked at his desk calendar. It was Saturday morning. He and Cindy had spent the previous night on call.

Another Friday night.

"Thanks," Callahan said. "Have a good weekend."

Cindy remained in the doorway. "You know, I'm still looking for someone for you."

He summoned his best look of contentment. "That isn't necessary."

"You're invited for the fireworks. I have a friend you should meet. She's cute. She—"

"Thank you," Callahan said. "But I'm heading to my parents' place for the Fourth."

Cindy sighed.

"You should get home," he said. "It was a long night. Frank and the kids, I'm sure they're missing you."

"Okay, but fair warning. I'm not giving up on you."

"And I appreciate that, but it's not necessary. Have a good weekend, Cindy."

"You too."

Callahan worked for several more minutes before turning off the computer. At the door, he reached for the light, pausing to look at a photo on the wall.

In the photo, the four tentmates in Izmir had just returned from a jog. Haas was flexing his biceps as the others laughed. In an adjacent photo from the Nicaragua excursion, he and Bryce stood together. Bryce had sent the photo and signed it.

There's no wrong friends can't right—Bryce

Callahan stared at the photo, Bryce's gaze cutting through him. Next to it was a photo Adams had sent of Lil holding their newborn son.

He scanned the other photos, emotion welling within him. His version of Alin's wall of vanity had become his own wall of emotions. He often thought about taking it down. Someday he would. But not yet. It was too much like saying goodbye.

He looked at a photo taken on the night he received his Purple Heart. He stood with Secretary Hawthorne, Matti, and Safiye. Safiye was smiling brilliantly. What the two of them had shared on the island disappeared in the time it took them to fly back to Washington.

On that morning at the house at 1 Observatory Circle, after walking Safiye down to the waiting taxi, he'd returned to the bedroom. A flash drive and letter were inside the envelope. He knew the letter by heart.

> My love, this drive contains Mehmet's research notes. He sent it to my home address. It was postmarked from Ankara on the day he died. I'm sure he would have wanted you to have it. I hope you find it useful in your research endeavors. Safiye

So easily he'd fallen into the old routines. He'd resumed his full teaching, research, and clinical activities. His free nights and weekends were spent replicating Mehmet's experiments. After verifying some of Mehmet's early work, he realized if the rest of the information on the flash drive was true, it would change the course of biomedical research. The remaining experiments had to be duplicated, however, and Mehmet's speculations further tested. It would be enough to keep a large research lab working indefinitely.

Mehmet's research was all behind him now. But it had served a purpose. It not only helped him through the long winter and dulled the pain of Safiye's absence but it reminded him of why he'd become a doctor.

From the time he'd stood in the back of Kate's hospital room as a nine year old, feeling his family's jubilation as the doctors told them his sister was in remission, his dream had been to become a physician. His life in the face of that unpursued dream would have been empty. What he did at the hospital was often larger than life. He'd come to realize, however, the key to his happiness was having a life outside the hospital that was larger than his work.

Safiye had sent postcards, keeping him up to date on her travels. In Istanbul, she'd signed on with the International Red Cross. Famine had subsequently brought her to Somalia, and the ravages of Syria's civil war had brought her to a refugee camp on Turkey's southern border. She too was immersing herself in something. He was glad.

He took one last look at the photo and then turned off his light. He locked the door behind him and drove home. Home was no longer an efficiency apartment but a century-old house he'd purchased outside of town. After retiling the kitchen in the spring, he was in the midst of painting the exterior and hanging new shutters. A less rigorous call schedule had provided the extra time.

He ate breakfast on the back porch and read the paper. Afterward, he filled a thermos with coffee and began the long drive to his parents' cottage, thankful for the time to do nothing but think.

Callahan drove along a gravel road. He turned past a weather-beaten mailbox and followed two trodden tire tracks through the grass to a quaint cottage. He parked behind a rental car.

In the great room of the cedar-paneled cottage, his mom and his sister Kate were preparing dinner. His father and brother-in-law were playing with the kids on the floor.

"Uncle Mike," the kids screamed as he stepped inside.

Callahan hugged his niece and nephew. His mother wrapped her arms around him, her eyes moist with tears.

"I normally don't get tears until I leave," Callahan said.

"Your mother is getting sentimental in her old age," Callahan's father said.

"Don't let him kid you," his mom said, wiping her eyes. "He's worse than me. Seeing you made me think about last summer. It all came back in a rush."

Callahan hugged Kate. "How was your flight?"

"Perfect," she said. "We flew into Green Bay. Dad picked us up this morning."

Callahan's niece clamped her hands over her ears. "Flying hurt. Mommy told us to hold our noses, but that didn't help. And Daddy had to take off his shoes."

"I'm not a big fan of flying either," Callahan said.

"What about your excursions?" his mother said. "You fly all over the world."

"You mean *flew*. I didn't go on the last one."

A month earlier, the relief team had traveled to India after a tsunami struck the Mumbai coast. None of Callahan's former tentmates had gone.

In March, Haas and Brooke had married. Callahan had served as best man at the wedding—a small ceremony in Iowa City, where the couple now lived. Scott and Lil Adams had attended the wedding, but Adams had since quit the relief team, citing family responsibilities after Lil became pregnant with their fourth child. Safiye had been invited but sent her regrets.

"Don't feel bad," his father said. "In the humanitarian department, you've already made a lifetime of contributions."

Callahan's mother walked to the kitchen. "Michael, dinner will be ready in twenty minutes. You have just enough time for your walk."

He laughed. "You're already trying to get rid of me?"

His mother turned to his brother-in-law. "The first thing Michael has always done when he gets here is run down to the water. He'd only come back to the house when it was time to eat or go to bed."

"When I was ten," Callahan said.

"It sounds like you'd better go for your walk," his brother-in-law said, smiling. "I know how these Callahan women can be when it comes to following tradition."

"Hear, hear," his father added.

"We're standing right here," Kate said. "We can hear you."

"Be back in time for dinner," his mother called out.

Callahan backed away, hands raised.

"Can I go with Uncle Mike?" Callahan's niece asked.

"No," Kate said. "You get to set the table."

"Mom!"

Taking that as his cue, Callahan stepped outside. His mother was right. He did have an impulse to go down to the water—not to swim, but to stretch his legs after the long car ride.

On the beach, he took off his shoes and socks and let his feet sink into the sand. He began walking, letting the waves crest against his feet.

With the holiday weekend, the normally deserted beach was busy. A few couples lazily strolled the shoreline. A dozen teenagers congregated around a fire. Ahead, near the tip of a peninsula, a lone person ran toward a flock of seagulls.

Callahan watched the seagulls take flight. He too enjoyed the childish act of running at the birds and watching them fill the air. As the birds circled, the figure spun.

Callahan looked back toward the cottage. The nose of the rental car was visible.

Dad picked us up this morning.

If that was true, his sister wouldn't have needed the car.

You have just enough time for your walk.

When his mother had said that, her eyes had been wet with tears.

He looked toward the peninsula. As he watched the figure spinning, the birds circling, he realized his mother's tears hadn't been tears of sorrow over last summer. They were tears of happiness regarding the present.

He broke into a sprint.

The kids by the bonfire whistled as he passed.

At the peninsula, he came to a stop.

The lone figure remained at the water's edge, watching the seagulls fly north, heading toward the next safe haven.

When she turned, their eyes met.

"Did you ever find yourself in the last place you expected to be?" she called out.

"More times than I care to think about," he said as she walked toward him. "Why? Are you having regrets about being here?"

"No. I've begun to realize there's a whole lot of stuff,

important stuff, I'm missing out on." She stopped in front of him, raising an eyebrow. "Do you ever think about the future?"

"I've recently made it a point not to."

"I've been thinking about it a lot," she said. "Every time I do, the one I envision, the one I hope for, starts right here. I love you, Michael. I always have and always will. The question is, can you love me again?"

Callahan spent a few moments looking at her. He then pulled a necklace from beneath his shirt collar. Snapping an object from the string, he held it out.

In the sunlight, the diamond sparkled.

"I never stopped."

EPILOGUE

"There are two Mustafa Kemals: One is me, the flesh-and-blood, mortal Mustafa Kemal. The second Mustafa Kemal I cannot express with the word "me," it is "we". That second Mustafa Kemal is you, all of you. That is the non-provisional Mustafa Kemal that must live and succeed."

—**Mustafa Kemal Atatürk**

Four years later

C allahan turned on the television and flipped to channel 309—a previously unused European channel. It was nearing 7 a.m., almost 1 p.m. in Stockholm. Sitting back, he wrapped his arm around Safiye, who held their four-month-old daughter.

A small boy walked into the room, rubbing his eyes. "Batman?" he asked, looking toward the television.

"No," Callahan said. "Come and sit."

The boy wedged between his parents. Safiye kissed his forehead. "Beyir, how are you this morning?"

"Good," the boy said. "Dad, are you going to work today?"

"Not today. It's Saturday. I get to stay home all day, and tomorrow too."

"Can we play hide-and-seek?"

"Sure. And baseball?"

"Yes!" the boy said.

On the television, an elderly man stood at a podium. The camera switched to a heavyset man walking up an aisle, wearing an ill-fitting suit. His graying red hair was pulled into a short ponytail. A gaunt man with dark hair and hunched shoulders followed. When the two men reached the stage, the audience stood and clapped. The two men looked toward each other. Laughing, they hugged.

"They look good," Callahan said. "Morticai got a haircut."

Safiye laughed. "And a comb."

A week earlier, Safiye had approached Callahan, holding out her phone. "It's Matti. She's excited about something."

"Michael, I have wonderful news," Matti Carlyle said when he took the phone. "We won."

"Won? What?"

"I thought you were a scientist, Dr. Callahan. The doctors from Koba Laboratories, along with Drs. Silverstein and Valance, just won the Nobel Prize for Medicine."

It had been four-and-a-half years since Callahan had flown to Northern Virginia University and given Mehmet's flash drive to Morticai Valance. He never would have known about Valance except for an excerpt in Mehmet's research notes describing his meeting with the epigeneticist. After Callahan's trip to Virginia, he'd called Matti and encouraged her to use her philanthropic skills to expand Valance's less-than-inspiring lab. At the time, Matti had just finished fund-raising for a new research wing at the NIH. She wasn't looking forward to testing her golden connections again so soon. "Maybe we can get a place for him at the NIH," she'd said. "I'll arrange a meeting with the new director, Dr. Saul Silverstein."

After being confronted with Mehmet's research notes and Callahan's verifying data, Silverstein became a fervent proponent of epigeneticism. For Morticai Valance, the notes were a second wind. He accepted a position at the NIH and moved back to Washington, DC, where he and Silverstein set aside their differences and worked together, not only validating Mehmet's data but testing his speculations and carrying them to their logical conclusions. The groundbreaking papers that poured from their collaboration posthumously listed Dr. Mehmet Koba as first author, followed by the PhDs at Koba Laboratories and then Silverstein and Valance.

On the one-year anniversary of the dedication of the NIH's new research wing, Silverstein and Valance had announced the beginning of clinical trials. The trials utilized a novel form of gene therapy employing the epigeneticists' creed that cancer cells were good cells behaving badly. Aimed at redirecting the cancer cell and not destroying it, the gene therapy blocked the function of the previously unknown Primidin molecule. The medication was modeled after a therapy postulated by Mehmet in his last research notes. The experimental trials had achieved miraculous results.

On the television screen, Morticai stepped to the podium. His exceedingly flowery tie glowed. As he spoke, Callahan turned up the volume.

"You can't see them, but standing with us are Dr. Mehmet Koba and his research team," Morticai said. "I think Saul will agree: Mehmet pulled us up here by our ears—two old men, screaming and kicking, entrenched in our own ways. Saul and I are better off for having met Mehmet Koba. And I can say, unequivocally, the world is better off because of him." Pausing, he scanned the audience and held out his arms. "On behalf of millions of cancer patients, I would like to thank Mehmet Koba and his colleagues at Koba Laboratories for giving them a second chance at life."

Safiye covered her mouth, unable to suppress a sob.

The camera panned back as the audience applauded. When it quieted, the camera moved in on Morticai, who remained at the podium.

For a moment, Morticai's penetrating gaze traversed the ocean. He started to say something but stopped, his voice choked with emotion. Composing himself, he held up a small red object. It was the flash drive Mehmet had mailed to Safiye's home and that Callahan had taken to Northern Virginia University.

"Michael, Matti, and Safiye," Valance said. "For giving a cynical old man another chance, thank you."

Northwestern Iran

In a sweat-drenched T-shirt, Enver Pasha walked slowly but steadily up the mountain road. He stepped out onto a rocky outcropping and savored the view.

To the unknowing eye, the valley spread before him, hidden between steep subordinate ridges of an unnamed peak of the Elburz Mountains, appeared untouched. On the opposing ridge, several sheep grazed as a covey of snow cocks flew overhead. A spotted eagle skirted the tops of the junipers blanketing the valley floor.

We have no friends but the mountains.

The Kurdish maxim had proven true. Mountain living had done wonders for him. It wasn't surprising. He was born to these mountains—the mountains of Kurdistan.

His gaze settled on the trees above the barracks where the boys lived. His time as headmaster had seen unprecedented expansion of the Enderun. With orphaned boys being an unfortunate consequence of the endless wars afflicting the Middle East, recruits were more numerous than ever. The Şebeke had also continued to grow, its tendrils spreading into more distant and greater spheres of influence. The Janissaries would soon be ready for another Sayişma. This time, they would be better prepared.

Enver's thoughts rarely turned to Iskender these days. His son was gone, but in his place was an entire school of young men. Men he could teach, shape, and be proud of. It was as close to being a father, the father he'd always wanted to be, as he could hope.

In the distance, his eye was caught by an unmarked jeep. The jeep made its way along a narrow dirt road—the only route into the valley. He hurried down the hill.

Cemil Kura had come to make his yearly visit. They had much to celebrate. Almost five years to the day after returning from the South Pacific, where a bulletproof vest had saved his life, Cemil had been appointed Turkey's commander-in-chief—its *başkomutan*.

At the foot of the mountain, Enver stepped from the dirt road onto one of the many paths crisscrossing the valley floor. Ahead, the jeep came to a stop. Cemil climbed out. From a nearby building, a door swung open. Maxwell Göttingen emerged. The two men shook hands.

After a recent shipment of plutonium, Göttingen had been busy. Hostile acquisition of radioactive material was no longer necessary. More than enough weapons-grade plutonium could be purchased on the black market. The Enderun's host country, Iran, also eagerly exchanged plutonium for training with Göttingen, whose hyper-fractionating and enrichment techniques, along with his miniaturized accelerator, allowed the building of smaller, more powerful bombs. Hidden from the prying eyes of UN inspectors and possessing an unlimited amount of radioactive material, resources, and time, Göttingen was developing an array of weapons that would soon make the Janissaries a world force.

From the building, boys streamed toward Cemil and clamored around him.

"Congratulations," Enver called out. "Your father would be proud."

Cemil motioned toward the boys. "He'd be proud for many reasons."

Enver looked from Cemil to Göttingen and then to the surrounding buildings. It had been over eighty years since Muhammed Tunç had rushed into the burning mosque and lifted him from the crib. Muhammed's dream of a unified Middle East, conceived as he bundled him in a blanket and carried him from the Kurdish village, no longer seemed so distant.

ACKNOWLEDGMENTS

I am very grateful to Lisa Akoury-Ross from SDP Publishing Solutions for her support and making this book a reality. I am also much in debt to Elizabeth Delisi, Stephanie Peters, Kellyann Zuzulo, Susan Strecker, Karen Grennan, and Kirkus Editing Services for their expert editing advice. I would like to thank Dr. Ethan Menchinger of The University of Manchester—an expert in Near Eastern and Ottoman studies and the author of *The First of the Modern Ottomans: the Intellectual History of Ahmet Vâsif*—for providing valuable feedback on the novel.

I have much appreciation for my early readers: Jane McAndrews, Lauren Pelkey, Kevin Kuske, and Ann Kuske. Their advice and words of encouragement have been greatly appreciated. Thank you to my sister Wendy Kneen for her concept for the cover and Ganbat Badamkhand for his artwork. Thank you to Howard Johnson for his creative layout designs.

Thank you to my high school English teacher and first writing teacher, Mr. William Scarpaci, for initiating a love to write. And many thanks to all the teachers throughout my life, including the pathology faculty at the University of Virginia. Mostly, I thank my wife Leslie for reading countless versions of this novel and for her boundless encouragement.

ABOUT THE AUTHOR

Tim Pelkey resides in Michigan with his wife Leslie. They have two grown children. Tim's first novel, *The Baljuna Covenant*, won three 2017 IBPA Benjamin Franklin Awards, was a finalist for the 2017 NIEA Political Thriller Award, and was a finalist for the 2017 Eric Hoffer Award. It made the recommended reading lists for Kirkus Indie Reviews, Stevo's Book Reviews on the Internet, and US Review of Books. *The Ottoman Excursion* is his second novel. timpelkey.com

The Ottoman Excursion
Tim Pelkey
Publisher: SDP Publishing
Also by the author: The Baljuna Covenant
www.timpelkey.com
Also available in ebook format

 **SDP Publishing**

www.SDPPublishing.com
Contact us at: info@SDPPublishing.com

CPSIA information can be obtained
at www.ICGtesting.com
Printed in the USA
FSHW010520180420
69262FS

9 781734 240252